ARLEN CLASSIC LITERATURE

A LIFE OF NO LIGHT TOIL

The Anna Maria Fielding Hall Reader

Portrait of Anna Maria Hall by Daniel Maclise (1833)
from S.C. Hall, *Retrospect of a Long Life: From 1815–1883* (1883)

A Life of No Light Toil

The Anna Maria Fielding Hall Reader

Edited and introduced by Marian Thérèse Keyes

A LIFE OF NO LIGHT TOIL
The Anna Maria Fielding Hall Reader

is published in 2022 by
ARLEN HOUSE
42 Grange Abbey Road
Baldoyle
Dublin 13
arlenhouse@gmail.com
www.arlenhouse.ie

978–1–85132–265–7, paperback

Distributed internationally by
SYRACUSE UNIVERSITY PRESS
621 Skytop Road, Suite 110
Syracuse
NY 13244–5290
United States
Phone: 315–443–5534
supress@syr.edu
syracuseuniversitypress.syr.edu

Typesetting by Arlen House

cover image:
'Annie Leslie'
frontispiece to *Annie Leslie and Other Stories* (1877)
Artist unknown

Contents

This volume is dedicated to
Emeritus Professor Mary Shine Thompson Ph.D
Barrister at Law
a passionate scholar
a brilliant mentor
and a dear friend

Acknowledgements

Huge thanks to Alan Hayes for commissioning this *Reader* of Anna Maria Fielding Hall's work. The tireless work of Arlen House in promoting the work of Irish women writers, past and present, is breathtaking. Time and again, women writers and artists disappear without trace despite being lauded and fêted throughout their working lives. I am deeply grateful to Alan for the opportunity to showcase the work of a complex and intriguing figure who was at her peak in the 1830s and 1840s, a woman who only came to my attention when I was cataloguing a large collection of nineteenth century children's books at the Victoria and Albert Museum in London during the 1990s. The high production values of her many publications reflect her close contacts with the artistic, publishing and bookselling communities of the period. It is hard not to be in awe of her unwavering ethic for hard work and her zeal to transform society as witnessed through her writings on nationality, childhood and gender.

This *Reader* is based on research carried out as part of my Ph.D. between 2007–2010 and articles published since then. I owe an enormous debt to my supervisor, Dr Mary Shine Thompson, my auxiliary supervisor, Celia Keenan and reader Dr Carole Dunbar. Thanks also to Curator Rosi Beech (aka Tessa Rose Chester) who encouraged my research into many aspects of the Renier Collection of Children's Literature in the V&A's Bethnal Green Museum of Childhood in the 1990s.

My academic work on Anna Maria Fielding Hall inspired me to become involved in the exciting world of children's books, 19th century to the present day, and I was thrilled to receive the Children's Books Ireland Award in 2021 in recognition for outstanding contribution to the world of children's books. As the Librarian at dlr LexIcon, I was pleased to coordinate the setting up of the Irish

Author Collection and Bookstore in 2017, with former Dún Laoghaire-Rathdown County Librarian Mairead Owens and current County Librarian Catherine Gallagher. Many of my colleagues have contributed to the growth of this important resource especially Nigel Curtin, David Gunning and Lisa Murphy but also the following: Patricia Corish, Bernie Doherty, Sean Downes, Caroline Flood, Fiona Jordan, Kevin Lynch, Maeve McElligott, Geraldine McHugh, Julianne Morgan, Éanna O'Keeffe and Eveleen Rooney. This Collection has been immeasurably enriched by many important and rare titles of Irish women's writing acquired from Arlen House in recent years.

Grateful thanks to Dr Éimear O'Connor, Director of the Tyrone Guthrie Centre, Annaghmakerrig for permission to reproduce the painting of Tyrone Power in *The Groves of Blarney* by Nicholas Crowley, Christopher Fitz-Simon for commentary on this painting and Richard Howlett of Concept2Print for assistance with scanning. I would also like to acknowledge the staff at the following institutions for their assistance: Dublin City University, Huntington Library California, Iowa University Libraries, National Art Library London, National Library of Ireland, National Library of Scotland, Royal Irish Academy, Trinity College Dublin and all my colleagues at Dún Laoghaire-Rathdown Libraries.

Finally, warmest and sincere thanks to my brother Matthew and his family in Belgium – Evelyn, Feargal and Alice, Owen and Orla; my brother Joe who is always incredibly helpful and constructive; my wonderful daughters Nora and Joanna who have followed this project with great interest and last but not least my husband Michael (certainly no Samuel Carter Hall!) whose support and love made this journey one of discovery and celebration.

ANNA MARIA FIELDING HALL: A LIFE OF NO LIGHT TOIL[1]

Introduction

During the mid 1990s, when I was cataloguing the Renier Collection of Historic and Contemporary Publications for Children at the Victoria and Albert's Bethnal Green Museum, the name Anna Maria Fielding Hall, A.M.H. or Mrs S.C. Hall, appeared repeatedly. In 1998, as part of Magda and Rolf Loeber's ongoing research for *A Guide to Irish Fiction 1650–1900,* they spent time researching the Renier Collection, and I compiled a list for them of her works held in the Collection. I was struck not only by the fact that Anna Maria was Irish, had spent her childhood in Wexford until the age of fifteen and wrote on Irish themes, but also by the quality of her illustrated books and by the range of her children's books, with well over 40 published titles.[2] I was particularly taken by a beautifully-bound, lavishly-illustrated copy of *Midsummer Eve: A Fairy Tale of Love* published in 1848 – many of the illustrators were Irish and I was surprised that the author had received relatively little critical attention.

As a curator in the National Art Library at the V&A, I noted the extent of her involvement in *The Art-Union*, later *The Art Journal,* and that she was married to Samuel Carter Hall, its editor. For art researchers of the nineteenth century, this journal is of seminal importance and was one of the most frequently requested items in the library. The potential intersection between her illustrated books and her husband's art connections became apparent. As an art historian with a particular interest in illustrated children's books of the nineteenth century and the ever-changing dialectic between word and image, my interest was certainly piqued.

During her lifetime, Anna Maria's publications were eagerly awaited and widely reviewed in all the major journals of the period. Significantly, she contributed to, and was reviewed by, the Irish periodical press at a time when this was a rare enough occurrence for an Irish writer living in England. Irish journals featuring her work included *The Dublin Literary Gazette, The Dublin Penny Journal, The Dublin University Magazine* and *The Irish Penny Journal*. But by the time of her death in 1881, most of her books were out of print; and assessments over the subsequent 140 years have been scarce, with an overall tendency to quote from the same sources, perpetuating earlier biases and inaccuracies. Since the publication of facsimile editions of four of her titles by Garland Publishing in 1979: *Lights and Shadows of Irish Life, Sketches of Irish Character, Stories of the Irish Peasantry* and *The Whiteboy*, it comes as no surprise to know that these titles have generated the most critical interest in the last forty years.

The chief critics who engaged with Anna Maria's work during this period were Robert Lee Wolff, Barry Sloan, James Newcomer and Maureen Keane. Wolff and Sloan rated her, as did many of her contemporaries, in the same league as John and Michael Banim, Gerald Griffin and William Carleton. The popularity of Carleton's stories in

Ireland may have overshadowed her reputation in her home country and there are frequent comparisons with Maria Edgeworth and Lady Morgan. James Newcomer 'discovered' Anna Maria's work in 1985 when researching books on Maria Edgeworth and Lady Morgan. Subsequently he spent many months studying her work in Cambridge and in the extensive Hall archive in Iowa and he wrote two sympathetic articles on her work. Maureen Keane produced a definitive account of Anna Maria in *Mrs S.C. Hall: A Literary Biography* in 1997, a balanced, exhaustively researched publication with a much deeper analysis of the individual stories than found in earlier critiques. It includes a comparative chapter on William Carleton and Charles Lever who both produced novels about the landlord/tenant relationship in 1845, the same year as Anna Maria's *The Whiteboy*.

In addition to the work of these critics, further commentaries and biographical dictionaries have emerged in recent years, including an extensive entry in the Orlando Project Database published by Cambridge University Press, *The Field Day Anthology of Irish Writing* (Vol. V, 2002), and most notably the Loebers' *A Guide to Irish Fiction 1650–1900* (2006). It is encouraging to see a number of developments in recent years where Anna Maria's output is examined from new perspectives, such as work on the 'remarkable 1849 didactic novel *Grandmamma's Pockets*' in Barbara Burman and Jonathan White's essay on tie-on pockets in *Women and Material Culture, 1660–1830* (2007). Likewise the new edition, as part of the Chawton House Library Series of Women's Novels, of *Sketches of Irish Character* edited by Marion Durnin (2014) includes nuanced essays on the text and also on the illustrated plates by Daniel Maclise that were used to accompany the 1844 edition.

I completed my Ph.D thesis in 2010 where I explored the pivotal role visual art plays in Anna Maria's ekphrastic[3] writing, the diversity of genres explored in her children's books and the challenges of the publishing world for a woman writer and editor. Central to my work was a study of the colonial, didactic and gendered elements of her writings. The dissertation is now available online and a selection of articles have been published based on this research. I was delighted to be invited by Alan Hayes of Arlen House to produce this anthology so that I could share my enthusiasm for an enigmatic and intriguing Victorian woman writer who deserves a wider readership.

On the jacket of Arlen House's important 2021 anthology, *Look! It's a Woman Writer! Irish Literary Feminisms 1970–2020,* questions are asked:

> Why have women been treated differently, and discriminated against, in the literary world?
> Why has gender been a 'problem' in the writing, publishing, funding and reviewing scene?

These self-same questions preoccupied me during my study of Anna Maria Hall, and they will be interrogated in this anthology – the extraordinary invisibility of a lifetime's work and the possible reasons for oblivion. According to her husband, she had written 150 books in her lifetime and Maureen Keane notes 400 joint publications with S.C. Hall, Anne Colman mentions 500 volumes. He also claimed that she could 'affix her signature to at least a thousand reviews of published books' – many reviews at this time were unsigned with anonymity preferred.[4]

For this anthology, I have chosen a range of works dating from 1829–1852, broadly chronological, to give a flavour of her *Sketches*, her work for the theatre, a variety of school and governess stories showing a range of stylistic writing, a ghost story, a fairy tale, a biographical 'Memoir', two short excerpts from a successful series of children's books for Chambers, an excerpt from her Irish novel, *The Whiteboy,* and a brief flavour of *Ireland, its Scenery,*

Character &c. Each section is briefly introduced, followed by a list of further reading. I have not provided excerpts from her other extensive travel literature apart from the 3-volume work on *Ireland*, nor from her English novels, all of which deserve further study. This introduction provides an overview of Anna Maria's life, her relationship with her husband and how it influenced her literary career, and finally, her life as a professional writer and editor – writing for women and with women. It was indeed a life of no light toil.

Biographical Overview

Anna Maria Fielding (1800–81) was born on 6 January 1800 in Anne Street, Dublin. Her father, William, was Irish and he died during her infancy. Her mother, Sarah Elizabeth, was of Swiss Huguenot extraction on her mother's side of the family. The young widow and child lived with Sarah's mother and stepfather, George Carr in Graige House in Bannow, County Wexford. When her grandmother died, fifteen-year old Anna Maria moved to London with her mother, where subsequently she married the Irish journalist and editor, Samuel Carter Hall (1800–89). He had left Cork for London in 1822 and although he had more exposure than his wife to Irish ways, he was more reticent about his Irish roots. Nevertheless, like his wife, he ceaselessly promoted Ireland, in his case by researching and publicising Irish folklore and antiquities.

Encouraged initially by her husband to write her Irish sketches, Anna Maria gained widespread success with her two series of *Sketches of Irish Character* when they appeared in 1829 and 1831.[5] The following three decades were immensely prolific as she produced further sketches, plays, novels and children's books. She also published a broad selection of travel literature, much of it jointly with her husband. She was an experienced editor, firstly with the *Juvenile Forget-Me-Not* from 1829–37 and later with

Sharpe's London Magazine from 1852–53 and the *St James's Magazine* from 1861–62. She wrote numerous articles for the burgeoning periodical press of 1830s–40s London, Edinburgh and Dublin, including serialised versions of her novels and many art-related works for her husband's *The Art Union*.

The artist and journalist, Henry Vizetelly in his *Glances Back over Seventy Years* (1893) was clear as to which of the Halls was the more gifted:

> True, he assumed an intellectual authority over her, and she blandly accepted the false position, but no one was taken in by it.

Whilst acknowledging what seemed to be a happy, compatible marriage, her strategy within her relationship and with the wider public was, I will argue, carefully cultivated to ensure that S.C. Hall was always convinced of her loyalty to him. Her success at maintaining such a role, coupled with the fact that he had the last word in his *Retrospect of a Long Life: From 1815–1883*, are two of the possible reasons she slipped so swiftly from the canon after her death.

The Halls lived in Firfield, Addlestone, Surrey from 1851–60

The Halls maintained their strong links with their native country and undertook at least five tours during the period 1825–41 and again before 1865. These early tours fed into their important three-volume joint publication entitled *Ireland: its Scenery, Character, &c* published between 1841–43. This work was published in many different part editions in later years, some focusing on one area such as *A Week at Killarney* (1843) or the four-volume *Hand-Books for Ireland* (1853). In her many sketches and in her novel *The Whiteboy* (1845) she highlighted the wretched plight of the Irish, in particular the consequences wrought by irresponsible absentee landlords and mercenary bailiffs. Her travel books and sketches aimed to encourage people to visit Ireland and to sample the unique 'character' of the Irish people.

"The Rosery" in Old Brompton
Letterhead used by the Halls c. 1840

While the Halls lived in 'The Rosery' in Old Brompton from 1839–49, they were active participants in the thriving artistic and literary scene in London. They entertained such notables as Charles Dickens, Nathaniel Hawthorne,

Mary and William Howitt, Jenny Lind, Thomas Moore, John Ruskin and William Wordsworth. Anna Maria corresponded enthusiastically with a cross-section of artists, writers and celebrities. She engaged in many philanthropic activities, played an important role in the setting up of the Hospital for Consumption at Brompton, was vocal in her support for governesses and women's issues, and both Halls worked tirelessly to support temperance causes. They were Evangelical Christians with a keen interest in Spiritualism, which they shared with many of their contemporaries.

Despite an earnest desire to have children, only one child, a daughter named Maria Louisa, was born alive in 1836 and she only survived for a few short days. They had an adopted daughter, Fanny, and her mother, Mrs Fielding, lived with them until her death in 1856. In 1868, Anna Maria was granted a £100 civil pension, and in 1874, six hundred subscribers helped the Halls to celebrate their fiftieth wedding anniversary with a £100 annuity, £670 in cash and an album containing five hundred congratulatory letters.

Fiftieth Wedding Anniversary Card (1874)

Anna Maria died on 30 January 1881 and her husband died eight years later on 16 March 1889. Both were buried at Addlestone churchyard in Surrey.

A Hard-Working Couple

Anna Maria's first stories owed much to her husband's position as editor of the annual entitled *The Amulet*, edited by him from 1826–37. He was able to provide opportunities for her work in this annual and also in his monthly periodical *Spirit and Manners of the Age* and most importantly in *The Art-Union*. The illustrated annual was a publishing phenomenon of the early nineteenth century which attracted women in particular, both as writers and readers. Annuals promoted contemporary literature and art amongst the rising middle classes as engravings were an integral and highly expensive part of them. They were expensively produced with decorative silk, stamped or leather bindings, numerous steel engravings and contributions by leading authors of the day. They were often given as tokens of friendship and affection, initially around Christmas time but eventually suitable for any year and any season.

It is worth noting that these early tales were to appear again and again in different guises over the coming decades. For example 'The Trials of Grace Huntley' was included in her publication *Tales of Woman's Trials* (Houlston & Son, 1834). An illustrated version was published by Chapman and Hall in 1847 and a play of the same title was performed in London in 1843. Westley and Davis, the publishers of *The Amulet* and *The Spirit and Manners of the Age*, made an offer of £100 in 1828 for Anna Maria to write several more sketches to add to the five already published in the annuals; her career was launched with the publication in 1829 of the first series of *Sketches of Irish Character*.

Anna Maria was a regular contributor to *The Art-Union*. Her average output per volume in a ten-year period from 1847–57 never dropped below twelve per cent of each issue. This figure is based on a survey of signed articles and commentaries, but in an era when exhibition and book reviews were frequently unsigned it is not unreasonable to suggest that she may have contributed more than this. An ad in *The Art-Union* in December 1847 proclaimed that the average circulation was 14,000 monthly, 'a circulation second to that of no periodical in the empire'. Whilst bearing in mind that periodicals frequently exaggerated circulation figures, it confirmed that it was a well-established title and an ideal vehicle to promote Anna Maria's writing.

As for the ethos of the periodical, Anna Maria's contributions could have been helpful to the aspiring middle-classes in a number of ways: attracting a female audience to the periodical; widening the appeal of the periodical to those not immediately involved in art practice; writing about topics such as the benefits of good illustration for children's books; and the lasting impact of exposure to the principals of fine art and design. Not only was S.C. Hall delighted that she helped to broaden the appeal of *The Art-Union* to a female audience but he readily acknowledged her contribution:

> And surely I may not forget the aid *The Art Journal* received in actual work as well as in sweet and wise counsel to me, its editor ... Here she gave to my dry details concerning 'The Thames' and 'South Wales' the sparkling episodes from which they derived great value.[6]

By all accounts, the Halls appeared to have a close and loving relationship over nearly sixty years of marriage. Anna Maria was loyal, trusting and supportive to her husband despite the fact that he made enemies and landed in financial and legal difficulties on a regular basis. The oft-quoted reference to Charles Dickens's dislike of him and the fact that he modelled the pompous Mr Pecksniff from *Martin Chuzzlewit* on S.C. Hall must have been a source of embarrassment to them. Anna Maria went to a great deal of trouble to ensure that domestic duties were never second to her responsibilities as an author and thus she was able to avoid humiliating her husband at such a crossroads in her own literary development. The portrait of Anna Maria by Henry MacManus at the height of her fame, depicts her holding not her own celebrated *Sketches of Irish Character* for which it was the frontispiece but her husband's *Book of Gems* (1836). While she never overtly contradicted or went against her husband, some pockets of resistance do emerge, however subliminal they may have been. This is particularly evident in many of her comments about men and marriage safely built into her fictional writings.

Frontispiece from *Sketches of Irish Character* (1844)
signed by Anna Maria Hall
from a painting by H. MacManus A.R.H.A, engraved by K. Ryall

S.C. Hall never achieved the kind of literary success his wife enjoyed. His real talents lay in his editorial abilities and the exceptional role he played in the promotion of British art in the nineteenth century. He produced some short tales in *The Amulet* but there is no easy relationship between author and reader as there is in his wife's tales – there is a dull seriousness and the plots are insubstantial. He was more comfortable with poetry but again, his poems were solemn and worthy.

He omitted to include his wife's name on the title page of any editions of *A Book of Memories of Great Men and Women of the Age,* despite noting in the introduction to the third edition how much aid he received from his wife. Likewise with *The Vernon Gallery of British Art,* she was not given fair acknowledgement. He also destroyed all her letters to him, so we are left with an incomplete account of their lives together. This readiness on his part to give her credit and yet withhold it in other areas resulted in an elevated sense of his own importance. Naturally it limited and diminished her actual output and reputation as a consequence, but most contemporary commentators saw her as the superior writer of the two.

What is in no doubt is that both of the Halls worked extremely hard and while Peter Finlay, whose study, 'Early Victorian Travel Writing on Ireland', is convinced that the bulk of *Ireland, its Scenery, Character &c.* was by Anna Maria, the superior writer of the two, there is no doubt that her husband worked hard to compile the information, images and legends from antiquarian authorities in Ireland. A glance at a series of letters in the Royal Irish Academy from S.C. Hall to John Windele provides a snapshot of the hard work, the deadlines, the frustrations of illustrators who let him down and the pressure of covering thirty-two counties in twenty-four parts. The full extent of who exactly did what in such an ambitious joint project may never be fully analysed.

Nonetheless, commentators then and now acknowledge their sincere dedication to the cause of encouraging the English to visit Ireland.

Anna Maria had to work in a male environment, amongst those who could create obstacles and make life difficult for her. She had to walk a fine line with her husband who found it difficult to be the less famous partner. In a reference to a visit to Hannah More when Hall was not long married, she recalled that whatever throwaway remark she had made, Hannah More quickly replied:

> Controversy hardens the heart and sours the temper. Never dispute with your husband, young lady; tell him what you think and leave it to time to fructify.[7]

Anna Maria appeared to have lived this advice at all times.

Portrait of Samuel Carter Hall by Paul De La Roche (1847) from his *Retrospect of a Long Life: From 1815–1883* (1883)

The Professional Writer and Editor

Anna Maria's growing reputation as a writer led to editorial appointments which in turn helped to market her own work. Her first major position was as editor of the annual *The Juvenile Forget-Me-Not.* Many of the women who earned a living with the annuals found a new and profitable audience in the juvenile market. These annuals adhered to the didactic school as expounded by Mary Sherwood, Maria Edgeworth and others, where moral stories, prayers and homilies were expected and delivered. Frequent themes involved childhood mortality, poverty and avoiding cruelty to others and to animals. The chief contributors during her reign as editor from 1829–37 included Anna Maria herself (19 items), Maria Jewsbury (14 items), Mary Howitt (13 items) and Letitia E. Landon (12 items).

Aside from Anna Maria, other women contributors found a steady source of income through their work with the annuals. Joanne Shattock listed Letitia Landon as earning £2,500 a year at her peak, with Caroline Norton reputedly earning £1,400 a year on her literary work alone. While popular demand existed, writing for the annuals proved lucrative. Anna Maria formed solid professional relationships with such women and many of them were personal friends and contributors to her later works. The compendium nature of the annuals and the timing of their production influenced publishing for the juvenile market, sowing the seeds of demand not only for the seasonal children's annual but also for beautifully illustrated books.

In July 1852, Anna Maria was offered the position as editor of *Sharpe's London Magazine*. She had high hopes and great enthusiasm for the new project and she extolled the many highly-regarded contributors. Though not remembered greatly today, writers such as Frederika Bremer, Dinah Maria Mulock, Ida Pfeiffer and Frank Smedley were sought after and wrote extensively for

Sharpe's. Anna Maria had a clear idea of what she hoped to achieve over the following months and pointed out the non-sectarian ethos of the magazine and also her keen sense of the family market. While she had a number of her own stories included in *Sharpe's* in the late 1840s and early 1850s, as editor this naturally increased. Her stories included 'Nelly Nowlan's Experience', 'The Lucky Penny' and 'Helen Lyndsey'. Two years was the average length for a Victorian serialised novel at this time but *Sharpe's* tended towards short instalments compared to other magazines. Unfortunately a new proprietor took over the magazine and whatever the nature of a disagreement was, she never had the opportunity to develop her plans for the magazine. Once the repeal of the stamp duty on paper came about in 1855, with the subsequent drop in paper prices and attendant competition in the market, *Sharpe's* did not itself survive particularly long.

Anna Maria's reign as editor of the *St. James's Magazine* was to last marginally longer than with *Sharpe's* (a year compared to six months with the latter) and at least she had the satisfaction of being invited by proprietor John Maxwell to set it up, thus having more control of it from the start. Rumour had it that her tenure would be brief. Mary Braddon, the successful 'sensation' author, succeeded her as editor and remained until 1867. Braddon was a common law wife of Maxwell's from the early 1860s and Maxwell had arranged in 1861 for her to work one day a week on the *Magazine* under Hall's supervision, ultimately groomed for the editorial chair. She learned first-hand from Anna Maria the necessary skills of copy-editing, how best to sooth and encourage authors and reviewers and how to deal with the endless constraints of finding suitable contributors, at the right price, out of the many unsolicited manuscripts that inevitably added to the workload of any popular magazine.

The *St. James's Magazine* was considered a more middle-brow rival to literary *Cornhill* and Anna Maria utilised her many literary connections. She had regular contributions from well-known novelists and poets such as Anthony Trollope, Thomas Hood, Mary Howitt and Frederika Bremer. One of her best novels, *Can Wrong Be Right?* was serialised throughout 1861–62, with accompanying plates by Hablot Knight Browne and was published in a two-volume publication in 1862. Browne was well-known by his pen name Phiz and illustrated books by Charles Dickens and Charles Lever amongst others. Anna Maria continued to publish children's stories in the *St. James's Magazine* and these were compiled and published as *Chronicles of Cosy Nook* by Marcus Ward in 1875.

Anna Maria's experiences with these two periodicals were significant though short-lived. The exponential growth of the illustrated press in the nineteenth century stimulated competition and there was an extensive demand for art, literature and news amongst the middle classes. The annuals and periodicals undoubtedly popularised the work of many contemporary writers and artists.

A Woman's Story

It was in her novel *A Woman's Story* that we find Anna Maria addressing the life of a professional woman writer with passion. It was serialised as *Helen Lyndsey – The Star* in *Sharpe's London Magazine,* the first episode in Issue 2, January 1853, and eventually published four years later as a three-volume novel by Hurst and Blackett. It is tempting to read into the novel many of Anna Maria's views of the literary world, the high and low points and the constant struggle to make a living. Helen, the heroine, was a playwright whose first work achieved instant acclaim and she was the new star in London, invited to all the soirées and fêted and courted by friends and socialites. Like Alice in "The Curse of Property", Helen had to work hard to pay off her father's many debts and she did not spare herself in the process. 'I have steeped my head in water and trimmed my lamp, and worked' (Vol. 1. p. 308). Keeping up with the social round of invitations and autograph-signing for a leading literary figure was challenging and took the author away from her art. How to unite the duties of society with the duties of literature was a problem both for Anna Maria and 'Nobody', her narrator in *A Woman's Story*. No doubt Anna Maria was thinking of her own lifestyle when she referred to the philanthropic work, committee work, her advice to writers and the frustration of other writers stealing ideas. In *A Woman's Story,* she highlighted the difficulty of making a living if not paid adequately for hard work. Helen's frustration is likewise expressed as follows:

> But what other reward have I for the long, long struggle with the rapacity of publishers – the ignorance of editors – the taunts of the illiberal against a working woman, – the long, long nights and days of labour? (Vol. 1. p. 307).

One cannot but think back to Anna Maria's editorial position at *Sharpe's* and how this very novel, *Helen Lyndsey,* was cut short due to the change of editor. In this light, it was no wonder that the vexations and vagaries of a writing career were foremost in her mind. The marketplace by the 1850s was competitive and Helen had to turn from her plays to make a living in other areas. Short poems only earned small sums and long poems were too difficult to dispose of because of the crowded market. Helen 'worked prose to order – so many pages of humour subdued by so many pages of pathos' (Vol. 1. p. 279). This self-consciousness regarding her work reflected the economic necessity driving the work of authors and the difficulties compared to several decades earlier 'when authors were not as numerous as roses in June' (Vol. 1. p. 252).

More than in her other novels and to a greater degree than in "The Curse of Property", Anna Maria had the freedom to express her opinions, through Helen, about how life differed for a woman. Boys had many options open to them from youth – professions, trades, a life as a sailor or a soldier, the ministry or the law. Whatever the youth's inclination, an effort is made to support his calling in life. However:

> ... no matter what are the differences made by nature in girls, they must all work in the same mill, be all pumice-stoned to the same consistency, and learn all the same things. (Vol. 2, p. 241).

Most tellingly, Helen spoke of her desire for immortality 'to bring proof that the mind is of no sex.' This was radical for Anna Maria, a plea for recognition of intellectual equality, not the assumed subservience and obsequiousness that was publicly acceptable and expected. Anna Maria's heroine can safely express all these opinions and at the conclusion of the novel be 'reformed', keeping the author's own reputation untarnished.

Communality of Women

The illustration of 'Regina's Maids of Honour' from *Fraser's Magazine* depicts an imaginary re-creation of the literary women of 1836 sipping tea together. It appeared a year after a related image of Fraserian men drinking claret and ale. Daniel Maclise provided the portraits and William Maginn the biographies. Despite the condescending and frequently lewd remarks of Maginn about his subjects, this image highlights the regard in which Anna Maria was held, a decade after her earliest writings. She knew all of the women present, had met them, corresponded with them and had written appreciations when Jane Porter and Mary Mitford died.

"Regina's Maids of Honour" by Daniel Maclise
Fraser's Magazine, 13 January 1836
Left and anti-clockwise: Servant, Anna Maria Hall, Letitia Elizabeth Landon, Lady Sydney Morgan (*back of seat facing out*), Caroline Norton (*pointing at book*), Marguerite Blessington (*standing far right*), Jane Porter (*with mantilla*), Harriet Martineau, Mary Mitford (*sipping tea beside Anna Maria*).

In addition to assisting with Mary Braddon's journalistic apprenticeship in the *St. James's Magazine,* Anna Maria was known as a kindly and helpful editor for other budding writers, such as Isabella Fyvie Mayo, Anna Eliza Bray and another author with Irish connections, Dinah Mulock Craik who counted Anna Maria as one of her most significant contacts when she moved to London with her parents in 1839. She regularly frequented the weekly soirées held at the Halls' house in Brompton. According to Sally Mitchell, Anna Maria was the young writer's 'literary angel', helping her to get some of her work published in *Chambers's Edinburgh Journal.*

Letters held in Princeton University Library show Anna Maria's friendship with Ellen Wood (the noted sensation author of *East Lynne* published in 1861) and also the

American poet Lydia Sigourney. The latter had been a regular visitor to the Halls, and in her letter asks Anna Maria if she could possibly gain autographs for her daughter of the following: 'Wordsworth, Southey and Mrs Southey, Joanna Baillie, Carlyle, Rogers, Mrs Opie, Mrs Hofland, Mrs Norton, Lady Blessington, Miss Mitford, L.E.L., Miss Barrett.' This indicates the extent of Anna Maria's contact with a range of eminent contemporaries, many of whom frequently alluded to her warmth and generosity.

Writing for Women

Anna Maria made no secret of the fact that she had a preference for her heroines over her heroes and also that she saw herself as addressing predominantly female readers. She idealised her Irish women but was dismissive and impatient with what she saw as the limitations of the Irish male. This pattern extended equally to writings set in England:

> A hero is supposed to deserve peculiar attention at a lady's hand: and yet I do not know how it is, but I take far more pleasure in recording the actions, and developing the character of my heroines. I love my own sex – I would rather, ten to one, repeat the conversations of Lady Ellen – of Mary Lorton – or even chronicle the occasion of Magdalene's tears, than describe the feelings of Harry Mortimer ... (*Uncle Horace,* 1838, Vol. 1. p. 74).

Her earliest novels did however engage with male protagonists such as the complex Hugh Dalton, Robin Hays and Oliver Cromwell in *The Buccaneer* (1832), Sir Everard Sydney and Ralph Bradwell in *The Outlaw* (1835). *The Whiteboy* featured a number of well-rounded central male characters such as Edward Spencer and Abel Richards. She wrote taut and exciting tales with complex plotting and gripping drama.

Within her domestic novels there were many instances when a husband or male character was portrayed in a less than flattering light. Mr Lyndsey in *A Woman's Story* was a man of few ideas and few words: 'Absent when present and had as well never be present at all.' The Brevet-Major Cobbs in the same novel had a somewhat similar dynamic: 'the Major had, to a certain degree his own way which, I have observed, is generally quite as much as any married man can accomplish.' Lady Bab's husband in *Marian* likewise was 'singularly tame and gentlemanly-looking' and:

> was a sort of hanger-on to his wife's reputation ... and frequently formed a sort of soft undulating accompaniment to his wife's eloquence, which he was very politely careful not to interrupt.

Novels by Hall formed part of the popular culture of her era and reading such literature meant that women were taking time out from attending to the family in order to focus on themselves. The text may provide pleasure to the reader in a number of complex ways; through the recognition of stereotypes, acknowledgement of the formula and comparison with others of the genre; and identification with heroines who assert themselves in a variety of dramatic situations. While domestic novels may appear at first glance to be deeply conservative, the reader is not by any means subsumed within what may appear initially to be a strict socialising narrative. The potential to display deviant opinions can be carried effectively within the novel.

Anna Maria's discourses around women and marital relationships ostensibly offer the reader the acceptable beliefs of the dominant ideology – the sacredness of the marriage bond and the centrality of moral behaviour. The family audience was an important market and her ideal reader was most likely a young girl on the verge of womanhood. A keen desire to prepare the reader for future potential trials and pitfalls lay behind her zeal to share her own experiences of this significant stage in a woman's life.

On a superficial level, Anna Maria preserved the status quo but she offers, often through her secondary characters, humorous and pertinent asides on social life, fashions and types that reflected her own experience, entertained her readers, and as has been demonstrated, also subverted in subtle ways this dominant ideology. Much has been written about the importance of popular culture and women readers by writers such as Kate Flint, Angela McRobbie, Nancy Baym and Janice Radway. Anna Maria gave her readers what they wanted and they were empowered by stories that imitated or anticipated aspects of their lives. Many of her characters mimic gendered stereotypes such as the devoted wife, the overbearing wife, the strong-minded 'Blue' and the ineffectual male. Their actions and reactions provide a foil that subverts the dominant ideology, yet at the same time unthreateningly entertain the reader. She was sure of a market until the rise of the lurid and frequently immoral sensation novels of the 1870s that ultimately eclipsed her more subtle insights into domestic life of the mid-nineteenth century.

Anna Maria as an Innovator

Anna Maria was a versatile writer, ambitious to extend her literary boundaries, driven by economic necessity, opportunism and an awareness of the marketplace. In this she exemplified the strong bourgeois values of industry, enterprise and ambition. She was pragmatic, as was evident in her sensitivity regarding the financial worth of her work. Her acute awareness of the shifting vagaries in literary trends is a recurrent theme in her correspondence with publishers such as Chambers and with close friends. Her letters overall paint a portrait of a confident, sympathetic and highly organised woman who was unafraid to pursue her goals, make use of her contacts and ask for assistance. She lived through an era of extensive change in literary fashions and book production, so the need to be flexible and adaptable was essential for survival. Her ability to turn her hand to any format or any genre meant that she was less restricted in her response to change when required. As a busy working woman who earned her living in a tough professional environment, Anna Maria was an exceptional figure who was unfailingly supportive to others who came within her sphere.

In a number of other ways, Anna Maria was an innovative figure: she was in the vanguard of an Irish regional short fiction movement; her fantasy writings saw her as an early exponent of the literary fairytale in Ireland; her illustrated books were lauded; she was sought after for her editorial skills, making a significant contribution to children's annuals and leading London periodicals.

Anna Maria was one of the first regional Irish writers, along with contemporaries such as the Banim brothers, Gerald Griffin and William Carleton, to use the short story format to focus on the lives of the Irish peasantry, set in a distinct and identifiable Irish location. Her preference, to study the characters of the peasant class rather than her own Anglo-Irish class, was well documented and there was a ready audience in Ireland and England for such stories from the mid-1820s–1830s.

She was also one of the first writers to experiment with the Irish literary fairytale. From the 1820s, Thomas Crofton Croker and Thomas Keightley had paved the way forward by gathering Irish fairy and folktales but Anna Maria's attempt to fashion these legends and folktales into her own creation was noteworthy. In *Midsummer Eve,* she created a cast of fairy characters and placed them in an Irish setting, merging Irish superstitions and legends such as that of the changeling and the O'Donoghue legend with those purely of her own imagination. Other Irish figures such as Patrick Kennedy and William Allingham were working in this field from the mid-1850s so she can be situated within a history preceding the explosion of interest in Irish fairytales later in the century with the work of Lady Wilde, Lady Gregory and William Butler Yeats.

Anna Maria's illustrated books can be seen to link the Georgian period with the heyday of Victorian book production in the 1860s. Indeed the history of book illustration from the 1830s–70s could be charted through a survey of her publications alone. Thanks to the Halls' friendship with many leading artists of the period, she was uniquely placed to avail of their work and she was at all times passionate about the importance of not short-changing children in terms of quality of text and illustration. As a woman writer and a writer for children, her work has been marginalised. Her child readers were her first audience and she edited annuals, gift books and anthologies for them, selecting the best writers and artists available and ensuring high quality production for this important audience.

Anna Maria was a progressive writer and can be seen as an important figure in the history of women writers of the mid-Victorian period. She was prolific, hard-working, adaptable and innovative. The central question as to how women writers slip from the canon so swiftly and so brutally is one that is not easily answered. It is thanks to the perception and passion of Arlen House that an anthology such as this can encourage renewed interest in the life and work of a figure such as Anna Maria Fielding Hall. Undoubtedly there is much work to be done to reclaim other women writers, not only from the nineteenth century but indeed from recent decades also.

NOTES

1 '... No rational person will, for a moment, complain of the necessity for labour which those not born to wealth must endure:

I know what it is, for mine has been a life of no light toil; mine has been daily and nightly hours of hard work for a series of years; but it has been remunerated in a double sense, and consequently, although fatiguing and anxious it has brought with it contentment and gratitude. But what would this incessant toil have been if unsuccessful! – if, as with scores of others, these blotted papers had grown mildewed with tears of disappointment, and like many of my less fortunate sisters, I should have signed forth, in words of touching helplessness – "I cannot dig: to beg I am ashamed!" ...' Mrs. S.C. Hall, 'A Visit to the Female School of Design', *The Art-Union* (July 1845) p. 231.

2 A list of her children's books is included at end of this *Reader*.

3 Ekphrasis describes how one medium of art relates to another, traditionally literature to visual art. It has many meanings but it can intensify the experience of an imaginary encounter, stimulate creativity or form the basis of an entire discipline such as art history. Anna Maria often related her writings to particular works of art, part of her wider aim to publicise the art and to make it better known.

4 'An ordinary reader would not care to have his books recommended to him by Jones; but the recommendation of the great unknown comes to him with all the weight of the *Times*, the *Spectator*, or the *Saturday*.' Anthony Trollope, *An Autobiography*. 1883 (London, Oxford University Press, 1953) p. 175.

5 Her earliest works were published in *The Amulet*, edited by S.C. Hall. These included 'The Murmurer Instructed' (1926), 'The Savoyards' (1927), 'The Gipsy Girl' (1928), 'The Mountain Daisy' and 'The Rose of Fennock Dale' (both 1829).

6 *Retrospect*, Vol. 2. p. 453.

7 'The Residence of Hannah More', *The Art-Union* Feb 1, 1848.

FURTHER READING

Bourke, Angela *et al.* (eds), *The Field Day Anthology of Irish Writing: Vol. V: Irish Women's Writing and Traditions* (Cork, Cork University Press in association with Field Day, 2002).

Burman, Barbara and Jonathan White, 'Fanny's Pockets: Cotton, Consumption and Domestic Economy, 1780–1850' in Jennie Batchelor and Cora Kaplan (eds), *Women and Material Culture, 1660–1830* (Basingstoke, Palgrave, 2007).

Carleton, William, *Traits and Stories of the Irish Peasantry* (Dublin, Curry, 1830).

Colman, Anne, *Dictionary of Nineteenth-Century Irish Women Poets* (Galway, Kenny's Bookshop, 1996).
Durnin, Marion, *Sketches of Irish Character by Mrs. S.C. Hall* (Chawton House Library Women's Novels; Abingdon, Routledge, 2016).
Finlay, Peter, 'The Irish as "Other": Representations of Urban and Rural Poverty in Early Victorian Travel Writing on Ireland', Diss. Queen's University of Belfast, 2005.
Hall, S[amuel]., C[arter]. Mrs. *Can Wrong be Right? A Tale*, 2 vols (London, Hurst & Blackett, 1862).
Midsummer Eve: A Fairy Tale of Love (London, Longman, Brown, Green and Longmans, 1848).
Sketches of Irish Character, 2 vols (London, Frederick Westley and A.H. Davis, 1829).
Sketches of Irish Character, Illustrated Edition (London, M.A. Nattali, 1844).
The Whiteboy: A Story of Ireland in 1822 (London, Chapman & Hall, 1845).
A Woman's Story (London, Hurst & Blackett, 1857).
Hall, S[amuel]., C[arter]. Mrs., and S.C. Hall, *Ireland: its Scenery, Character, &c.* 3 vols (London, How and Parsons, 1841–1843).
A Week at Killarney (London, Jeremiah How, 1843).
Hall, Samuel Carter, *The Book of Gems: The Poets and Artists of Great Britain* (London, Saunders and Otley, 1836).
Retrospect of a Long Life: From 1815–1883, 2 vols (London, Richard Bentley & Son, 1883).
(ed.), *The Vernon Gallery of British Art* (London, Virtue, 1854).
Keane, Maureen, *Mrs. S.C. Hall: A Literary Biography*, Irish Literary Studies 50 (Gerrards Cross, Colin Smythe, 1997).
Kelleher, Margaret and Philip O'Leary (eds), *The Cambridge History of Irish Literature*, 2 vols (Cambridge, Cambridge University Press, 2006).
Keyes, Marian Thérèse, 'Adding Sparkle to the Dry Details: Folkloric Themes, Tales and Tangents in the Work of Anna Maria Fielding Hall' in Anne Markey and Anne O'Connor (eds), *Folklore and Modern Irish Writing* (Dublin, Irish Academic Press, 2014).
'Paratexts and Gender Politics: A Study of Selected Works by Anna Maria Fielding Hall' in Marian Thérèse Keyes and Áine McGillicuddy (eds), *Politics and Ideology in Children's Literature* (Dublin, Four Courts Press, 2014).
'"Taken from the Life": Mimetic Truth and Ekphrastic Eloquence in the Writings of Anna Maria Fielding Hall (1800–1881)', Diss. St. Patrick's College, Dublin City University, 2010.

Loeber, Rolf, Magda Loeber, and Anne Mullin Burnham, *A Guide to Irish Fiction 1650–1900* (Dublin, Four Courts Press, 2006).

Newcomer, James, 'Mr. and Mrs. S.C. Hall: Their Papers at Iowa', *Books at Iowa,* 43 (1985), 15–23.

Ní Dhuibhne, Éilís (ed.), *Look! It's a Woman Writer! Irish Literary Feminisms 1970–2020* (Dublin, Arlen House, 2021).

Shattock, Joanne, *The Oxford Guide to British Women Writers* (Oxford, Oxford University Press, 1994).

Sigourney, Lydia Huntley, Letter to Mrs. Hall, 24 Sept. 1842. Carter Hall Papers Box 1/43 (Princeton University Library, Princeton).

Sloan, Barry, 'Mrs. Hall's Ireland', *Éire-Ireland: A Journal of Irish Studies* 19:3 (1984), 18–30.

Vizetelly, Henry, *Glances Back Through Seventy Years,* 2 vols (London, Kegan Paul, 1893).

Wolff, Robert Lee (ed.), 'Introduction', *Sketches of Irish Character* by Anna Maria Hall (New York: Garland, 1979).

"The Library" by F.W. Fairholt
Midsummer Eve (1848)
Anna Maria working at her desk in her magnificent baronial style library in The Rosery, Old Brompton, Kensington, the Halls' address from 1839–50

I

Sketches of Irish Character

Old Frank (1829)

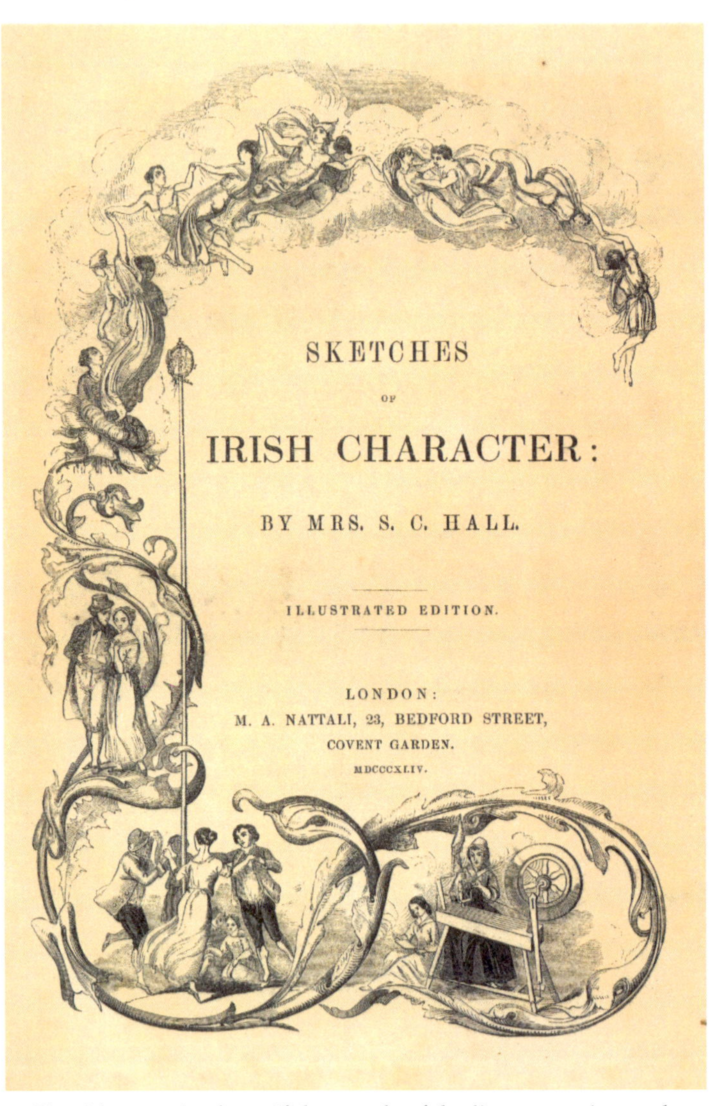

The title page is a beautiful example of the *livre romantique* style
Title page from *Sketches of Irish Character*
ill. by J. Franklin, engr. by Jackson

"OLD FRANK": A SKETCH

Anna Maria's earliest writings were a series of Irish sketches, stemming largely from an oral storytelling tradition, and although she wrote nine novels, three plays and numerous travel books, the bulk of her writing consisted of literary sketches, much of it destined for periodicals. Many of the individual sketches reappeared in different editions as publishers frequently included them in suitable anthologies.

S.C. Hall took full credit for his wife's initiation into the world of letters in his *Retrospect* as follows:

> In 1825 Mrs Hall had written nothing ... One evening she was telling me some anecdotes of her old Irish schoolmaster, 'Master Ben.' Said I, 'I wish you would write about that just as you tell it.' She did so. I printed her story in *The Spirit and Manners of the Age*, a monthly periodical I then edited, and from that day dates her career as an author. (Vol. 2. p. 425)

Anna Maria's fondness for the characters that peopled her early childhood in Wexford, coupled with her facility with language and an ability to capture a turn of phrase with consummate ease, meant that her *Sketches of Irish Character* proved immediately popular. As a child, she had listened to her coachman and storyteller, Old Frank, who time and again told her the fairy and folk stories that were to influence so many of her works. Her memory was prodigious and her recall of her life in Wexford was to provide much material for her stories.

In addition to the tales she heard from her servants and local peasants in Wexford, her grandmother had a store of tales from her Swiss/French background and these likewise were woven into her wider output. As with the Irish peasantry, she was drawn to the poor people of the Savoy region of the Alps rather than the urban wealthy. Her focus on the Irish peasant was also part of what she felt was the wider philanthropic duty of a woman of her class towards the needy in society. As a writer, she could highlight the plight of the poor, thus bringing about social change and awareness. Although her intentions were admirable and she genuinely sought to assist the Irish, she also could be seen as falling into the trap of the pursuit of the "exotic", a relationship of subtle domination akin to that outlined by Edward Said in *Orientalism.* She manipulated the voices of the peasants for her own purposes and didactic aims. Despite this, her *Sketches* launched her career in Ireland and in England.

The sketch was a familiar format during the early nineteenth-century and Anna Maria returned to it repeatedly throughout her writing career. The word "sketch" appeared in many publications of this time such as Washington Irving's *The Sketch Book* (1820*), Sketches and Fragments* by Lady Blessington (1822) and *Our Village: Sketches of Rural Characters and Scenery* by Mary Russell Mitford. The looseness or flexibility in the structure of the sketch has been examined by Richard Sha in his account of *The Visual and the Verbal Sketch in British Romanticism* where he argued that the sketch in art and literature was seen to be less finished in the classical sense but was in fact more truthful because it captured the essence of the character or the scenery. The Romantics viewed the sketch as a fleeting first impression, non-judgmental but aesthetically more powerful and closer to the truth. Sha has argued that the unfinished nature of the sketch meant that, for women, it had less pretension to gravitas and was thus attractive for women artists and writers who often had to preface their writings with a "veil of self-effacement." Sketching was assumed to be one of woman's amateur accomplishments and it was not seen as a threat which would detract from her primary duties towards her husband and household. For all of those reasons, the sketch therefore was the perfect vehicle to showcase Anna Maria's spontaneity and her search for truth and propriety.

Heather Ingman refers to the instability of the sketch, "veering between travelogue and morality tale" in the writings of Anna Maria Hall and Maria Edgeworth. Anna Maria's sketches were a distinct form of short fiction, and like the work of her contemporary William Carleton, they can be seen to represent an important phase in the development of the Irish short story.

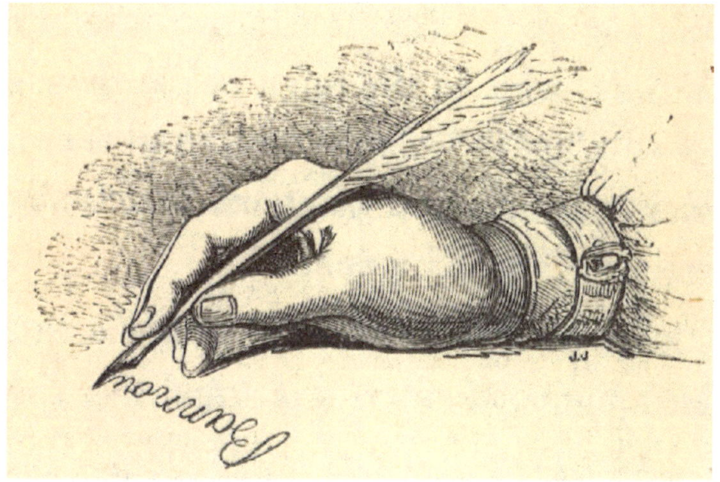

The Bannow Hand from end of 'Introduction' to 1844 edition
The Pen, ill. by J. Franklin, engr. by Jackson

Anna Maria dedicated her first series of *Sketches* to Mary Russell Mitford, renowned for her series of sketches entitled "Our Village" ten years earlier for *Lady's Magazine.* She became a celebrity and people flocked to visit the village of Three Mile Cross in Berkshire where the stories were set. In her introduction, Anna Maria addressed Mitford, noting that Bannow would be the setting for her own sketches. She saw Bannow as being an exceptionally favourable specimen of an Irish village. She was very proud of Bannow, above all with its residents. As in

Mitford's work, the reader meets many of the same characters in various stories. For example, the Roman Catholic priest Father Mike, appears in a number of tales, apart from the one which bears his own name, such as "Captain Andy," "Old Frank," "The Bannow Postman," and "Jack the Shrimp." Her vivid descriptions of the area enable the reader to visualise such local landmarks as the mountain of Forth, Johnstown Castle and the Tower of Hook. They are referred to with the same frequency and affection as her favourite characters and this specificity is one of the strengths of her narrative style.

"Old Frank" is a lively sketch, authentically and energetically portrayed. As with many of her sketches, Anna Maria employs a framing narrative within which she introduces one story that reminds her of another. Tales are recounted and the characters mull over the events and the underlying moral is highlighted. She transitions effortlessly to her description of her warm and happy memories of her old coachman to his store of folk and fairy tales and how much she enjoyed listening to his tales. He is persuaded to relate "The Stout and Strong of Heart", a favourite for them both. It is full of drama and deals with one of her recurrent themes, that of the changeling and the relentless mischief of the fairies. The second half of the sketch gives a flavour of the political situation in the recent past and Frank's 'true and faithful service' to his master during the rebellion of 1798.

The reader is captivated by the strength of the story-telling, the lively and humorous dialogue, the warmth and depth of Anna Maria's love for her coachman and the vivid sense of place and character. Marion Durnin champions the *Sketches* and deplores how they have been either ignored or misunderstood by her critics:

> Far from being pretty tales of cottage girls and careless youths, they are riven with death, abandonment, orphanhood, even

> gothic strangeness, and bear witness to a way of life on the cusp of extinction (p. xxiii).

The illustrations are taken from the highly successful third edition of 1844, created by many well-known Irish and English illustrators. Each sketch had a large half-page illustrated vignette at the beginning and a smaller closing vignette. Note the main scene chosen for the opening vignette for "Annie Leslie", an entirely different image to that used thirty years later for the book *Annie Leslie and Other Stories* (1877) chosen for our own book cover.

The 1844 edition also includes a frontispiece portrait of Anna Maria by Henry MacManus and five further plates by Daniel Maclise.

The Rivals, from the sketch "Annie Leslie"
Ill. by H.J. Townsend, engr. By Jackson

Further Reading

Durnin, Marion, *Sketches of Irish Character by Mrs. S.C. Hall* (Abingdon, Routledge, 2016). Chawton House Library: Women's Novels.

Hall, S[amuel]. C[arter]. Mrs. *Sketches of Irish Character*, 2 vols (London, Frederick Westley and A.H. Davis, 1829).

Sketches of Irish Character (London, Frederick Westley and A.H. Davis, 1831).

Sketches of Irish Character, illus. ed. (London, M.A. Nattali, 1844).

Hall, Samuel Carter, *Retrospect of a Long Life: From 1815 to 1883*, 2 vols (London, Richard Bentley & Son, 1883).

Ingman, Heather, *A History of the Irish Short Story* (Cambridge, Cambridge University Press, 2009).

Keane, Maureen, *Mrs. S.C. Hall: A Literary Biography*, Irish Literary Studies 50 (Gerrards Cross, Colin Smythe, 1997).

Mitford, Mary, "Our Village." *Lady's Magazine*, 1819.

Said, Edward W., *Orientalism* (London, Penguin, 1991).

Sha, Richard, *The Visual and the Verbal Sketch in British Romanticism* (Philadelphia: University of Pennsylvania Press, 1998).

The Rescue from the Fairies
ill. by J. Franklin, engr. by Walmsley
Half-page vignette at beginning of "Old Frank"

Old Frank

As long as I can remember, Frank was called – "Old Frank." He was a little, crabbed-looking man, bent nearly double; had a healthy colouring on his cheek, and a few, very few, grey hairs straying over his bald and shrivelled forehead; with a halt in his walk; and was always either singing or coughing: somewhat "cranky" in his temper, and, in his capacity of coachman (which situation he had filled for a period of forty-two years in our family), exercised despotic away over horses, dogs, and grooms. He was singularly faithful, and strongly attached to his master and mistress, his horses, and myself; indeed, as to the two last, it was a matter of doubt which he loved best; however "snappish" he might have been to others, he was to me, in my childish days, one of the kindest and firmest of friends; no matter how I tormented him – no matter what pranks I played (and they were not a few), "Miss Maria" was always right, and everybody else was wrong. Having lived so long in the family, he was hardly looked upon as a servant, and neither master nor mistress disputed his dictum; indeed I do not know why they should, for, whatever his authority extended, matters were well managed. The coats of his carriage-horses shone like French satin, and the carriage, an old lumbering thing of the last century, could not have existed at all under the care of any other coachman, Frank, the carriage, and horses, had grown old together; they were all of a piece, and cut a remarkable appearance, whenever they walked (for that was their most rapid pace) out in the bright, sunshiny summery. But it was not alone in this, his principal situation, that Frank was entitled to, and treated with, respect. All the perfect and all the embryo, sportsmen of the neighbourhood came to consult him on every matter connected with dogs and horses; he was famed, all over the county, for educating pointers on the most approved principles, and was permitted to have three or four constantly in training for the neighbouring gentry, who always remunerated him handsomely for his trouble. He had been an excellent sportsman in his youth, and took much pride in boasting that, except his head, all the bones in his body had been broken; indeed, even his head exhibited a sufficient quantity of bumps to puzzle a phrenologist; the old man still loved sporting, and it was owing to this circumstance that Frank and I were great friends.

I certainly was "a country child;" and to escape from study, and stroll with Frank, Frank's dogs, and Frank's daughter, "my kind and gentle nurse," was one of the greatest of my simple enjoyments. I can hardly tell why, but Bannow, in my remembrance, always seems like fairy-land – its fields so green – its trees so beautiful – its inhabitants so different from any I have elsewhere met!

The aged man used to make it a constant practice to take out a steady old pointer, with a young, untaught, roving, but well-grown puppy; and I believe Joss (the old one) was as much interested in the business of educating the young dog, as Frank himself. Be that as it may, we used all to wander among the green lanes and fields, and, when I was tired, nurse would seat me on an old grey stone, or rustic style, and Frank would lean on his gun, and tell me some of the fairy tales, or legends, with which his memory was so well stored. He had a most confirmed belief in banshees, cluricawns, fairies, and mermaids; and if Mary, who was very superior to the general order of servants, ever presumed to doubt the truth of one of her father's stories, he reproved her in no gentle terms; and no wonder, - he had a mark in his hand, which was actually given by an arrow, shot at him by a fairy queen, one evening, when he was returning home after a quiet carouse at Mr. Talbot's. He could never be prevailed upon to root up large mushrooms (fairy tables), or to pull bulrushes (fairy horses), lest he might offend the good people.

His most favourite walk was across some young plantations, admirable covers for game, to a small hill, thickly wooded at either side, where there was a singularly fine oak, one of whose branches jutted suddenly from the trunk, and formed a rustic seat, which, in childish sportiveness, I used to call my throne. From thence the prospect was very beautiful: the long, white chimneys of my old home sprang, as it were, from amid the trees, that, from this particular point of view, appeared to fringe the ocean's brink; while the many-coloured foliage of the lofty poplar, dark cedar, feathery birch, or magnificent elm, gave richness and variety to the landscape.

But in our own summer-house – a comparatively rude structure, yet which in those days, was, to my mind, the most perfect example of elegance and good taste that was over erected – how I did love to sit, during the long evenings – nurse's arm around me, to prevent the possibility of any irregular and restless movements terminating in an upset, and listen with delight to Frank's fairies, about whom the good old man so dearly loved to talk, only interrupting his narrative, now and then, by a necessary word of caution to his dogs. Whenever I urged him to tell me a story, he used to shake his head, and say, "Och! Miss, honey, ye'll, maybe, think of ould Frank and his fairies, when ye'll be far from your native land, and my poor smashed bones at rest. But my blessing be about ye," he would add, patriotically, *"never deny your country."*

My favourite story was, "The Stout and Strong of Heart," and I believe it was Frank's favourite also; for many a time and oft has he repeated it to me, and always have I listened with attention, pleasing the old man, while I was myself delighted. I will give it my readers, although I fear it will lose much, from the absence of my ancient friend, who, with so much earnestness and native humour, related it.

"There was plenty of mirth, and of everything else, in the little cabin of Jerry Mahony, for his daughter Ellen had just become a bride, and the merry party were beguiling the time while the dinner was in preparation. The blind piper was sitting on the hearth-stone, making beautiful music, and now and again taking a sup of potheen, to the long life of the wedded pair. Jerry himself was listening to all the compliments and good wishes of the neighbours; his wife, Biddy, busily placing all her own and the borrowed delf upon the table, and bustling her mind Peggy with a continual 'Make haste, hurru! – 'tis only once in a long life;' while the bride and bridegroom, James and Ellen Deasy, sat in a corner, talking over their future arrangements, and planning ways and means to make themselves happy and comfortable; and, to be sure, the mother of the girl got everything in order. And Ellen was lovely and beautiful enough for a queen, let alone a poor man's wife. But, although she was made much of, by rich and poor, no one thought more of her than Kit Murtough, the blind piper; and good right had he so to do; for she had the pity for him, the poor, sightless creature: – and it was he who made the beautiful music that night; so beautiful was it, that the priest himself could stand it no longer, but capered like a China-man. Well, the next morning, Biddy Mahony went to the foot of the ladder that led to her daughter's room –

"'Ellen, honey,' says she, 'come down, I have some nice tay for ye both.' She waited, and there was no answer; so she went up a few steps, 'James, agra! Won't you waken for me?" Still no answer: well she went into the room, and stopped, and said, 'Why then won't either of you spake to yer own mother, that gave birth to one, and a wife to the other? Jemmy, Nelly, dears! – get up and look at the morning that's so smiling and happy.' Still not a word: so she went and pulled the wisp of straw out of the window, and let in the light. She then looked on the bed, patted her child on the cheek, and felt that she was a cold corpse. Her bitter shrieks soon woke the husband; and the neighbours came running in, in crowds; and black grief was in that cabin where the night before, there had been so much joy.

Many suspected that James Deasy, had a hand in his wife' death, and there were some who told him so. But sobs, from the very depth of his heart, were James's only answers. The evening came, and the young bride was laid out for the wake. All was got in readiness for the 'berring,' which, according to custom, was to be on the third day. Now, nobody took the death of poor Ellen more to heart than did Kit the piper, who wandered about the neighbourhood of her dwelling, playing only dismal tunes, until the night before the funeral, when he was sitting, between lights, under the corn-rick that stood in the sheltered corner of Jerry Mahony' field, while the mournful music made the place more melancholy. Suddenly he felt a sudden gush of wind pass by him, and then all was still; he paused for a while, and again struck up the same tune, the tune that poor Ellen so dearly loved; then the wind came stronger by him, and again he paused; once more he began the air, and the wind beat furiously against him. He now crossed himself, and called on the blessed Virgin, when he heard the voice of the dead bride speak to him, and say, 'Kit Murtough, go to my husband, and tell him not to weep for me, for I am a living woman, but the fairies carried me away. Bid him come here at nightfall, and bring a pail of new milk from the cow; but tell him, be careful not to spill a drop of it, or he'll lose me forever, but to be STOUT AND STRONG OF HEART; and when he hears the blast rush past him, let him throw it upon me, so that it may drench me all over, but, if he misses me, he'll never see me more'. A joyful man was Kit that minute, and off he posted, and told it, word for word, to the husband, who, to be sure, put but little faith in it, yet the love to the wife made him try. So, to make all sure, he milked the cow himself, without spilling a drop, and off he went to the corn-rick, very much troubled in his mind, with the hope of recovering his bride, the doubts as to the piper's story, and the fear that he should 'miss drenching her, and then lose her forever.' But James was a bold man, and feared nothing else. So he waited patiently until the first blast of wind passed him. He took up the pail, but his heart misgave him, and he laid it down again. Once more the blast came, and more strongly, but still James Deasy was only half a man. The third time it came furiously upon him; then James was ready, and threw every drop upon the blast, when, all at once, he saw his wife before him, as plainly as when she stood beside the priest; and he clasped his arms about her, while a loud whirling tempest – full of the good people – came all round them. But she was safe from harm, and they returned smiling to her father's cottage.

"No one but a mother can tell Biddy Mahony's joy to see her child come back to her again. And the evening of that day saw happiness returned to Jerry's cottage, where the piper had his old seat, in the chimney-corner, sung many a merry song, and drank a double portion of whisky to the health of the bridegroom and the bride.

"But James Deasy, when he came in, went straight to the coffin, and, in the place of the corpse, he saw a great log of wood, with the shroud upon it. This he quickly put upon the fire, when they heard a loud screech, and the log went up the chimney with a noise like a thunder-storm, that almost shook the roof off the old cabin. The neighbours came running in to know what was the matter; and there they saw James Deasy, and Ellen his wife, sitting in the corner, as if nothing had happened; she looking as beautiful, and he as happy, as when Father Peter blessed them both, a few days before.

"Some months had now passed away, and Ellen was about to become a mother, when she called her husband to her bed-side, and said, 'James, dear, happy have we been, and happy will we still be if you do my bidding; which is, when my little baby is born, put three crosses on its forehead, and three on mine, and don't leave me for a minute, however they may try to wile you away, for the fairies will be after the both of us." Well, James never left her bedside, but watched her night and day, for fear the fairies should be waiting to take off both the wife and the child; which, when it came, was a glorious boy. But, all at once, James heard a scream outside the door, and a small voice calling 'Ellen Deasy;' he looked round, and saw the latch raised, and the door opening gently, then ran towards it, and pushed it to violently, when, all in a minute, he heard a loud laugh, as if from many persons, and, when he looked on his wife's bed, he saw that both mother and child were dead. James remembered the crosses, and remembered that his wife warned him to let nothing tempt him from her bed-side. But 'twas too late, they were both gone, and James Deasy was indeed a wretched man.

"They kept poor Ellen and her little one for a long time above the ground, and then they buried them both in the churchyard. But James could not rid himself of the idea that the bodies were not those of his wife and child, so he would not let the priest say mass or anything over them; a thing which brought much shame and scandal upon him. But he had his own reasons for it.

"Now, it happened, one morning, that James Deasy was hoeing his little garden, and thinking, as he did every day, of his poor Ellen, that he had lost nearly a twelvemonth, when his hoe struck against a sod as green as ever was spring leaf, although his spade had been into it many a time, and it had been long covered with black clay. All of a sudden he heard music under it – beautiful and sweet music, such as he had never heard before. He remembered his poor wife's warning, to 'be stout and strong of heart', so he raised up the sod, and looked down. There he saw, at a depth that seemed many miles underground, a number of little people dancing most merrily; they were all dressed in green leaves, and had fine forms and faces; for, to his great wonder, he could distinguish them plainly, although they were so far off. He thought that one of the little people resembled his dead wife; and he knew it must be her, when he heard her say, 'to the corn-rick at midnight,' while the rest of the fairies repeated her words, 'to the corn-rick at midnight;' and then the music ceased, and the ground appeared the same as it had always been; for James could not discover the green sod heh had just raised. The more he thought upon the words, 'to the corn-rick at midnight,' the more he was convinced they had some meaning, and that they were addressed to him. So he waited impatiently till the night came, and went off to the appointed place.

"Now, the green island was well known over all the country as the pet of the fairies. There he waited till he heard the sound of the merry pipes, and saw a long train coming along the path. He stood quite quiet, as if he was minding nothing at all but the road-stones he pretended to be breaking, until the whole of the crowd had passed him; when up from the ground starts James, seizes the last woman of the group, tears off the cloak from the shoulders, signs three crosses on the brow, snatches the child, and does the same to it, when, lo and behold! his own wife, Ellen Deasy, on her knees before him, and his own beautiful little baby in her arms! The sign of the cross has driven all the fairies away, and, safe and sound, James, and Ellen, and their little one, returned to their cottage, and never more was the life of either disturbed by the good people.

"They are still living in Dumraghodooly, and James is ever and always ready to tell his story over a glass of whisky punch; but no inducement has yet prevailed on Ellen to give any account of her adventures in fairy-land."

"Oh, Miss, don't laugh," Old Frank would add – "it's as true as I'm a sinner, and it's bad to disbelieve the fairies. Sure I was an unbeliever once myself, and this was my punishment – one of their arrows right through the flat o' my hand; I shall carry the mark to my grave. Come, Miss, it's time to go home; – bad luck to the dog! Joss, where's Rover? – Rover! Oh, that young dog wants as much attindance as a Mullenavat pig!"

"How is that, Frank?"

"Why, Miss, the Mullenavat people are Munster, ye know, and quite inferior to the Wexfordians, and depind on the pig to pay the rint, and, on that account, trate him with all the respect possible – why not? – and so they pick out the big pratees for the pig, and ate the little ones themselves; and they give the pig the clane straw, and sleep themselves in the dirty; and they give the pig the candle to go to bed wid, and go to bed themselves in the dark."

"And is that true, Frank?"

"As gospel, Miss; upon my word it is. Here, Rover! the only way to steady that dog will be to hang him. Rover – Rover!"

Frank delighted in telling stories of the rebellion, but he left it to others to recount what true and faithful service he had rendered his master and mistress in that perilous time; and they were nothing loath to do him ample justice. I have often heard how he buried the best wine in the asparagus beds, to save it from falling into the hands of the rebels; and how he concealed his favourite horses in the hen and turkey-houses; and how, at the risk of his life, he carried a forged order to General Roche, who commanded the rebel forces in the town of Wexford; which order purported to come from another rebel chief, and demanded the instant freedom of his master, whose life was thus preserved.

It was in the summer of 1798, that my grandfather, who had been, for a few days, in Dublin, on business of importance, embarked with his constant attendant, Frank, on board a small Wexford trading vessel. Intelligence had reached them of the disturbed state of the country; and, as land travelling was unsafe, the "boat" was engaged to convey them direct to the Bay of Bannow.

As they passed Dalkey Isle, and coasted along the beautiful shores of Wicklow, glowing in the full richness of summer, the sea-breeze tempering the fervid heat with its invigorating freshness, my grandfather thought he had never seen the country look so tranquil or so happy; the lowing of cattle, the bleating of sheep, the cooing of the wood-pigeon, even the subdued warblings of the forest birds, were heard on board their light bark; but when the day passed, and the night darkened, unusual fires sparkled on the hills; and, along the shore, lights would blaze for a moment, and then suddenly disappear. The anxiety of both master and servant to arrive home was intense, and they were much pleased to perceive, through the grey mist of the succeeding morning, the spire of Wexford Church. As the day advanced, Mr. ________ distinctly saw green flags floating from the masts of the several vessels in the harbour.

"We must sport one too, sir," said Rawson, the Captain of the brig; "if we do not, they will board us." He unfurled his flag immediately, after which, Frank went off deck into the cabin, and slyly took out his master's pistol from his portmanteau; he then (as he subsequently stated), poured a little water into the pans of a fowling-piece, a blunderbuss, and other firearms, that he had perceived lying under some coiled rope and canvass sacks. The fact was, he had ascertained, by overhearing some conversation between the Captain and one of his crew, that Rawson was a United Irishman, and one in no way to be trusted. He then crept on deck, and placed himself beside his master's elbow. My grandfather kept his eye fixed on Rawson's movements; but, to say the truth, if he had been tacking for the bottom of the sea, he could hardly have discovered it, being utterly ignorant of all naval tactics.

The channel into the harbour of Wexford is very narrow; nor was it until the prow of the vessel was passing between the two embankments, Mr. __________ observed that Rawson, instead of steering for Carnsore Point, was making direct for the town. He instantly sprang at the Captain, who was at the helm, and seized him by the throat; while Frank, nothing loath, presented a pistol to his head, swore vehemently that, if he did not tack about, he would throw him overboard. Rawson, who was a man of great bodily strength, drew a pistol from his bosom; it missed fire; but, at the moment when my grandfather had overpowered his antagonist, he received a blow on the head from Frank; he was almost stunned, staggered a few paces forward, and fell. At that instant, two or three musket balls whizzed past, and Frank whispered, – "I humbly ax yer honour's pardon, but it was the only way I had left, to make yer honour get out of the way of three blackguards in that boat, who took prime aim, and would have had ye down as clane as a partridge, but for my taste of a knock; the game's up now, but that bit of a blow wouldn't hurt a pointer, sir."

In another instant they were boarded by the rebels, and Mr._____ was soon bound hand and foot. He would, most likely, have been piked on the spot, but that the insurgents were, at this period, anxious, if possible, to obtain the sanction and assistance of some of the leading gentlemen of the country. They, therefore, secured him, to prevent the possibility of escape, and Frank was suffered to depart. The poor man arrived at Bannow when it was near midnight, and found my mother and grandmother marking the minutes by their tears. The whole country was in a state of open insurrection; and, although they had hitherto been treated with respect, through the kind interference of the good priest and Captain Andy, yet the uncertain fate of my grandfather, and the continued stories of death and destruction they had heard, kept them in perpetual agitation. Frank's account was not likely to soothe their misery, and they asked each other what was to be done, without receiving consolation from any plan that was suggested. Captain Andy was with his rebel regiment at the mountain of Forth. The priest had gone, it was supposed, to Ross. What plan could be adopted? – "Frank, can you not devise any mode?" 'Frank coughed, – "Can nothing be done?" – Frank replied to this question by asking another: "Can ye tell me, madam, if they have taken Grey Bess for the devil's sarvice yet?"– "She was in the stable this morning, with two or three of the old horses." – "Hem! I'm glad of that, I'll jist step out – I wonder they passed her; she's as fine a slug of a mare as there's in the whole country."

The ladies thought Frank's attention to his quadrupeds ill-timed, but he went his way; and, first concealing the carriage-horses in the fowl-houses, mounted Grey Bess, whose strong, well-made limbs merited the encomium he had passed on her, and, without imparting his intention even to his fellow-servants, set off at a brisk trot to the mountain of Forth. Arrived at the encampment, he soon found out his friend Andy, and, in a few moments, they were in close conversation at a little distance from the mass of the people, who were either sleeping, drinking, or singing, in scattered groups over the mountain, canopied by the clear, moonlit sky. "We must get him off, Frank; General Roche is in command – yet I don't know how! Can you write?" – "Is it me?" replied Frank; "not I – can you?" "No; an order from General Keough would do it, but he's for making a bonfire of the town."

"The baste!" exclaimed Frank, "would there be any sin in jist signing his name to a little taste of an order to General Roche, to let him go free on particular business, to be returned when called for? If we had him safe in Bannow, 'twould be asy to hide him away in an ould cave, or castle, or cask, or ship him off, like a sack of pratees, to Wales. Where there's a will there's a way: but he's clane gone if he remains in Wexford. Is Father Mike here?" Andy bent his thumb back to intimae that he was in the camp. "I thought so God be wid ould times! He'll never forget my mistress's attintion to him, and she an Englishwoman, let alone my master's. If ye see a man an' his bit of a wife go past in the morning on Grey Boss, *bathershin.* God be wid ye!" and Frank went off to seek the priest. He was easily found, and soon understood what Frank wanted.

"My simple order would be of no use, Frank, for they think me faithless enough, because I cannot spill blood – blood of the innocent as well as the guilty. General Keough's would do it; "the kind-hearted man paused: "every imprisoned Protestant will, I know, suffer before tomorrow night."

"Mu poor master, sir, and mistress! – I'll tell ye what, if yer reverence will jist give me the scrapeen of an order, who'll know ye iver wrote it? – and sure it's I that 'ud write it in the crack of a whip, if I knew how. Oh, sir, think of all the good they did the poor Catholicks in the hard winter!"

Father Mike hesitated no longer, drew from his pocket a little inkhorn, and wrote the order on the top of Frank's hat, the moon shining brightly on them at the time.

Away went Frank and Grey Bess into Wexford, and the day had dawned by the time he arrived at the Court-house. He unhesitatingly presented his order, and my grandfather was much delighted to find himself at liberty.

"I wonder the General wrote," said the man who let him out, "for he'll be in Wexford himself in an hour!"

This intelligence alarmed Frank much, and he hurried his master to a dwelling, the fidelity of whose inmates he could depend on; it belonged to his uncle Kit's third daughter, who was married to Mickey Hays, the grocer, at that time Commissary-General to the rebel quartered in Wexford. There Frank equipped his master in a good frieze suit, a long coat, straw hat – mounted a bunch of laurel at one side, and a green feather at the other, and presented to him a sturdy pike; he then arrayed his own little person in "his uncle Kit's daughter's" red petticoat and hooded cloak.

"And now," said he, "yer honour will remember that yer name's Pat Kennessy, and that ye're going to the blessed priest's house and that I'm yer wife – that 'll ride on Grey Bess behind ye."

They arrived safely at Bannow; and my grandfather often said – when the troublesome times were passed, and he jested at the remembrance of by-gone dangers – that, three times within forty-eight hours, Frank saved his life – when he damped the powder – knocked him down – and became his wife.

Honest Frank's services did not go unrewarded; he was suffered to indulge all his little peculiarities, without let or hinderance, and to be as cross as he pleased, without the possibility of a reprimand. Although an ample prevision was made for his latter days, he mourned most bitterly our coming over to what he always designated "the could-hearted English country;" and his affection was so strong, that he would have left his children, to follow us, had he not been (to use his own expression) "past travelling, at eighty-five."

Good old man! I well remember him when the moment of parting arrived, and we were to take our departure for "the great metropolis of nations." He stood foremost of a troop of weeping domestics; his hat held reverentially in his withered hand, while the sleet of a January morning mingled with his grey hairs; tears rolled abundantly down his wrinkled cheeks; we were seated, yet still he held the coach-door open - "God bless you all! shut the door, Frank," said my dear grandfather, almost as much affected as his faithful servant. Frank still held it, cast a farewell look upon us, and then, turning to a man who was close to him, exclaimed, "You do it, James; I can't close the door that shuts me out for ever from –" the horses went on, and I saw my kind story-teller no more.

I have said that Frank loved his horses; he also loved the old family carriage. And when we left the country, my grandfather presented it to him, thinking of course he would sell it. No such thing. Frank went to live with his daughter, my old nurse, at the village of Duncormuck; and there he erected a spacious shed, under cover of which he deposited his favourite chariot; the poor old man's delight was to wheel it in and out. Until within a few days of his death, he attended to it with the most scrupulous exactness, and invariably got into a passion whenever the propriety of selling it was hinted at.

"Who knows," he would say, "but they may come home of a suddent? – and what a comfort it would be to them to find the ould carriage, and ould Frank, ready for sarvice!" POOR OLD FRANK!

Closing vignette at end of "Old Frank"
The Temple at Graige
ill. by W.H. Brooke, engr. by Mason

II

A Tale of Landlords and Peasants

The Curse of Property (1830)

from *Tales of Women's Trials*

Maria Edgeworth was an important influence on many aspects of Anna Maria's work. She corresponded regularly with her, visited her in Edgeworthstown, and subsequently described this visit in *The Art-Journal*. Edgeworth was impressed with her early sketches and the fact that the second series of Anna Maria's *Sketches of Irish Character* was dedicated to "Miss Edgeworth" was testament to the strength of her friendship and homage. Anna Maria's view that Ireland was best served by a benevolent Anglo-Irish ruling class who would direct the peasants fairly, live in Ireland on their estates and manage the land for the peasants, stemmed largely from Edgeworth's influence. As in Edgeworth's *Castle Rackrent* and *The Absentee*, the dissolute lives of careless landlords, the loss of fortunes through mismanagement, and the ruinous consequences of absenteeism were captured time and again in many of Anna Maria's sketches such as "The Last of the Line," "Hospitality," "Independence" and "The Curse of Property". She was attracted to complex characters like Thady Quirke, the steward in Castle Rackrent who recounts the tale of four generations of Rackrent heirs. Jeremiah Keg, the "valet by inheritance" serves a similar purpose in her own account, albeit less central than the main narrator Sir Charles Stanley. Anna Maria, like Edgeworth was to make ample use of the device of the unreliable narrator in her tales, frequently none other than the author herself – confirming for the reader the authenticity of the unfolding events.

In the introduction to this anthology, I discussed aspects of Anna Maria's novel *A Woman's Story* (1857). This earlier work, "The Curse of Property" was first published in *The Iris: A Literary & Religious Offering* (1831) and in numerous editions of *Tales of Woman's Trials*. A manuscript exists in the National Library of Ireland dated circa 1830.

Despite an almost three-decade difference, similar themes emerge: the need to be independent due to economic factors; the meteoric rise to fame; the social obligations that went with a literary career; and most importantly the potential conflict between femininity and authorship. Alice Lee, the heroine of "The Curse of Property" had to leave Ireland due to bad debts by her Anglo-Irish family but she settled in Paris and thanks to "some persons of literary distinction" discovered that "her powerful and clear mind was capable of great efforts, and much usefulness." She was the toast of Paris, much to the chagrin of the relatives who had treated her so badly.

> The thing was impossible – what! The little pug-nosed girl, who had never been to school, to be praised in the newspapers, and thought much of by learned people, – for *her* to write a book, a whole book, who had learned to hold her pen from a village school-master!

Anna Maria emphasised that Alice was not one who put on airs just because of her superior intelligence. She was certainly not one of those "morbid literary ladies ... who sigh and sentimentalise over their being obliged to appear before the public, and yet use every justifiable and unjustifiable mode of forcing celebrity." She remained humble and above all, Christian, and, as in many of Anna Maria's tales, the heroine did her duty according to the state of life that it had pleased God to call her. The driving force behind Alice's efforts to make a success of her literary career was the necessity to be independent. It was the lack of this vital quality that destroyed the estate of her clan at Barrybrooke. Thanks to Alice's Christian ethos, she got her "revenge" on her despicable relatives by helping them in every way that was within her power.

Anna Maria described the nobility of Alice Lee's motives and the real secret of her popularity thus: "Though she became an *author*, she had not ceased to be a *woman*." Anna Maria outwardly rejected the vulgarity of the "blue" (bluestocking) or the "strong-minded" woman but all her writings show her deep concern for women and the trials confronting them in all areas of their lives.

Anna Maria always ensured that she herself was never perceived as anything less than a "proper" woman according to the conventions of the age – the "Angel of the House" as outlined in Mary Poovey's *The Proper Lady*. The Proper Lady was devoted to her husband, self-sacrificing, self-effacing, passive and pure. In *The Proper Lady*, Poovey examines how some women authors became professional writes despite the strictures of propriety and the conventions of proper femininity. She addresses the important link with the spread of evangelicalism and the focus on spiritual reformation and social improvement, both cornerstones of Hall's mission. The virtues of hard work, self-discipline and temperance coupled with the extension of women's domestic activities into her local sphere through charitable work were central in Anna Maria's oeuvre.

FURTHER READING

Edgeworth, Maria, *Castle Rackrent: An Hibernian Tale* (London, J. Johnson, 1800).

Hall, S[amuel]. C[arter], Mrs, "The Curse of Property: a Sketch of Irish Mismanagement." Ms. 34,260. [c. 1830] National Library of Ireland.

"The Curse of Property." *The Iris: A Literary & Religious Offering* (1831).

"The Curse of Property." *Tales of Woman's Trials* (New York, Wallis & Newell, 1835).

"Edgeworthstown, Memories of Maria Edgeworth." *The Art-Journal*, July 1849.

Tales of Woman's Trials (London, Houlston & Sons, 1835).

Tales of Woman's Trials (London, Chapman and Hall, 1847).

Keane, Maureen, *Mrs. S.C. Hall: A Literary Biography*, Irish Literary Studies 50 (Gerrards Cross, Colin Smythe, 1997).

Poovey, Mary, *The Proper Lady and the Woman Writer: Ideology as Style in the Works of Mary Wollstonecraft, Mary Shelley, and Jane Austen* (Chicago, University of Chicago Press, 1984).

Poor Barry!" exclaimed Mr. Newton. "Poor Barry! It was sad to see that once fine property melted away, one could hardly tell how, until even the noble dwelling of his ancestors was sold in lots to a fellow who printed 'Architect' on his card."

"I was his uncle's friend," sighed old Sir Charles Stanley; "and the remembrance of that family – it is strange, but, nevertheless, true – affords me at once exceeding pain and sincere pleasure. I mourn over the love of display, and the pauperising system, pursued by poor but proud relations, by which that fine estate was utterly ruined; and I grieve for it the more, because it is far from being a singular instance of ruin, effected by similar means. You, my dear friend, will readily believe that the pleasurable reminiscences I experience arise from the noble conduct of that little black-eyed girl, Alice Lee, whom all the family, excepting Claude, the heir-at-law, strove to injure; and to whom even now they grudge the fair name and the fair fame acquired by her own industry and exertions."

"I should like to hear you tell the tale, Sir Charles," replied Mr. Newton. "I have heard portions of the history; but the loss of property, consequent upon mismanagement, is unfortunately so common in our poor country, that many such events may have been confused in my memory with this particular one."

"My old friend, Charles Barry," commenced the venerable baronet, "had the misfortune to inherit, with his estate, the charge of some five or six half-brothers and sisters, who married, and had a greater number of 'blessings,' in the form of children, than usually fall to the lot even of Irish gentry. The person he at that time loved most in the world, was his own sister, a young woman nothing differing from other girls of her age and rank, and who, in due time, married two thousand a year (it was so called) and a fox-hunting 'Squire. Mr Barry's health had for some months been on the decline, and he resolved to visit Bath, then esteemed the most fashionable and health-giving place on earth.

"A little scene which occurred at Barrybrooke the evening before his departure, will best illustrate the ménage of an Irish bachelor's house in the year eight-two. I was staying with him at the time, and we had agreed to travel together. I must, however, tell you, that he had determined upon not letting any of his numerous relatives – who came for 'sea air' to Barrybrooke, with the intention of remaining, some for three, others for nine, and others again for twelve months – know aught of his movements. In the evening he summoned, into his study, Jerry Keg – valet by inheritance – and whom I always remember the same stiff, upright, honest-looking fellow, with a grave air, a twinkling eye, and a twisted nose. Jerry entered, his high shoulders propping his ears, his head projecting like that of a tortoise, his hands folded behind his back, his old-fashioned, richly-laced livery sticking out on either side like the fins of a flat-fish.

"'Jerry," said his master, 'I wish my valise filled with rather a better supply of things than I require when I visit my sister; I wish Black Nell saddled, and as you accompany me, you must take Padreen I suppose. Have all things ready by six o'clock tomorrow morning, and tell Meg we shall not return for a month.'

"It's a clane impossibility, yer Honour,' replied Jerry, bowing; 'Black Nell, I heard the groom say, wanted shoes, and I ade an oath never to cross Padreen since he flung me into the apple-tree, over the fence. As to the valise, sir, honey! Mrs. Mooney's little Jack cried for it to make a cart for Bran; indeed, it 'ud surprise yer Honour to see the 'cuteness of that child – how he settled it car-fashion behind the dog's tail, and made the natest little harness ye ever see, out o' one of the new traces o' yer Honour's gig.'

"'And how dare you, sir,' said my friend, incensed at this new proof of his not being master in his own house, 'how dare you suffer Mrs. Mooney, or anybody else, to destroy my property in that way?'

"'Sure, she's yer Honour's half-sister, and I hope I know manners too well to contradict a lady; much less one of yer Honour's blood relations.'

"Well, pack the things in a trunk, and we can all go in the carriage.'

"'O, boo-boo-boo! – the carriage, is it? Sure, yer Honour's own second cousin, Mr. Finnerty, sint that off yesterday, to bring his nurse and the twins here, and his wife along wid 'em, to give ye an agreeable surprise, as he said, seeing yer Honour's so fond o' children; and it's my own opinion, that sorra a thrunk in the house 'ud hould thegether; they've been all let to drop to pieces, because it's so long since they've been wanting.'

"'What am I to do, Stanley?' said my friend, looking at me despairingly.

"'Simply thus,' I replied; 'let us leave our servants to follow, put a few things into my portmanteau – for I promise you, the outward man will need refitting when we arrive at our destination – and I will ride Dorton's horse.'

"This was agreed upon, to Jerry's mortification, who muttered, 'He could ride the mule any way, tho' it was a stubborn devil, and it was no thing for a gintleman of family and fortune, like *his* master, to lave his own place without an *attindant*.'

"'What do you mean to do with the horde, at present in possession of the house?' I inquired, laughing. I always tried to laugh him out of his faults, for, like most of his countrymen, he was more proof against *reason* than *ridicule*.

"'What can I do with them?' he replied; 'they are my own kith and kin; and as I am the head of the family, and a bachelor – poor creatures! – ay, it is easy for you to laugh – you English folk know nothing, and care less, about long-tailed families; with you, the junior members of a family, both males and females, contribute to their own support; with us – '

"'The senior,' I said, 'is expected to provide for all, and is soon rendered, by that means, incapable of providing for himself. In the name of goodness, my dear fellow, if you must play almoner to such a tribe, do it in a rational way; – pay them so much a year – say ten, twenty, or thirty pounds each – but I defy any income to stand the constant drains to which yours is exposed; – men, women, and children = dogs, horses, and servants – make an eternal inn of your house. My life on't! you never know, from one year's end to another, how many eat at your board.'

"'Meg does – and she is a faithful old creature.'

"'True; but she has so long been accustomed to this Castle-Rackrent system, that it is for you to commence the reform – you cannot expect *her* to do it.'

"'Faith, Charles, you are right,' he replied; 'but you cannot enter into my feelings. To tell you the simple truth, I could not afford to pay half the people I support ten pounds a year.'

"'Permit me to ask how much their support costs you?'

"'Eh? – O! a mere trifle, I suppose: but seriously' (and he fixed his fine blue eyes upon me as he spoke), 'you do not suppose me capable of the meanness of calculating what people eat and drink?'

"'I would only wish you capable of the wisdom of considering whether, in justice to others, you can literally *give* more than you possess.'

"'Justice! What do you mean?'

"'Forgive me, my dear Barry, but have you paid off any of the embarrassments which hung over the estate when you came of age?'

"'I cannot say I have.'

"'If you have not paid off the principal, I trust the interest has been punctually discharged.'

"'I cannot say that it has. I am never pressed for it; and somehow or other, the rents slip through my fingers before I have time to think of my debts.'

"'Of course you investigate the accounts of your agent and steward regularly?'

"'Strange beings you Englishmen are! My agent's a glorious fellow – exact as a dial, punctual as a dun. O, no! no necessity in the world to look after him; and as to my steward, faith! He's a clever fellow – so ingenious! Cannot write much, but has a way of his own of keeping accounts – particular sorts of crosses he makes – amazingly curious, I assure you.'

"I smiled and sighed. Jerry knocked at the door.

"'I want to spake to yer Honour.'

"'Speak out, then, at once.'

"'It's Mr. Maberly, the grazier, called about the three fat bullocks he sold yer Honour last Christmas, to kill for the poor; and if it 'ud be convenient jist to let him have the money, now.'

"'Tell him it is *not* convenient, and send him to Dennis; why should he pester me about his dead bullocks? I thought he was paid long ago; there, leave the room.'

"'The widdy Rooney is below, on account that her son is kilt intirely, and as good as dead, by the Spillogue boys; and she thought, maybe, ye'd help her in her throuble.'

"'Poor thing! There, give her that,' tossing a guinea on the table; tell her, I'll commit her son if he gets into any of these broils again.'

"'God bless you, sir! I'll tell him not to brile agen – if he can help it.'

"'What, is he below?'

"'As much as is left of him, yer Honour;' and away went Jerry. The just creditor, therefore, was dismissed without even an apology – the riotous youth, with a reward! I noted this, and more! – I urged his remaining even for a day or two longer, for the purpose of arranging his accounts. It was useless; he laughed me off, and promised, that on his return he would – 'see about it.' Alas! How many of the bright and shining lights of this poor country have been extinguished by PROCRASTINATION!

"His easy manners, his good-nature, and really handsome person, made him a universal favourite at Bath, and many a lady of large fortune would readily have bestowed upon him hand and heart; but Charles was no fortune-hunter – he considered the lust of gold 'The last corruption of degenerate man,' and fixed his affections upon a young and beautiful widow lady with one daughter, whom he had accidentally met at the house of a mutual friend. Although his passion was violent, I saw good reason why it should be lasting. United to feminine loveliness, she possessed the rare endowments of judgment and gentleness; there was a steadiness, a sobriety about her, which made Barry often say, in the words of the poet:

> I have a heart for her that's kind,
> A lip for her that smiles;
> But if her mind be like the wind,
> I'd rather foot it twenty miles.

"'She is so uniform,' he would add, 'that I almost think her too good for me, who am so volatile; yet I love her the more for the contrast."

"It is exceedingly difficult to throw off the trammels that have grown with our growth; and when he was accepted by this interesting woman, he positively wanted courage to write and inform his sister of his intended marriage.

"'Poor thing,' said he to me, one morning, 'she will so grieve at my being married; for she has even now instilled into the mind of her only son, Claude, who is about six years of age, that he is to be sole heir to my property.'

"'If,' I replied, 'she has been absurd enough so to act, she deserves punishment. In addition to supporting the cousin-clan, is it usual for the head of a family to remain in a state of single blessedness to please his relations?'

"He smiled; but not until after they were united did he communicate his attachment to his sister. He went further; – he wrote to old Megg, to say, that grieved as he might feel, it was necessary that no visitors should remain at Barrybrooke, as Mrs. Barry disliked company. So far, so good; would that he had persevered in a course so decided!

"I could not repeat, if I would, the innumerable mortifications which Mrs. Barry experienced on her visiting Ireland for the first time. The manners and habits of the people ill accorded with her English feelings. From being the admired and beloved of a circle of intellectual and accomplished persons, she found herself shut up in a castellated, dilapidated house, with bare-footed housemaids (I speak of what *was* forty years since) and other servants, to whom the English language was totally unknown. Everything, from the kitchens to the attics of the rambling building, wanted arrangement; and she was bewildered where first to commence a reformation. Out of two-and-twenty servants, to discharge ten appeared the most likely mode of getting anything done properly; and this step immediately made her unpopular with the peasantry. Then she blundered dreadfully as to the management of her parties, – asked Orangemen and their wives to meet the priest of the parish; and placed the rector's wife, at table, above a lady who was second-cousin to the Great Earl of Ormond! These offences were not to be forgiven in a neighbourhood where every circumstance formed an event, and where, if truth must be told, the women envied her beauty; – the men feared her intellect. Then the family! – how was it to be expected they could pardon Mr. Barry for marrying, at all, in the first place, and for not consulting them, in the second? The thing was impossible, and they acted accordingly.

"Harriet, the daughter of Mrs. Barry by her first marriage, was a proud and silent girl, but possessed of exquisite feeling. Her troubles were hard and many; but they were not of long duration; she pined; and wasted, and wept in secret; and at last, as the only way left of escaping from a place where she felt every eye glared suspiciously on her, clandestinely married, and, in less than twelve months afterwards, gave birth to a female child, and died. Mr. Barry, with the pure kindliness of spirit which always characterized his impulses, gave the little orphan into his wife's arms, and bursting into tears, exclaimed – 'It is your grandchild, – it shall be also mine; I will be unto it a true parent.'

"You know that my friend had not been blessed with children; the feeling, therefore, on his part towards the helpless innocent was but just and natural. The person most displeased, when my little friend Alice Lee took up her abode at Barrybrooke, was Mr. Barry's sister; her son, Claude Barry, as he was always called (his father, by the way, two years after his birth, broke his neck at a steeple-chase), was naturally considered heir to his uncle's property; and it was a grievous thing, in her opinion, for a stranger to take even a small part of the good things she expected her son to possess exclusively. Claude himself was always a good-natured boy, though not much given to reflection.

"'I can't think why you all hate that little child,' he would say; 'she is a merry soul, and gets my uncle out of his nervous fits sooner than anyone else, with her innocent prattle; she is quite a comfort in the long winter evenings when the place is too dull for us to remain there.'

"'Innocent, indeed!' replied one of the family coterie, when the observation was finished. 'I wonder how *she* could be *innocent*, tutored as she is by her grandmother.'

"'I am astonished you have not more discernment, Claude, than not to see,' said his mother, 'that the little imp is brought up with mighty high notions: the very last time I was there, she cried because there was no sugar in her bread and milk.'

"'It's a comfort,' kindly added a third, 'that the child is indisputably ugly; a little bit of a thing, notwithstanding all the cramming she gets, with a monstrous forehead towering over her eyes, making her look as if she had water on the brain.'

"'We may all be obliged to her yet, for all that,' said Claude, laughing, and making the remark more from a love of tormenting, than aught else; 'poor thing! I shall be the only one among you, who never thought or said an unkind word of her!'

"'And more fool you!' and 'you'll repent it!' and that always safe and wise saying. 'Time will tell!' was echoed about, through the scandalous council, until poor Claude wished the holidays were over, and he was fairly back at school. The following summer, many of the same party were staying at Barrybrooke; for disagreeable as they certainly were to Mrs. Barry, she bore their society with praiseworthy forbearance; unfortunately, some words had arisen between her and Claude's mother, on a very unimportant matter, and the lady was anxious for an opportunity of mortifying her sister-in-law. Mr. Barry was from home; but after dinner, when the dessert was placed on the table, Mrs. Barry desired the servant to send in Miss Alice, who was then about six years old. The little girl came, as usual, to her grandmamma's knee, and at the moment Claude was helping himself to some currants.

"'Give a few of those to Alice, dear,' said Mrs. Barry.

"'Help yourself first, my darling,' observed his mother; adding in a bitter under tone, 'It is not meet to take the children's bread and give it to the dogs.'

"Mrs Barry rose as she spoke; and I shall never forget the dignity with which she crossed the dining-hall, to leave the apartment in which she had suffered so gross an insult: – those who felt justly (I was one of the number) followed. Alice perfectly understood what had passed; and the little thing stood where her grandmamma had sat, swelling with range. Claude heaped the plate with currants, and called her affectionately to his side. Alice looked at him with an expression I shall never forget.

At last, swallowing her passion, she shook her head, and turning to his mother, said, very quietly, –

"'I am no dog; I am, as you have often called me, a little ugly girl: but the time may come, when those who hate me now, may be glad to pick crumbs from *my* table, and thank me for them too.'

"This spirited reply coming from one so young, drew forth many and various observations from the party. Claude was indignant at the cruelty of his parent, and followed his aunt with apologies, and even tears. This was only one incident in a thousand of the dislike evinced to this hapless child, of whose father, I should have told you, nothing had been heard for a considerable period, as he want abroad on the death of his wife. In the meantime, the circumstances of my old friend were far from improving; his habitual neglect of money matters, and his eternal procrastination, were swiftly leading to a ruin, which, as Mrs. Barry was ignorant of its extent, she could not avert. Indeed, the very exactness with which she conducted household matters, was attributed to her as a crime.

"'Where's the use of painting palings, for the rain to batter against?' said one; – 'such expense, indeed!'

"'Then,' said another, 'there was an enormous bill for building two pig-sties: even if the bastes *did* get into the garden, now and then, what grate matter was it? Where's the good of flowers?'

"'Couldn't she let the tenants go on as they used,' exclaimed a fourth, 'and take the spinning and duty fowls from their wives, as others did before her? What was the time of the poor to them? Talk of extravagance! Wasn't it the height of extravagance to pay women for spinning, when it could be done for nothing?'

"Mrs. Barry's system, whatever might have been the prejudice entertained against her by the peasantry, as 'a fine lady from foreign parts, who was come to reign over them,' was productive os so much good to the poor, that they soon regarded her as their best friends, and their gratitude and affection were proportionate, while increasing difficulties pressed hard upon Mr. Barry, and he wanted resolution to tear himself away from family and party feuds. These circumstances soured his temper, and made him at times capricious and severe. It is well known, that at home or abroad, whatever goes wrong with a married man, is avenged upon his wife. Perhaps I ought not to say *avenged*, but I can hardly find a term to express the ill-temper which is too often shown at home, when adverse circumstances are encountered out of the domestic circle.

"Your own poet has expressed in language so chaste and beautiful the peculiar feelings which this sort of thing generates, that I will repeat you the lines: –

A something light as air – a look,
A word unkind or wrongly taken, –
Oh! Love, that tempests never shook,
A breath, a touch, like this, has shaken.

"'Are they not beautiful?' exclaimed the old gentleman again. Not that matters were so bad with them either; but certainly, something was fast undermining Mrs. Barry's constitution. I would not have said that her chief happiness arose from the consolation afforded her in the affection of her tenants, had I remembered the devoted tenderness of her grandchild, and the delight she took in attending to her education. The development of the girl's mind was both rapid and powerful. Distant as they were from towns, no aid of masters could be obtained. Mrs. Barry knew enough of music to teach the child its rudiments; and Alice, gifted with a fine ear, and a genuine love for the charming science, made swift progress in the art she loved. Many studies were resorted to, with a view to occupation, that would not have been thought of under other circumstances, or if the little maid had enjoyed the society of persons of her own age. Her grandfather taught her Latin, and the priest of the parish instructed her in Italian. Of what are usually called children's books, she never possessed any; but could repeat, almost by heart, the *Histories of Hume and Rollin,* with many of the ancient chronicles. Her light reading varied from the *Arabian Nights* to the *History of the Robber Freny,* with odd volumes of Irish History, and now and then a romance of the Radcliffe school. Shakespeare she loved; Milton she revered; but there was ONE book that was invariably perused morning and evening, which laid the foundation of her good conduct and future prosperity. Her grandmother saw hat her romantic and rambling mind needed a powerful corrective. Situated as she was, and feeling that the child was debarred from amusements suited to her age and sex – observing also the avidity with which she obtained information, and unable, from the increasing delicacy of her health, to guide her as she wished – she wisely felt the necessity of strengthening her religious impressions. The imagination of my young friend readily caught at the *beauties* of Scripture, but her grandmother wished her reason to be convinced of its *truths;* this she happily effected, and the silence and solitude of her sick room often echoed the pure doctrines of salvation, and the breathing prayers dictated by faithful hearts. Barry procured for his wife, at an immense expense, the best medical advice the county afforded. His affection had cooled, but never changed; and the prospect of losing one so dear, redoubled his attentions. It was, however, of no avail: and after a tedious illness, I followed her to her grave. Alice had never left her sick bed: it was a touching sight, to see the expiring effort the pale but still beautiful woman made to place the hand of the weeping child within that of her husband: he fell on his knees, and solemnly swore to protect Alice Lee to the latest hour of his life, and to bestow upon her a handsome income at his death.

"'I do not want that last promise,' she said in a trembling voice, 'she can make riches for herself. Protect her, but let her be independent!"

"'*Independent* was the last word this excellent woman uttered; no wonder than that it was a hallowed feeling and a hallowed sound to the heart and the ear of her grandchild.

"'I will be independent," said the sweet girl, as she strewed the flowers in which her grandmother had delighted, over the silent corpse, and placed to her cheek the blooming roses which she had so loved to cultivate; and then she laid her own head on the same pillow, and read in the Book of Life, of eternity, and heaven, and worlds beyond the grave – and was comforted in her affliction!

"She had watched from her chamber window the slowly pacing funeral pass from the courtyard, the coffin supported by eight of the oldest tenants, who claimed the privilege of carrying it to its resting-place, and Claude

Barry, in right of kin and as the representative of his uncle (who was too ill to perform the melancholy duty), following as chief mourner. She had seen the procession, attended by a multitude of people, wind round the hill side, till it was concealed from her view by a dense wood that overshadowed the road, and drying her tears, she entered the dark room where her grandfather was nurturing in secret the bitterness of grief. She seated herself quietly by his side, and made a sign of silence to old Jerry, who had followed her into the apartment, and whose infirmities prevented his attending the funeral: surprised that he motioned her towards the window which looked out upon the avenue, she opened the shutter so as to peep forth and ascertain his meaning. The old porter at the second gate was engaged in evidently a fierce contention with some four or five men, who demanded free passage to the house. Poor Alice trembled all over, for she had heard of writs and execution, as calamities threatened against her grandfather; but as he had 'managed to keep them off' (alas! For such management), she never thought they would really arrive at Barrybrooke. The appearance of the men, the agitation of the servant, and, above all, their suddenly pushing past the porter, while Jerry exclaimed so loud as to startle his master: 'I'll bar the doors,' confirmed her in her feeling that they were sheriff's officers. And she flung herself on her protector's neck, exclaiming 'What shall we do!'

"Poor Barry looked for a moment on the men as they wheeled round the house to approach the door. 'I see who they are, 'he said in a quiet voice; 'alas! And was not my heart sufficiently broken? And have I already lived to see the time when I return thanks to the Almighty for having taken from me the wife of my bosom – so that she has been spared this misery?'

"He walked to the hall, where his faithful servant, in the true spirit of Irish fidelity, had drawn the bolts, and established himself with a rusty musket, that had done the rooks and magpies much mischief, resolved to protect the dwelling 'bailiff or sheriff.'

"'Open the door, Jerry,' said my friend.

"'What, yer Honour?'

"'Open the door.'

"'For what, plaze yer Honour, 'ud I do that same?'

"'To admit these men.'

"'Lord bless yer Honour, and keep ye in yer right mind, which y are not in at this present time, or yed niver give way to the like o' them.'

"'Fool,' exclaimed Mr. Barry, as they thundered at the portal, 'do as I command you.'

"'Master, darlint!' replied the poor fellow, 'you may trample on me if ye like, and call me what ye plaze; but I'll never be the manes of letting shame into the house, in the shape o' the law, – only the boys are all at the funeral, it's long till they'd suffer such sarpents to walk the county. – Well, since ye'r determined on it, do it yerself, sir. I niver opened a door to a limb of the law, nor niver will.'

"Jeremiah flung down his musket, and hastily left the hall, while Alice clung closely to her grandfather's arm.

"'Come in, gentlemen, come in,' said he, with a frightful calmness of manner; 'here I am, you see; – be seated, and tell your business.'

"'The business was soon told; a writ against his person at the suit of Benjamin Maberly, *Esquire,* for cattle furnished during a period of sixteen or eighteen years – a sort of running account, with now and then a nominal settlement; bills bearing interest, and sundry other expenses; – this claim alone amounted to the enormous sum of two thousand pounds; for my poor friend had often taken it into his head to stock farms, and speculate in sheep, pigs, and oxen – speculations that always terminated badly, from his unfortunate habit of never attending to his own business, but leaving it to others to manage for him. Another of these men of law had an execution against his goods and effects, for the sum of three thousand pounds, he having bestowed upon a favourite cousin a bond for fifteen hundred pounds, upon his commencing 'professional man;' the interest of this, of course, was never paid nor demanded, but on his refusing to lend the young hopeful some two or three hundred pounds, which he thought proper to require, he placed the affair in an attorney's hands, who urged immediate proceedings on the bond, the interest of which had amounted to a sum equal to the principal. Mr. Barry was very unfit to think or set; but Alice prevailed on the officer who made the arrest, to wait until the arrival of his friends; he proceeded calmly to take an inventory of the furniture; while the master of the mansion seemed perfectly torpid. Claude returned with me and three or four others from the melancholy funeral to the house of mourning. As to poor Claude, he had all the family taste for expenditure, and the property he inherited from his father was mortgaged to its full value. This did not prevent his living in style; he had a good stud, fine dogs, and a machine to drive in, that almost broke one's neck to look at; he had given a ball on his coming of age, which cost almost as much as the fee-simple of his estate was really worth; and his mother, with her usual wisdom, observed it was of little consequence, considering her son's expectations.

"Claude, therefore, could do little – except join me in bail, which was entered into immediately; in less than an hour after our return, Jerry had the inexpressible satisfaction of banging the hall-door after 'the *sarpints*,' and of drinking (a ceremony, by the way, the poor fellow never omitted) 'Destruction to the law,' in a bumper of pure whisky. I remained at Barrybrooke, and endeavoured to unravel the difficulties with which my friend was encompassed. I confess they far exceeded my anticipations. To enter into details would be useless. Suffice it to say, that on his marriage, to pacify his relations, he had granted annuities, which had never been regularly paid, and then had given securities on his property for the various sums that accumulated he knew not how; then, none of the old incumbrances had been paid off; and the fine domain, which could have supported the establishment if properly farmed, was positively nothing more than a common for the neighbours' horses, cows, sheep, pigs, and poultry to revel on. Mrs. Barry had retrenched most considerably the household expenses; but as my friend, Alice Lee, said, 'grandmamma was never suffered to know grandpapa's affairs; and what she saved, even from her own personal comforts, was expended out of doors.' Claude's difficulties were quite as perplexing. The advice I gave to both parties was as follows; – Mr. Barry to sell off as much property as would discharge all pressing demands (for when one creditor comes down on an estate, the rest are sure to follow), to let Barrybrooke, and go abroad for five or six years, live on a small allowance, and thus clear what was spared. Claude we recommended to marry a rich widow, who was known to look favourably on him, and pay off his debts with her fortune, providing an annuity for her from his estate.

"'Cousin Claude,' said Alice, quietly, 'take *my* advice: they say you have fine oratorical talents, go to the bar, and make a fortune for yourself.' It may be easily imagined, that the advice given was not relished by either. Barry's pride revolted at the idea of selling a single acre; and Claude did not like the widow, because he had chosen to fall in love with a girl without either character or fortune. Some accommodation was made with the creditors, and my friend resolved to go abroad. A noble lord offered to take the house, and reside there; but no! again family pride was up in arms: – and although the certainty that Barrybrooke could not be kept in even decent order, except at great expense, was dwelt upon by his true friends, he disdained to let it; decided that three old servants should remain to take care of it, and as quickly as possible bade adieu to the halls of his ancestors, leaving the property to nurse for his creditors, and reserving only an income of three hundred a-year for himself. All his relatives objected strongly to his being accompanied by Alice Lee. – 'She'll be sure to come round him,' they exclaimed one and all, 'and if only sixpen'oth of property is left, it's only just that right should have it.' It was all in vain: Barry took a proud, cold leave of his 'dear relations' and 'particular friends;' his spirit had been bitterly wounded by his late misfortunes; but it was by no means subdued.

"'Jerry,' said he, as the poor fellow held open the carriage door, 'see that the widow Murphy has the milk as usual and the children at the school their clothing at Christmas; the agent will attend to it.' (I must tell you I had used every exertion to prevail on him to appoint a new agent, but in vain,) – and Barry was trying to conquer his emotion, when Alice, her face swollen with weeping, sprang into the carriage. The only living thing she possessed – a pet lamb, attempted to follow her, and looked up bleating in her face. 'Keep it, Jerry,' she said, 'it is all I have to give you, and I give it you as a remembrance.'

"The carriage drove on: at the gate, a concourse of tenantry, and the poor he had so often relieved, awaited him. They stopped the carriage: some of the men, who had grown grey on the estate, came forward. 'We have lived and flourished under yer Honour, and them that's dead and gone, for many years; and ye've never distressed us, nor offered to do it. If yer Honour 'ill stay among us, and keep from foreign parts, we'll make an advance on our rents, and pay up at once to next half-year; don't lave us to the marcy o'strangers, and we'll work for ye, and fight for ye, and never let a writ or a sheriff come near the house.'

"'Och! Don't go to lave us,' exclaimed a poor woman, laying her thin hand on the coach-window. 'Oh! Don't agra! Miss, don't let him – and the mistress, God mark her soul to glory! Nor *could* in her grave yet!' All this was too much for my friend; he could only reply, covering his face with his hands, 'God bless you all! I must go now; but I will return to you in happier times.'

"Mr. Barry proceeded to France: the idea of cheap living is connected, perhaps, truly, with the Continent. An Irish gentlemen is sure of a kind reception abroad; and the intelligent and cheerful manners of my friend Alice, equally free from English stiffness and French levity, increased the felling of kindness into esteem. Barry, however, could not long remain contented in the Provinces, and determined on a visit to Paris. This certainly was not wise; but Alice Lee had the happy art of extracting sweets from poison. She was introduced to some persons of literary distinction there, who discovered that her powerful and clear mind was capable of great efforts, and much usefulness. They taught her to soar, and directed her flight with judgment and kindness. Her attempts were made without even the knowledge of her grandfather, who read and approved her first production without having an idea from whose pen it proceeded; – his feelings can be better imagined than described, when he discovered that 'his little cherished child,' – the scorned, the despised one – had not only received, but, merited the praise of some of the most celebrated persons in France; he was not slow in sending this intelligence over. I, indeed, heard it with far more pleasure than surprise; but it threw every member of the long-tailed family into utter consternation. 'The thing was impossible – what! The little pug-nosed girl, who had never been to school to be praised in the newspapers, and though much of by learned people, – for *her* to write a book, a whole book who had learned to hold her pen from a village schoolmaster!' Fancy, my dear sir, all the exclamations of vulgar astonishment, and even then you can hardly have an idea of the hubbub the news occasioned. – Happily for Alice, she was not one of those morbid literary ladies, who mourn at their hard fate, and pretend to sorrow because their minds are superior to their neighbours, – who sigh and sentimentalise over their being obliged to appear before the public, and yet use every justifiable and unjustifiable mode of forcing celebrity. Alice was in the purest sense of the word A Christian, and she felt the necessity of doing her duty in that state of life to which it pleased God to call her. She shrank not from the useful exercise of her abilities, and she had the good sense enough to perceive that the odium, which at that time, even more than now, attached to literary women, proceeded from the attention they exacted, and the airs of superiority they assumed, in society. She did not neglect the cultivation of simple flowers, because she was skilled in botany; she did not cease to charm by the exercise of her fine melodious voice, because she comprehended the nature of sound; nor did she delight less in the mazes of the dance, because she understood the laws of motion. Though she became an *author*, she had not ceased to be a *woman*: her motives were noble – her actions pure; so that she neither needed, nor work, a mask: – this was the grand secret of her popularity.

"The creditors of Mr. Barry's estate had lately become clamorous and declared that the sums stipulated for had not been regularly discharged. My friend found it necessary to go over to Ireland, and settle matters, the derangement of which he could not account for; even his stipend had not lately been remitted, and but for the exertions of Alice Lee, he would have suffered much pecuniary difficulty. He felt that he ought to clear himself from the imputation of connivance where evidently, on the agent's part, mismanagement, if not dishonesty, must have been practised: he came upon the man unexpectedly, and the fellow paled and trembled before him. Conscious and confused, he fixed the next morning for the explanation of his accounts, but that very night set off for America, taking with him a very considerable sum, which he had prevailed on the tenants to advance, in addition to their rents, under the idea of ministering to their landlord's necessities. This was a dreadful blow to my friend's feelings: Alice had suffered much from delicate health, and he would not subject her to the fatigue of the journey; but earnestly did he long for her presence, to support and cheer him. About three weeks after he had quitted Paris on this unfortunate business, Alice Lee received the following letter, sealed with dismal black; the first page was in the handwriting of her beloved guardian and relative. She afterwards permitted me to copy it.

"'Barrybrooke, December, 18 –,

"'My BELOVED CHILD, – I ought not to have written you so gloomy an account; it was sadly selfish of me to disturb your mind when I know how much depends on the work you are now engaged upon. You would gladly support your poor grandfather – would you not? Even if he had not an acre left. No account of that villain since he sailed from Cork. Alice, pray for me – pray that my senses may be spared. The ingratitude I meet with, is the scorpion's sting that festers in my heart. Pray for me, Alice Lee! I suppose it must come to a sale. Sell Barrybrooke! And the trees and flowers *she* planted! But I shall have one unfading flower left; – you, Alice! Poor Claude is even worse off than myself. Oh! *The curse of property,* managed as it is in this unhappy country. Would that I had been bred a common tradesman; I should then have been *independent,* and not afraid to look every man I meet in the face, lest he should ask me for money. Do you know that my sternest creditors are those of my own kin? I am sick at heart, my child, and you are not here. Do you remember the evening you left that splendid conversazione at the

Count de Leonard's to come home, that you might give me the medicine with your own hand? Yet I would not have you *here* now for the world. Jerry grows young again, and Sir Charles is kind as ever: it is too late to wish now, – but if I had taken his advice, – good night, my child. You are the only being related to me who never gave me cause for anger. Good night – God bless you! Tomorrow I will finish my letter.'

"Poor fellow!" exclaimed Sir Charles, as he lifted his eyes from the painful record. "When the next sun rose, his spirit had met his God: – his heart was indeed broken. The remainder was written by his old servant."

"'May it plaze ye, Miss, to put up with me to tell ye the sorrowful tidings, – that next morning when I wint as us usual into his Honor's room, he was clane gone, and as *could* as a stone; they worried the soul out o' him, that they did; and my curse, and the curse o' the poor, 'ill rest heavy on 'em on the day o'judgment for that same. I wish ye could see how eautiful he looks this minute; jist smilin' in his coffin. So best; for he's beyant trouble now. – God be praised! They couldn't keep his sowl from glory! Poor Master Claude is lie one mad, and Sir Charles is forced to order the funeral: it 'ill be the thing to do honour to the name, and a grand berrin, as ever was seen in the country; priests and ministers, and all the heart's-blood o' the gentry – and it's my intention, now that the dear master's gone, to travel into foreign parts myself, and wait upon you, Miss, who must want someone to look after ye; seeing (no offence, I hope!) that ye are all as one as my own born child; and so keep up yer heart, and God's fresh blessin' be about ye, prays yer humble and faithful servant (till death) to command. – JEREMIAH KEG.'

Very soon, the estates of the *late* Charles Barry, Esq. were advertised to be sold by the sheriff, for the benefit of the creditors of the said estates. The sorrow of sweet Alice Lee was agonizing to witness or think upon; and even now she has not ceased regretting that she did not accompany her grandfather on his *last* journey. Agitation brought on a nervous fever; and her friends in Paris, for more than a month, dreaded what its final effects might be. She recovered slowly; and one day I was sitting with her in the drawing-room (as I found I could be of no service in Ireland, I went to see her), when the lady she was staying with, endeavouring to divert her mind, observed, with the good-humoured playfulness of her country, that Alice's last work had made a conquest of an old half-Indian gentleman, a Mr. Clifton, an Englishman, she believed, who wished he were young enough to make love to her.

"'Clifton was my dear grandmother's name,' replied Alice; 'and she had a brother once, but he died, I believe.' A vague idea, which I could neither account for nor express, took possession of my mind. The next morning I waited on the old gentleman; and judge of my delight and astonishment when I found, after much investigation that Mr. Clifton was indeed the brother of her grandmother, who had gone abroad when his sister was too young to remember aught about him, and who had returned a wifeless and childless man: and the discovery of such a relative was a source of extraordinary happiness to him. He was a proud, stern man, very unlike the parent she had lost; yet he soon proved that he was anxious to bestow upon her what the world calls substantial proofs of his affection. Being the avowed heiress of a rich Indian merchant could add nothing to the lustre of Alice Lee, but it increased her power of doing good. The idea of Barrybrooke being sold rendered her very miserable. Her uncle, who might well be proud of her, when I mentioned her wish to him, caught with avidity at the idea of gratifying her, and agreed to give money for the purpose, just as if he were bestowing upon her a splendid toy. He wished to visit Dublin, and we set out for that once splendid city with many and varied feelings. But I tire you,

– a moment more and my tale is ended. We were grieved, on our arrival there, to find that the sale had been hurried forward: by the desire of Alice Lee, I wrote to the sheriff, offering terms for the house, &c. of Barrybrooke. Through some precious mistake, my letter miscarried. We drove down to the estate; and here you must let me mention an instance of the delicacy of my favourite's mind – she would not travel in her uncle's carriage, but only in a post-chaise.

"'It would insult their distress,' she said, 'to go in splendour, when the family of my benefactor is reduced to almost to want. The auction was going on when we drove into the town; we were ten minutes too late, the very house of Barrybrooke had been sold to the architect I spoke of! The kind and generous feelings of my young friend were thus thrown into another channel; she purchased an annuity for 'Cousin Claude,' and to the hour of his death he never knew from whom the income came, that enabled him to live with so much comfort during the five years he survived his uncle. She practised the revenge of a Christian: she did good to those who had despitefully used her, nor were they averse to partake of whatever *crumbs* she chose to bestow."

Mr. Newton looked at his watch: – the kind-hearted, garrulous old gentleman took the hint, only adding, that the motto adopted by Alice, was INDEPENDENCE, – the device, a little bark passing through a stormy sea, with Hope at the helm, and the haven in view; and adding, "Thank God, all the trails of Alice Lee were endured in youth: her after-age was free from them, save and except those inherent in, and doubtless necessary to, human nature."

III

ANNA MARIA HALL'S THEATRICAL WORK

The Groves of Blarney, 1836

Tyrone Power as Connor O'Gorman in *The Groves of Blarney*
painted by Nicholas Crowley in 1837
oil on canvas, 635 x 762mm
Courtesy: The Tyrone Guthrie Centre at Annaghmakerrig,
Newbliss, County Monaghan

Anna Maria's plays included *The Groves of Blarney: A Drama in Three Acts* (1836); *Mabel's Curse: A Musical Drama in Two Acts* (1837); and *St. Pierre, the Refugee: a Burletta in Two Acts* (1837). Lytton Bulwer (Lord Lytton) was impressed with her talents as a writer and S.C. Hall reproduced Bulwer's account in the *New Monthly* in 1832 quoting as follows: "Mrs Hall evinces in it, as in 'The Buccaneer,' very marked talents for the stage, and if she would devote her time and skill to a village tragedy that should contain the simplicity and power of 'Grace Huntley,' I feel confident that it would have a startling success."[1]

Women authors appeared to enjoy success in writing for the theatre during the early Victorian period. Apart from her three main plays, some of which enjoyed long and successful runs, there is evidence to suggest that she adapted some of her stories from *Tales of Woman's Trials,* including *The Trials of Grace Huntly; or, The Struggles of Poverty and Crime* (1843 at Victoria, London) and her sketch "The Last in the Lease" was performed in Greenwich as a 3 act play *The Last Life* (1874). H. Philip Bolton notes in his entry on Mrs S.C. Hall in *Women Writers Dramatised* the many difficulties tracking down manuscripts and references:

> ... while the somewhat archaeological enterprise of women's literary studies continues apace and unearths writers forgotten by male literary historians, the task is a large and long one that remains incomplete.

He highlights a number of published versions of Anna Maria's plays, notably 3 dramatisations of *The Groves of Blarney* and references to it appearing in April and May 1838 at the Adelphi in London and elsewhere that it ran for a 'whole season' . He remarks that this was one of the few occasions that a woman writer dramatised her own work for the stage.

The Groves of Blarney first appeared as part I in a three-volume publication by Anna Maria – *Lights and Shadows of Irish Life,* published in 1838 and was dramatised 'with considerable success' according to the *Dictionary of National Biography*. Thanks to her high profile *Sketches of Irish Character* (1829 and 1831), she continued in a similar vein for Parts II and III of *Lights and Shadows of Irish Life* and again for *Stories of the Irish Peasantry* (1840). Many of these stories first appeared in the periodical press before they were compiled as publications, due to requests from her publishers who recognised commercial potential. As always, Anna Maria continued to work long and hard on her literary career and was keen to explore a variety of formats. In the same decade she produced four English novels – two historical romances, *The Buccaneer* (1832) and *The Outlaw* (1835) and two contemporary novels *Uncle Horace* (1837) and *Marian* (1840). These were well reviewed and enhanced her reputation. *The Groves of Blarney* was therefore written by a woman who was at the height of her literary powers, unafraid of expanding her range by writing with a view to staging her work in the popular theatre of the day.

Anna Maria acknowledges her debt to Thomas Crofton Croker for the history of the area and she notes that the melodramatic story of disguise, kidnapping and revenge was based on a real incident in Blarney in County Cork in 1812. Her Irish characters translated particularly well to the theatre. There was a lightness of touch in her delineation of her characters and the humour and energy permeates the dialogue keeping a lively pace throughout. This was the era of the stage-Irish play with lovable rogues, romance and farce which was to reach a peak later in the century with the melodramatic plays of Dionysius Lardner Boucicault (1821–90). *The Groves of Blarney* deserves a place in the history of Irish theatre, one that is frequently overlooked, especially in the evolution of melodrama in the pre-Famine period. Anna Maria's understanding of timing, cliff-hangers, villains versus virtuous characters and high octane escapist action has been underestimated and under-examined to date.

Several sources note that the play was written with renowned actor Tyrone Power in mind. He portrayed the dashing central hero Connor O'Gorman, "a true hearted Irishman" as announced in the playbill at the Adelphi. According to Christopher Fitz-Simon, the painting depicts Tyrone Power in three distinctive poses from the play, a triple portrait in honour of the romantic swain. Painted by Nicholas J. Crowley who moved from Dublin to London in 1837, it was exhibited at the British Institution in 1840. Sadly Tyrone Power was lost at sea in March 1841 when the SS *President* disappeared in the North Atlantic. It was reputed that he had the only copy of Anna Maria's new play *Who's Who*? on board with him at the time.

NOTE

1 S.C. Hall, *Retrospect*, vol. 2. p. 455.

FURTHER READING

Bolton, H. Philip, *Women Writers Dramatized: A Calendar of Performances from Narrative Works Published in English to 1900* (London, Bloomsbury, 1999).

Cullen, Fintan, and Foster, R.F. *'Conquering England': Ireland in Victorian London* (London, National Portrait Gallery, 2005).

Fitz-Simon, Christopher, *"Buffoonery and Easy Sentiment": Popular Plays in the Decade Prior to the Opening of The Abbey Theatre* (Dublin, Carysfort Press, 2011).

The Irish Theatre (London, Thames and Hudson, 1983).

Hall, S[amuel]. C[arter], Mrs, *The Groves of Blarney: A Drama in Three Acts* (London, [Webster's?] 1836).

Lights and Shadows of Irish Life (London, Henry Colburn, 1838).

Mabel's Curse: A Musical Drama in Two Acts (London, J. Duncombe [1837]).

St. Pierre, the Refugee: A Burletta in Two Acts (London, n.p., 1837).

Hall, Samuel Carter, *Retrospect of a Long Life: From 1815 to 1883*. 2 vols (London, Richard Bentley & Son, 1883).

Keane, Maureen, *Mrs. S.C. Hall: A Literary Biography* (Gerrards Cross, Colin Smythe, 1997).

The Groves of Blarney

Part 1

"The groves of Blarney, they are so charming."

I take it for granted there are few persons in our English world, who have neither seen nor heard of "The Groves of Blarney," so celebrated in history and song. Their celebrity, however, is mainly derived from the virtue possessed by the famous "song" – which I, by virtue of my privilege, may safely describe as THE GREAT IRISH SMOOTHING-IRON. This magic slab is perched upon the most inaccessible part of the castle; and many risk their necks with a view to polishing the most unruly of all unruly members. Indeed, it would be an admirable speculation to bring over a fragment of the wonder-working granite to the good city of London, where it would no doubt effect a desirable change in the habits and manners of society in general. After saluting the precious relic, husbands would become positively polite to their wives – and wives would continue as gentle as if still unwed; at public meetings, speakers would greet each other with a "Save ye, sweet gentleman;" and there would be no end to the compliments paid by blustering citizens to their opponents, at Hall or Common Council. Ladies of a certain age would eulogise the loveliness of their younger sisters; men would confess each other handsome; and the streets would resound with the compliments of cads and coachmen. Critics would learn politeness, at the expense of justice; and members of parliament, even in the House of Commons, would remember they were, or ought to be, gentlemen. But as it is probable the stone would lose its power if removed, we venture to recommend that all rude people be compelled by act of parliament to visit it, at least once in their lives and imbibe its virtues.

The following tale is one of strictly domestic interest, and derives its title from an occurrence which took place in the village of Blarney, as nearly as I can ascertain, about the year 1812. Yet my readers (long acquaintance has made me consider them my friends) my like to know, that Blarney Castle, its groves, and its once picturesque and beautiful village, are about four miles north-west of Cork.

For the history and character of the place, I refer them to the details of my friends Mr. Crofton Croker – to whom Ireland is so largely indebted. He has employed rare talents and industry in her cause; and was among the first to direct the attention of England to the vast stores which she possesses, – stores from which profit, information, and amusement may be largely drawn. His name is intimately and honourably connected with his country.

And now to my story. In the immediate neighbourhood of the village of Blarney, there resided a gentleman of large property, who, anxious to promote agriculture, and improve the condition of his tenants, brought over an intelligent and industrious Englishman to superintend his farms, cultivate his lands, and watch over his hot and green-houses.

Mr. Francis Russell had received an excellent education, and understood the habits, feelings, and prejudices of the people, without which knowledge, I very much doubt whether any practical agriculturist can be useful in Ireland. Moreover he was a Roman Catholic, without being a bigot. The gentleman who had secured so excellent and useful person to superintend the management of his estate, considered it an advantage that Russell was of the same religious persuasion as those it was hid duty to oversee; and he had been long enough in England to know that English Catholicity is divested of all the bitterness with which it is unhappily so frequently associated in the sister country. Francis Russell brought over his wife and two young daughters, the youngest almost an infant, to a very pretty cottage ornée on his employer's estate, adjoining the village, and for a time every thing went on astonishingly to his satisfaction. But, alas! For poor Ireland! I said the gentleman had a large property in the neighbourhood – and so he had; but it was dreadfully embarrassed – not irretrievably so, if he had taken the bee's motto, "economy" – followed Russell's advice, and retrenched: but prudence unhappily formed no part of his kind and generous nature. Nothing could restrain his perverted desire for improvement. He opened mines which he had not the means to work; built a factory – that was never roofed – at the time, too, when the house of his ancestors was tumbling about his ears; projected roads – saw company – and for every hundred he really received spent a thousand. When he engaged Mr. Russell, he had just raised several thousand poinds by "custoniams," and money was flying in all directions; but days of reckoning came, and nothing to reckon with. As if to increase the unfortunate gentleman's difficulties, his valuable overseer died suddenly, and his wife and their children were left totally without provision; for, relying on his patron's false (unintentionally so) representations, he had given up all other prospects to settle at Blarney. The only thing the ruined gentleman could do, he did – he executed a deed of gift at a peppercorn rent of the pretty cottage (which Russell had fancifully christened "Bee's Nest") to the widow and her girls. Poor man! He did not live very long to see the final result of his mismanagement; and, as if a blight was over all he touched, sickness, aided by sorrow, brought Mrs. Russell to the brink of the grave before her eldest daughter, Margaret, had completed her eighteenth year. Margaret was a genuine English girl, fair and lovely to look upon – gentle and fervent, docile, yet deep-hearted, skilled in the arts of thrifty housewifery, and managing their still pretty cottage and the two acres of land attached to it with the wisdom of an experienced farmer. The fairy estate chained them to the village of Blarney; and the warm affections bestowed on them by their neighbours rendered the place very dear to the widowed mother. Still poverty came – the cow died; – in truth, I must give another reading of the old tale of "Auld Robin Gray." Margaret – poor Margaret – was at once the sacrifice and the heroine. For the "Jamie" of the song, who would have made the "crown a pound," read that Connor O'Gorman, a handsome Irish youth of twenty, would, in the enthusiastic phraseology of his country, "have walked barefoot through the world to sarve her;" and yet saw her the wife of Hector Lee – a Robin Gray – rich, if not well-favoured, and one whom the "Flower of Blarney" would have been well satisfied to call father. The preface to my tale is little more than a record of deaths. Margaret had hardly written her name Lee instead of Russell, when the parent for whose dear sake she had apparently sacrificed her all of happiness in this world was called to another, and she was left with the charge of a child-like sister, wild as a young fawn of Killarney, and obstinate as a mule.

Flora was sparkling and pretty, and if good man Lee (as she always called him) had not been a farmer of as much courtesy as wealth, she would have stood a fair chance of being exiled for her mischief; but the old man bore with everything for the sake of her he loved – I might almost say, worshipped; and when at the end of two years Margaret presented him with a young Hector, it would be utterly impossible to describe his joy. To oblige his wife, he had left his old farm-house, and resided in the cottage she so much loved; and when his child began to walk, he would sit for hours under the shadow of a bower se had trained with English skill, from whence he could see through the deep arch of Blarney-bridge the towers of the old castle. But it pleased God to call the gentle, kind old man to himself before his boy was two years old; and "well-knowing," to use his own words, "that his warnings were for death," after he had received the extreme unction enjoined by his religion, he desired that Margaret might remain with him alone, and taking her soft hand within his horny and withered palms, he said,

"Shade back the curtain, Peggy bawn, for my eyes re dim; there, now I can see ye'r face, just the same as ever, God bless it! My will is made, gra! You have a hundred good acres at a nominal rint, and not an acre of *bouchlawns* on the whole – thanks to you for that and everything; two cows and the horse, besides the mare – for your life, and to your own blessed child afther – at your disposal till then, my Peggy; and the long acre fields, as good as twinty acres, at your disposal for ever. But it isn't about *that* I wanted to spake. My soul is made, and but for the panting of my heart, like an ould eagle struggling with the chain, I'd be bravely still; 'tis about yerself, Margaret; you'll be the flower of Blarney again in yer widow's cap – just three-and-twenty – and the sun nor the storm never dare look in yer face since I had ye –did they, Peg?

But Peg, as he loved to call her, could not answer for her tears.

"Crying for the ould man?" he continued, as she bent to kiss him; "bless you, darling, bless you! It's the first time the sight of yer tears ever did my heart good. I'm glad you can shed a tear for the ould goodman Lee, for I've seen yer tears before, Peggy, when ye didn't think I did, and *they scalded my heart,* for I knew what they were shed for; there was no sin in them, darlint – no sin, only sorrow – that the May-meadow sweet, and the ould winter ivy, should twist on the one stem; – but, reach me a drink; – thank and bless you, honey dear. Now, as to yerself; there's Ulick O'Sullivan, Ulick Rhu, and faith (God forgive me for swearing) his head is not redder than his hand, if he had an opportunity – have nothing to say to him, Margaret. I've got my prosperity by minding the laws, and if report speaks true, he's got his by breaking them. He'll want you to marry him – I know he will; – but shun him, for the sake of yourself and our child, Margaret dear; shun them all – all but one – I needn't name him; I don't say, Peggy, that while you were a wedded wife, you thought of him; no, no, he might cross your memory sometimes as a shadow crosses the sky; but when I am in my grave, it is only natural that a young thing like you should take another husband. Connor O'Gorman, dear, loved you – I don't think he loved you as well as I did – I don't think, but I don't know – even now, when the thickness of death is over my eyes, I look at you, and the blessed Virgin, (blessed saints forgive me if I spake sin!) she could hardly be more beautiful or pure than yourself. You were too good for me, and I think you far, far too good for him; and yet, if you love him, you ought to have some reward for spending the flower of your youth with an ould man."

Margaret (and she spoke as she thought at the time) said she would never marry – never. She had her child to love; and she would love nothing else.

But the dying man prevented her continuing in such a strain.

"It would ill become me, Peggy, to be selfish on my death-bed: you have been not only a blessing to me but to the town land, and to everyone you came near; and I hope, at the end of a twelvemonth and a day, you'll be quick about thinking of another husband. And, Peggy, Connor loves you, and if you could lay any law upon him, to keep quiet and steady – the sort of thing you like – he would make a good husband. He could have had his pick of the girls in the barony, if he had liked, but, sure, any one who once thought of you could think of no one else! It's a hard thing to part ye, Peggy, if it wasn't God's will; but as it is, why you have my leave and blessing to make yerself happy; only, darlint, the boy – our child – but I needn't tell you to take no one who in the way of all kindness and goodness would not be a father to him. And the ould mare – grey Nelly – don't let Flora taze the life out of the beauty, as she does out of everything else. The hundred pounds I've left her, will buy the neat and tidy odds-and-ends for a house when she marries, which you English-born think so much of. And when I'm gone, Peggy, I wouldn't like you to forget me – that I would not – and should like you to spake of the ould man by the fire of an evening, or about the farm, and to be kind (as, indeed, you always war) to anything I liked – to think and speak of me, Peg, as of one whose dying breath will be spent in blessing you, and who only wishes he had been more near your own age, that he might have been left long on the world to make you happy. I trust we shall meet again above, jewil. And Margaret, dear, in regard of the funeral, let the people, my people, avourneen – have their own way. You're all for quiet and that, in England, and you don't like the wakes, I know; but somehow, I think it would make all belonging to me very quare and uncomfortable, if I could not go the way all my people did, and have Kate Harrington, the finest and most ancient keener in Cork county, to keen me, – and plenty of everything; – and, dear, don't be hurt at the noise, for it's the more noise the more respect. At my father's funeral (heaven be his bed!) there were more games of 'the walls of Troy'* (Peculiar to wakes) and 'short castle' played than had been known at any wake in the country for many a year. And mind, dear, that my head's turned to the foot of the bed, for your sake, to keep misfortune from the family. I know, Margaret, you've no favour towards these things, but O think of the ould man, and forgive it – it's the last time he'll trouble you."

Margaret promised, and faithfully performed, all he requested; and having in broken sentences repeated his desire, that at the end of a twelvemonth and a day she should begin to think of another husband, and murmured prayers on prayers for her happiness, and kissed his child, he sunk into a sleep, from which he awoke in about two hours to repeat his blessing on the head of his young wife, and to assure her with his feeble and dying lips that she had never once angered him during their marriage. Flora was then called for and knelt by his bed-side; loudly did she weep, for he had been like a fond father to her ever since her mother's death.

"You give breath to your sorrow, and it flies, Flory," he said; "but my young wife's sorrow settles in her heart. Mind all she says, for I was like an ould red deer of the mountains larning from a little lamb. And remember I bare witness that a loud or sharp word was what I never heard from your lips, or felt on my heart, Margaret Lee, since the hour the priest – God help him! – declared May and January to be the one month. And Flora, merry maid," continued the old man, smiling in death, " that's more than your husband will be able to say when ye'r only a day married."

Again he old man slumbered even while the slight jest passed from his lips; and long did Margaret watch him, and more than once move from his cheek the silver hair which the light summer breeze that entered through the casement had disturbed. He laid quite still, and the beams of the setting sun entered the chamber with that noiseless joy which steeps the green hill and valley in hues of happiness. "When he awakes I should like him to see how bright it is," thought Margaret, and she removed the curtain: the eye-lids were half open, the – but details of the gentlest death are painful. Old goodman Lee awoke no more.

Margaret obeyed her husband's desires in all things touching the funeral. Mr. Lee's were all more or less disappointed, as relations always are when they are not mentioned according to their own estimation of their own deserts in "the will;" though he had left many small tokens of regard to those he considered worthy, of course they were not satisfied. But the liberality of the funeral arrangements were such as to admit of no complaint; the favourite keener exerted her talents to the uttermost; she seated herself on the floor, closed her eyes, clasped her hands round her knees, and began first, in a low and monotonous tone, to set forth the domestic and neighbourly virtues of the deceased. Her Irish poetry would bear the following translation: –

"Kind and gentle were you, and lived through frost and snow – sorrow and tears – with an open house and an open heart; the sun of heaven shone on you, and you reflected its beams upon others; the Flower of Blarney saw and loved you; – and though she is of a strange country, you taught her to love the green and weeping Island – to dry the widow's tears – to feed the orphan, to clothe the naked. –

"Oh! Why did you die, and leave behind you all the good things of life, – the big barn, the grey mare, the high-trotting horse, the most elegant farm of the town-land, and, above all, the beautiful boy, who will be the young oak of the forest yet. Oh! The justice and the mildness were you of the country's side; and while grass grows and water runs we will cry for goodman Lee. The beggar walked from his door with a full sack, and he turned wormwood into sweetness with his smile.

"But now his wife is desolate, and his full and plentiful home has no master." –

I know nothing more picturesque than an Irish funeral, when viewed, as all picturesque objects ought to be, in the distance. Mr. Lee had been respected by rich and poor; his good-nature, good-humour, and punctuality in the discharge of his business, had brought their sure reward; and it certainly was with a feeling of pride that Margaret looked, with weeping eyes, from her curtained window, upon the crowd of horse and foot that attended her true and generous friend to his grave. The coffin was placed, after the fashion of the country, on an open hearse, with a course canopy, supported by four pillars; the famous keener was seated by the side of the body enveloped I her blue cloak, – and when the motley procession moved on, she commenced her wild chaunt, bending over the coffin, her hood concealing her features with its heavy drapery, her action expressive of the wildest grief, and her voice at times swelling into loud and powerful tones, which were repeated at intervals by the crowd. When they reached the cross-road, such being considered symbolic of their creed, the procession stopped; the men uncovered their heads, and the priest said a few words of prayer for the repose of the soul of the deceased. Then again Margaret's ear caught the chorus of the death-song, and, in a few more minutes, all view of the funeral was obstructed as it wound round the hill; then Margaret caught her child to her bosom, and wept over him long and bitter.

Part II

"Flora, will you hold your tongue?"

"Margaret, you have just told me you do not mind a word I say; so what harm can there possibly be in my talking?"

"Oh, none in the world, if it amuses you."

"But it amuses *you*, sister," persisted Flora Russell; – "it amuses you, I am sure it does. What would you do without me? It is now more than eleven months since we have been living in this blessed cottage, like two nuns in a cell, with nothing to enliven us but little Hector; I should have died only for Hector and" –

"Marcus Roche," put in Margaret.

"Well, sister, – there, I do not blush, not one bit, you see – not one bit of blush; and I do confess that Marcus Roche is, as old Monica calls it, 'very divartin.' In the first place, you know he must be very learned, or Squire Callaghan would never suffer him to instruct his sons, as he does, in English, and French, and writing, and – what is it they call it? – the round thing, you know – oh the use of the globes, and all that. Then he has taken such pains with me; I really write a very beautiful hand now; and as to accounts, indeed, sister, I can sum up" –

"What! Cast this for me, to prove your skill," said Margaret, pushing that rare thing in an Irish house of any grade, an account-book, towards the giddy Flora; – "here – the profits on the dairy during the past month. Nora O'Brian says our butter is the best in the market, and really the three cows have turned out so well –"

"Thanks to your management."

"And Norah," continued Margaret, "now manages the poultry so cleverly."

"Only it is so hard to make her keep them clean. What do you think she told me? – that none of the O'Briens were born with brooms in their hands to go sweeping afther the bastes of the creation."

"If you would let her alone about trifles she would do much better, Flora. My dear father always said that Irish reform ought to be read Irish alteration; you must effect the change little by little, nor attempt too much at once, but go cautiously and gently about your improvements, not startling, but undermining their prejudices, and never quarrelling with them; for, if you observe, Flora, they are so ready-witted, that in a quarrel they have always the best of it, catch you up in no time, and overturn all your wisdom by a merry laugh. There, give me the book now, the casting up is done, I suppose; – give it me. What is this? Well, Flora, you are really too bad; you have written "Marcus Roche" three times across the pounds, shillings, and pence – that's a pretty way of casting accounts."

"The pen did it of itself, sister Margaret," said Flora, with a penitential look; "it was one Marcus made – it did it of itself."

"You are very silly, Flora, and I must say you do not try to improve."

"I know one who does not say so," observed Flora, observed Flora, and her mobile features assumed a very arch expression; "someone told me yesterday, as I was coming from chapel, that I was very much improved, and growing very like you."

"Indeed!" exclaimed Margaret.

"Why do you not ask who it was?" said Flora.

"Because – because –"

"Because, Madam Margaret, you know very well it was Connor O'Gorman. I wonder who blushes now."

"Flora, you are both thoughtless and unfeeling; and if Connor O'Gorman has desired you directly or indirectly to" – Margaret paused. Ever since her husband's death the conduct of Connor O'Gorman towards one he so deeply and dearly loved had been marked by the most especial reverence; he seemed to regard the young English widow as if she were his patron saint, and they had rarely met, except at chapel. Margaret felt this delicacy, and loved Connor ten times the better for it; it spoke to her heart far more eloquently than words could have done; and when contrasted with the coarse impatience of those who thought they could not speak too soon, Margaret felt that he had more delicacy of mind than she supposed, and came to the very just conclusion, that Irishmen often, and Irishwomen always, have sensitive and delicate perceptions.

"But I am sure," Margaret added, after her brief pause, "that Connor did not authorise you to deliver any message for him – he would not do so."

"Not a message, Margaret, but I told him we were very dull and lonely – and he carried Hector in his arms – and said Hector must be dull too."

"Who said Hector was dull?"

"Why, how particular you are. I said Hector was dull, and so Connor said, would he like a little puppy to play with – if it was mine – and I said I would like it, and so Connor is going to bring the puppy here by'n-by; and now," added Flora sulkily, "the murder's *out*, and I'm *in* for a scolding."

Margaret looked annoyed, very much annoyed; Flora's unceasing activity of mind was a source of perpetual trouble to her. No Irish mountaineer was ever more wild or wilful than her generous, inconsiderate sister. "You know," she said, "how anxious I have been not to receive Connor here – at least not yet; besides, he may have altogether changed; he has rather avoided me, though I like him the better for it. Your accepting his gift is a sort of encouragement – in short, you have done very wrong."

"Shall I send him word that you will not let me have it?" inquired Flora.

"No, that would be giving his visit an importance it does not deserve."

"You never forbade Ulick O'Sullivan, nor Terence Dacey, nor the Cork attorney, whose love was so very energetic, from coming – though to be sure *one* visit always settled their business; but that fine noble fellow, who has behaved so delicately (for I know he loves you a hundred times better than you deserve) –"

"He has not told you so, has he?"

"Law, sister, a person need not speak out the words; do you think I don't know when a man's in love, and who he's in love with? Well, here's Marcus Roche; I am sure I don't want the puppy, and he can tell Connor O'Gorman that I'm not to have it."

It was impossible to look at Marcus Roche without feeling interested; he was slight, rather under the middle size, of dark complexion, and that Spanish form and expression of face which is almost peculiar to the people of the county of Kerry. He had received the education supposed to qualify men for the Catholic priesthood, in France; but unfortunately (for his mother had *promised* him to the Church) he, as they term it, *"lost his vocation"* – fell absolutely in love with Flora Russell, but with more prudence than belongs to the generality of his countrymen, reloved to wait until one or two events, likely to occur, had taken place; he had some rich relations and really very good prospects. In the meantime he gave lessons in French and tolerable Latin to several respectable families, and bestowed his leisure on the improvement of his future bride. He loved Ireland with all the unspoiled enthusiasm of an Irish heart, and, in the simplicity of his earnest and confideing nature, believed every tradition of the ancient grandeur and learning of his "darling country." He was a tolerable antiquarian, and so anxious to discover antiquities that he not unfrequently committed blunders, which were a source of perpetual amusement to Flora, who loved to banter and plague him in every possible manner. His education had given him habits of retirement which young Irishmen seldom possess. In that respect, and in the gentleness of his disposition, he differed essentially from his friend Connor, who was worthy of being considered an Irish Dandie Dinmont. Having said so much in favour of Connor O'Gorman, I must only add that in him Dandie's perfections and Dandie's faults were exaggerated; and that, moreover, he was as handsome a fellow as ever twirled a shillelagh, or danced a t a fair. His deep blue eyes were full of expression, and could sparkle with either love or anger, as occasion required. He did not deserve the stigma of imprudence, for his ancestors, once possessed of much wealth, left him but little to squander, and *that* little he had rather increased than diminished. His farm, if not neatly, was vigorously managed; and he was, in the expressive phrase of the country, *"born to good luck,"* for whatever he undertook prospered – except, indeed, his love.

It was certainly a smiling fortune that sent Marcus to the Bee's Nest Margaret respected young Roche, and, without affectation, told him of Flora's imprudence, at which Marcus shook his head, and Flora pouted over her work. He, however, seized the opportunity to tell Margaret how devoted his friend was to her, and how fondly he hoped, that at the expiration of her year of widowhood, he might be permitted to address her in the language of love. He spoke of his delicacy, of his bravery, of his fidelity, of his uprightness; told Margaret how perfectly just it was for her to return to the object of her first affection, and pleaded Connor's cause if not as warmly, more eloquently, than Connor could have done himself.

Flora was secretly delighted, though she had the good sense to hold her tongue, judging wisely, that her sister was still displeased with her. But then Margaret told Marcus, that supposing the year of widowhood expired, supposing that she really liked Connor, supposing he really loved her, she had made up her mind that he (Connor O'Gorman) must serve a sort of apprenticeship to peace and quietness; that he must, in fact, before she consented to think of him as a husband, during a period of twelve months abstain from everything bordering on a FIGHT; that he must avoid altogether, or dwell in peace and quietness with Ulick O'Sullivan, when the said Ulick got from under the cloud that overshadowed him, and leave the O'Sullivan faction and the O'Gorman faction to settle their disputes, which one would imagine had been decided long ago; (for they had quarrelled at every fair, pattern, and wake, during the last two hundred years;) that he must deprive the O'Gormans of his counsel and presence; that during the same period he must not taste whiskey, which Margaret, like all sensible women, considered the curse of Ireland; and that, moreover, he must break himself of a foolish trick he always had – (and Margaret almost smiled as she spoke it) – a foolish trick of laughing and jesting with all the pretty girls in the parish; upon these terms only could a notion of the contract be entertained; but after making the declaration, Margaret drew herself up in all the dignity of second mourning, and told Marcus that even *then* she would not bind herself to marry Connor.

"Then," said Flora, "Connor is not the man I take him to be, if he consents."

"Consents!" repeated Margaret, with the air of a queen; "*consents!* Flora, pray mind your work, you have put the hooks of Hector's pin-before on the wrong side."

"There's a wrong and a right to everything," said Flora, tartly, for she did not like to be reproved before Marcus; "but at all events, here comes Connor and the puppy; am I to take it?"

"I have nothing to do with it," replied Margaret; "but, Marcus, I can trust to your honour; I am not authorized – I" – and Margaret, in greater confusion than she had ever felt since the time when that same Connor breathed into her ear the first love vows she had ever heard, left the room, followed, however, by the trusty Marcus, who gave her a letter from her old lover, which he had at all risks promised to deliver.

The letter may possibly exist in the Chronicles of Blarney, and some other Crofton Croker, assisted by the extraordinary kindness of "the good people," may hereafter find and bring to light its contents; but if truth must be told, I confess I have never seen the original, and can therefore only form an opinion as to the nature of its contents from the subsequent conduct of Mistress Margaret Lee.

Collecting herself – which means summoning her courage – she entered the room where Connor waited to know his doom, at one door, just as Flora's pretty figure disappeared at the other.

She was quite right in the belief that Marcus, and Flora, and Connor, had all conspired against her; and that, delicate as Connor's conduct had been, he was, nevertheless, determined to renew his suit, and have a direct answer as to its probably termination.

Margaret had nothing to urge against his love, except the fear that habits, which, being an Englishwoman, she considered wild and reckless, would militate, not only against her own happiness, but prejudice the well-doing of her child; "Had I no one but myself to think of,[2] she said, "the case, Connor, would be different; but I have a my duty as a mother to perform: and though I might be justified in giving my hand with my heart, had I, as I say, no one but myself to think of, I owe it as a duty, an imperative duty to my child, to give him no father, as God has taken his, unless it be one who will keep him free from the faults which mar the noblest natures in the world. It rest with yourself to say whether you will or will not comply with my – what shall I call it?"

"Say it's your wish, just say it's your wish," exclaimed Connor, "and then the only sorrow I'll have will be, that instead of one year you did not say a hundred, so that I might prove my love and constancy by waiting all that time. Oh, Margaret, the hope that was frozen in my heart has burst into life again, and is destroying me entirely. I – I –" and, overpowered by his feelings, the stout and true-hearted man rushed out of the room to conceal his emotion. He soon returned, however, and, truth to say, Margaret did not see him enter without a gush of proud and happy feeling, clouded, but not overcast, by a fear which it is difficult to overcome when you feel there is a want of stability in the person upon whom your heart reposes. He looked so handsome and so animated; his lithe boyish figure had ripened into such full and graceful proportions; his manner, so softened by disappointment, was now buoyant with joy, and the tones of his voice, despite the deep rich brogue (in which after all there is something *heart-warming*) were so full of fervour, so cheering – the sort of voice to hasten on the morning – to call hope from the depths of despair – to wake the echoes of an enchanted cave – to talk love in – whether in sport, or the soft, low whispers of confidence and joy. His voice, I say, was the perfection of Irish voices, and no one with a heart can have listened to the richness of a well-toned Irish voice without feeling its power; at least, such as have ear for music and heart for affection; Margaret *had* both an ear and a heart, and, in good truth, if truth must be told, she felt quite as happy as her lover, and, during the remainder of the day, did not think a great deal of the obligation he had taken on himself to abstain from fights and whiskey. Margaret did not persist in her desire that he should refer to his lovemaking propensities in the resolution, "feelings," Flora said, "perfectly conscious of the influence of her own charms, as far as that went."Connor would not be satisfied with a simple promise; no war-horse ever manifested so much delight in the trappings of his slavery as did Connor O'Gorman. Margaret assured him that his word of honour would be sufficient, that she only wanted to be convinced he had the power of forbearance. But Connor knew it would be a much easier task for him to refrain altogether than to forbear, and so he determined to put it, as he termed it, "out of his own power to do wrong." The next morning Father Horragan, the best-hearted and most jovial of priests, registered an oath on behalf of Connor O'Gorman, which he would have been sorry to take himself – against whiskey and fighting. In his zeal to prove to Margaret how gladly he would do anything to obtain his long courted prize, he added various items, so as to show how joyfully he would rest her bondsman.

There was no loop-hole in his oath – no way of escape – no possibility of drinking with one foot inside and the other outside the door, so as to be neither in nor out; no saving clause by which he might soak bread in the spirits and so *eat* the liquor he did not *drink*; no mode of avoiding his "obligation" not to touch a drop *on earth,* and then climbing into a tree with his bottle. Such devices for cheating themselves are by no means uncommon with those who, in a fit of repentance, have sworn against the besetting sin – the darkest and deepest curse under which Ireland labours – the enemy they are always ready to put into their mouths to take away their senses; "the drop of drin" is to the Irish peasant a far more bitter draught than "the draught of slavery." Connor was too right-minded, too anxious to be what his long-loved Margaret really wished, to condescend to stratagem. He had never been what in Ireland would be called *"over-fond* of his tumbler," but he had liked it well enough to know that he would miss the "warm drop of comfort" his pale and gentle sister Alice never failed to mix for him every evening. Still, what was that – what was anything to the chance, the almost certainly, of obtaining one known all through the province as the "Rose of Blarney" – the fair and rich young widow "who had refused such a power of men" – who was the best match in her sphere, ay, or above it, in the barony – the woman upon whom he had lavished the earliest and strongest affections of his young impetuous heart – whose determination to sacrifice herself for her mother's sake would have driven him to desperation, had he not resolved that he would at least make Margaret respect him. Marcus Roche had watched Margaret closely since her widowhood, and frequently told Connor he was convinced she loved him, and both Marcus and Flora laboured unceasingly to keep up a felling, which, if they had known the depths of Margaret's heart, they might have been assured would have ceased only with her existence.

Connor's delight was so overwhelming that he never fancied the second clause in his "obligation" would be more difficult than the first. The O'Sullivans and the O'Gormans were, as we have said, perpetually quarrelling, and a quarrel in Ireland invariably terminates in a fight. Nothing could exceed the dismay of the O'Gorman faction when they found that Connor was "book sworn" against any sort of a fight for a year and a day; they declared unanimously that "the back-bone of the country was broken," and hinted that none but a weak-minded "Sassenach" would think a man worth having who did not twirl a shillelagh and break a head.

Margaret, when her promise to Connor was known, received a just proportion of that sort of advice which is so often given and never followed; her prudent friends, who had other views for her, shook their heads, and said she was throwing herself and her lands away; her English relations wrote remonstrance on remonstrance, declaring their belief that he would never keep his oath, to which Margaret replied with a sigh, the bitterness of which was not only known to herself – that if he did not, she was absolved from her promise. On the other hand, Connor's "people," who were as proud as possible of their descent, thought Margaret Lee, the daughter of an humble English agriculturist, in "the very height of good luck" to get such a "fine, handsome, respectable young man as Connor O'Gorman, with the best blood of the O'Gormans in his blue veins;" and moreover, they thought her "proud and overbearing, to be setting herself against the customs of the country, and she only an Englishwoman, *without a back*; and no great things of a Catholic either, consorting with Protestans, and taking tea (if you please) with the minister's wife, and singing a Protestan hymn betimes of a

Sunday evening; and she afther soothering Father Horragan, so that he doesn't heed it – not he."

Connor did not meet the reproofs and sneers of his former companions in arms and whiskey as philosophically as Margaret encountered those she received from her friends; and had he not sworn agains single-stick, I very much doubt if, at the end of three months, his head would have been in a state of perfect preservation. He, however, shunned all public gatherings of the people, set his house and farm in order, and almost worried his sister Alice to death with plans and improvements.

"Brother dear, let the chickens eat the two or three grains of stirabout as they always used, out of the saucepan, it's more natural to them – they're not acquainted with the trough, and are losing flesh. O my! 'twould be no wonder if my head was grey with the new fashions – no wonder in life, Connor; but I'll try and get into them if I can."

"That's a good girl, and a dear sister," was Connor's reply; "and Alice, the pigs got out of the sty yesterday – there are no pigs in the country, though I say it, that have so comfortable a home as ours, and yet they're the most unruly bastes in the town-land."

"Ah, Connor, it's hard to get over old customs, and Nelly never contradicted till you put a door up in her face; it's hard to bear the craythur's grunts when she looks at the cause of her sorrow. She's a beautiful mother to the bonneveens, and never did hurt nor harm to mortal – barring now and again when she'd sweep up a young duck or a gosling, – the chickens were always too nimble entirely for her – but I'll fasten the sty; and, brother, Mick says there need be no hurry in life about the hay, that there's no sign of rain."

"Now," said Connor, "it's true what Margaret Lee says; that unless you watch the people, the hay-harvest goes to destruction, just as if we war waiting for bad weather when God sends us good. She got in every blade of her hay-harvest last week."

"The Griffin was here this morning," said Alice, doubtful as to how her information would be received; "and she says –"

"What does she say?" demanded Connor, sharply.

"Why, she says, that the farmering boys find it hard staying with Mistress Margaret."

"What do they mean by hard staying? Where everyone else pays a tenpenny, she pays a shilling; she gives them full and plenty of oaten and barley-bread, good stirabout, and never asks them to eat potatoes more than once a-day! O the ingratitude of the world, to call *that* hard staying. The upper servants at Squire Callaghan's hav'n't better food, nor, maybe, as good; indeed, I know it. What else did the Griffin say? Speak up, Ally."

"She said nothing in the world against her on that account, brother dear. Only, ye see, you can maybe put in a word that Mistress Margaret would heed, and not worry the boys so about being exact to time, and finishing the work what she calls neat. She sent poor Jimmy Casey off his job."

"Because," said Connor, "he never came to it sober."

"But he meant no harm," observed Alice; *"it was his luck, poor boy."*

"Margaret Lee spakes a true word," continued Connor, while he tied a green silk handkerchief round his throat, in a style very becoming, if not very fashionable. "Margaret Lee says very truly that it's hard to know how to serve the lower orders of the people. I see it very plain now. Margaret has a way of making everything plain; they won't thank you to serve them in your way, and would rather have a couple of noggins of whiskey (Ally, I don't feel the want of the tumbler at all at all now) than a weight of potatoes or half a loaf of bread to take home to their children. It's true I'm saying. And everything she does, and everything she says, is for the good of the country, if they'd only think so. Sure, if she hadn't a heart in it, she need not have remained amongst us, nor – but I'm ashamed of you, Ally, to let the lies and the tittle-tattle of that ould, heartless bogthrotter, Mabel Griffin, that's neither a witch nor a wizard, but part of both, take hold of such as you. She's eating the heart out of that marauding scoundrel, Ulick O'Sullivan, who's afeard to show his face in the valley these two months: one day soothering down his faction, and then buttering them up and abusing us, and then the next she's down the Bograh Mountains oiling you; and if she daren't speak out against the Rose of Blarney under this roof, (I only pray, if she did, that the wattles would knock her down of themselves,) she comes with a tail of one story, and the head of another, and then she fits the right tail to the wrong head, and the wrong head to the right tail, and so she goes on; and that's the birth of mischief all over the world. Only, Alice, I've not been a bad brother to you, and I take it very unkind to me, and very unjust to her, that was, as you well-know, and ever will be, the light of my eyes, the joy of my heart – my delight – my life – my HEART'S BLOOD, Ally, – I take it not right of you to let the first breath of a May morning touch your cheek, if it whispered a word against Margaret Lee. I'm out with you, Ally." And so saying, Connor threw that heavy accompaniment to a respectable Irish farmer, a "top-coat," over his arm, and was about to sally forth, when Alice clasped her arms round his neck, and kissing him affectionately begged his forgiveness with many tears.

"You know," she said, "I love Margaret with all my heart. I'm proud ye'r likely to win the Rose of Blarney that you thought of so long, and I'm proud that now *you can put the first rose of summer in yer hat, and not a man dare lift his finger against it*; but somehow, brother, ye seem altogether gone from everything but her, and that's always hard upon a sister, and the reason, maybe, why sisters-in-law, are seldom sisters in love."

"But you will be so, Ally – I know you will; it's the prate of that Griffin, that spreads as much disunion in a country as foxes with firebrands would in a field of wheat; and that being the case, mavourneen, why don't have anything, good, bad, or indifferent, to say to her – that's the best way."

"Well, indeed, Connor," replied Alice, "I'm thinking ye'r right, only what am I to do? If a woman crosses our own hearthstone, what can we say but 'kindly welcome?' Sure there's not an O'Gorman on earth who'd say an unkind word in his own house, even to the Griffin. And then the woman (if woman she is) is convenient, with her knowledge of England and foreign countries; and a little morsel of finery, dog chape, and quite new, and willing to take anything in exchange; and if a body takes a fancy to a shawl, not formenting for the money."

"Ay, Ally dear," said Connor, kindly, while he pushed the hair from his sister's pale forehead, "Margaret says that's what ruins the principles of half the girls in the country; the egg-women and basket-women taking anything, even to a handful of whate, from the colleens, in exchange for a bit of riband or a crooked comb, or anything that way; and the girls taking the whate unknown from their parents, – it isn't the value of the thing, but the desate – (Connor did not observe that his sister looked confused) – and so, dear, when you see the Griffin coming, just shut the front door, and slip out at the back – there's one use I've found for the back-door you hated because it was an English fashion – and then you're not at home, you know, like the quality; and if you meet her outside the house, why there's no harm in life, then, in your looking distant, and so drop her easy."

"Drop who asy?" inquired a voice at the door.

Connor turned round, and there, fully equipped, stood the very "Griffin" of whom he had been speaking. Her appearance was striking, and yet she might have passed in a crowd without exciting observation, – but when once you had looked on, you could not easily forget her. She wore the long blue-hooded cloak peculiar to the south of Ireland; and those who knew her longest, never remember the hood drawn over her head, or her grizzled hair defended from sun or storm by any better covering than a white muslin cap – *very* white – with a high crown or cawl, and a double border of what, even in those tasteful days of long ruffles, would be called magnificent lace; the cap was bound round the head with a broad riband, and by the colour of the riband it was easy to determine what party the Griffin wished to please. If she was on the forage amongst the country-people, she invariably mounted one of green, tied at the side in a *flahoulagh* bow; if she had something to tell, or show, the gentry, she pinned on one of a dainty blue or pink, and took good care to say that "indeed she was a paceable craythur, who never made or bothered with politics, or troubled about religion, madam!" No one doubted the truth of the latter assertion. Her eyes, or rather eye – for one of them she had lost – was small, bright, black, and restless, and certainly did double duty in "right good style." Her hair hung in spiral and abundant ringlets at each side of her face. Her upper-lip was shaded by a dark line, resembling a moustache. Her features, though large and heavy, were decidedly expressive of two feelings, however opposite: when bent upon cajoling, or insinuating, there lurked an infinite fund of humour about the corners of her mouth; but when contradicted or annoyed, nothing could exceed the deadly expression of revenge that contracted her brows, and flashed from beneath their penthouse. Sometimes a large pedlar's pack was strapped under her cloak, across her brawny shoulders; but more frequently she *apparently* contented herself with a basket slung on her arm, and well-filled with Birmingham finery, and the fag-ends of antiquated ribands. She was gifted with extraordinary aptness and quickness of perception, and if she had had the power of commanding her temper, she would have been as complete a rustic Machiavel as ever plotted or executed plots. Nobody exactly knew what part of the country she came from, or seemed to remember when she came. She said she was a sailor's widow, and she was very fond, like too many in the polite world, of interlarding her conversation with scraps of what certainly were foreign tongues. Her fingers were always adorned with thick brass rings; her high shoes, clasped over her instep by square silver buckles, and her throat encircled by coral beads. She had an air half-savage, half-cunning, and though universally disliked, was received with more than usual courtesy by the always courteous peasantry of Ireland, who applied to her the various epithets of "a knowing woman," "a grate card," "a fine woman with rather more larning than a quiet God-fearing man would like in a wife;" while others hardly dare whisper lest she might hear it, "that she was no better than she should be, was up to all sorts of smuggling and deceiving, and the country would have a good riddance if she was out of it."

"Drop who asy?" she repeated, while her hands rested on the top of an iron-shod staff with which she occasionally assisted her speed. "Who do you want her to drop asy – is it me? For here I've been standing for more than a minute, the wind blowing away my gray hair, the way the world blows off ould friends. Mounseer – as the Frinch say – neither you nor Ma'mselle have offered 'Kindly welcome, Mrs. Griffin,' or *the* Griffin, as they calls me, the sons o'Cain, out off left-handed compliment to my beautiful fingers;" and she stretched forward her expanded hands, showing that each digit was armed with a hooked nail, more resembling the claw of a kite, than the nail of a woman."

"I never refused the welcome at my own door-stone to friend or foe," said Connor, not with a good grace, certainly; "so if you come in ye'r welcome."

Alice advanced a chair, and then asked the pedlar if she would like to step into "the room," meaning the parlour, which, however excellent in the house of an Irish bachelor farmer, would have been little thought of in an English cottage; still, the clay floor was free from holes, clean swept, and well sanded; there was a picture of the Virgin over the chimney – a corner-cupboard, filled, or nearly so, with delf and china, the broken portions of which were not always turned to the wall – six chairs – a dark mahogany table, above which, on an antique bracket, was placed a duc an durras glass, a relic of Irish hospitality that had been in the family for I dare not say how many years. The table was covered with a piece of good stout frieze, being what the honest tailor gave up out of "the makings" of Connor's last "topcoat," and on it, in solitary grandeur, stood an old filigree tea-caddy, that some priest or friar had bequeathed to Honor O'Gorman, Connor's mother; coloured prints of the saints, in black frames, hung upon the walls, and the window was adorned, if not shaded, by a white dimity curtain.

The Griffin accepted the offer, "swayed" herself into the room, and placig her basket on the floor, repeated her question; to which Connor replied, "Faith, ma'am, I was only giving a piece of advice to Ally, that when anything is neither useful nor ornamental, it's better to drop it."

"And am I neither useful nor ornamental, Mr. Connor O'Gorman, tell me that?" persisted the virago.

"Sure, Mrs. Griffin, I wasn't spaking to you at all," said Connor; "it's quite enough for a lone gentlewoman like yerself to have to stand against what's said to you, without gathering maneings, as a sparrow gathers straws, and for as little good, out of everything you meet on an Irish highway, or hear at an Irish door."

"If it was on the highway I met an affront," continued the unappeased Griffin, "I'd know how to punish it better than, – (if the wind of the word that crosses the mountains spakes truth, joli garson, as the Frinch say,) – I'd know how to punish it better than Mr. Connor O'Gorman, who must whiten his hands and perfume his breath with O de Coloney instead of shiskey, to plaze the Rose of Blarney. There's three black thorns up the chimney, I see, Mister Connor – seasoning,* I suppose.

**(The Irish peasants dry their fighting-sticks, by hanging them up the chimney, and grease them frequently).*

Time was, whin it would be a *bon Chrettien's* office to tell Ulick I'Sullivan of the black thorns; but Ulick may fight the spirits that do be dancing, *bon grey, mol grey,* on the Bograh Mountains, or divert himself with the ghosts of the Macarthies, in the vaults of Blarney Castle, for anything you care; but it's fine to be obedient to the laws, and gentle and quiet, like sucking calves – only lately come to the O'Gormans, that's all."

"Don't heed her, brother," whispered Alice to Connor; "never heed her, *she's very dark this morning*; don't heed her, Connor dear."

"I'm not going to heed her, never fear girl," replied Connor, with a bitter laugh; "I'm not going to heed her. But I'll tell you what, Mrs. Griffin, I'd scorn myself if I wanted strength to tell the truth, even to one who has more to do with evil words and evil winds than becomes an honest woman." – The Griffin started from her seat, and looked furiously at the young farmer, but he continued – "I *did* tell Ally to drop you easy."

"O brother!" exclaimed Alice, turning pale.

"And I repeat it. Alice O'Gorman, you're no sister of mine if you keep any communion with her. My door shall never be shut in your face, Mrs. Griffin, nor in the face of any wanderer, no matter how poor, no matter how ill-spoken of – I never will close my door against the houseless."

"Indeed, Mr. O'Gorman, we're not behoulden to your house, sir, we've plenty of homes, thank God!"

"You have, ma'am, I dare say – by sea and land, over land, and *in* land too – among the distilliries, maybe; and I'll tell you why I don't like the honour of your polite company for my sister, ma'am: she's a little simple, quiet girl, and I hold it, that every honest brother, father, or husband, through the country, ought to keep the women's hearts over which he has power, pure; and that it's the duty of a pathriot to watch over the religion and innocence of his countrywomen. For look here," continued the young farmer, and he snatched a white rose from his sister's bosom, and held it above his head, "this is woman as she should be – above the reach or touch of anything low, or mean, or dirty, or desateful; – but this is what she becomes," and he illustrated the figure by dropping the flower upon the clay-sanded floor, and crushing its petals beneath his foot; "this is what she becomes when mixed up with the talk and the scandal, the sin, and the badness, that's carried through the world by idle and mischievous bog-throtters, who shoulder sin lie a musket, and whose lips are foul with black and bitter words."

"Are *my* lips foul?" inquired the Griffin furiously; "Mister Connor O'Gorman, Mistress Griffin says, Are *my* lips foul?"

"If they're not, I wish the country joy of the change, that's all. Now keep off, ma'am – I'll not suffer ye to strike me – I'll spancel yer hands with that strong gad I made for the kicking cow, and she never kicked since. I'll have no carrying of stories from the Bee's Nest here, or from here to the Bee's Nest. And so, ma'am, you may rest yourself as long as you please, and then we'll walk out of the house together, for Ally will be none the worse of spending the heel of the evening by herself."

"Let her pay me what she owes me," said the Griffin, "and then I'll go bail it will be many a long day before anything but *my curse* darkens your door."

"Oh! Mrs. Griffin! Mrs. Griffin!" expostulated Ally.

"Owes! What does she owe you?" inquired Connor, glancing angrily at his sister.

"Three thirteens, for a crooked comb; two testers, for black tags; seven tinpennies, for an illigant shawl; and half a crown for she knows what herself."

Alice trembled like an aspen, and dared not look at her brother, who put his hand into his pocket, and drew forth a small leathern bag which was tied round the neck by a piece of string.

"Here, now; if it's not too much trouble, will ye say that riddle-ma-ree over again, Mrs. Griffin."

"If it's more convenient to you, Mounsieur," said the woman insolently, though she was marvellously appeased by the sight of the money – a thing in her particular way of dealing she seldom saw except when she carried her barter to Cork, "I'll take it out, as I have done before, in – "

"Hush, Mrs. Griffin, for the Virgin's sake!" exclaimed poor Ally, who, from the love of finery, had been led to exchange her brother's corn, and property of even more value, for the trumpery which this genuine huxter palmed upon the village girl as "genteel."

Connor's generosity prevented his taking any notice of the interruption, further than saying, (what by the way was a great boast,) "that such thrifles couldn't inconvenience an O'Gorman at any time. First of all, he counted down the "three thirteens," then the "two testers," then the "seven tenpennies." "And now, Mrs. Griffin, ma'am," he said, "what was the last ingenious article for working the money out of a foolish girl?"

"She knows herself," said Mrs Griffin, dropping the coins carefully into a large blue worsted stocking, which she had pulled from the depths of her capacious pocket.

"But *I must* know," persisted Connor.

"Then," said the Griffin, without noticing the imploring expression of Ally's face, who felt that she was rapidly falling in her brother's estimation – "then, Mister O'Gorman, it was a – *sirop*."

"Speak English, ma'am, if you please."

"I never am in the habits of confining myself to one language, Misther O'Gorman," replied the Griffin, throwing back her head; "but I'll do my best this time; it was a love-powder the young lady bought, to win – "

But Ally would not permit the mischievous creature, who had lured her on to so much folly, to finish her sentence. She threw herself on her knees before her, and implored her not to speak the name. "You said it would work harm," she exclaimed, "you said it would work harm, not good, if the name was spoke except at – oh! Why did I heed ye – why did I heed ye!"

Connor raised his sister from her servile position and forced her into her bedroom; then turning to the Griffin, he indignantly flung her the half-crown. Fond as the adventuress was of money, she was fonder of revenge; seizing the coin, she threw a leer of bitter hatred at O'Gorman, and then fixing her malignant glance on the duc-an-durras glass, which she knew was the most precious relic Connor possessed of all his family's former wealth and station, she deliberately flung the half-crown at it; and the goblet, which would have formed the glory of an Irish antiquarian, fell into a dozen glittering fragments upon the floor. The woman looked at the destruction she had caused with malignant triumph, and exclaimed,

"May every one be so kilt, and spilt, and smashed, that turns their tongue on the Griffin; and may the seed, breed, and generation of Connor O'Gorman be in smithereens upon Ireland's ground, like that meminto of his glory – Amin."

And, fierce with passion, the violent and evil-hearted woman passed from the farm, leaving its master with an irritated, yet bruised spirit. He gathered up the fragments of the glass, and placed them in the venerable caddy, and I am not very certain that his eyes were dry while her performed their obsequies; he remembered how often in his childish days his tall old grandfather had presented that glass, full to the brim of scalding punch, to the priest, or any other honoured guest, after he had mounted his nag at the door; he remembered the exultation with which he used to listen to the tales the old man recounted of those who, of high rank in ancient times, had drunk the stirrup-cup of gratulation and good-will a the castle gates of his ancestors, then the possessors of lands and rivers, where their descendant now could claim but a few poor acres. It had, indeed, been to Connor a magic glass – a sort of mirror, in which he saw the past, and on which when he looked he thought more brightly of the future. After he had locked the ancient caddy, fearing to trust his voice in converse with his sister, he placed his elbows upon the table, and covered his face with his hands. A low moaning roused him at last, and, upon looking up, he saw the fond, weak-minded girl, whose folly had smitten him to the heart.

"Indeed, brother," she whimpered, "I'm raly sorry, and ashamed, and often thought to tell you, only my mind failed."

"Your principle failed, you mean," said Connor, sorrowfully. "Oh! Ally, it is not the value of a few grains of corn that I think of, but the deceit. We were for many a long day but two together in a could world; I never refused you anything I could give; at wake or fair I took care no girl was better dressed than my little sister; I loved you Ally, – I thought you loved me – but no, Ally, there is no love where there is not perfect trust, you, as well as the rest of my people, have been more like millstones to drag me under the strame than feathers to float me on it. Put on your cloak and bonnet, and come with me."

"Oh! Not to Margaret! Not to Margaret! She is so perfect herself, she would hate me."

"No, not to her," he replied, sadly; "for I could hardly look her in the face if I thought she knew my sister had been –"

"Not a thief – oh! No!" she interrupted; "it was the Griffin said you'd never miss, or think bad, of fhte thrifle of meal or barley."

"I do not want to hear what she said," exclaimed Connor; "we're done with her now; that's one comfort. But come to the priest, Ally, and tell him yer fault – it is long since you have been to your duty; make a clean breast, Ally, and then – why I am sure I'm hardly able to guide you, you poor lamb, that had no mother, as I had, to watch over you – only was laid in her could grave, and you a dawshy thing, *like a young green rush in a lonely pool,* bent by every passing breeze, and nothing to strengthn you but the sun of heaven – and if that shone too strong, why it would scorch up the water of life round you, machree. I'm a great deal your elder, Ally, and I thought I taught you honour and honesty – there, don't cry, like a good girl – I'll never even mention it to you, and no one will be the wiser of it for me, and it will tache you a lesson; and when you've made a *clean breast,* and heard what his reverence says, why dear, make Margaret your friend, as I wanted you, long ago; sure if she's above you in learning, so much the better for you – as the star said when she had the moon to look at . Please the Almighty to strengthen my good resolve, she'll be your sister, I hope, in four months and eleven days – the saints between us and harm! And keep up yer heart, my sister, and avoid all such as the Griffin – though, to be sure, like her distant cousin the Phoenix – there's not many of the family – "

"But the glass, brother, the glass," repeated Ally.

"Say nothing about that, Ally," said Connor, in a sorrowful tone, "the least said soonest mended – which *it* can never be – so there's an end of that; but by all the books that were ever shut and opened – wait till my time's up – "

"O brother, brother!" exclaimed Ally, "she's a woman, and no O'Gorman ever struck a woman, even when he had too much – "

"I think," he replied, "she is an incarnate devil, that's what I think; and I think his reverence ought to see to it – she's not right, one way or other – "

"And yet," said Ally, "they say she can talk the birds off the bushes, as indeed I know, to my cost; and if you knew how, you would not look so could on me; and, brother, I remember onct she chated yourself about the knee-buckles, and in three months after, the riding-whip – but to be sure it was your *own* – not all as one as my fault."

The generous, superstitious, honest, confiding, and yet, on particular subjects, keen-sighted fellow, kissed his sister affectionately.

I would not have detailed this incident so fully, but that after events proved the truth of the adage – the injured may forgive, but the injurer never does. Connor, when requested to do so, forgave, (and he seldom did things by halves) though he disliked the Griffin, who from her knowledge of every person and every circumstance, possessed an extraordinary influence over man, woman, and child. Persons of acute observation and strong minds always have large power over their fellow-creatures; but, if they are badly disposed and can stoop to mould weakness and superstition to their own purpose, they become more dangerous to the well-doing of my countrymen, than the serpents St. Patrick got so much credit for banishing from the Emerald Isle.

IV

School Stories and Governess Stories

The Young Rebel (1829)
Marian (1840)
The Governess (1852)

MASTER BEN.

Half-page vignette at beginning of sketch
"The Schoolmaster" from "Master Ben"
Ill. by H. MacManus
engr. by Landells
from *Sketches of Irish Character* (1844)

School stories as a genre had their gestation in the mid-eighteenth century. Sarah Fielding's *The Governess* (1749) and John Newbery's publication *Goody Two Shoes* (1765) were early examples of the moral tale within a school setting. These were followed by Dorothy Kilner's *The Village School* (c. 1795), Maria Edgeworth's *The Barring Out* (1796) and Elizabeth Sandham's *The Boys School* (1800) at the turn of the century. By the time Anna Maria penned her school stories, it was an accepted subject within which to explore behaviour, friendships and adventures, invariably couched in didactic terms. In the mid-nineteenth century many of Charles Dickens's novels such as *Nicholas Nickleby* (1839), *Dombey and Son* (1848) and *David Copperfield* (1850) had school story elements. *Jane Eyre* (1847) by Charlotte Brontë was one of the most celebrated with *Tom Brown's Schooldays* by Thomas Hughes (1857) one of the most influential.

Anna Maria had definite ideas about how a child could be educated which may be summarised as follows: A child fared best in a rural environment, educated at home and not at a boarding school. Care must be taken not to force feed a child with an abundance of meaningless facts and figures and the freedom to play and roam in the countryside was a vital part of education. Repeatedly, these views were expressed in her work and they show her familiarity with the work of the leading theorists in the field John Locke, Jean-Jacques Rousseau, Hannah More and Maria Edgeworth.

Her very first Sketch featured "Master Ben," her schoolteacher in Bannow in Wexford. He was engaged to try to teach her the multiplication table, "an act no mortal man (or woman either) ever could accomplish". She had the utmost respect for him:

> His steps were strides: his voice shrill, like a boatswain's whistle; and his learning – prodigious! – the unrivalled dominie of the country, for five miles round, was Master Ben.

Significantly, Anna Maria's earliest full-length publication, *Chronicles of a School Room* (1830), revealed her commitment to education for young women. She indicated in her dedication to Mrs Hofland that the stories within were "not for childhood but for those emerging from it." As in many of her stories, the author set out to convince the reader that there was an element of autobiographical truth framing the structure. The author was staying in Sussex where she made the acquaintance of Mrs Ashburton a former governess and the chronicles referred to the governess's recollections of memorable children under her tutelage. Students included one who had fled the French Revolution, an Irish student, a Scottish Laird's daughter, two from Bengal, and a Quaker who had journeyed from America, one who was born blind and another deaf. The device of focusing on one character's tale at a time could easily have its origins in the much-imitated formula adopted by Fielding in *The Governess, or The Little Female Academy* (1749).

The question whether to educate young girls at home or away was a regular predicament in many of Hall's stories. In *The Whisperer* (1850), Aunt Tart the guardian of Clementine, Isabella and Edward, had a thorough dislike of girls' schools. At their very best, she considered them necessary evils. In *The Swan's Egg* (1851), Miss Lyddy confided her worries to Simon, the Irish servant, about the education of Kate and Jane and his advice, as always, was solid, that "a young bird learns best in its own nest."

Anna Maria's most extensive treatment of the boarding school genre was in *Marian* (1840), the story of a foundling who was taken into a wealthy household. Marian was a novelty for Mrs. Cavendish Jones until she tired of her and abandoned her to Miss Arabella Womble's establishment.

Womble was the epitome of the heartless money-grabbing school mistress, always ready to exercise petty tyrannies to save money and torment her charges. The loss of Marian's treasured books which were confiscated and thrown onto the fire as a punishment was a pivotal act demonstrating the irrational behaviour of the Womble philosophy. Half-starved under a harsh and unenlightened regime, Marian ended up with an education that was "superficial and frequently erroneous; ... which left her much to undo in after-life." In the novel, the author deplored the system of female education available for girls:

> The mania that possesses many rational persons in middle life, to send their young daughters from their comfortable homes to a third or fourth-rate starving and perverting academy, that they may imbibe a little bad French and a little tuneless music, which is of no earthly use afterwards, is truly a matter for marvel.

Anna Maria was not the only author expressing concerns about education at this period. She corresponded with Charles Dickens over the infamous Mr Shaw who ran Bowes Academy in Yorkshire where damages of £300 had been awarded against Shaw for his brutality causing blindness in several pupils. Dickens admitted to her that Shaw was indeed the inspiration for the villainous bully Wackford Squeers, headmaster at the appalling Dotheboys Hall in *Nicholas Nickleby*. Though not comparable to the level of physical degradation found in *Nicholas Nickleby*, Arabella Womble was capable of inflicting mental and emotional abuse that was almost as harrowing as that described in Lowood in *Jane Eyre*, published in 1847, seven years after *Marian*. Jane Eyre is one of English literature's best known governesses but the governess novel was a popular genre in the early nineteenth century, one that Anna Maria revisited on many occasions.

GOVERNESSES

The governess novel could easily be considered as a genre of its own in the nineteenth century according to Cecilia Wadsö Lecaros, not just as a sub-section of that of school stories with which it is often included. According to M. Jeanne Peterson, there were over 25,000 governesses in England in 1851 but over 750,000 female domestic servants at the same period. Kathryn Hughes in *The Victorian Governess* suggested that although the figure for governesses was a relatively small proportion of nineteenth-century working women, she attracted a great deal of literary interest because she came from the same class as did the authors and library subscribers. The readers knew full well that a change in circumstances, the death of a father or political upheavals could mean that they were one step away from a similar fate or "one man away from the schoolroom," as Sally Mitchell described it in her review of Hughes's book.

A familiar figure therefore in many Victorian novels, the governess appeared in a high percentage of Anna Maria's writings, most frequently depicting a heroine who had fallen on hard times, who proved her worth through her independence and hard work. The fascination with the governess stemmed from the fact that she was a middle class woman who had to work outside the home at a time when there were very few options available for those who had to work for a living. It was socially acceptable to do this as it was a womanly job that took place within a family setting so it was not frowned upon although it offered a poor salary without any kind of pension or comfort on retirement.

The governess could be treated very badly by her host family, neglected and treated as a servant and instantly forgotten when dismissed after completing her course of education of the young ladies of the family. Anna Maria did a great deal of philanthropic work highlighting the plight of governesses including the publication of *Stories of the Governesses* (1852). This collection encapsulated the range of her views on the topic of governesses, many poignant and tragic tales but others that had more positive dénouements.

Governesses generally had three options open to them. They could teach in a school (either their own or with other governesses), they could live at home and travel as a daily governess to their employer, or, as was most common between the 1840s–60s, they lived at the employer's home, teaching and providing companionship to the children. According to Peterson, a governess earned anything from £25–£100 per year but the average was around £20–£40 per year compared to an average low agricultural wage of the same era bringing in £30 per year.

Hughes outlined that the accepted protocol for children's education was that a nurse cared for children up to the age of five. A preparatory governess tutored boys and girls up to the age of eight, teaching the rudiments of reading, writing and arithmetic. Boys were then sent away to preparatory school once they reached the age of eight. Girls remained at home to continue lessons generally consisting of a combination of English, History, Geography, Music (Singing and Piano), Dancing, Drawing and Needlework. This continued for girls until the age of twelve when a finishing governess was employed to prepare the girls for their social debut when they reached the age of seventeen.

The threat of the governess introducing a destabilising force within the family is explored by Lecaros and Hughes in detail. There was the perception that the position could be used by those lower in society to gain a foothold higher up the social ladder. Anna Maria had many Irish nannies, nurses, cooks and washerwomen in her fiction but they never made it to the ranks of governess from the lower classes. Any Irish governesses who featured in her stories, such as Gertrude Raymond in "Hospitality," came from the Anglo-Irish class, usually women who needed an acceptable form of independent employment to survive. There was also the question of religion and a Roman Catholic governess simply would not have been acceptable. While she respected those who upheld their religion faithfully, she had definite lines of demarcation beyond which she would not be drawn.

In regular monthly missives of *The Art-Union* in 1848, Anna Maria includes advertisements for Bazaars and fund-raising activities in support of the Asylum for Aged and Decayed Governesses. She describes how 'Every day – every hour teems with instances of the great necessity that demands a Refuge for the aged disseminators of the knowledge we so dearly prize.' Through her writings and her activism on their behalf, she proved herself to be a passionate advocate for the plight of governesses.

FURTHER READING

Brontë, Charlotte, *Jane Eyre*, 1847 (Oxford, Oxford University Press, 2000).

Dickens, Charles, *Nicholas Nickleby* (London, Chapman and Hall, 1839).

Fielding, Sarah, *The Governess or the Little Female Academy*, 1749 (Charleston SC, BiblioBazaar, 2007).

Hall, S[amuel]. C[arter], Mrs, *Chronicles of a Schoolroom* (London, Frederick Westley & A.H. Davis, 1830).

Marian; Or, A Young Maid's Fortunes (London, Henry Colburn, 1840).

Marian; or, A Young Maid's Fortunes, 2 vols (Leipzig, Bernard Tauchnitz, 1877).

Stories of the Governess (London, J. Nisbet, 1852).

The Swan's Egg (Edinburgh, William and Robert Chambers, 1851).

The Whisperer (Edinburgh, William and Robert Chambers, [1850]).

"The Young Rebel." Mrs. S.C. Hall (ed.), *The Juvenile Forget Me Not. A Christmas and New Year's Gift, or Birthday Present, for the Year 1829* (London, N. Hailes, 1829).

Hughes, Kathryn, *The Victorian Governess* (London, Hambledon, 1993).

Hughes, Thomas, *Tom Brown's Schooldays*, 1857 (Oxford, Oxford University Press, 2008).

Lecaros, Cecilia Wadsö, *The Victorian Governess Novel* (Lund, Lund University Press, 2001).

Peterson, M. Jeanne, "The Victorian Governess: Status Incongruence in Family and Society." *Victorian Studies*, 14 (1970), 7–26.

"Nor grandeur hear with a disdainful smile
The short but simple annals of the poor."

It was a bright and cheerful morning – the sunbeams danced merrily on the gay river which skirted the village of Callow – and the dewdrops hung like diamonds round the clustering vine that, in those days, overshadowed the humble school of Dame Mabel Leigh. Dear Dame Mabel! She was one of the governesses of the olden time, who ruled by the assistance of a large birch rod, and sundry other aids which are now out of fashion. She was a very excellent old woman for all that; and although she thought it beneath the dignity of a school-mistress to *reason* with her pupils, yet she possessed so many good and valuable qualities, that even the vicar's lady treated the dame with deference and respect. She had held undisputed sway over all the girls and many of the boys, from two to ten years of age, for more than forty years: but do not for a moment imagine that the worthy dame kept one of those fine "Establishments," whose blue, green, or red signboards announce that "Ladies and Gentlemen are here taught French and English Education, and all fashionable Accomplishments;" – No such thing; the simple one of Dame Mabel, which was more than half covered with clustering grapes and vine leaves, only promised that there children were "taught to read:" and the villagers of Callow were quite satisfied if their daughters could read the Bible, sew, hem, and stitch neatly.

Thomas Hill, indeed, the rich, fat, and rosy landlord of the Plough Inn, had only one daughter; and to make her *genteel,* as he called it, he sent her for six months to a boarding-school. When she had been there a short time, such a box arrived at the Plough! everyone in the village thought it must be something very beautiful as it came from Mary Hill's school; and when it was opened, appeared a piece of embroidery, in a fine gold frame. People were somewhat puzzled at first to know what it was. There was an animal, which might be either a pig or a mule, with its heels in the air; and there was a boy somewhat taller than a tree, and another brown-black looking thing: however, the *poetry* underneath explained the matter –

"The vicious kicking donkey
Has thrown my brother and Pompey"

The silly people of Callow (for there are silly people everywhere) thought that Mary must be wonderfully improved; but the wise ones knew that it was not right for a girl in her situation of life to waste so much time on such useless work. Indeed poor Mary was not the better for her six months' trip; she has brought home a great many airs; and it was very evident that she had not been properly instructed; for I am almost ashamed to say that she despised her parents, because they were not as rich or as fashionable as the *"Pa's"* and *"Ma's"* of the *young ladies* she knew at school. However, I have said enough about her.

Monday was always a busy day with good Mabel; the little floor of the school-room was fresh sanded; laurel, gemmed with bright hedge roses, graced the chimney; the eight-day clock, towering even unto the ceiling, seemed to tick more loudly than ever; Tom, a venerable old white mouser, had a new blue riband round his neck; and the high-backed chair was placed so as to command not only a good view of the four corners of the room, but of a large cupboard, where books and work were arranged, and where the *very* little people often congregated like a nest of young wrens, and whispered and twittered, whenever the dame's back was turned; – then a little black-looking carved table was placed on the right-hand side of this throne, and on it, ready for use, every Monday morning, appeared a new well-made birch rod. The good dame seldom wore out more than one a week, which, considering all things in those days, was not thought too much. But I wish I could describe the dame to you, for I am sure you will never see any one like her, as even the village school-mistresses now are very different to what they were twenty years ago: her apron was always white as snow, and round it a flounce full two fingers deep; her neckerchief, clear and stiff, neatly pinned down in front; the crown of her cap in the highest part might measure perhaps half a yard, somewhat more or less, and under it her nice gray hair was turned over a roller; and although her eyes were dark and penetrating, and her nose long and hooked, yet her smile was so sweet that every little child's heart felt happy when she gave such a mark of approbation: but there were times when in very truth the good dame's anger was excited; and then she certainly did look what the young ones called "very terrible."

"I'll certainly try this new rod on your bare shoulders, Fanny Spence," said the old lady, one "black Monday morning," to a little arch-looking girl with blue eyes, who amused herself by eating the corners of her spelling-book – "I'll teach you how to munch your book as a rabbit does clover. Mercy on me! you have half torn out the pretty picture of 'The Fox and Grapes', and you have daubed over as many as ten leaves with – How did you get at my rose pink? – Oh! you wicked, wicked child!" – 'The dame, I am sorry to say, now lost her temper, and elevated her rod and voice at one and the same moment. Fanny, who had opened her mouth to commence squalling, thought it better to tell the truth; so, keeping as far from the rod as she could – "Indeed, if you please ma'am, it was Dick Shaw – he painted 'em for me – and he stole it out of your basket yesterday, while you were taking up the stitches little Kate dropped in the toe of her stocking."

Before Dame Mabel had decided what punishment to inflict, her attention was attracted by little Kate herself, who crept slowly to her seat with hanging head and downcast eyes.

"This is a very pretty hour for you to come to school, miss, – Why, all your strings are out, and your hands and arms torn and dirty. I see how it is; – open your mouth – black, as I supposed; – You have been down the lane after the blackberries; – Very well – I'll find a way to punish you." The old lady stooped, and with great dexterity drew off her garter (it was twenty years old), and was about to tie the culprit's hands behind her, when, in lisping tones, the little thing declared it was all Dick Shaw' fault:

"He showed me the bush, ma'am, and he promised to hold it; and I did not eat more than two or three, when he pulled it away, and I fell into the ditch." – "And serve you right too," said the dame: "Girls have no business to play with boys; – but your arm is much scratched just here. Well," she continued, her tone instantly softening (for she was really very kind hearted), "give me my blue bag, and I will bind it up with some of the old linen the good vicar's lady gave me." – The bag was brought, and emptied; but no old linen was to be found. The children were severally questioned; and at last little Phoebe Ford, a merry laughing thing of six years old, who, though she had many faults, always spoke the truth – a perfection which made her even at that age respected – said that she saw Dick Shaw pull out the roll of linen at twelve o'clock on Friday, and that he said it would do nicely to fetter White Tom.

"That boy," said the dame, "shall be expelled from my school; and I certainly ought not to have kept him since his trick of the spectacles, nor would I, indeed, were it not that *others*" – and her eye glanced at a red-faced, red-armed girl of ten, with a fuzzy head and little twinkling eyes – "were almost as bad as he. I only said *almost,* Mary, – and you have been very good since."

By the way, I must tell you that the affair of the spectacles occurred two days after Dick came to Dame

Leigh's school. Dick took a fancy to fit his governess's spectacles on Farmer Howit's big pig – and Mary, romping Mary Green, agreed to hold the pig while they were fitting on. Now as the pig, who in this instance showed more wisdom than either Dick or Mary, could see better without than with spectacles, he soon pushed Dick into a stagnant pool of green water, and left the luckless Mary sprawling like a great frog in the mire; while he rejoined his brothers and cousins, grunting triumphantly, and curling his little tail, which the fallen Dick had unmercifully pulled in the contest. But nothing could cure the boy's love of mischief; and everything that went wrong in the village was laid to his account. His poor mother's heart was almost broken; his father even, hard-working man as he was, had been seen to shed tears over his son's wilful ways; and his sister, a fine, good industrious girl of sixteen, could have been of great service to her parents, were it not that her entire time was taken up in trying to keep Dick out of mischief, or to repair the mischief Dick had done.

"It was he pinned Kitty Carey's frock to Aunt Colwell's red petticoat, and it tore such a great piece; and Kitty cried because it was a new London chintz," said Mary Doyle.

"Hush, don't speak so loud," said Liddy Grant; "the dame will hear ye."

"She's not looking, she's mending little Kate's arm; and I just want to show you the bright new housewife my mother gave me, because I would not play at 'touch wood' with Dick Shaw on Sunday; – and I know that no good will come of him or anybody else who breaks Sunday."

"I tink," said Anna Miles, who could not speak plain. "I tink Dick very bold; for he" –

"Bless me, look!" interrupted Mary Doyle. "Hark! Did ye ever hear such a screaming? – It is Dick Shaw himself; and Patty is dragging him to school; – he kicks like a donkey, – there goes his shoe."

"His bran new spelling-book – and his hat, that cost his poor father five shillings," said the prudent Liddy – "He has the best of it; Patty will never be able to bring him up."

"She has the best of it now though," cried Mary, who, unable to sit still any longer, got one foot on the lower step, and held fast to the door-post, as if afraid that Dick would break loose and do some more mischief.

"The Young Rebel" by W. Holmes
The Juvenile Forget-Me-Not (1829)

"The Young Rebel" by Hablot Browne
The Juvenile Budget (1840)

Patty pulled – Dick kicked and roared, – no young lady singing the *do re mi fa,* that gives master and pupil so much trouble, ever opened her mouth so widely as Dick – you could see all the way down his throat. And Patty looked quite as calm and tranquil as Dick looked wild and furious. Everybody, yes even the pretty face which is now gazing over this pretty book, looks ugly in a passion. At last Patty's firmness conquered Dick's violence, and she carried him into the school-room.

Here a fresh mortification awaited the young Rebel: he had been conquered by a *girl*; – that was bad enough; but it was still worse to be expelled from a *girls'* school. Dick stood stiff and sturdy, while the good dame read him a lecture, which, though simply worded, conveyed many useful lessons, and ended by saying, "that evil communications corrupt good manners," and he should no longer remain in her school. Dick was formally expelled; and in a little time Dame Mabel's scholars became as peaceable as they had been, before Obstinate Dick set so bad an example; even romping Mary Green became a very good sort of girl.

Dick, I am sorry to say, did not improve; for poor boys as well as rich ones can never be respected or prosper in their several spheres of life, if they are wilful, violent, disobedient, or Sabbath breakers.

The young Rebel's father, finding that he continued so very wicked, permitted him to go to sea; and for many years no one heard anything of Obstinate Dick. Dear Dame Mabel grew so old that the vicar got a new mistress for the school; but the old woman continued to live there; and though she was blind and nearly lame, she never wanted for any thing; for the poor are often more grateful than the rich, and the villagers remembered the care and pains the dame took with them when they were little troublesome children.

One fine spring morning, when Patty Shaw was placing her aged friend on a nice green seat at the school door (for old people love to breathe the pure air, and Mabel felt the sun's rays very warm and pleasant, though she could not see its brightness), a young man, with a wooden leg and but one eye, in a tattered sailor's dress, stopped, and looked earnestly up the village. "Do you want to see any one, young man?" said Patty, in her clear calm voice – "or, as you seem very much fatigued, is there anything I can give you?" – "Is there an old man, a carpenter, of the name of Shaw in your village?" replied he; "and can you give me a draught of water? For I have walked far, and have not a penny to buy food."

"Patty, Patty!" cried old blind Mabel, "if your brother Dick is a living being, that is his voice."

And she was right. Dick Shaw's temper had prevented his advancement; and he returned in poverty to his native village, where, but for the kind exertions of his sister he must have become an inmate of the workhouse; for his parents were both dead, and he had not received even their blessing. But Patty was beloved by everyone; and poor Dick was sincerely sorry for his former obstinate ways: and he now manages to go more quickly on the messages of those who employ him with his wooden leg, than he used formerly when he had two good ones. And said he the other day, "If sincere penitence could restore my eye and leg, which I lost through my own wilfulness, I might then be really useful; but that cannot now be; so I must do my best, and be thankful that God did not cut me off in the midst of my sins."

Marian; or a Young Maid's Fortunes

Marian at School

Chapter X

"Miss is in sulk," said the French woman to the teacher, at the schoolroom door, "but she get out of dem agin."

"Are you sulky, little girl?" inquired the fag of the school, in a voice which constant insult had ground into a whisper, so that "Miss Kitty" never spoke loud enough to be heard across the room.

"I don't know."

"Then go and sit down; there are not many girls returned yet, so you may have your sulks to yourself," continued the withered teacher, as she pressed her hard iron fingers into the soft dimpled hand of the foundling.

No one, to have looked on the remnant of mortality, would have imagined she was that lovely, beloved, and tender thing, called woman. Her features were pinched together from the constant habit of controlling her feelings; so that her mouth had acquired a rigidity of muscle which rendered it almost immovable; her hair, thinned by premature old age, was streaked with grey, frizzed out into two curls on either side her temples, twisted into a knot behind, and fastened by a horn comb; her complexion was saddened; her eyes, dimmed by late watchings and early rising. Her brow was the reverse of Miss Womble's; it was expanded and full, indicating an observant, if not a very comprehensive, mind. Bred up to be a teacher, she had never heard the voice of sympathy and affection since her mother, rising her dying had with a last effort, from her pillow, said, "God help you, my poor Kate! I leave you pennyless, in a cold heartless world."

The succeeding years of poor Kate's life proved the strength of that mother's observation. No mere school-girl ever dreamed of loving a teacher; and, had one of Miss

Womble's pupils committed such an indiscretion, she would have been prevented from repeating it by the governess's jealousy – she being firmly resolved that her teacher should be her slave, and that nothing should ameliorate her condition. It is not to be wondered at that fifteen years of such discipline should have turned the milk of human kindness in this bereaved woman's bosom into gall and bitterness, or that she vented that bitterness in sundry acts of petty tyranny upon the little ones, who certainly aided Miss Womble in tormenting "the teacher." Miss Kitty held Marian's soft hand within hers, and led her into that desolate school-room, without one feeling of pity for the tears which rolled down her cheeks, or one sympathising thought as to the sufferings she must undergo. A single shovel-full of coals was burning in the grate, which was walled in by a high green wire fender, and it must be confessed the bars were much brighter than the fire; the floor was destitute of carpet, the windows of curtains or drapery; two long, narrow, deal table, were fixed in the middle of the room, and equally long deal forms, narrow and hard, flanked either side; on the table were piled sundry slates, boxes, and heaps of school-books; there was a reclining board behind the door, two pair of stocks, and two or three back-boards; the floor was mottled with spots of ink, and the table had sundry marks expressive of the propensity which young ladies, as well as young gentlemen, sometimes have of writing and drawing in wrong places.

Over the chimney-piece, in a square black frame, were several rules and regulations, fines and maxims, all very good, taken separately, but, like most maxims, unfit for general society or general use. Indeed, it would have been impossible to select or arrange an apartment more completely at variance with every idea of comfort and home than that which Miss Womble ostentatiously designated in her advertisements, a "spacious and lofty school-room."

Miss Kitty left Marian standing in the middle of this cheerless apartment, desiring her to sit down. The poor child looked timidly round; it was evident, even to her, that but few of the pupils had yet arrived. One, however, was sitting upon her trunk, which had not yet been carried upstairs, crying very bitterly; two others (Indians) were standing over a basket filled with winter fruits and cakes, which they were dividing and devouring much to their own satisfaction; a fourth, a lanky girl, was seated, in a sort of half-melancholy, abstracted mood, looking at the fire she dared not approach, her long nose and long fingers being admirably matched, in a red, purply tint, denoting extreme cold. Marian glanced round on her companions, but, meeting no returning glance, did what strangers always do in a strange house, she walked up close to the fire-place.

"Mustn't go there," said the long girl, "read the rules – 'Every young lady placing her hands on the fender to pay one penny to the poor-box, and learn an additional column of French spelling.'"

Marian moved to sit in a comfortable easy chair, which I forgot to enumerate in my catalogue of the school furniture, and which stood in solitary dignity between the windows.

"Mustn't sit there, that's the governess's chair. Read the rules," persisted the purple young lady – " 'The pupils to keep their regular seats except when in the stocks on the reclining board, or in class; any young lady taking over than her proper seat to pay a penny to the poor-box, and do one extra sum in arithmetic.'"

"But I have no seat yet," remonstrated Marian.

"Do as you like," replied the long young lady; "only, no one ever sits in that chair, except the governess, or Kats!"

"Cats!" echoed Marian.

"Yes, Kats," replied the thin girl. "We always call Miss Kitty, Kats, she's so cross. Mind, little one, you don't tell. I've been here five years, and mum's our word!"

"Mum!" said the perplexed novice.

"Yes, Mum; that's our word. Why, you little stupid, mum means hold your tongue."

Marian made no reply.

"What's your name, little one?" persisted Miss Kemp.

"Marian Winter."

"Have you ever been at school before?"

"Never."

"Poor child! I dare say you were very sorry to leave Pa' and Ma', and brothers and sisters?"

"I have none."

"Oh, dear! – How odd! No Pa' or Ma', or brothers or sisters. Well perhaps you're better off; they torment one sadly. Brothers – particularly brothers. Do you come as a boarder of half-boarder?"

"I don't know."

"Oh, as a boarder, I suppose; you are too little for a half. However, we shall soon know."

Although Marian did not understand the difference, she innocently inquired "How!"

"Oh", replied her informant, laughing, "because pupils – whose pupils – get bread and butter, halfs, get bread and scrape."

Marian was again at fault, but she did not feel inclined to prolong the conversation with a companion who continued humming a tune, and knocking first one heel and then the other against the ground, to mark the time and keep her feet from freezing.

Miss Kemp (that was the thin young lady's name) was, as Miss Womble elegantly expressed it, "the crack music pupil of the school" – foremost rattler at the ill-used piano, and still more ill-used harp, whose very strings murmured terror and dismay at the approach of Miss Kemp's footstep; and when, with a triumphant air, she threw up the lid of the one, and drew, or rather hauled, the other towards her, it was acknowledged by all who had a feeling of sympathy with the suffering instrument, that great must be its tortures, past, present, and to come; nevertheless she had all the elements of a great performer, if they had been properly developed.

Marian continued sitting and shivering on the narrow form, as, one by one, the different pupils entered – for Miss Womble's school had degenerated, since our first introduction to her, into quite a preparatory school, on an extended scale. She was most anxious it should be believed that this was her own choice, and also that all the children belonged to the "upper classes." Accordingly, the butcher who supplied her school-table with indifferent meat, exchanged his beef and mutton for a certain portion of polite education bestowed upon his daughter, but the government always designated him as a "provision merchant in the city!" Her grocer, on the same principle, was a "China merchant;" and her milkman, though his daughter – Heaven help her! – was as an apprentice, only destined to pick up the educational crumbs which fell from Miss Womble's ill-supplied table, yet even Miss Jay, poor, despised Miss Jay, was spoken of as "the daughter of an agriculturalist!"

Some of the children, as they entered, greeted each other with that warm affection which is the sweet offspring of innocence and love; but the first day at school after the Christmas holidays is always a sad one. Eyes look red, and many have severe colds, and others have been crammed at home into an overfed stupidity, which it takes them a week to get rid of; though they have to tell each other, they are not in spirits to tell it yet, the establishment harmonising as a whole but on one point, that of staring at the new pupil, for Miss Womble had but one *"that half."*

Marian endured the stare with a good deal of the composure of a well-bred lady, neither returning nor shrinking from it; and when Miss Womble entered the room and spoke a word or two to each, her cheek, for the first time, flushed, for she felt something like pleasure in recognising a face she had seen – there are times and situations when we would hail a foe almost as a friend.

Miss Womble's greeting to each was in exact proportion to the sum paid by the parent for the pupil; and, as no abatement had been desired for Marian, she was patted on the head, kissed, and told to go upstairs. Quite aware of Marian's extraordinary genius for music, she hoped that she might soon succeed Miss Kemp as "crack pupil" in that material department of display.

"Miss Kemp, you must make a pet of this little girl; you will find great pleasure, I am sure, in superintending her practice – it is already a pleasure to hear her play."

"Oh, oh," thought cunning Miss Kemp – Miss Womble's was the third inferior school she had practised in – "Oh, oh," thought she, "Miss Womble thinks to make me useful in nursing a rival, does she?" and she walked up-stairs after Marian, for the purpose of ascertain more about her.

Solitary as the foundling had often been at Mrs. Jones's, that solitude was happiness to the feelings she experienced when, after being half-washed and assisted to dress by the fagging off-spring of the "agriculturist," she descended, in the dim-twilight, to the dim and freezing atmosphere of the school-room, where Miss Kitty murmured over the prayers, with a total absence of interest or sympathy in their holy import. Then followed the bustle, the riot, the discontent of the first morning, as to who was to be monitor, who was to sit here, who there, complaints of Misses This and That, sneers and snaps, with a muttering of questions and replies as to what they had seen and what they had not seen during the holidays; while Miss Kitty, perfectly unmoved, sat in Miss Womble's chair, arranging lessons, marking quantities, naming books, appointing classes, lecturing the two apprentices, calling "silence," in her suppressed voice, which was itself a silence, "doing the school business," which, to be "done" properly for thirty girls, would have fully occupied two if not three teachers.

At last "Miss Winter" was called.

"Got any books?"

"Yes, Ma'am."

"Fetch them."

Marian went upstairs and brought down her hoard – a heap of ignorant story-books, selected *by herself* during her walks with Kitty or Ma'mselle; two volumes of Shakespeare's Plays; "Elegant Extracts;" the "Arabian Nights' Entertainment;" a Bible and Prayer-book; Bunyan's Pilgrim's Progress" – these last being gifts from Mr. Jones; and two or three others, as dis-similar as can possibly be imagined.

Miss Kitty turned them over one by one – placed the Bible and Prayer-book by themselves, and laid the others in a heap; Marian standing by, her eyes glittering with pleasure, as she surveyed her treasures, Miss Kitty then marked down and placed aside a heap of Pinnock's Catechisms, Goldsmith's brief, imperfect, and mangled Geography, and Magnell's questions, and a pile of necessary and unnecessary books – necessary, as regarded making out the bill – unnecessary, as far as the education of a child of nine years old was concerned, and Marian was desired to remove them to her locker. Marian was pleased to be allowed to have such nice new books, "all for herself," and was about adding her old to her new store, when Miss Womble entered; the school rose *en masse,* and Miss Kitty abdicated, having first directed Miss Womble's attention to Marian's favourites. After looking at one or two, the governess said –

"You cannot have these books any more, Miss Winter."

"They are my books, Ma'am."

"That does not matter: they are not yours now; I take them from you."

"They are mine, Ma'am," repeated the little lady resolutely; but Miss Womble, when afterwards telling the story, quite forgot she had provoked that obstinacy.

"Not when I say they are not," said the injudicious governess, committing an act of tyranny where she should have reasoned. Had she told Marian they were not books fit for her to read at school, and that she would take care of them for her, then, indeed, Miss Womble would have conquered, as a teacher ought, by the strength of superior *reason*; and it is a power which a child seldom attempts to withstand.

Marian burst into tears. And how frequently do the ignorant and the unfeeling misunderstand and misrepresent the tears of childhood! How difficult it is to judge what string has jarred of the heart's mysterious chords! How impossible, *at first*, to comprehend the feelings and affections of a young child! How cruel to irritate, where it is a duty to investigate and to soothe! How fatally easy to strengthen bad habits, and absolutely *create* evil passions, by harsh and unjust treatment! Nothing galls a sensitive or high-minded child so much as injustice.

"You cry because you cannot have your own way," said Miss Womble.

"No, Ma'am," sobbed Marian; "it is for my 'Elegant Extracts,' and 'Gulliver,' and the 'White Cat.' My dear, dear book! – oh! leave me them; only to look at, and indeed I will not open them!"

"I shall not trust you, little obstinate miss. Here, Miss Jay, throw those trumpery pamphlets on the fire, and take these to my room. Be quiet; Miss Winter! I must show you that there is to be but one mistress here. Little obstinate minx! She does not care for the books: it is the spirit of contradiction, that's all!"

Anyone who remembers the nature of the highly-wrought temperament of the foundling will at once perceive how little Miss Womble knew of her disposition. Marian really loved her books; they had been her only companion; each was endeared to her warm young heart. There could be no doubt whatever of their being unfit for her, and it was necessary to remove them; but the manner of doing it should have been different. When she saw her cherished friends blazing on the fire, she screamed, and used the most violent efforts to rescue them from the flames – of course, without success. But her flagrant disregard of Miss Womble's power was too serious a breach of school discipline to remain unpunished; she was compelled to stand in the stocks for more than an hour; and, on refusing to apologise or reply, sentenced to solitary confinement.

Miss Womble had never considered how dangerous it is to a teacher's authority to hazard strong measures with a child until fully acquainted with its disposition; and she hardly knew how to act when Marian obstinately refused to ask pardon.

"The books were mine," she repeated; "and, even if she took them from me, she had no right to burn them: they were mine! – they were mine!"

A sofa was put into the dark closet, and there Marian was doomed to sleep.

"Little obstinate thing, giving so much trouble!" grumbled the housemaid. "Why don't you say 'sorry,' and be done with it?"

Marian was sadly fearful of darkness, yet her obstinacy overcame her terror; and she was awoke out of one of those sound sleeps, which only the young know, by the key turning in the door.

"It's only me – me, Tom Kemp, as the girls call me," muttered a voice, which Marian recognised. – "It's only me, little stoopid: here, I have brought you some cake and fruit. We always have a key on the sly for this dunny – we call this room dunny – because we never know who may be sent here and it wouldn't do to be starved, you know, by any of them. Why don't you beg pardon at once?" she continued, as Marian sat up and ate the cake with avidity. "Where's the good of holding out?"

"They were mine!" repeated Marian; "and I'm not sorry."

"But you ought to be sorry."

"Why, Miss Kemp?" inquired the child.

"Call me Tom: those who love me call me Tom; you know the governess said you ought to be sorry, and that's enough."

"But, I think –" recommenced the child.

"Think! – Well done, little fairy-finder! Think! – Why, you didn't come to Miss Womble to *think*, but to obey! Who ever heard of a school-girl thinking? and such a little one as you, too! I tell you what it is; say 'sorry' tomorrow – there's a dear! and we'll lend you story-books out of school-time."

"Those were mine!" repeated Marian, sadly, "and she had no right to them."

"Brother!" exclaimed the good-natured but ineloquent Miss Tom. "Who ever heard of a girl's right at a preparatory school? I'd have left this long ago, only my pa's a poor Irish officer, with five sons and my beautiful self, and he can't afford to pay for my finishing; so I shall never be finished, I suppose – go into the world unfinished, live unfinished, *die unfinished!* But you must learn not to contradict a governess; no good ever comes of it – only starvation and double lessons and black-hole, that's all – and enough too! I don't like to see you up here, though you are to cut me out – but it will be a long time first, clever as you are; there; kiss and good night. Now, say 'sorry,' like a good girl. You won't? Then indeed, Marian, you are an obstinate little fool. Why, if you had a mother, you would be obliged to beg pardon if you were naughty."

"Beg my mother's pardon!" exclaimed Marian; "so I would a thousand times; but I have no mother!"

And the child hid her face in the pillow and cried bitterly. Miss Kemp again advised her to go to sleep, and beg pardon. Marian, however, held out much longer than it could have been supposed a child would continue of one mind; but hunger and harshness, and, above all, solitude at last conquered, just as she had established a character for the most unflinching obstinacy – which, I must confess, she deserved. A teacher of Miss Womble's class always experiences a pleasure in exaggerating the early defects of her pupils: it is a sort of commentary upon the perfections of a system which she insinuates will overcome such faults; and, accordingly, Marian's offence was repeated, with variations, both to Mr. and Mrs. Jones, until the latter cast up, as usual, her hands and eyes, and prayed that Heaven would forgive her for having been instrumental in prolonging the existence of such a demon. Fortunate was it that Mr. Jones remained firm to his resolve; and two years were added to Marian's existence without any occurrence which novel-readers would consider worthy of recording. But those who would seek to know the *cause* of the *feelings* and *actions* of men and women must go back to childhood and its impressions for their origin. The information Marian obtained was superficial and frequently erroneous; for the errors of what were then, and, into many instances, *still are, school-books,* left her much to undo in after-life. The system was one of duplicity and harshness. Sunday, instead of being rendered a day of religious and rational happiness, was one of gloom and discontent, Miss

Womble being in the habit of selecting *punishment lessons* from the New Testament – a course quite sufficient to make any child dislike the book, to which, of all others, she ought to turn for consolation. These tasks repeated on Sunday: indeed, the day was invariably one of tears. The only girl who seemed to enjoy the day was Miss Kemp: she had the piano all to herself to play Handel's music. – Moreover, there was always roast beef, preceded by Yorkshire pudding, for dinner, of which she was particularly fond; and, altogether, "Tom" was the only really happy girl on, what *she* called, "Miss Womble's Sabbath."

Marian had acquired a considerable proficiency in music – having, thanks to Miss Kemp, learnt to read it fluently; and even Mrs Jones, during the one week in which she tolerated her during her second vacation, was obliged to confess her musical progress far beyond her expectations. Her beauty increased, so as to render her remarkable; and her governess, in consequence, always placed her in the foremost rank during their show walks; and when the bitterness of their first quarrel was past, the governess praised the superiority of her system, and latterly grew rather kind to a child who gave her so very little trouble, and produced, certainly, four-fold for all seed sown.

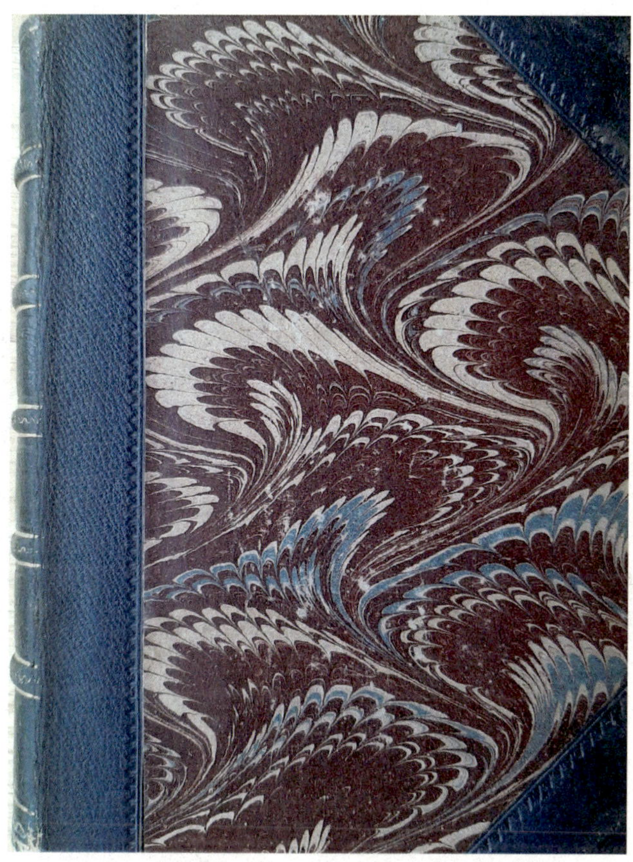

Binding of *Marian; or A Young Maid's Fortunes*
(Leipzig, Bernhard Tauchnitz, 1877)

Scene from "The Governess"
Artist unknown
Stories of the Governess (1852)

The Governess

Part the First

Head my advertisement thus – "Wanted – a governess," commenced Mrs. Gresham: – who had called upon her sister, Mrs. Hylier, to consult concerning the important document; Mrs. Gresham and Mrs. Hylier being both in want of resident governesses to educate their children. A visitor was also present, a Mrs. Ryal, confessedly the "most clever woman" of the neighbourhood – an astonishing manager; but although the ladies desired her advice, there were somewhat in dread of her sarcasm.

Mrs. Gresham had repeated, "Wanted – a governess," when an old gentleman, a Mr. Byfield, was announced. The trio of wives and mothers looked at each other, as if to say, "What a bore!" – and then Mrs. Hylier rose gracefully from her *chaise longue,* and smiling sweetly, extended her hand, and welcomed Mr. Byfield with exceeding warmth of manner; while Mrs. Gresham and Mrs. Ryal declared aloud their delight at being so fortunate as to meet a neighbour they had so rarely the pleasure to see.

The party thus assembled were all inhabitants of the bustling yet courtly suburb of Kensington; and Mr. Byfield being a rich and influential, though a very eccentric, man, was sure of the deference which people of small means are too prone to exhibit towards those whose fortunes are ample.

"Do not let me interrupt you in the least, ladies," said the old man, quietly taking his seat near the window. "Mr. Hylier promised I should look over these pictures by daylight; and when you have talked your own talk, there will be time enough for mine." The ladies, one and all, declared their conviction that his "talk" must be more pleasant and instructive than theirs. He smiled – shook his head – touched his hat (which he had laid at his feet), as if to say he would either go or have his own way; and so Mrs. Gresham recommenced reading – "Wanted – a governess. Any lady possessing a sound English education, a thorough knowledge of the theory and practice of instrumental and vocal music, and a perfect acquaintance with the French, Italian, and German languages; also with the rudiments of Latin:"

"Latin!" interrupted Mrs. Ryal. "Latin! Why, what *do* you want with Latin for a pack of girls?"

"I thought," answered Mrs. Gresham, meekly, "that as there are but three girls, Teddy might do his lessons with them for a little while; and that would save the expense of a tutor."

"Oh, very good – very good," replied Mrs. Ryal; "then add also, Greek; if the governess is anything of a classic, you'll get both for the same money."

"Thank you, dear Mrs. Ryal; how clever you are! G-r-, there are two 'ees' in Greek? – also the rudiments of Latin and Greek."

"I beg your pardon once more," said the provokingly "clever lady;" "but make it Greek and Latin; that is the correct way."

"Greek and Latin, and the principles of drawing – if her character will bear the strictest investigation, may hear of a highly respectable situation by applying to Z.P."

"Post-paid," again suggested Mrs. Ryal.

"Of course," continued Mrs. Gresham, " and as the lady will be treated as one of the family, a high salary will not be given."

"Well," said Mrs. Ryal, "I think that will do. You have not specified writing and arithmetic."

"English education includes that, does it not?"

"Why, yes; but you have said nothing about the sciences."

"The children are so young."

"But they grow older every day."

"Indeed that is true," observed pretty Mrs. Hylier with a sigh, and a glance at the pier-glass. "My Ellen, though only ten, looks thirteen. I wish her papa would let her go to school; but one of his sisters imbibed some odd philosophic notions at school, so that he won't hear of it."

"Certainly," observed Mrs. Ryal, "I will never again take a governess into my house to reside – they are all *exigeants*. One was imprudent enough to wish to get married, and expected to come into the drawing-room when there was company of an evening. Another would have a bedroom to herself; though, I am sure, no one could object to sleep n the same room with my own maid. Another – really the world is very depraved – occasioned a painful difference between Mr. Ryal and myself; and let *that* be a warning to you, my dear friends, not to admit any pretty, quiet, sentimental young ladies into your domestic circles. Mr. Ryal is a very charming man, and a good man; but men are but men, after all, and can be managed by anyone who will flatter them a little. Of course, he is a man of the highest honour; but there is no necessity for having a person I the house who plays and sings *better* than one's-self."

"Oh, my dear Mrs. Ryal!" exclaimed both voices, "you need never fear comparison with anyone." The jealous lady looked pleased, but shook her head. "Well, at last I resolved to be my own governess – with the assistance of a *young person,* who comes daily for *three,* and sometimes I get *four,* hours out of her; and she is very reasonable – two guineas a month, and dines with the children. She is not all I could wish. Her manners are a little defective, for she is not exactly a lady. Her father is a very respectable man, keeps that large butter shop at the corner – I forget – somewhere off Piccadilly; but I prefer it, my dear ladies, I prefer it – she does all the drudgery without grumbling. Your officers' and clergymen's daughters, and decayed gentlewomen, why, their high-toned manners – if they never speak a word – prevent one's being quite at ease *with* them, though, they are, after all, only governesses."

"But," suggested Mrs. Gresham, mildly, "lady-like manners are so very necessary."

"Yes," answered Mrs. Ryal, "so they are; for you and I –"

"And the children so easily imbibe vulgar habits, that it is really *necessary* to have a lady with them."

"Well," said Mrs. Ryal, with a sneer, "ladies are plenty enough. I dare-say you will have fifty answers. What salary do you mean to give?"

Mrs. Gresham was a timid but kind-hearted woman; one who desired to do right, but had hardly courage to combat wrong. She was incapable of treating anything unkindly, but she would be guilty of injustice if justice gave her much trouble; she hesitated, because she required a great deal and intended to give very little.

"*I* cannot give more than five-and-twenty pounds a year to anyone," said Mrs. Hylier, in a decided tone. "My husband says we cannot afford to keep two men-servants and a governess. He wanted me to give the governess seventy, and discharge Thomas; but that was quite impossible; so I have made up my mind. There are only two girls; no boys, like my sister Gresham's little 'Teddy;' she can spend every evening in the drawing-room when we are by ourselves – have the keys of the piano and library – amuse herself with my embroidery – go to church in the carriage on Sunday – and drive at least once a-week with the children in the Park. There!" added Mrs. Hylier; "I am sure there are hundreds of accomplished women who would jump at such a situation, if they knew of it."

"Washing included?" inquired Mrs. Ryal.

"No. I think she must pay for her own washing, unless there was some great inducement."

"You allow no followers?"

"Oh, certainly not. What can a governess want of friends? Her pupils ought to have all her time."

"God help her!" murmured the old gentleman. The murmur was so indistinct that the ladies only looked at each other; and then Mrs. Hylier said, "Did you speak, sir?" There was no answer; the conversation was resumed with half a whisper from one lady to another, that perhaps Mr. Byfield was not deaf at all times.

"And what do *you* intend giving, Mrs. Gresham?" questioned Mrs. Ryal.

"I have three girls and a boy," she replied; "and I thought of forty."

"It will be impossible to prevent your governess from talking to mine, and then mine will get discontented; that is not fair, Fanny," observed her sister; "say five-and-thirty, allowing for the difference of number."

"And plenty, I call it," said Mrs. Ryal. "What do they want but clothes? They never lay by for a rainy day. There are hundreds – yes, of well-born and well-bred ladies – who would be glad of such situations."

"I am sorry for it," said the old gentleman, rising and advancing to where the three Kensington wives were seated; "I am very sorry for it."

"Indeed, Mr. Byfield! Why, we shall have the better choice."

"Forgive me, ladies, for saying so – but still more am I grieved at that. Permit me to read your advertisement."

Mrs. Gresham coloured; Mrs. Hylier had sufficient command over herself not to appear annoyed; but Mrs. Ryal, the oracle of a *clique*, the "clever woman," who had, by dint of self-esteem and effrontery, established a reputation for intellectual superiority over those who were either too indolent or too ignorant to question her authority, evinced her displeasure by throwing herself back in her chair, loosening the tie of her bonnet, and dressing her lips in one of those supercilious smiles that would mar the beauty of an angel.

"Wanted, a governess," read the old gentleman, who frequently interrupted himself to make such observations as the following: – "Any lady possessing a sound English education – that in itself is no easy thing to attain – a thorough knowledge of the theory and practice of vocal and instrumental music – a thorough knowledge of the theory and practice of either the one or the other requires the labour of a *man's* life, my good ladies – and a perfect acquaintance with the French, Italian, and German languages – how very useless and absurd to found professorships of modern languages in our new colleges, when, in addition to the musical knowledge that would create a composer, a single person, a young female, can be found possessed of a *perfect* acquaintance with French, Italian, and German! Oh, wonderful age! – also, the rudiments of Greek and Latin – may hear of a highly respectable situation by applying to Z.P. post paid, Post-Office, Kensington. Much as you expect in the way of acquirements and accomplishments, ladies," continued the critic, still retaining fast hold of poor Mrs. Gresham's document, 'you have not demanded a great deal on the score of religion or morality – neither are mentioned in your list of requisites."

"Oh!" exclaimed Mrs. Hylier, "they are taken for granted. No one would think of engaging a governess that was not moral and all that sort of thing, which are always matters of course."

"To be sure they are," added Mrs. Ryal, in that peremptory tone which seemed to say, Do you dare to question my opinion? "To be sure they are; and everyone knows that nothing can be more determined with respect to religion and morality than my practice with my children. Rain, hail, or sunshine, well or ill, the governess must be in the house before the clock strikes nine. Psalms read the first thing; and if they have not got well through the French verbs, a chapter besides *for punishment;* catechism, Wednesdays and Fridays; and the Collect, Epistle, and Gospel, by heart, every Sunday after church. I always do two things at once, when I can; and this strengthens their memory, and teaches them religion at the same time. I never questioned my governess as to religion; it looks narrow-minded; and yet *mine* never dreams of objecting to what I desire."

"I should think not," was Mr. Byfield's quiet rejoinder; "strange ideas your children will entertain of the religion that is rendered a punishment instead of a reward."

Mrs. Ryal grasped the tassel of her muff, but made no reply.

"Oh," he continued, "here is the pith in a postscript – 'As the lady will be treated as one of the family, a high salary will not be given.' Ladies!" exclaimed the old man, "do you not blush at this? You ask for the fruits of an education that, if it be half what you demand, must have cost the governess the labour of a life, and her friends many hundred pounds. It is your DUTY to treat as one of your family the person who is capable of bestowing upon your children the greatest of earthly blessings; and yet you make the doing so a reason for abridging a stipend, which pays a wretched interest for time and money. Shame, ladies, shame!"

The ladies looked at each other, and at last Mrs. Hylier said, "Really, sir, I do not see it at all in the light in which you put it. I know numberless instances where they are glad to come for less."

Tears came into Mrs. Gresham's eyes, and Mrs. Ryal kicked the ottoman violently.

"The more the pity," continued Mr. Byfield; "but I hold it to be a principle of English honesty to pay for value received, and of English honour not to take advantage of distress."

"Suppose we cannot afford it, sir – am I to do without a governess for my children because my husband cannot pay her sixty or seventy pounds a-year?"

"But you said just now, madam, that Mr. Hylier wished you to pay that sum."

"Yes," stammered the fair economist, "if – if' –

"If you could manage with one footman," said the old gentleman, "instead of two. In my young days, my wife, who had but one child, and we were poor, said to me – 'Joseph, our girl is growing up without education, and I cannot teach, for I never learned, but we must send her to school.' I answered that we could not afford it. Oh, yes, we can,' she said; 'I will discharge our servant; I will curtail our expenses in every way, because I am resolved that she shall be well educated, and honestly paid for.' It never occurred to that right-minded, yet simple-hearted, woman to propose lower terms to a governess, but she proposed less indulgence to herself. Thus she rendered justice. She would sooner have worked her fingers to the bone than have bargained for intellect. Ay, Mrs. Rayl, you may laugh; but of all meannesses, the meanest is that which depreciates mind, and having no power but the power that proceeds from a full purse, insults the indigence which often hides more of the immaterial world beneath a russet gown, than your wealth can purchase."

"My wealth!" exclaimed the offended lady; "*your* wealth, if you please; but though *your* wealth, and your oddity, and your altogether, may awe some people, they *can* have no effect upon *me*, Mr. Byfield – none in the world; everyone says you are a strange creature."

"My dear Mrs. Ryal," said Mrs. Hylier, "you positively must not grow angry with our *dear* friend, Mr. Byfield; he does not mean half what he says."

"I beg your pardon," interrupted the eccentric old gentleman; "I mean a great deal more. I only wish I had the means of giving to the world my opinion as to the inestimable value of domestic education for females. I would have every woman educated within the sanctuary of her own home. I would not loosen the smallest fibre of the affection which binds her to her father's house; it should be at once her altar and her *throne*; but as it is a blessing which circumstances prevent many from enjoying, I would command the legislature of this mighty country to devise some means for the better ordering and investigation of 'ladies' boarding schools.' To set up an establishment for young ladies is very often the last resource for characterless women, and persons who, failing in all else, resort to that as a means of subsistence. Such temporary HOMES should be under the closest superintendence of high-minded and right-thinking gentlewomen. I look upon the blue-boarded and brass-plated schools that swarm in our suburbs," he added, as he turned away to hid an emotion he could not control – "I look upon them as the very charnel-houses of morality."

Mrs. Ryal elevated her eyebrows, and shrugged her shoulders, while the gentle Mrs. Gresham whispered her "not to mind; that Mr. Byfield was half-mad on the subject of schools."

"Ladies," said the old man, apparently recovered from his agitation, and in his usually quiet, calm, yet harshly-toned voice; "ladies, you are, in different degrees, all women of the world; you live with it, and for it, and you are of it, but you are also mothers; and though your Ellen, Mrs. Hylier, does grow so fast as almost to overtake her mother's beauty, and you, Mrs. Ryal, stand in open defiance of vulgar contagion, because you fear a rival in a well-bred governess, and get more time out of your daily labourer than you would expect from your milliner for the same money; and you, Mrs. Gresham – but I cannot say to you more than that you all love your children – some more, some less – still, according to your natures, you *all* love then dearly. So did I mine. My child was all the world to me! I told you what her poor mother did for her improvement – the sacrifice she made. But though we had the longing to secure for her every advantage, we had no skill as to the means of obtaining the knowledge we so desired her to possess. We placed her at a 'first-rate school,' as it was called, and thought we had done our duty; but this going from her home loosened the cords of love that bound her to us. And when a sudden stroke of good fortune converted a poor into a rich man, and we brought our child to a splendid house, we found that our daughter's morals had become corrupted through the means of her companions – an evil the most difficult of all for a governess to avert – and that she had imbibed moral poison with her mental food." The old gentleman became so agitated, that he could not proceed; and angry as the ladies had been with him a few moments before for a plain-speaking which amounted to rudeness, they could not avoid sympathising with his feelings.

"But we are not going to send our children to a school," suggested Mrs. Gresham.

"I know that, madam," he replied; "but I want to convince you, by comparison, of the blessings that await the power of cultivating both the intellect and the affections under your own roof and so argue you into the necessity of paying honestly, if not liberally, the woman upon the faithful discharge of whose duties depends the *future* happiness or misery of those dear ones whom you have brought into the world. It is now twenty-two years since I saw that daughter; I shall never see her again in this world; I thought I had strength to tell you the story, painful as it is, but I have not. I would have done so, in the hope that I might have shown you how valuable, past all others, are the services rendered by a worthy and upright woman when entrusted with the education of youth; but when I think of my lost child, I forget everything else. She stands before me as I speak. My blue-eyed lovely one! All innocence and truth – the light, and life, and love of that small four-roomed cottage; and then she loved me truly and dearly; and there again she is – most beautiful, but cankered at the heart, fair, and frail! Lay your children in their graves, and ring the joy-bells over them rather than intrust them to the whirling pestilence of a large school, or the care of a *cheap* governess!"

"He certainly is mad," whispered Mrs. Ryal to Mrs. Hylier, while the old gentleman, folding his hands one within the other, walked up and down the room, his thoughts evidently far away from the three wives, who were truly, as he had said "mere women of the world." And yet he was right – they all loved their children, but it was after their own fashion; Mrs. Gresham with the most tenderness – she wished them to be good and happy; Mrs. Hylier's affection was mingled with a strong desire that they might continue in a state of innocence as long as possible, and not grow too fast. Mrs. Ryal had none of that weakness; she did not care a whit whether she were considered old or young, as long as she was obeyed; so she determined her girls should have as little of what is called heart as possible, that they might be free to accept the best offers when they were made. She was continually contrasting riches and poverty. All the rich were angels, and all the poor thieves; there were no exceptions; those who married according to their parents' wishes rode in carriages, with two tall footmen behind each; those who married for love walked a-foot with draggled tails, and died in a workhouse. Of all the women in Kensington, Mr. Byfield disliked Mrs. Ryal the most, and seeing her at Mrs. Hylier's had irritated him more than he cared to confess even to himself. Mrs. Ryal entertained a corresponding animosity towards Mr. Byfield; she had resolved, come what would, to "sit him out;" but she was afraid if she remained much longer, that Miss Stack, the daily governess, whose mother was ill, might go a few minutes before her time was up, and she had more than once caught her shaking the hour-glass – so much for the honesty of one party and the consideration of the other; she knew perfectly well that as soon as she was gone, she would be abused "by the old monster;" for she was conscious that, if he had gone, it would have given her extreme pleasure and satisfaction to abuse him. The old gentleman had not spoken for several minutes, but continued to walk up and down, pausing every now and then to look at her over his spectacles, as if to inquire, "when do you mean to take your departure?" Mrs. Ryal was too exalted to notice this; but after consideration, she rose with much dignity, shook hands with her two "dear friends," dropped a most exaggerated curtsy to Mr. Byfield, who, the moment she was out of the room, threw himself into an easy chair, and drew a lengthened inspirations, which said plainly enough, "Thank heaven, she is gone!"

"And now, ladies," he exclaimed, "finding that *you* want a governess, I want to recommend one – not to you, Mrs. Gresham; notwithstanding 'little Teddy,' she would be too happy with you. I should like her to live with *you,* Mrs. Hylier."

"With me, Sir? Why, after the censure you have passed upon us both, I should hardly think you would recommend us a dog, much less a governess."

"I expect you will treat your governess hardly as well as I treat my dog," was the ungracious reply.

"Really, Mr. Byfield"

"Psha, lady!" interrupted the strange old man; "no words about it; I have not been so long your opposite neighbour without knowing that your last governess did not sit at your table; that when you had the hot, she had the cold; that when a visitor came, she went; that she was treated as a creature belonging to an intermediate state of society, which has never been defined or illustrated – being too high for the kitchen, too low for the parlour; that she was to govern her temper towards those who never governed their tempers towards her; that she was to cultivate intellect, yet sit silent as a fool; that she was to instruct in all accomplishments, which she must know and feel, yet never play anything in society except quadrilles, *because* she played so well that she might eclipse the young ladies who, not being governesses, play for husbands, while she only plays for bread! My good madam, I know almost every governess who enters Kensington – by sight; the daily ones by their early hours, cotton umbrellas, and the cowed, dejected air with which they raise the knocker, uncertain how to let it fall. Do I not know the musical ones by the worn out boa doubled round their throats, and the roll of new music clasped I the thinly gloved hand? – and the drawing ones – God help them – by the small portfolio, pallid cheeks, and haggard eyes? I could tell you tals of those hard-labouring classes that would make factory labour seem a toy; but you would not understand me, though you *can* understand that you want a governess, and you can also understand that I, Joseph Byfield, hope you will take one of my recommending."

The sisters looked at each other, as well as to say, "What shall we do?"

Mrs. Hylier assumed a cheerful, careless air, and replied – "Well, sir, who is your governess?"

"Who she exactly is, Mrs. Hylier, I will not tell you; and she does not know, though she imagines she does; *what* she is I will tell you. She is handsome, without the consciousness of beauty – accomplished, without affectation – gentle, without being inanimate – and I should suppose patient; for she has been a teacher in a school, as well as in what is called a *private* family; but I want to see her patience tested."

"Is she a good musician?"

"Better than most women."

"And a good artist?"

"That was not in the bond; but she does confound perspective, and distort the human body as excellently as most teachers of – the art that can immortalise" –

"My dear sir" –

"Ay, ay; half a dozen chalk heads – a few tawdry landscapes, with the lights scratched out, and the shadows rubbed in – a bunch of flowers on velvet, and a bundle of handscreens" –

"My dear sir," interrupted Mrs. Hylier, "these sort of things would not suit my daughters; what they do must be *artistic.*"

"Then get an artist to teach them; you go upon the principle of expecting Hertz to paint like Eastlake, and Eastlake to play like Hertz. Madam, she is a well-informed, prudent, intelligent gentlewoman; with feeling and understand; consequently doing nothing ill, because she will not attempt what she cannot accomplish. She will not undertake to *finish* (that's the term, I think) pupils in either music or drawing, but she will do her best; and as she has resided abroad, I am told (for I hate every language except my own) she is a good linguist; and I will answer for her accepting the five-and-twenty pounds a-year."

"Very desirable, no doubt," muttered Mrs. Hylier, unwilling, for sundry reasons of great import connected with her husband, to displease Mr. Byfield, and yet most unwilling to receive into her family a person whom, judging of others by herself, she imagined must be a spy upon her *ménage.*

"*I* knew you would so consider any one I recommended," said the old gentleman, with a smile that evinced the consciousness of power; "and when shall the '*young person*' (that is the phrase, is it not?) – when shall she come?"

"I think I should like to see her first," answered the lady, hesitating.

"Very good; but to what purpose? You know you will take her?"

"Anything to oblige you, my dear sir; but has she no female friend?"

"Some one of you ladies said a few moments ago that a governess had no need of friends."

"You are aware, Mr. Byfield, it is usual upon such occasions to consult the lady the governess resided with last; it *is* usual; I do not want to insist upon it, because I am sure you understand exactly what I require."

Indeed, madam, I do not pretend to such extensive information; I know, I think, what you *ought* to require, that is all. However, if you wish, you shall have references besides mine," and Mr. Byfield looked harder and stiffer than ever. He walked up to a small watercolour drawing that hung above a little table, and contemplated it, twirling his cane about in a half circle all the time. The subject was ugly enough to look at – a long chimney emitting a column of dense smoke like a steamer, and a slated building stuck on one side, being a view of the "Achilles saw mills," which Mr. Hylier had lately purchased, a considerable portion of the purchase-money having been advanced by Mr. Byfield.

"No matter how odd, how rude, how incomprehensible our old neighbour is, Caroline," Mr. Hylier had said to his wife only that morning; "no matter what he does, or says, or fancies; if you contradict or annoy him, it will be my ruin."

Her husband's words were forcibly recalled to her by the attitude and look of the old gentleman, and she answered – "Oh, dear no, sir, not at all; one cannot help anxiety on such a subject; and I must only endeavour to make the lady comfortable, and all that sort of thing, although I fear she may complain to you of" –

"No, no, madam," he interrupted; "I do not desire her to be treated in any way better than your former governess; I wish to see how she bears the rubs of life; I *particularly* request that no change whatever be made in her favour; if I wished her to be quiet and comfortable, I should have sent her to my gentle little friend Mrs. Gresham."

Mrs. Hylier bit her lip. "Good morning, ladies; when shall Miss Dawson – her name is Emily Dawson – when shall she come?"

"When you please, sir."

"To-morrow, then, at twelve."

He shut the door; Mrs. Gresham rang the bell; and Mrs. Hylier, in a weak fit of uncontrollable vexation, burst into tears.

"Did you ever know such a savage?" exclaimed Mrs. Gresham.

"I am sure *you* have no reason to complain – if it was not for the hold he has over Hylier" –

"I wonder if she is any relation of his?" said Mrs. Gresham, who was a little given to romance.

"Not she, indeed; he is as proud as Lucifer, and has money enough to enable him to live in a palace."

"Could it be possible that he intends to marry," suggested Mrs. Gresham.

"Marry, indeed; would any man that could prevent it, permit the woman he intended to marry to be a governess? No. I'll trouble my head no more about it; let her come; one is pretty much the same as another; the only thing that really gives me pain is, that Mrs. Ryal should have heard so much of it; she's a regular bell-woman; likes to have the earliest information of whatever goes on in the world, so as to be the first to set it going. She was the means of the dismissal of five governesses only last winter, and there is no end to the matches of her breaking. She will declare the girl is – God knows what – if she finds all out."

"Well," said Mrs. Gresham, musingly, "after all, it is very odd; only fancy Mr. Byfield taking an interest in a governess *at all*. Still, I must insert my advertisement, and I think I might substitute dancing for Greek; they are about equally useful, and one must not be too unreasonable."

"Very considerate and good of you, Fanny," said her sister; "but believe me, the more you require the more you will get; and I am not sure that Mrs. Ryal was wrong about the sciences; every day something fresh starts up that no one has ever heard of before, and one must be able to talk about it; it is really very fatiguing to keep up with all the new things, and 'somehow I do not think the credit one gets by the knowledge is half enough to repay one for the labour."

"Mr. Gresham says the whole system, or, as *he* calls it, *no* system, of female education is wrong."

"My dear Fanny, how absurd you are" What can men possibly know of female education? There is my husband, a worthy man as ever lived, and yet he will tell you that the whole object of female education should be to make women – now only imagine what?"

"I am sure I do not know."

"Why, good wives and mothers."

"Both ladies laughed, and then Mrs. Hylier exclaimed, "to think of my taking any one into my house under such circumstances? But at all events, I must prepare the children for their *new governess*."

Scene from "The Governess" by J.N. Paton
Tales of Woman's Trials (1847)

The Drawing Room Table-Book (1848?)

GEORGE VIRTUE:
LONDON AND NEW YORK.

V

Spiritualism and Ghost Stories

The Dark Lady (1848?)

Spiritualism

Spiritualism was important to both of the Halls. They believed that communicating with souls proved the existence of the afterlife, thus confirming the basis of their strong religious beliefs. The Halls held and attended Spiritualist meetings regularly and S.C. Hall wrote a pamphlet entitled *The Use of Spiritualism* which was first printed in 1863 with numerous later editions. It gives insight into a movement that had widespread influence on the literature and art of the period and found followers from all walks of life. Numerous prominent people were involved, including the painter Sir Edwin Landseer, the author Sir Arthur Conan Doyle, members of the Trollope family, Mrs Browning and William and Mary Howitt. Not all were keen to announce their Spiritualist interests publicly as Spiritualism received a great deal of bad press and practitioners were frequently ridiculed for their beliefs.

In the 1884 edition of *The Use of Spiritualism,* S.C. Hall recorded episodes relating to his wife, "the good woman, who, after she left earth, was mercifully permitted to continue her influence, to give me counsel, to bring me messages ..." He described in some detail that he received over 160 messages from her, delivered through half a dozen different mediums in the three years since her death. It was notable that no conflict was at any stage seen with their religious faith – if anything Spiritualism enhanced and deepened it.

Ghost Stories

On occasion Anna Maria included dramatic and even melodramatic references to ghosts and haunting in her sketches and stories. One such story was contained within her discussion of "Memories of Pictures IV: The Miniatures of Peter Oliver" in *The Art-Union* in 1843 and in it she comes closest to a reference to a Spiritualist episode. It is a dark tale that fills the narrator with terror, the story of a brother and sister who dabbled in the occult and had no belief in any world beyond this. When the brother left home to travel, they made a pact that if either should die they would visit from the spirit world and leave a token as proof. Several years later, her brother appeared to her one dreadful night to tell her that: "There is an hereafter" and he left a token as proof: "The form glided to the bedside, pressed the fingers upon her wrist ... it was marked by the impression of the dead man's wrist ... it was blackened as it burned." Anna Maria was talented at tales such as this and the reader is caught up in the drama and horror of the tale.

Her tale of "The Dark Lady" or "Le Femme Noir" is her best known ghost story. It appeared in two nineteenth-century publications, the first in *The Drawing-Room Table Book* (1848?] and the second in *The Playfellow and other Stories* (1866). It has also been included in two recent anthologies *What did Miss Darrington See? An Anthology of Feminist Supernatural Fiction* (1989), *Bending to Earth: Strange Stories by Irish Women* (2019) and in several science fiction and horror websites such as www.horrormasters.com. She focused on a tale told her by her great-grandmother, a Huguenot and native of the Canton of Berne in Switzerland. The setting of the story in the castle of her great-grandmother's childhood friend Amelie de Rohean, surrounded by the ravine and the raging torrents of the Alpine rivers, all added to the romantic melodrama for her eager listeners. Anna Maria gives her opinion at the beginning of the story saying:

> People may laugh at ghosts then, if they like, but as for me, I never could merely smile at the records of those shadowy visitors. I have large faith in things supernatural, and cannot disbelieve solely on the ground that I lack such evidences as are supplied by the senses.

As with all of her stories, they are imbued with a feminist subtext, albeit from a mid-nineteenth century angle. There are lessons to be learned, wealth does not bring happiness, only love can achieve this. Above all, the female spirit is a force for good contrasting with the cruelty of the tyrannical Count.

Ghost stories were an important branch of short fiction that emerged during the Victorian era. Commentators in *The Oxford Book of English Ghost Stories* saw the 1850s as a crossroads with authors turning their back on the Gothic elements of earlier writings to forge a distinctive genre of ghost stories. The ghost story played with the insecurities behind the confident and well-ordered society presented by the Victorians. Instead of the distant castles and macabre events common to the Gothic, the Victorian ghost story found horror close to home, often on a more domestic level. The nightmarish illustration accompanying Anna Maria's temperance tale "The Drunkard's Bible" demonstrates this effectively. This tale, originally published in the 1840s was reprinted by temperance publishers in Norwich and republished with this illustration by W.J. Allen in 1875 in *Boons and Blessings*. In the story, the evils of drink brought ruination to the family, conjured up by the image of the wraith-like forms hovering over the uneasy sleeping man.

"The Drunkard's Bible", ill. by W.J. Allen
Boons and Blessings (1875)

Her didactic message brought the supernatural back from the castle turrets and brooding Swiss Count firmly within the ordinary domestic sphere. S.C. Hall noted in his *Retrospect* that over half a million copies of this particular tract had been circulated.

As with other stories included in *The Drawing-Room Table-Book,* the engravings were provided for the publication in advance and Anna Maria ensured to weave them seamlessly in her text. The portrait of Amelie was typical of fashionable society ladies, popular in the Annuals and Keepsakes of the period. Likewise, the cliff-hanger scene in the brooding Alpine setting was the perfect inspiration for her text.

FURTHER READING

Cox, Michael, and Gilbert, R.A. (eds), *The Oxford Book of English Ghost Stories* (Oxford, Oxford University Press, 1986).

Giakaniki, Maria, and Showers, Brian J., (eds), *Bending to Earth: Strange Stories by Irish Women* (Dublin, Swan River Press, 2019).

Hall, S[amuel]. C[arter]., (ed.), Mrs. *Boons and Blessings: Stories and Sketches to Illustrated the Advantages of Temperance* (London, Virtue, Spalding, and Co., 1875).

The Drawing-Room Table-Book (London, George Virtue, [1848?]).

The Playfellow and other Stories (London, T. Nelson and Sons, 1866).

Hall, Samuel Carter, *The Use of Spiritualism* (London, E.W. Allan, 1884).

Salmonson, Jessica Amanda, (ed.), *What Did Miss Darrington See? An Anthology of Feminist Supernatural Fiction* (New York, The Feminist Press, 1989).

Amelie de Rohean portrayed in "The Dark Lady"
ill. by F. Stone, engr. by C. Rolls.
The Drawing-Room Table-Book (1848?)

People find it easy enough to laugh at "spirit-stories" in broad daylight, when the sunbeams dance upon the grass, and the deepest forest glades are spotted and checkered only by the tender shadows of leafy trees; when the rugged castle, that looked so mysterious and so stern in the looming night, seems suited for a lady's bower; when the rushing waterfall sparkles in diamond showers, and the hum of bee and song of bird tune the thoughts to hopes of life and happiness; people may laugh at ghosts then, if they like, but as for me, I never could merely smile at the records of those shadowy visitors. I have large faith in things supernatural and cannot disbelieve solely on the ground that I lack such evidences as are supplied by the senses; for they, in truth, sustain by palpable proofs so few of the many marvels by which we are surrounded, that I would rather reject them altogether, as witnesses, than abide the issue entirely as they suggest.

My great-grandmother was a native of the canton of Berne; and at the advanced age of ninety, her memory of "the long ago" was as active as it could have been at fifteen: she looked as if she had just stepped out of a piece of tapestry belonging to a past age, but with warm sympathies for the present. Her English, when she became excited, was very curious – a mingling of French, certainly no Parisian, with here and there scraps of German done into English, literally – so that her observations were at times remarkable for their strength. "The mountains," she would say, "in her country, went high, high up, until they could look into the heavens, and *hear* God in the storm." She never thoroughly comprehended the real beauty of England' but spoke with contempt of the flatness of our island – calling our mountains "inequalities," nothing more – holding our agriculture "cheap," saying that the land tilled itself, leaving man nothing to do. She would sing the most amusing *patois* songs, and tell stories from morning till night, more especially spirit-stories; but the old lady would not tell a tale of that character a second time to an unbeliever; such things, she would say, "are not for make-laugh." One in particular, I remember, always excited great interest in her young listeners, from its mingling of the real and the romantic; but it can never be told as she told it: there was so much of the picturesque about the old lady – so much to admire in the curious carving of her ebony cane, in the beauty of her point lace, the size and weight of her long ugly ear-rings, the fashion of her solid silk gown, the singularity of her buckled shoes – her dark-brown wrinkled face, every wrinkle and expression, – her broad thoughtful brow, beneath which glittered her bright blue eyes – bright, even when her eyelashes were white with *years*. All these peculiarities gave impressive effect to her words.

"In my young time," she told us, "I spent many happy hours with Amelie de Rohean, in her uncle's castle. He was a fine man – much size, stern, and dark, and full of noise – a strong man, no fear – he had a great heart, and a big head.

"The castle was situated in the midst of the most stupendous Alpine scenery, and yet it was not solitary. There were other dwellings in sight; some very near, but separated by a ravine, through which, at all seasons, a rapid river kept its foaming course. You do not know what torrents are in this country; your torrents are as babies – ours are giants. The one I speak of divided the valley; here and there a rock, round which it sported, or stormed, according to the season. In two of the defiles these rocks were of great value; acting as piers for the support of bridges, the only means of communication with our opposite neighbours.

"'Monsieur,' as we always called the Count, was, as I have told you, a dark, stern, violent man. All men are wilful, my dear young ladies," she would say; "but

Monsieur was the most wilful: all men are selfish; but he was the most selfish: all men are tyrants." – Here the old lady was invariably interrupted by her relatives, with, "Oh, good Granny!" and, "Oh fie, dear Granny!" and she would bridle up a little and fan herself; then continue – "Yes, my dears, each creature according to its nature – all men are tyrants; and I confess that I do think a Swiss, whose mountain inheritance is nearly coeval with the creation of the mountains, has a *right* to be tyrannical; I did not intend to blame him for that: I did not, because I had grown used to it. Amelie and I always stood up when he entered the room, and never sat down until we were desired. He never bestowed a loving word or a kind look upon either of us. We never spoke except when we were spoken to."

"But when you and Amelie were alone, dear Granny?"

"Oh, why, then we did chatter, I suppose; though then it was in moderation; for Monsieur's influence chilled us even when he was not present; and often she would say, 'It is so hard trying to love him, for he will not let me!' There is no such beauty in the world now as Amelie's. I can see her as she used to stand before the richly carved glass in the grave oak-panneled dressing-room; her luxuriant hair combed up from her full round brow; the discreet maidenly cap, covering the back of her head; her brocaded silk, (which she had inherited from her grandmother,) shaded round the bosom by the modest ruffle; her black velvet gorget and bracelets, showing off to perfection the pearly transparency of her skin. She was the loveliest of all creatures, and as good as she was lovely; it seems but as yesterday that we were together – but as yesterday! And yet I lived to see her an old woman; so they called her, but she never seemed old to me! My own dear Amelie!" Ninety years had not dried up the sources of poor Granny's tears, no chilled her heart; and she never spoke of Amelie without emotion. "Monsieur was very proud of his niece, because she was part of himself: she added to his consequence, she contributed to his enjoyments; she had grown necessary; she was the one sunbeam of his house."

"Not the *one* sunbeam surely, Granny!" one of us would exclaim; "you were a sunbeam then."

"I was nothing where Amelie was – nothing but her shadow! The bravest and best in the country would have rejoiced to be to her what I was – her chosen friend; and some would have periled their lives for one of the sweet smiles which played around her uncle, but never touched his heart. Monsieur never would suffer people to be happy except in his way. He had never married; and he declared Amelie never should. She had, he said, as much enjoyment as he had: she had a castle with a drawbridge; she had a forest for hunting; dogs and horses; servants and serfs; jewels, gold and gorgeous dresses; a guitar and a harpsichord; a parrot – and a friend! And such an uncle! He believed there was not such another uncle in broad Europe! For many a long day Amelie laughed at this catalogue of advantages, that is, she laughed when her uncle left the room; she never laughed before him. In time, the laugh came not; but in its place, sighs and tears. Monsieur had a great deal to answer for. Amelie was not prevented from seeing the gentry when they came to visit in a formal way, and she met many hawking and hunting; but she never as permitted to invite any one to the castle, nor to accept an invitation. Monsieur fancied that by shutting her lips, he closed her heart; and boasted such was the advantage of his good training, that Amelie's mind was fortified against all weaknesses, for she had not the least dread of wandering about the ruined chapel of the castle, where he himself dared not go after dusk. This place was dedicated to the family ghost – the spirit, which for many years had it entirely at its own disposal. It was much attached to its quarters, seldom leaving them, except for the purpose of interfering when anything decidedly wrong was going forward in the castle. 'La Femme Noir' had been seen gliding along the unprotected parapet of the bridge, and standing on a pinnacle, before the late master's death; and many tales were told of her, which in this age of unbelief would not be credited."

"Granny, did you know why your friend ventured so fearlessly into the ghost's territories?" inquired my little cousin.

"I am not come to that," was the reply; "and you are one saucy little maid to ask what I do not choose to tell. Amelie certainly entertained no fear of the spirit; 'La Femme Noir' could have had no angry feelings towards her, for my friend would wander I the ruins, taking no note of daylight, or moonlight, or even darkness. The peasants declared their young lady must have walked over crossed bones, or drank water out of a raven's skull, or passed nine times round the spectre's glass on Midsummer eve. She must had done all this, if not more: there could be little doubt that the 'Femme Noir' had initiated her into certain mysteries; for they heard at times voices in low, whispering converse, and saw the shadows of two persons cross the old roofless chapel, when 'Mamselle' had passed the foot-bridge alone. Monsieur gloried in this fearlessness on the part of his gentle niece; and more than once, when he had revellers in the castle, he sent her forth at midnight to bring him a bough from a tree that only grew beside the altar of the old chapel; and she did his bidding always as willingly, though not as rapidly, as he could desire.

"But certainly Amelie's courage brought no calmness. She became pale; her pillow was often moistened by her tears; her music was neglected; she took no pleasure in the chase, and her chamois not receiving its usual attention, went off into the mountains. She avoided me – her friend! who would have died for her; she left me alone; she made no reply to my prayers, and did not heed my entreaties. One morning, when her eyes were fixed upon a book she did not read, and I sat at my embroidery a little apart, watching the tears stray over her cheek, until I was blinded by my own' I heard Monsieur's heavy tramp approaching through the long gallery; some boots creak – but the boots of Monsieur! – they growled!

"'Save me, oh save me!' she exclaimed wildly. Before I could reply, her uncle crashed open the door, and stood before us like an embodied thunderbolt. He held an open letter in his hand – his eyes glared – his nostrils were distended – he trembled so with rage, that the cabinets and old china shook again.

"'Do you,' he said, 'know Charles le Maitre?'

"Amelie replied, 'She did.'

"'How did you make acquaintance with the son of my deadliest foe?'

"There was no answer. The question was repeated. Amelie said she had met him, and at last confessed it was in the ruined portion of the castle! She threw herself at her uncle's feet – she clung to his knees: love taught her eloquence. She told him how deeply Charles regretted the long-standing feud; how earnest, and true, and good, he was. Bending low, until her tresses were heaped upon the floor, she confessed, modestly, but firmly, that she loved this young man; that she would rather sacrifice the wealth of the whole world, than forget him.

"Monsieur seemed suffocating; he tore off his lace cravat, and scattered its fragments on the floor – still she clung to him. At last he flung her from him; he reproached her with the bread she had eaten, and heaped odium upon her mother's memory! But though Amelie's nature was tender and affectionate, the old spirit of the old race roused within her; the slight girl arose, and stood erect before the man of storms."

"'Did you think,' she said, 'because I bent to you that I am feeble? Because I bore with you, have I no thoughts? You gave food to this frame, but you fed not my heart; you gave me nor love, nor tenderness, nor sympathy; you showed me to your friends, as you would your horse. If you had by kindness sown the seeds of love within my bosom; if you had been a father to me in tenderness, I would have been to you – a child. I never knew the time when I did not tremble at your footstep; but I will do so no more. I would gladly have loved you, trusted you, cherished you; but I feared to let you know I had a heart, let you should tear and insult it. Oh, sir, those who expect love where they give none, and confidence where there is no trust, blast the fair time of youth, and lay up for themselves an unhonoured old age.' The scene terminated by Monsieur's falling down in a fit, and Amelie's being conveyed fainting to her chamber.

"That night the castle was enveloped by storms; they came from all points of the compass – thunder, lightning, hail, and rain! The master lay in his stately bed, and was troubled; he could hardly believe that Amelie spoke the words he had heard: cold-hearted and selfish as he was, he was also a clear-seeing man, and it was their truth that struck him. But still his heart was hardened; he had commanded Amelie to be locked into her chamber, and her lover seized and imprisoned when he came to his usual tryste. Monsieur, I have said, lay in his stately bed, the lightning, at intervals, illumining his dark chamber. I had cast myself on the floor outside her door, but could not hear her weep, though I knew that she was overcome of sorrow. As I sat, my head resting against the lintel of the door, a form passed through the solid oak from her chamber, without the bolts being withdrawn. I saw it, as plainly as I see your faces now, under the influence of various emotions; nothing opened, but it passed through – a shadowy form, dark and vapour, but perfectly distinct. I knew it was 'La Femme Noir,' and I trembled, for she never came from caprice, but always for a purpose. I did not fear for Amelie, for 'La Femme Noir' never warred with the high-minded or virtuous. She passed slowly, more slowly than I am speaking, along the corridor, growing taller and taller as she went on, until she entered Monsieur's chamber by the door exactly opposite where I stood. She paused at the foot of the plumed bed, and the lightning, no longer fitful by its broad flashes, kept up a perpetual illumination. She stood for some time perfectly motionless, though in a loud tone the master demanded whence she came, and what she wanted. At last, during a pause in the storm, she told him that all the power he possessed should not prevent the union of Amelie and Charles. I heard her voice myself; it sounded like the night-wind among fir-trees – cold and shrill, chilling both ear and heart. I turned my eyes away while she spoke, and when I looked again, she was gone! The storm continued to increase in violence, and the master's rage kept pace with the war of elements. The servants were trembling with undefined terror; they feared they knew not what: the dogs added to their apprehension by howling fearfully, and then barking in the highest possible key; the master paced about his chamber, calling in vain on his domestics, stamping and swearing like a maniac. At last, amid flashes of lightning, he made his way to the head of the great staircase, and presently the clang of the alarm-bell mingled with the thunder and the roar of the mountain torrents: this hastened the servants to his presence, though they seemed hardly capable of understanding his words – he insisted on Charles being brought before him. We all trembled, for he was mad and lived with rage. The warden, in whose care the young man was, dared not enter the hall that echoed his loud words and heavy footsteps, for when he went to see his prisoner, he found every bolt and bar withdrawn, and the iron door wide open: he was gone. Monsieur seemed to find relief by his energies being called into action: he ordered instant pursuit, and mounted his favourite charger, despite the storm, despite the fury of the elements. Although the great gates rocked, and the castle shook like an aspen-leaf, he set forth, his path illumined by the lightning: bold and brave as was his horse, he found it almost impossible to get it forward; he dug his spurs deep into the flanks of the noble animal, until the red blood mingled with the rain. At last, it rushed madly down the path to the bridge the young man must cross; and when they reached it, the master discerned the floating cloak of the pursued, a few yards in advance. Again the horse rebelled against his will, the lightning flashed in his eyes, and the torrent seemed a mass of red fire; no sound could be heard but of its roaring waters; the attendants clung as they advanced to the hand-rail of the bridge. The youth, unconscious of the *pursuit*, proceeded rapidly: and again roused, the horse plunged forward. On the instant, the form of 'La Femme Noir' passed with the blast that rushed down the ravine; the torrent followed in her track, and more than half the bridge was swept away for ever.

The Escape of Charles le Maitre in "The Dark Lady"
ill. by W. Purser, engr. by E. Goodall
The Drawing-Room Table-Book (1848?)

As the master reined back the horse he had so urged forward, he saw the youth kneeling with outstretched arms on the opposite bank – kneeling in gratitude for his deliverance from this double peril. All were struck with the piety of the youth, and earnestly rejoiced at his deliverance; though they did not presume to say so, or look as if they thought it. I never saw so changed a person as the master when he re-entered the castle gate: his cheek was blanched – his eye quelled; his fierce plume hung broken over his shoulder – his step was unequal, and in the voice of a feeble girl he said – 'Bring me a cup of wine.' I was his cupbearer, and for the first time in his life he thanked me graciously, and in the warmth of his gratitude tapped my shoulder; the caress nearly hurled me across the hall. What passed in his retiring-room, I know not. Some said, the 'Femme Noir' visited him again: I cannot tell, I did not see her; I speak of what I saw, not of what I heard. The storm passed away with a clap of thunder, to which the former sounds were but as the rattling of pebbles beneath the swell of a summer wave. The next morning Monsieur sent for the Pasteur. The good man seemed terror-stricken as he entered the hall; but Monsieur filled him a quart of gold coins out of a leathern bag, to repair his church, and that quickly; and grasping his hand as he departed, looked him steadily in the face. As he did so, large drops stood like beads upon his brow; his stern, coarse features were strangely moved while he gazed upon the calm, pale minister of peace and love. 'You,' he said, 'bid God bless the poorest peasant that passes you on the mountain; have you no blessing to give the master of Rohean?'

"'My son,' answered the good man, 'I give you the blessing I may give: – May God bless you, and may your heart be opened to give and to receive.'

"'I know I can give,' replied the proud man; 'but what can I receive?'

"'Love,' he replied. 'All your wealth has not brought you happiness, because you are unloving and unloved!'

"The demon returned to his brow, but it did not remain there.

"'You shall give me lessons in this thing,' he said; and so the good man went his way.

"Amelie continued a close prisoner; but a change came over Monsieur. At first he shut himself up in his chamber, and no one was suffered to enter his presence; he took his food with his own hand from the only attendant who ventured to approach his door. He was heard walking up and down the room, day and night. When we were going to sleep, we heard his heavy tramp; at daybreak, there it was again: and those of the household, who awoke at intervals during the night, said it was unceasing.

"Monsieur could read. Ah, you may smile; but in those days, and in those mountains, such men as 'the master' did not trouble themselves or others with knowledge; but the master of Rohean read both Latin and Greek, and commanded THE BOOK he had never opened since his childhood to be brought him. It was taken out of its velvet case, and carried in forthwith; and we saw his shadow from without, like the shadow of a giant, bending over THE BOOK; and he read in it for some days; and we greatly hoped it would soften and change his nature – and though I cannot say much for the softening, it certainly effected a great change; he no longer stalked moodily along the corridors, and banged the doors, and swore at the servants; he rather seemed possessed of a merry devil, roaring out an old song –

> Aux bastions de Genéve, nos cannons,
> Sont branquez;
> S'il y a quelques attaque nous les feront ronfler,
> Viva! Les cannoniers!

And then he would pause, and clang his hands together like a pair of cymbals, and laugh. And once, as I was passing along, he pounced out upon me, and whirled me round in a waltz, roaring at me when he let me down, to practise *that* and break my embroidery frame. He formed a band of horns and trumpets, and insisted on the goatherds and shepherds sounding reveilles in the mountains, and the village children beating drums: his only idea of joy and happiness was noise. He set all the canton to work to mend the bridge, paying the workmen double wages; and he, who never entered a church before, would go to see how the labourers were getting on nearly every day. He talked and laughed a great deal to himself; and in his gaiety of heart would set the mastiffs fighting, and make excursions from home – we knowing not where he went. At last, Amelie was summoned to his presence, and he shook her and shouted, then kissed her; and hoping she would be a good girl, told her he had provided a husband for her. Amelie wept and prayed; and the master capered and sung. At last she fainted; and taking advantage of her unconsciousness, he conveyed her to the chapel; and there beside the altar stood the bridegroom – no other than Charles Le Maitre.

"They lived many happy years together; and when Monsieur was in every respect a better, though still a strange, man, 'the Femme Noir' appeared again to him – once. She did so with a placid air, on a summer night, with her arm extended towards the heavens.

"The next day the muffled bell told the valley that the stormy, proud old master of Rohean had ceased to live."

VI

An Irish Fairy Tale

Midsummer Eve: A Fairy Tale of Love (1848)

Front cover of *Midsummer Eve* (1848)

MIDSUMMER

EVE:

A FAIRY TALE

OF

LOVE.

BY

MRS. S. C. HALL.

LONDON:

LONGMAN, BROWN, GREEN, AND LONGMANS.

MDCCCXLVIII.

Title page of *Midsummer Eve*
by J. Lecurieux (1848)

"The Mother's Blessing"
drawn by R. Huskisson, engraved by W.T. Green
Midsummer Eve (1848)

Arrival of the Literary Fairytale

The literary fairytale arrived in England rather later than in other countries such as France and Germany, and this delay has been attributed by commentators such as Jack Zipes and Stella Beddoe to the rise of Puritanism in the post-Civil War period. For different reasons, influential writers such as Maria Edgeworth and Sarah Trimmer frowned on oral folk and fairytales and considered them to be unsuitable for young middle-class readers. Trimmer actively condemned fairytales in her periodical *The Guardian of Education,* and Edgeworth, along with her father, dismissed the genre. Edgeworth's philosophy was based on a rational approach to education whereas Trimmer's preference was for greater emphasis on religious and instructional material. Anna Maria referred to the books she read as a child such as *Beauty and the Beast* and *Cinderella.* Then "when fairytales all of a sudden were considered foolish if not injurious, I had no reason to complain of the change to Maria Edgeworth's "Early Lessons" and Mrs Hofland's "Son of a Genius.'"[1] As an avid and eclectic young reader, she appeared to be adaptable.

However, oral tales and customs survived amongst the peasants of Ireland and this is one major reason why Anna Maria was attracted to the customs and tales of the Irish peasantry. While she emphasised the importance of instruction, she also championed the desirability of entertainment as an important ingredient in the mix and she had no difficulty reconciling Christian mores coexisting in a fairytale medium. Her experiments with fairytales can be considered in the context of an evolving and important stage in the development of the English fairytale tradition. From the 1820s was a growing shift towards an acceptance of fantasy for children brought about by the influx of newly translated works from abroad. Edgar Taylor translated *German Popular Stories* by the Grimm Brothers in 1823, Edward Lane's *Arabian Nights* appeared from 1838 and Mary Howitt translated Hans Christian Andersen's *Wonderful Stories for Children* in 1846. Children and adults wanted books that stimulated their imagination. The stage was set for the growth of more fanciful literature for children that would culminate later in the Victorian period with such important works of fantasy as Charles Kingsley's *The Water Babies* (1863), Lewis Carroll's *Alice's Adventures in Wonderland* (1865) and George MacDonald's *At the Back of the North Wind* (1871).

From the early 1840s, fairytales were found to be ideal vehicles for inculcating didactic lessons. Zipes has outlined how fairytale worlds moved in two directions from mid-century, either conventionalism, where the plots upheld the status quo of Victorian society; or towards those that were more utopian in outlook. Anna Maria's fairytales belonged to the former perspective. At the heart of both of her major fairytales, *Midsummer Eve* (1848) and *The Prince of the Fair Family* (1867) is a conventional concern with the moral growth of the central protagonists. The distractions provoked by the fairies were not profoundly threatening and the morals were by no means heavily disguised. In *Midsummer Eve,* once the fairies were acknowledged, and humoured rather than antagonised, the story continued (beyond Part 1) with little or no interference from them beyond the initial danger at Eva's birth and at important key moments coinciding with her birthdays. Anna Maria took the local folklore as her starting point and fashioned fairies of her own to suit her tales. Honeybell and Nightstar, the fairy queens of day and night were her own creations in *Midsummer Eve,* as were King Rosemary and Queen Foam in *The Prince of the Fair Family.*

Title page for *The Prince of the Fair Family* (1867)
An example of the 'stick' frame or border,
favoured in many *livre romantique* books

Setting and Influences

For Anna Maria, fairytales were useful in many ways. They were a nostalgic reminder of the characters and storytellers of her childhood. She was interested in the tales from an antiquarian point of view, and the stories helped to enliven their travel books of Ireland. They were also an important inspiration and resource for her many sketches and novels. *Midsummer Eve* is her first and only full-length Irish fairytale – *The Prince of the Fair Family* was set in Wales.

The setting of Killarney was an important choice for her. Between the years 1825–1841, the Halls made five tours of Ireland, culminating in *Ireland, its Scenery, Character &c.* followed by *A Week at Killarney* (1843) and *A Companion to Killarney* (1878). These publications highlighted history, social conditions, customs and legends associated with the area. The town had attracted many artists and poets in the eighteenth century and the Halls acknowledged the influences of Isaac Weld and Thomas Crofton Croker on their own work. Anna Maria was ambitious in her attempt to bring to fruition a romantic tale in a romantic setting, peopled both by real and supernatural beings. She referred repeatedly to the legends and folklore of Ireland, to the pookas and banshees she first encountered in the tales told by her servants in Wexford and later in the writings of Crofton Croker and Thomas Keightley.

In *Midsummer Eve*, Anna Maria used many of the motifs of the cautionary tale coupled with Christian, moralistic overtones. It is a triangular love story: two cousins, Sidney and Cormac Talbot vie for Eva Raymond's attention. It draws on familiar motifs such as the reversal of fortune, jealous lovers and mischievous fairies. There is a strong moral sentiment throughout where those who give in to passions or who value material possessions at the expense of the spiritual fare badly in the story. The tale of the life of a simple but honourable country girl whose father had died before her birth echoed elements of Halls' own life in the country with her mother but no father figure. Randy the woodcutter in *Midsummer Eve,* assumed the role of the central male figure who keeps the heroine away from supernatural danger.

Anna Maria was undoubtedly influenced also by Shakespeare's *A Midsummer Night's Dream* – we know from her biographical account in *Grandmamma's Pockets* that "She began reading – perhaps for the twentieth time Shakespeare's Midsummer Night's Dream ..." The German romantic tale *Undine* by Friedrich de la Motte Fouqué, translated into English in 1818 was another likely influence and two engravings of *Undine* by the fairy painter Robert Huskisson, a favourite artist of the Halls, appeared in *The Art-Union* in 1846 and 1847, testifying to the popularity of the story. Finally, in other tales, Anna Maria recalls a young servant in Wexford who had a great store of tales about mermen and mer-maidens and also about changelings, which was to become a recurrent subject throughout her writing. It was a theme in folklore worldwide, a changeling was the offspring of a fairy, troll, elf or other legendary creature that has been secretly left in exchange for a human child. Rooted in ancient beliefs, it echoed the very real fear of losing a child in an era when child mortality was very high. In reality the child was most probably suffering from illnesses such as metabolic disorders, wasting illnesses, hydrocephalus, spina bifida, all of which could have brought about gradual changes in a child who initially presented as healthy. It was easier for parents to blame an outside cause such as a bogeyman or the fairies than to deal with the inexplicable.

The Livre Romantique *or Romantic Book Style*

Midsummer Eve highlighted the depth of Hall's desire to create a fairy fantasy in the idyllic Killarney setting. It was ambitious but ultimately, as a narrative, it was not sufficiently fantastical to match the many striking illustrations accompanying her text. *Midsummer Eve* is a beautiful example of the *livre romantique* style.

The format which captured the spirit of illustrated book production in the mid-nineteenth century was the *livre romantique*. There are many examples amongst the Halls' publications, in particular their stunning three-volume *Ireland: its Scenery, Character, &c.* (1841–43). From 1820–60 the term was used to describe a style of book production characterised by numerous wood-engraved vignettes that were invariably integrated with the text, in contrast to the individual unpaginated plates added either at intervals throughout the book or at the end of a text block. Notable features included decorative initial letters, the decorative panel or slip, the "stick border," a range of decorated letter forms on the title-page and greater textual and visual unity achieved through rule borders creating picture frames around each page.

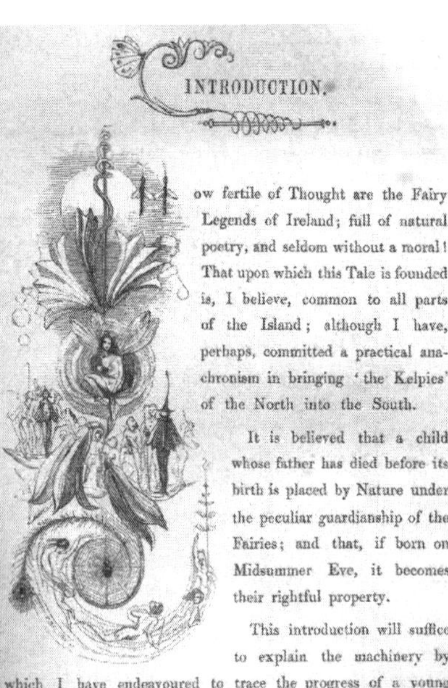

INTRODUCTION.

How fertile of Thought are the Fairy Legends of Ireland; full of natural poetry, and seldom without a moral! That upon which this Tale is founded is, I believe, common to all parts of the Island; although I have, perhaps, committed a practical anachronism in bringing 'the Kelpies' of the North into the South.

It is believed that a child whose father has died before its birth is placed by Nature under the peculiar guardianship of the Fairies; and that, if born on Midsummer Eve, it becomes their rightful property.

This introduction will suffice to explain the machinery by which I have endeavoured to trace the progress of a young

Decorative initial letter, two dragonflies resembling the letter 'H' for the Introduction to *Midsummer Eve* (1848)

Many up and coming artists provided designs for these books and it is notable that they included fairy painters, landscape artists, animal painters and antiquarian artists – sometimes this could lead to some confusion for the reader. This can be seen in the portrayal of Eva and Sydney in a very anglicised Dovecote interior by Joseph Noel Paton compared to F.W. Fairholt's more realistic portrait of the cabin with the dried hams and fish "intermingled with bunches of herbs" suspended from the rafters, the dresser stacked with crockery and pewter, the settle and wheels for spinning flax and wool. Paton's sumptuous interior was more redolent of a leafy cottage in Hampstead than in Killarney!

Later in the Victorian era the "one artist one author" approach to illustration was to prevail which provided a more homogenous approach overall. However, there is no doubting the splendour of the *livre romantique* to capture the spirit of gift book production mid-century. The Halls with their easy access to the finest artists of their day were uniquely placed to produce a series of sumptuous examples of the *livre romantique* at the height of its popularity.

FURTHER READING

Edgeworth, Maria, *Early Lessons* (Charleston, SC, Nabu Press, 2010, orig. 1815).

Hall, S[amuel]. C[arter], Mrs, *Midsummer Eve: A Fairy Tale of Love* (London, Longman, Brown, Green and Longmans, 1848).

Midsummer Eve: A Fairy Tale of Loving and Being Loved (London, John Camden Hotten, 1870).

The Prince of the Fair Family: A Fairytale (London, Chapman and Hall, [1867]).

Hofland, Barbara, *The Son of a Genius: A Tale for Youth* (London, Griffith and Farran, 1879, orig 1812).

Zipes, Jack (ed.), *The Oxford Companion to Fairy Tales* (Oxford, Oxford University Press, 2000).

"The Portrait" by J.N. Paton, *Midsummer Eve* (1848)
Eva Raymond and Sidney Talbot in Dovecote Cottage

"Dovecote interior" by F.W. Fairholt, *Midsummer Eve* (1848)

"The Storm King" by J.N. Paton
Midsummer Eve (1848)
Fairies attempt to rouse the storm king from his uneasy rest
'... as he pillowed his head beside the Daemon punch-bowl – set like the eye of a Cyclops in the rough brow of Mangerton; but the old fellow who was still too wearied by the exertions of the long past winter to attend their summons, grumbled his displeasure in a tone which the echoes of Glena repeated in thunder' (pp 2–3).

Midsummer Eve

Part the First

It was as bleak and chill a Midsummer Eve as the oldest dweller in the Lake-country of Killarney could call to mind. The wind, although it did now absolutely roar through the Gap of Dunloe, or round and about the Purple Mountain, and 'lofty Mangerton of the Hoary Head,' disturbed by its harsh murmurings and audible discontent the young trees and lowly shrubs that grow beneath the shadows of the evergreen woods. All know that unearthly spirits hold their revels on Midsummer Eve; it is their fête-night: when they show the elements, of the past and future, that a power mightier than theirs can rule them. The wind knew this well; yet, on this evening, was neither entirely submissive nor absolutely rebellious. At times, it started from its dull quiet and prowled abroad; fretting everything it touched; shaking the light branches of the silver birch and drooping willow, ruffling the narrow forms of the slim laburnum, wrestling roughly with the stout holly, and scattering the delicate arbutus, whose leaves, fruit, and flowers are as fair and bright amid December's snow, as in the sunshine of July. The wind was not only out of season, but unnatural; it brought the chill of winter into the very midst of summer. It was, in truth, a sharp-toothed and biting wind; forcing its way into ill-built cottages – through broken windows and shrunken doors, where poverty sought warmth from peat-smoke rather than fire; piercing through every hole in the torn blanket or tattered cloak; whistling in bitter mockery of the poor man's moan; stirring the flax upon the rock which the feeble fingers of age, or the firmer ones of youth, twisted into threads; causing the lamb to nestle closely into its mother's wool, and the foolish calf to low complainingly at its chilling howl, as it passed through the half-roofless out-house. Anon, it pelted the ivied ruins of old Mucross, terrifying the very owls, who hooted it onwards, without stirring from their hermit-cells; and scourged the angry bats who ventured forth on their wonted errands. The Beings who held sway over earth that night were so bent on mischief that they exerted their utmost skill to rouse the STORM KING from uneasy repose, as he pillowed his head beside the Daemon punch-bowl – set like the eye of a Cyclops in the rough brow of Mangerton; but the old fellow who was still too wearied by the exertions of the long past winter to attend their summons, grumbled his displeasure in a tone which the echoes of Glena repeated in thunder. Compelled to be content with the efforts of his sharp and bitter satellite, they sought, so aided, to accomplish great things before the last hour of midnight – scudding with it bravely and boldly through the open country; at length it grew conscious of impotence, and retreated to narrow defiles and crowded inclosures – like those who, lacking power to disturb the world, delight in the minor evils of inflicting misery in their neighbourhoods and homes; but when, after ruffling the waters of the Flesk, it sprang upon the bridge of many arches, it gave a wild howl of delight to see old DOCTOR MAGRATH bowed to the neck of his grey pony. "At him – at him – keep him back – keep him back," muttered a thousand voices to the wind; and surely there must have been some mysterious understanding between them, for right glad did it seem of encouragement to worry the old man, as he had never before been worried; his hat and wig flew over the bridge, and his poor bare head was buffeted as by a forest of shillelas; but while he moaned and murmured at the rough handling of the elements, two stout fellows followed to see that he neither tarried nor turned back; and who, having neither hat nor wig to lose, cared for the wind as little as the pony, who, bending his head until his eyes were sheltered by his long shaggy mane, went steadily, though slowly, onward, as if perfectly conscious that his master's services were required by no other than the fair GERALDINE RAYMOND, the young widow of a brave officer, whose premature death was about to call into the world before its time, an infant – who was destined never to feel a father's kiss or hear a father's blessing. The cottage in which the young widow resided, was near the pretty village of Cloghreen; it was sheltered by the deep woods of MUCROSS – the venerable ABBEY that never seems so beautiful and hallowed as by moonlight – cheered by the music of the Torc waterfall and blessed by the view of the tiny church of Killagher, which tops the rising ground. Now, however, the woods failed to shelter her home from the assaults of the fearsome wind, that rasped against the windows, insinuated itself into every crevice, and lamented in sighs and moans – not for her struggles, but its own. Her only companion was a 'cross-grained,' but most faithful, attendant, who had been her NURSE, and looked to discharge the same office for the infant for whom she waited. Kitty Kelly was not superstitious – at least so she said; but she felt it a sort of solmn duty to provide the house with blessed salt and holy water; she had nailed a horse-shoe to the door at morning, well knowing there was a stern resolve among the 'good people' of the elements – Air, Earth, and Water – to obtain possession of any fatherless child that commenced existence on Midsummer Eve: such possession being the admitted right of whichever of the three POWERS first entered the house where the baby was 'expected.'

She now prayed earnestly against all fairies; those of the air she knew could endow a baby with most precious gifts; while the fairies of earth – those who dwell among glowers, and partake more of our own natures – those, she thought, might do 'a good turn to a fatherless child;' but still, 'she'd rather have nothing to do with them;' with the – with whom; surely Kitty knew herself better than to have any sort of fear of, or faith in, such follies – nor had she –

only her grandmother, her own mother's mother, had once seen the blackest and the worst of the whole race, the real KELPIE QUEEN – the Queen of the most obnoxious class of 'good people' – they who were banished by the other fairies from all the sports and pastimes in which the tribes are permitted to indulge; they, who are never allowed to rise from the sedges of the Lower Lake – except on their own 'Eve,' that they may have a chance of adopting some newborn child of earth into their community – a chance which seldom becomes a reality – although it is theirs by royal charter – the charter of the Prince O'Donoghue, lord of a thousand palaces that lie fathoms deep beneath the surface of Loch Lene. Kitty's grandmother had seen the Kelpie Queen in all her magnificence, arise on one of these festive occasions, from her water-palace, on the back of a huge frog, who seemed proud of his burden, and carried her with the air and bearing of a racehorse, while her dark air streamed on either side her sallow face, and her attendant court were endeavouring to press into their service everything they could take – from a tadpole to a water-rat; she had often recounted this to Kitty, in her childhood; and Kitty, even at that early period, affected to doubt a tale, which, despite her seeming, crept through her bones, and made her very heart freeze within her bosom. She would now have given all she possessed in the world, to have had any one with her beside her sick lady; she started at every noise.

A certain wise man – known as Randy the Woodcutter – had been sent off for the Doctor; and while she waited his return, she had, she thought, frequently heard him 'whisperin and cosherin at the door;' and yet he came not. At length, however, his well-known step was distinctly audible.

"Is all right, Randy?" she asked,from within.

"All *will* be right when I knock," he answered, "and then open quickly."

"Is he on the road?" inquired the Nurse, heedless of the warning; but before he could reply, a sharp blast rushed inward, and extinguished the flickering light of the lean candle she held with a trembling hand.

A cross and a blessing about us, Kitty Kelly!"exclaimed Randy, falling on his knees. "God, he knows I couldn't help it. Why did you open the door before I knocked? I done all for the best, as the end will prove. Oh, murther! Why don't you shut the door, instead of standing there like a rock in the lake – there's something more than the wind pass'd in now! – bless yourself, woman, dear! Oh, then, sure it's impossible to tell what would be on the wings of the wind this Midsummer Eve!"

"Nothing worse than yourself," stammered the Nurse, bravely, though she perceived, at once, that THE HORSE SHOE was gone, and even fancied she saw 'something' flying off with it. Turning eagerly to Randy, who, pale and shivering, was gazing on the kitchen rafters – "Is the doctor coming!" she exclaimed.

"'Deed is he; and for fear he'd stop or turn back from his duty, on account of the hardness of the night, I set my two cousins to keep the road after him. He'll be here soon. Oh, sure it was only my duty I did, madam."

"Is the man mad to madam me!" exclaimed Kitty. "Stand on yer legs, and shut the door, and put the chair against it, and don't keep staring and bowing to the rafters; dear me, but it is a blast; and I didn't think there was more than a whisper going."

"Kitty Kelly, you're not altogether of this country," exclaimed Randy, in a low tone: "you've only been two hundred years in it – for you came in with ould Oliver Crommell; so give way to your prayers – it's no wind that we're trembling in: of the three we're watching, one came in with me – the mistress will thank me for that; there was a second – and there will be a third. You may strive against them; I *dare* not!"

"I DARE!" replied Kitty, whose courage had in part returned – and then she started, for she fancied she heard shouts of ironical laughter; but, little daunted, she attempted to close the door violently. In this, however, she did not succeed; the wind pushed against her, and not only had the best of it, but flung her to the other end of the kitchen.

"Make the blessed sign," said Randy, yet without moving to her assistance.

"I can't," she replied; "my hand's weighed down by a ton weight." She had hardly uttered the words, when a gust of wind, freighted with most extraordinary noises – sighs, and snatches of music, atoms of laughter, and fragments of old songs, mingled with the sound of rushing waters – entered the cottage, and filled it as with an atmosphere.

"It will shut asy enough now," observed the Woodcutter, rising from his knees, and wiping his brow. "Air, Earth, and Water! Oh, I'm not afraid to say my say about the good people, day or night; they never did me an ill-turn, and never will; quiet, and kindly, and good they are, and mane nothing but good to the dear lady;" and his huge head nodded, and his long limbs bent and twisted, in a peculiar sort of homage to something invisible to all eyes but his own. The Nurse thought it probable that Randy made the speech and performed his gesticulations, in the hope of propitiating the good offices of the company whom she now knew had come to the birth. It was currently believed that he could see and understand more than beseemed an honest man; and yet Randy *was* an honest man, and had the unbought happiness of being more loved than feared. Still, the all-powerful 'they,' whispered he, was a 'fairy man;' and, as such, he was consulted by many who would scruple to confess they had any faith or trust in the existence of the 'good people.' This opinion had strengthened wonderfully during the last few months; indeed, ever since the young widow had given promise that the child of a dead father was to visit a care-full world, his hours had been spent, even more than usual, beside THE FAIRIES' OAK – a withered and time hollowed tree, which hung its decayed branches over the sedges that skirted the base of the far-famed 'Eagle's Nest' (the most wonderful of the lake's many wonders); and he had been more than ever attentive to keep free from pebbles and worm-heaps, 'the ring,' which tradition and his own knowledge assigned as the favourite trysting-place of the 'good people.'

The door was now easily closed, and the candle relit at the kitchen fire; the Woodcutter threw upon it an additional heap of bog-fir: the old cat's hair stood out like porcupines' quills; every now and then she opened her mouth to hiss, but closed it again without a sound; she would lift a paw, and stretch it forth, bristling with claws – then draw it back again, each claw returning to its downy sheath.

"Sit down, Randy, and don't be showldering the chimney, as if there wasn't a chair in the place," said the Nurse, through her chattering teeth.

"I know better manners than to disturb any one from their sate," he answered, bowing round, respectfully.

The Nurse crossed herself with the thumb of her right hand, and retreated to the bed-room of her mistress. The fire burned brightly – yet the cat tookno pleasure in its blaze, but kept moving, uneasily, from one side to the other, – 'wrinkling' up her coat, as if water had been thrown upon it – her tail twitching and bristling in restless discomfort.

"It's hard on you, pusheen gra!" said Randy, addressing the cat; "but you can't help yourself. They'll neither hurt nor harm you, pusheen." "They've got possession now, and they'll keep it," he thought to himself.

"They will!" whispered a soft voice in his ear.

Randy caught hold of the fore-lock of his hair, pulled it, and jerked his head rapidly forward. "And for good," he said aloud, wishing to compliment NIGHTSTAR, THE QUEEN OF THE FAIRIES OF THE AIR, whose voice he knew, and whom he had often seen descent to earth with her train of attendants shining in the distance, like a silver halo in the moonlight.

And many a time, in the cool of a Midsummer night, when the grateful flowers drank in refreshing dews poured into their bosoms by considerate clouds, had he seen HONEYBELL, QUEEN OF EARTH'S FAIRIES, pass on her favourite humble-bee, whose flight was guided by her page; while Nightstar descended with her train of attendant sprites, simply by the action of her own will. "And for good!" he repeated.

"Don't speak," replied the fairy, in a dignified tone; "there is no necessity; we see your thoughts as they are formed, and notice them if we please."

"The dickens a doubt I doubt ye," thought the Woodcutter; for despite his caution, thoughts would come.

"Now, don't swear, Randy; it's vulgar."

The Woodcutter could not prevent himself from thinking an earnest prayer, that power might not be given them to change the child, at its birth, for one of their onw.

"And why not?" was the inquiry, in a low and gentle tone – the very shadow of a sound. "Why not? Are your world's children so free from care, and all the sorrows and troubles of life – that tug at your hearts, furrow your brows, weigh you down before your time – spectres leading you to graves – are they so very happy, that you do not wish them to be with us, who, you know, spend our lives in enjoyment?"

"From sunset to sunrise," thought Randy, "no mortal ever knew what you do be doing when the sun shines."

"Even so," replied Nightstar, whom, on turning round, he saw seated in the very centre of a cobweb, while HER PAGE was engaged in combat with the dispossessed spider, who, dangling by his thread, endeavoured to defend himself against the wee-poised spear of the active elf. "From sunset to sunrise," she repeated, rocking herself backward and forward on her seat; "even so; and surely that is better than spending it as you and the rest of you spend it – in heavy sleep or midnight brawling."

"You never could lay that last to me, or to any of the Kerry boys," replied Randy, speaking out boldly; for he believed Ireland the finest country in the world, and Killarney the greenest spot in the Emerald Isle. He had no sooner spoken than he heard a loud clapping of hands, and little cries of "Bravo!" and, fully aware of the compliment, he gave another pull at his head-tuft, and, to his great astonishment, found, on opening it, that he had caught A FAIRY IN HIS HAND.

"Why didn't you hold me when you had me," exclaimed the creature, springing on a moonbeam that had just entered the window; "and then I would have told you of hidden treasure, as well as the Leprehawn you are so fond of hunting."

"Sure, it's not misdoubting your honour's generosity I'd be," replied the Woodcutter. "You can give me the information, or the gould, which ever your honour plases, all the same;" and then there were shouts of merry laughter; and it seemed to the enlightened eyes of the bewildered man, that a multitude of the fairies of the three elements completely occupied the kitchen – twirling round the rafters, and filling every crevice and corner – some even clinging to the feathers of the cock's tail. The earthly good people were far more slow and heavy in their movements than those who appertained to the purer element; they ate and drank whatever they could find, and fought sham fights with each other – and real ones with the Kelpies or water fairies. The Woodcutter's unsealed eyes had no difficulty in distinguishing the three distinct races, who had attended their liege ladies to be present at the birth of the fatherless, on Midsummer Eve: he knew that the change of the earthly for the unearthly child, would belong of right to whichever of the three had first entered the house, and he congratulated himself on having so managed that Nightstar and her court had been the earliest arrivals. Honeybell, Queen of the Earthly Spirits, would, he thought, yield honourably to the claims of her royal sister; but he had no such faith in the Queen of the Kelpies. She was a yellow, damp, distorted, little creature, who diverted herself in a huge tub, by causing the elves who make up, what may be called 'the people' of the other tribes, to be ducked whenever they were caught by her frog-like subjects. Randy had *his* own purposes to work out, and he dreaded the Kelpies' influence: his mind filled with hope when he contemplated the gentle dignity and kindly expression of Nightstar, her attendants floating around her with ineffable grace – many of them perfectly transparent, their bosoms illumined from within, by a little spark of light like that which flashes from a diamond. He looked upon the Queen reclining on the cobweb with as much ease as an Eastern lady in a palanquin, and having attracted her attention by what he intended to be a gentle sigh, but which shook the web, so that her majesty caught hold of the banner of her standard-bearer for support, he composed his thoughts.

"You might have conveyed to us your desire to *think,* without blowing a hurricane," said Nightstar; "but you mortals are so very boisterous. Yet I must forgive you, Randy; you are an honest fellow, and I don't think I ever yet found a black ugly thought at nurse in your mind: evil gets there, to be sure, sometimes; but it does not stay; it meets with no entertainment; you are an innocent soul, Randy, and we love you much; otherwise, we should have granted you no such royal privileges as you possess. You have a great regard for this poor lady, I know: she will have a daughter, I can tell you that. And now what is to be done with the little maid who is to be with us in a few minutes?" "She'll come to the poor mother, plase your gracious majesty, like a beautiful summer butterfly rising from HER FATHER'S GRAVE," thought the Woodcutter.

The Queen nodded twice, and smiled. "If she is not very, *very* pretty, Randy, I think I shall give her up to my royal sister, Honeybell."

"You're a mother, yourself, I'll go bail, my lady," thought Randy, "though you are so mall and youn."

"Oh, yes! I was a mother more than two hundred years ago," answered the Queen.

"What a little darling of a beauty she is," thought the Woodcutter, and the fairy smiled her pleasure at the compliment. "And looks as fresh as the first drop of May-dew," so ran his thoughts. The fairy smiled again, and drew herself up with gentle pride. "She's every inch a queen," thought Randy, as her own particular court gathered about her. "If she as six feet high in her stocking vamps, she could not be more stately." Queen Nightstar had certainly much of mortal woman about her; she was lovely – witty – kind – and generous; but very, very small – even for a fairy; and yet the little creature prided herself upon her stateliness, upon her dignity, and queenly presence. She had never been so well pleased with Randy, though she had patronised him for years; she had hitherto thought him a good-natured creature; *now*, she fancied him endowed with exceeding penetration. "You're might fond of the young prences and prencesses, I'll go bail," thought Randy.

"I am, of course," she replied.

"Might I make bould to ask how many your majesty has?"

"About three dozen," was the gracious reply.

"And you couldn't fix upon one you'd like to part with?"

"Part with!" she exclaimed – "I would yield my life rather than one of my children! Man – man – do you think I could have a choice! – My dear, dear children! – a mother's heart is large enough for all. I could love ten times as many, and yet one does not rob another of a hair's breadth of love."

"Why, then, if you are so fond of the whole three dozen, won't you allow that it's hard to take an only child from its mother – and she a widow?"

"You are very provoking, Randy," said her majesty, in answer to his thoughts – "and cunning in reasoning; but we merely exchange – we leave her one of ours."

"One of the ne'er-do-wells – that she'll see pine and die (to all appearance) before her eyes, at the end of three months: the grass isn't green yet over poor Mary Mackay, who fretted the life out of herself, after one of your changelings."

"Not one of mine – one of Honeybell's," replied Nightstar, thoughtfully.

"The baby will be all in the world left to comfort her; and sure there's plenty of children born in Killarney this holy night, by twos and threes – not wanted; where there's no house to hold, nor clothes to cover them: wouldn't one of them do for you?"

"I don't like low-born children," answered Nightstar, with a toss of her lovely little head.

"The highest born may have the lowest bed, when all is over; anyway, your majesty could make them what you plase; and it's yourself that knows that many a fine brave spirit rises from under the cabin roof; but no matter what they are; you could give them the gifts that would make them great people – and beautiful women, like yourself – my lady!"

"I'm sure I don't want to take the mortal's only little one, if she thinks so much about it: no doubt she will be very fond of it," sighed the Queen. "Honeybell is in such a sweet temper – so well-pleased with the cream and cakes, that she would, I daresay, instead of changing the child, help me to endow it. But there are the Kelpies; and you know their Queen is no friend of ours. Air has the first right of choice, Earth the second, and Water the third. She won't give it up, I am certain, even if Honeybell did."

A sudden thought crossed Randy's brain.

"I see, I see! – do it, do it," continued Nightstar, as rapidly as the thought was formed in Randy's mind; and, suddenly turning round, she addressed an observation to one of her courtiers, while the Woodcutter seized a little platter of blessed salt, and tossed it into the tub where the Kelpies were sporting. It was quickly and cleverly done; instantly the hands of Randy hung as awkwardly as usual by his sides; but great was the consternation that followed; such splashing of water and whistling of wind: the Kelpies rushed out of the house in the wake of their insulted Queen, threatening revenge on the fairies of earth, by whom they imagined the trick had been played them. Randy quickly shut-to the door, and could not help admiring the dignified self-possession of Nightstar, who called to Honeybell that the time was come. Immediately the court attendants prepared to follow their royal mistresses, but Nightstar expressed a wish that they should ENTER THE CHAMBER alone; and it was a beautiful sight to see them floating onward, Honeybell holding in her hand her sceptre of fairy foxglove, and wearing a necklace of diamonds that circled her throat with a wreath of light; eclipsed, however, by the star that glittered above the head of her sister queen. They moved on, hand-in-hand to the birth-chamber; while poor Randy, bewildered by the perfume of dews and flowers, and the gentle music, that whispered all around him, sunk upon his knees.

"Remember, gracious Queen," he thought; "remember, every crow thinks its own bird the whitest." In a little time, a low wail and bitter cry told him that a struggle had commenced between a living spirit and a bitter world.

His entreaty, addressed to the Fairies, did not, however, content the Woodcutter; the attitude he had assumed suggested another – a higher and holier petition; he prayed with all the fervency of his warm and honest heart, that the dear young lady might be saved in her hour of trial, and that her baby might be spared to her, to be the blessing and the hope of after years. Prayer gives strength to the feeble and invigorates the strong. He arose much comforted, and looked round with a smile of satisfaction upon the tiny court, who, freed from the restraint which the august presence of their Queens imposed, unbent their spirits, and played such madcap pranks that Randy could not but feel his freedom of sight a rare privilege; it amused him greatly to contrast the buoyant and thoughtless energy and activity of the younger members of the two regal courts, with the bearing, impressive even to solemnity, of the high official personages who, upon occasions such as this, were always in close attendance upon their sovereigns. Randy watched them with more than common interest, for he knew they would soon be summoned to council. This man, though cast in so rough to mould, was gentle and gracious in heart and mind. He had been known for years to the good people, and they delighted to do him kindnesses. The led him to where THE RED DEER SHED THEIR HORNS – and brought him the richest and earliest of the Wood Strawberries. When the sky looked blue above, and the summer breath stirred the trees – so that all said, 'the fair weather is with us now;' they showed him where the little cloud was rising, herald o the Storm King; they taught him to dye wood, so that common fir could not be known from the arbutus or the charmed yew, so prized by strangers; they gave him knowledge of the virtues which dwell in herbs and flowers – of palmistry – of murrain stones and fairy strokes – and filled his mind with fables and old tales. Had he lived in earlier times, Randy would have suffered wizard's martyrdom. As it was, he was as often called 'Randy, the Fairy Man,' as 'Randy, the Woodcutter,' – and he had certainly imbibed some of the spirit-feeling with the spirit-repute: he was keenly alive to the beauties of Nature; heard sweet music in the murmurs of brooks, and tuneful melodies from the leaves of trees. He could tell, it was said, what the south breeze whispered to the west, and gather the birds of the air around him – be they ever so wild. He wore a four-leaved shamrock in his bosom, and a wreath of mountain-ash circled his conical hat. The wildest deer on Glena would neither harm him, nor fly from him. Whenever he passed through a village, or rested himself beneath a tree, CHILDREN WOULD CROWD ABOUT HIM; and if he gave them but the blossom of a daisy, they would think themselves happy. His only enemies were the eagles; the echo of their screams, or the shadow of their wings, were the only natural sights or sounds that damped his spirits. His haunts were the ancient hollow oak and the green grass slopes whereon grew THE FOXGLOVE – flower chiefest in favour with the Beings of whom Randy did not scruple to own himself the faithful and fond ally.

He would have enjoyed the pranks and oddities of the fairy tribes much longer, but that his attention was aroused by a smart tap on the cheek from the wand of the chancellor. "I am commanded by his lordship," said a dapper little official, his secretary, in a dark cobweb robe, and a wig composed of the down of the wild rush, "to tell you to do something rational for his amusement; we have taken much pains with your education, Randy," he added, "and would fain see its fruits."

"Would his honour like a story grave or gay – of his own, or of our people?" Having obtained leave to use his own discretion, Randy bethought him once or twice, and then, with a low bow to the great dignitary of fairy-land, he said: – "Flowers, my lord, are very beautiful to look at, and very sweet to smell; but if you were much among the tip-tops of the family, you would be surprised at the odd ways some of them have, and the airs they give themselves. Well, those I am talking about had been used to a deal of tenderness, and were brought up under the warm shade of a fine glass-house; and the beautiful lady that tended them said, one day, 'The roses in the flower-knot last twice as long, and are much sweeter.' Well! Yer Honour never heard anything like the rustling of leaves the flowers got on with, when they understood what the lady said; being brought up lonely and grand, and looking out on the world through glass windows, they thought everything in a garden must be low and common. Yer Honour, they looked down on the flowers of the garden, just as much, or may be more, than the flowers of the garden look down on the flowers of the field – instead of *looking up* to the GREAT CAUSE of all the sweetness and beauty they possess – who knows that if fine flowers are the most admired, the flowers of the field make glad the hearts of the greatest number of innocent children, who enjoy a heaven of happiness in the gathering the cowslip, the wild violet, and the star-eyed daisy: to say nothing, yer Honour, of the favour your people show – in preference to all the flowers that ever grew in a garden – for the banks of the thyme, the blue-bells, the silver cuckoo blossom, and the purple foxglove."

This procured Randy a round of applause.

"To go back, my lord, to the pampered flowers; some change of fortune coming on the lady, she was obliged to leave her palace of a house, and take shelter beneath the roof of a cottage – 'There's some of my dear flowers,' said the sweet lady, 'able to bear removal as well as myself, and who knows but we may be all the stronger and better for it; I hope we are not too far gone in luxury to prevent our enjoying comfort.' So she placed them in her cottage-garden; her favourite white rose folded the protecting moss closely over her bosom, lest she should catch cold, and – a – I forget the name of it – shut itself as safe up in its leaves as if it was going a journey of a thousand miles; and looked with a wave of contempt upon the manner in which the garden flowers strove, out of civility, to make room for it; while one or two grave blossoms – of the sage class – knew they should get stronger and better from being in the fresh pure air of heaven, and admitted that their new neighbour – the rose of the garden – was in every respect as much the lady as the rose of the glass-house; in the morning, the garden rose unfolded to welcome the sun, and to hear the early hymn of the birds, and to see how her buds were growing; and as the dew-drops, one by one, ascended to the clouds that had left them during night, for her refreshment, she perfumed them for their journey, and graciously thanked them for their care: but the pampered flowers bent beneath the dews, and complained of the damp and chill; and the delicate rose said that her dress was *tossicated*, and shook off the dew-drops so roughly in her pet, that the tender things broke into atoms, and the proud flower desired they should visit her no more, as she was too high-born to be treated like a common flower; and needed no help from common things; what was a refreshing blessing to others, her refined ignorance – "

"She should have learned of us," interrupted the chancellor: "we know how to bring refreshment to, and take refreshment from, every flower that grows in garden or in field: they are our drinking cups, a thousand times richer than the things made of the world's dross, which you earth-worms call 'precious gems.' Your rose should have learned of us."

"She learned of NATURE, my lord, at last," continued Randy, "for the next night not a sparkle from any cloud visited her leaves, and she saw the fleecy moisture enveloping the other flowers, and felt that the Nature she had scorned, was comforting her children, and whispering to them to be of good cheer, for that next year their blossoms should be fairer and wax strong: and the gentle loving dews clustered upon the buds and leaflets; and at last, as morning drew near, a sharp dry air made the most impertinent inquiries concerning her quarrel with the dew-drops, and whistled spitefully in her face, and ruffled her leaves, so that, the next day, the hot sunbeams entered into her heart; and in the deepest humility she petitioned to be treated as a common flower, convinced that –"

The moral of Randy's tale was scared from his lips by a message from Queen Nightstar to the chancellor, and by the noise made by Honeybell's page in rousing his lordship from the heavy slumber into which he had fallen.

"Keep up, mistress," said the Nurse to the widowed mother: "The jewel it is! So like its father. A girl's born lucky that's like its father! What do you say? – 'it has no father?' It has two, lady dear: one in heaven, and one over – about – around us all! – the very King of Heaven is the Father of the earthly fatherless! – may He mark it to grace! Think of the comfort she'll be to you – to be your own; the weight of the world isn't half weight to the young mother who looks at her dawshy babby. 'You want to see it?' I'm sure you do; but wait till Nurse puts on its pretty cap, and makes it sit up like a lady. I tell you, dear, it's the very *moral* of its father."

"His child! – his child! – his own child! To smile like him – to speak like him! Are you sure, Nurse, nothing will happen it – nothing take it from me? I have a strange feeling, as if my child were in danger. But what danger? – there is nothing could have the heart to take my baby from its lone mother."

Randy felt the tears gathering in his eyes, but they were quickly changed to tears of joy – for he saw the WRITHING, MISSHAPEN SHADOW, that was to have been substituted for Geraldine's infant, forced by a number of the attendants to leave the cottage. He then thought he would peep into the interior. There was no doubt about it; Queen Honeybell looked sulky; but the lamp in Nightstar's bosom shone more brightly than ever, and her words fell on his ear more full of music than the robin's winter song.

"Let us endow her for the world, and against the world; it is some time since we have permitted the child of our choice to remain exposed to the temptations and imperfections of mortality: let us guard her, and yet leave her with her mother." What music and tenderness were in Nightstar's words, as she continued – "I am looking at this moment into that young mother's heart: I see how new feelings stimulate its pulsations: I see it expanding – welling forth its very essence into the new life which, though mysteriously parted from it, is dearer to it than ever; there is a whole universe of love – pure, unselfish, spotless love – love without limit, boundless as ocean, and deeper than its deepest caves – in that sweet mother's heart, towards the little lump of half-animated clay that is *her* child. Oh, sister! If it were given you to see the future that whirls through her brain! The great Power of all has poured into her a new nature – a stronger motive and firmer principle of life: her very heart is enlarged.

"A child deprived of its father, and born on Midsummer Eve, is by right our own," said Honeybell, pouting; but you have always some whimsey in your head about these creatures of earth. I do not envy you your power of seeing thoughts and hearts, believe me!"

"Let it *be* ours," persisted Nightstar; "let us pour into its heart and mind whatever of good we can; but let us not take it from its mother." The Queen of Earth's fairies bent her head in no very cordial acquiescence; and the aerial troop, seeing that their Queen had vanquished, were mightily pleased thereat, and played sundry fantastic tricks; now opening the baby's sleepy eyes, to ascertain their colour, sleeking its small quantity of downy mole-like hair with their tiny hands, endeavouring to straighten its little wrinkled fingers, and sadly retarding the Nurse in its adornment, by untying the strings as fast as she tied them.

"Sister," persisted Nightstar, "help me to endow my favourite."

"We never agree on educational matters," answered Honeybell: "you are too ideal for me – better have her all to yourself."

"You do yourself injustice, sister. Let us wave our wands, and show the young mother, as in a dream, what may be the future qualities of her soul's idol: let us bestow on the fairest of earth's blossoms the most precious of all gifts that woman can receive or bestow: let us gift her with LOVE."

"Love! Rubbish!" answered Honeybell, pettishly – "the sourceof woman's misery."

"And happiness!"

"I would gift her with beauty, wealth, and spirit; the world's treasures: that she may dubdue the world."

"Let her mother determine," said Nightstar; "let her mother determine. Do you offer your gifts, and I will offer mine!"

The pallid mother trembled in every limb while the Queens performed their spells above her couch. At first, her vision was perplexed: she saw, floating around her, those animated atoms of the mysterious world that have so much power over our destinies – without recognising what or who they were. At length she singled out the two Queens – Nightstar, as a living thing of light – Honeybell, as only a creature, beautiful and minute. The Nurse saw that Geraldine's eyes were fixed, and that she seemed entranced; this she fancied, was but a wile to get her to take her eyes off the child. Presently, her lady's lips moved, and she spoke softly and slowly, as if she were replying to certain questions, which the Nurse did not hear. "Whatever will give her most happiness, and make her most beloved – no woman was ever happy who was not BELOVED," she said. There was a pause after she had spoken these disjointed words; and the Nurse observed that her soft eyes wandered first to one side, then to another. She tried to call Randy, but her tongue refused its office; she clutched the infant firmly in her arms, and kept her eye steadily upon it. Again words came faint and wearily from the mother's lips. "Thank you, thank you – if you cannot prevent the world from assailing her – it is well to teach her to endure – we must all do that – the more love, the more endurance – riches, honours, and beauty, are fine things – but LOVE IS THE PERFUME OF LIFE!" There was another pause, and the young other's eyes were illumined by an expression of tenderness, resignation, and joy, such as had never gladdened them since her widowhood. Her lips quivered, and after a time, large tears welled forth, but disappeared before they reached her cheek – removed by some invisible agency. "There is good to be gathered from both sponsors," she said again; "but *you* think my thoughts – to be LOVING and BELOVED. So let it be!"

A soft mild light shone through the chamber – the atmosphere was filled with most sweet fragrance, and music soft and low. The Nurse urged by an irresistible influence, arose, and placed the infant on the mother's bosom. And as it drank its first draught of LOVE, it became imbued by that regenerating essence which cheers us from the cradle to the grave!

"The Fairy Ring"
drawn by W.E. Frost A.R.A., engraved by G. Dalziel
Midsummer Eve (1848)

"Barley Wood", the home of Hannah More
Ill. by F.W. Fairholt, engr. by Langton

VII

Biographical Memoir

The Residence of Hannah More (1848)

Hannah More's *Cheap Repository Tracts* were enormously influential when they appeared from 1795–98. At least two million copies were distributed by 1795 alone. Her target audience was the semi-literate lower classes and the aim was to improve their religious convictions and personal consciences. As with her participation in the Sunday School movement, much of the ethos behind this development was the conservative message to reduce the possibility of revolution amongst the lower orders. A distinctly anti-radical, anti-revolutionary message pervaded what Mitzi Myers called her "socialising literatures".

Middle class readers such as Anna Maria would have read her tracts as children, so More's public was wider than initially intended. Her evangelical message, about how the individual faces a personal struggle within, her belief that stories could change public attitudes and the impeccable ethical stance of the authorial voice all emerged later in Anna Maria's work. In the following account of a visit to Hannah More's residence, Anna Maria describes how More was her "Polar Star since infancy." She was profoundly influenced by More's emphasis on home, family, duty, love and respect and the evangelical priority to correct the corrupt influences of Original Sin as outlined in her influential *Strictures on the Modern System of Female Education*.

Anna Maria's position on childhood was unfailingly and unashamedly didactic. Adults are omnipresent in her children's books, serving to control, protect and guide the child along the correct path and ready to warn of ill-consequences if this path is not pursued. There is never a situation where the child is more knowing than the adult and she always asserts the necessity for obedience and honesty. Like More, Anna Maria believed that children learn best through kindness and encouragement, not terror. Most importantly, More emphasised the importance of making the best use of one's situation in life and advocated the preservation of the status quo. Social order depended on everyone carrying out his or her duties. The wealthy had responsibilities to the poor who likewise had to fulfil their duties. More never advocated a radical restructuring of society. The life of virtue lay at the backbone of her philosophy.

Figures such as Hannah More and Maria Edgeworth were important but it is worth noting that while Anna Maria refers to her debt to such mentors, her ideological position was not always identical. Towards the end of her account, Anna Maria remarks that 'We do not now adopt her opinions quite so implicitly as we did then ...' It is also interesting to read what amounts to her own manifesto on the duties of women –more pronounced in her non-fiction accounts than in her novels and short stories where she can provide a chorus of varied voices expressing differing views – even if the ultimate conclusions remain the same! The threat is also ever-present of 'the *malaria* of those unhealthy influences' from across the Channel – from the dangers posed by the spread of revolutionary principles to the insidious vogue for French literary trends mid-century.

The choice of format for Hall's writings was an important consideration. While her output was varied, certain formats were less likely to be sneered at by the male establishment. In Rohan Maitzen's article on historical biographies by Victorian women, she wrote of the significance of writing "Lives" or "Memoirs" rather than "Histories." She quotes from critics such as J.M. Kemble, writing in *Fraser's Magazine* and Francis Palgrave in the *Quarterly Review*, who were hostile to the idea of women historians. Palgrave's comment referring to Mrs Forbes Bush's historical writings, that "the confidence of the public is abused at present by literary ladies, who ought to be contented with marking pinafores and labelling pots of jam," was representative of mainstream attitudes towards women writers. Rather than rock the male preserve of history writing, Maitzen demonstrated that many women writers chose not to attempt to compete with them, preferring what was deemed the more subordinate route of memoir writing. She pointed out that "the memoir is colourful and lively instead of grave, trifling and intimate yet authoritive." This could well describe much of Hall's writings on a wide variety of topics and could explain her popularity as a writer for the journal press. The use of the sketch in particular served her purposes very well with its short, personal, animated format.

Many of Anna Maria's writings for *The Art-Union* were in the form of "Memories," "Sketches," and "Visits," – feminine and full of her signature anecdotes. In her series "Memories of Pictures" or "Pilgrimages to English Shrines", the incidental snippets of information that peppered her discussion of the lives of the artists and authors were full of domestic detail, preambles and asides. They were a rich source of extra information and indeed material culture and would undoubtedly have appealed to a female audience interested in background information about the artists and authors that Anna Maria knew personally.

According to the advertisement to the 1850 publication, it is noted that "To the pen and the pencil of the author's excellent coadjutor, Mr. F.W. Fairholt, the reader will be largely indebted for much useful information concerning the subjects treated of in these pages." Anna Maria also refers to the pencil of Mr. Tucker of Bristol "to whose graceful pencil we are indebted for these valuable aids to memory." Engravings invariably required artists and engravers working together on such publications. The artist and antiquarian Frederick William Fairholt (1814-66) was a close friend of the Halls who accompanied them on many of their travels, especially in Ireland. He provided thirty-four illustrations for the third volume of *Ireland, its Scenery, Character &c.*

FURTHER READING

Atkinson, Juliette, *French Novels and the Victorians* (Oxford, Oxford University Press, 2017).

Hall, S[amuel]. C[arter], Mrs, "The Residence of Hannah More", *The Art-Union,* 1 February 1848. Pilgrimages to English Shrines series. (This was serialised over four years from January 1848–October 1852 and, Hannah More's was the second pilgrimage published in *The Art-Union*).

Pilgrimages to English Shrines (London, Arthur Hall, Virtue & Co., 1850).

Pilgrimages to English Shrines (New York, D. Appleton & Co., 1854).

Maitzen, Rohan. "This Feminine Preserve: Historical Biographies by Victorian Women", *Victorian Studies,* 38:3 (1995), 371–393.

More, Hannah, *The Shepherd of Salisbury Plain, and other Tales* (New York, Derby & Jackson, 1857, orig 1795).

Strictures on the Modern System of Female Education (Salem, Samuel West, 1809, orig 1799).

Mitzi Myers, "Hannah More's Tracts for the Times: Social Fiction and Female Ideology", *Fetter'd or Free? British Women Novelists, 1670–1815* (Eds) Mary Anne Schofield and Cecilia Macheski (Athens, Ohio University Press, 1986).

In the month of January, 1825 – during a fall of sleet and snow, we left Bristol to pay a visit to Hannah More at BARLEY WOOD, her then residence, close to the pretty and retired village of Wrington, in Somersetshire.

Trembling on the threshold of a Life of Literature – quivering with apprehension as to what our fate might be if we dared to pass its iron gates, and ask to sit in the awful presence of those had raised the veil of the Inner Temple,

'whose names
In Fame's eternal volume live for aye!'

a note of invitation from Hannah More, written by her own hand, was an event that made the heart thrill with delight – not altogether unallied to fear: and even now, after the lapse of nearly a quarter of a century, with its mingled burthen of triumphs and depressions, it recalls one of the most impressive memories of a long and active career of authorship to which that valuable and admirable woman was the earliest, if not the strongest, prompter. We had previously made acquaintances with many memorable women of the epoch: we had bowed to the turbaned head of Miss Benber; gossiped with Miss Spence; been affectionately greeted by the excellent and accomplished sisters, Jane and Maria Porter: attracted, as by a golden link, to the lofty genius and generous heart of unhappy Laetitia Landon; corresponded with Felicia Hemans; been stirred to activity by honoured and venerated Maria Edgeworth; and received from good Barbara Hofland encouragement to 'appear in print' – notwithstanding the too popular opinion which refuses faith in the possibility that women may think and write and yet keep their homes in order, and augment the comforts of all around them. But none of these had inspired us with the awe which seemed inseparable from the idea of an interview with Hannah More, whose great work in life had been accomplished before we entered it; whose lessons had been our guides from youth upwards, and whose friends were the now buried immortalities of a gone-by age. Her 'Strictures on Female Education' had been our Polar star from infancy; and its author could not fail to be, in imagination, so wise, so lofty, so self-contained, so far above, and so different from, all other women, that while we eagerly desired, we feared, to meet her.

The snow was deep on the ground, and the friends with whom we sojourned said it was 'madness' to set out for Wrington on such a morning, particularly as the venerable lady's hours for reception were but from twelve till three; but we were decided, and the journey of some ten miles was passed in speculations as to what she would say, how she would look – and also as to what we should say! 'Say?' why nothing; how could *we* speak to Hannah More, or before Hannah More! Who had depicted so truthfully the character of 'Lucilla Stanley' in 'Coelebs', and of course expected every woman to be a Lucilla; who had written 'Practical Piety', and 'Christian Morals;' who had suggested to Royalty how a Princess should be educated, who had been complimented by Dr. Johnson, who had sat to Sir Joshua Reynolds, exchanged wit with Sheridan, enjoyed the social eloquence of Burke, had sufficient bravery to set Walpole in the right path, and been the honoured counsellor of Portous and Wilberforce, and the familiar friend of David Garrick!

We had too much faith in the righteousness of her name – we honoured her too devoutly to imagine her – Mrs. Hannah More – anything like any other human being we had ever seen; we recalled to memory how she had been fêted, and 'embroidered for,'[1] by Royalty, we could hardly conceive how she could have put off the 'stiff stays' of such 'grand' society to wander amid the Mendip hills, enduring – not the rusticity, for *that* might interest, or the vulgarity, for *that* might be pardoned – but the deep, and dark, and dangerous ignorance which had sent her humble neighbours to a fortune-teller to discover if the lady who wanted them to learn to read, and work, was not a 'Methodist;' while some expected to be paid for permitting their children to attend a Sunday School, and others suggested that she wanted to sell them as slaves for the colonies! But the darker the ignorance, the greater became the necessity for her exertions, – such exertions as she never wearied of, until physical strength gave way beneath mental energy. All that she had written, and all we had heard of her, gathered about our memory, as the wheels rolled softly in the snow, or sinking still deeper, crackled upon the frozen paths. We knew that her mind when she resided with her sisters in Bristol, engaged in the actual business of scholastic education, had drawn inspiration and health from her visits to the beautiful neighbourhood in which she was now spending the twilight of her radiant day; we attempted to rub our frozen breaths from off the starry glass, and look out, but we could only discern lofty hedges through the mist of snow; we knew that we were in the centre, round which her 'Practical Piety' had been evidenced by the perpetual exercise of universal benevolence; whose liberality, true as it was to the Divine precepts of her Master, was in advance of her period; we counted up the schools which owed their existence not only to her money and influence, but to her actual bodily exertion, and that while struggling with infirm health, and years that will exact augmented toll as they roll on. Her friends had told us she was totally unspoiled by the flattery and attention of the great; escaping from the society she never loved more than when she quitted it, but which she left from *a sense of duty*; zealous without bigotry; and liberal with a Christian spirit; and the more we recalled her excellences, the more did we desire that the interview so longed for, might be over – simply from a deep sense of our own unworthiness. At length we saw the chimneys of Barley Wood above the trees, and driving along between high hedges of ever-greens, whose bright leaves occasionally pierced through masses of snow, we drew up with a frosty crash at the door of the school-master's daughter.[1]

It was a pretty cottage – simply and purely rustic; even in winter, it looked cheerful, with its caves where swallows build, its covering of English thatch, and its many homely props – pillars hewn from the adjacent wood which the axe of the woodman had not desecrated by fashioning. It has been accurately copied by Mr. Tucker of Bristol, to whose graceful pencil we are indebted for these valuable aids to memory.

A country serving girl gave us entrance; and we stood for a moment in the hall. We had pictured to ourselves an old lady shrouded in black velvet, of a stately and severe presence, leaning (if she might to receive us) on an ivory-headed cane, and resuming quickly her seat on a carved and dignified high-backed chair; and we fancied that a large Bible, clasped with silver, should rest on a table beside her; we were kept waiting for a few minutes in the parlour, in which were hung several old and interesting engravings. The stillness and torpor of a frosty atmosphere had hushed all external noise, save the cold chilling whistle that moves no leaf – monotonous and dull; the snow was cleared away from the porch, and food for the wild birds had been strewed within the circle; several songsters, their feathers all on end, looking like fuzz-balls, were still there, and the earth's white covering was marked with the impress of their feet; the long slender toes of the fragile lark, the broad foot of the wood-pigeon, the deliberate prints of the thrush and the blackbird – told of the considerate charity that ministered to their wants; once a glittering shower of crystals fell from a spangled bough, and a flock of starlings wheeled up, but to return again to the same spot. While watching these stranger birds, a demure-looking servant ushered us up-stairs, and though all was so still without, within we heard voices and the very merry laugh of a child – a glowing fire diffused through the half-opened door the heat and light which are so delightful after a chilling drive. When we entered, a glance showed that the room was not too large for comfort, that the walls were lined with books, and that a group consisting of three ladies and a little boy were round a table, upon which there was an abundant supply of cake and wine; to the cake the little fellow was doing ample justice, and a diminutive old lady was in the act of adding another piece to that already upon his plate; she moved to meet us – it was the least possible movement, but it was most courteous. Instead of black velvet, Hannah More wore a dress of very light green silk – a white China crape shawl was folded over her shoulders; her white hair was frizzed, after a bygone fashion, above her brow, and that *backed,* as it were, by a very full double border of rich lace – the reality was as dissimilar from the picture painted by our imagination as anything could well be; such a sparking, light, bright – 'summery' – looking old lady – more like a beneficent fairy, than the biting author of 'Mr Fantom', though in perfect harmony with 'The Shepherd of Salisbury Plain.' The visitor and her son took their leave; 'Mrs. Hannah' stooped and kissed the boy, not as old maidens usually kiss children – with a kiss of necessity, or a kiss of compliment: she took his smiling rosy fearless face between her hands, and looked down upon it for a moment, as a mother would; then kissed it fondly more than once.

'And when you are a man, my child, will you remember me?' – The boy's eyes glanced from her to the remnants of the cake, – 'Well, remember the cake at Barley wood,' she said, reading his thoughts by the light of her own, and laughing.

'Both,' replied the little fellow with enviable fearlessness – 'It was a nice cake, and you are so kind.'

'That is the way I like the young to remember me,' she replied, 'by *being kind* – then you will always remember old Mrs. Hannah More.'

'Always, Ma'am,' he answered, his face at once becoming serious as he returned her gaze with his large well-opened eyes – indexes of truth and honest purpose; 'I'll try and remember it always,' he repeated, and then there was another kiss.

'What a dear child,' said Mrs. Hannah after they were gone, 'and of a good stock – that child will be as true as steel! I so enjoyed his glance at the cake, it was so much more natural he should remember *that* than an old woman so very little taller than himself – children always connect size with respect – a dear child – I hope he may be spared to his lonely mother' – and her eyes were in an instant suffused with the light of coming tears, as if there had been something sad in that young mother's history.

There were some South Sea curiosities scattered about the room, as if they had been recently examined; the lady who was residing with Mrs. Hannah More, her tried friend and companion, directed our attention to these things, and while the venerable lady drew nearer to the fire, seeing that our interest proceeded not from curiosity but veneration, this friend showed us translations of many of her works into various continental languages; the eleventh edition of one, the tenth of another, and so on: every spot in the room was distinguished by having some treasure in its keeping, and every article of virtù had its story: one in particular attracted us – an inkstand made of Shakespeare's real mulberry tree, the gift of David Garrick. It was impossible not to congratulate her on the possession of such mementos.

'Yes,' she said, 'this place is in itself a great blessing from the hand of Heaven, and the trees you praise are well grown, and have taken deep root; and old as I am, there are times when I feel it a duty to be careful lest I become too deeply rooted in a soil sanctified by friends and friendships!' Her voice had a pleasant tone, and her manner was quite devoid of affectation or dictation: she spoke as one expecting a reply, and by no means like an oracle. And those bright immortal eyes of hers – not wearied by looking at the world for more than eighty years, but clear and far-seeing then, – laughing, too, when she spoke cheerfully; not as authors are believed to speak –

'In measured pompons tones,'

but like a dear matronly dame, who had especial care and tenderness towards young women. It is impossible to remember how it occurred; but in reference to some observation we had made, she turned briskly round and exclaimed, 'Controversy hardens the heart and sours the temper; never dispute with your husband, young lady; tell him what you think, and leave it to time to fructify.' Her friend said she had been fatigued sooner than usual that morning by visitors, but would recover and 'be herself' presently: she drew close to the fire, and seemed inclined to repose or to muse, we could hardly tell which.

Of all women, Hannah More combined in the happiest manner the perfection of spiritual existence and temporal good. Her hopes were with the future, her activity with the present. She lost no friends, no fame, no homage, by living for the *future,* because she never neglected the work of the *present*; her sympathies were as active as her benevolence, and thus she carried conviction with her. She established her Schools, her 'Female Associations,' with as firm a hand as that with which she wrote – despite much that is impracticable and the introduction of some conventionalities inseparable from the period – the best religious work we have on female education – the most difficult of all subjects, from the mere fact that no two children in the same family require the same training. The only undeviating rule to secure this right training is instant, unreasoning, and implicit OBEDIENCE; and if this task be commenced in infancy, both child and parent will be spared an infinity of after sorrow.

No woman was ever so universally acknowledged as the reformer of education, the interpreter of morals, the expositress of piety: [1] these distinctions shed around Hannah More a lustre far eclipsing that which dimly points out the memories of the Sewards, The Piozzis, and the Montagus. It was a privilege to look at her for the few moments she 'rested,' and to think of all she had done; when so far from 'Education' being, as it is now, 'the fashion,' it was something so new as to be considered dangerous, – particularly to women, and to the born 'thralls' of humble life. Her brow was full and well-sustained, rather than what could be called *fine*: from the manner in which her hair was dressed, its formation was distinctly visible; and though her eyes were half-closed, her countenance was more tranquil, more sweet, more holy – for it *had* a holy expression – than when those deep intense eyes were looking you through and through. Small, and shrunk, and aged as she was, she conveyed to us no idea of feebleness; she looked, even then, a woman whose character, combining sufficient thought and wisdom, as well as dignity and spirit, could analyse and exhibit in language suited to the intellect of the people of England, the evils and dangers of revolutionary principles. How bravely had that woman stood in the gap during the crisis of England's moral as well as political peril, and sent forth in the 'Cheap Repository' [1] tracts after tracts, that were devoured by the people with more than the avidity with which they now swallow the paper pellets whose best apology is, that they do no harm! How fine and brave and true was her exposure of the speech of M. Dupont, ringing, as it did, with the hideous clanger of Atheism throughout Europe; and how noble her sacrifice of the sum produced by its sale (240*l.*) to the relief of the French emigrant clergy, – a charity again proving her practical piety – for her dislike to the tenets of the Church, whose ministers she succoured and protected, was well known. There were no traces of the sarcasm she evinced in her clever story of 'Mr. Fantom' upon her most peaceful face; perhaps the mouth had the power of satire, yet it was softened by time and religion. Alas! the race of 'Fantoms' are by no means extinct; there are still plenty such, who, like this hero of false philanthropy, neglect every duty of common humanity, and leave their neighbours' cottage and children to burn, and poor wayfarers to perish of hunger, while devising plans to extinguish the fires of the Inquisition, or to drag the wheels off the chariot of Juggernaut.

It had ceased snowing, and though the sun cast what seemed rays of fire through the atmosphere without dispelling the thick rimy substance that hazed the air, we resolved to brave the cold and see the monuments erected in the pleasure-grounds to the memory of Locke and Forteus. We felt as if breathing icicles, but we persevered, and knew that beneath that expanse of snow lay the lawn, where Mrs. More had assembled, at stated periods, those best monuments of her Christian love – the schools born of her will, and perfected by her example – perfected according to the light of the period; and a beautiful sight it must have been, when some of the most able and best in the country came to witness the gatherings of these hitherto poor uninstructed children there.[1]

The very humbler classes of society have, it is to be feared, gained but little by the exchange which modern theories have put in motion – of the coldly moral for the warmer inspirations of spirit teaching. We are in this norther land of ours more prone to reason than to feel, and do not like to be too much troubled by emotions of any kind; we are becoming altogether material, and a few years more will test the good or evil of such training, on our national character. One thing is certain: as far as it went, nothing could be better than the plan pursued by Mrs. Hannah More; and certainly, one of the perfections of her system, for all classes, was her upholding of the *useful* as preferable to the merely *ornamental*. This is a theory which, when broached in the upper classes of society, is sure to meet approval; but it is not one mother in ten who, finding that her daughter has only capacity for the more ordinary business of life, is content to cultivate that only, and not force her mind into what is called the higher range of intellect – forgetting altogether what a noble field for all that is of truest value in woman, is that which is connected with the ordinary business of life.

Mrs. Hannah More had a thoroughly English hatred to the unreal – to the untrue – and the useless: her total *deadness* to the heavenly enjoyments of music rendered her somewhat hard upon an accomplishment which her want of ear must have taught her to think waste of time; but the balance of education can be well preserved even where a taste for this most enviable talent predominates. It is very rarely indeed that persons can appreciate – not so much what they do not understand, as what they do not feel.

The two monuments we spoke of are in the grounds, each surrounded by shrubs and arched by trees. That to the good Bishop contains this inscription: 'To Beilby Porteous, late Bishop of London. To grateful memory of long and faithful friendship. H.M.'

That to Locke is thus inscribed: 'To John Locke, born in this village, this monument is erected by Mrs. Montagu, and presented to Hannah More.'

We returned, shivering, from our scramble through the snow; our venerable hostess had become quite herself –

vacated her seat by the fire, and insisted upon our occupying it. She spoke with fervour and affection of the advantages she received from her long friendship with Porteous and laughed while she said that Lord Oxford had called him her Father Confessor; she seemed quite alive to the *on dits* of Clifton, and referred to her long residence at Bristol more than once: she spoke with animation of Wilberforce, and his exertions on behalf of the Negro. Her friend drew her back from what she called 'modern times' to Mrs. Thrale, and Mrs. Carter, and Dr. Johnson, who, she said, was never at all 'savage' to her, though once he nearly made her cry concerning an apology she offered for Popery: then she spoke of Garrick, and the expression of her countenance became more earnest, more affectionate, than it had been at the mention of any other name. Certainly, her eyes in youth must have been glorious; for even then they were dark, and, almost painfully, penetrating, except when softened by emotion: when she spoke of this great Master of his Art, they expressed the utmost tenderness, – 'Ah', she said, 'if HE had been alive, it would have been indeed a trial to have retired from the world!' She considered him in every way a man of extraordinary genius; her reverence for Garrick was the true 'Hero-Worship:' his very faults she looked upon as accessories to his perfections. How beautiful it is to see this enthusiasm outliving its inspirer, and animating with fresh life the slow pulsations of age. 'I should have liked,' she said, 'to have looked upon his face once more, but they only showed me his coffin.' Her friendship for Mrs. Garrick only terminated with that venerable lady's life.

After a moment's silence she smiled, and observed, 'I must show you some mementos of my wicked days.' She opened a *bureau,* and took out some cards and a play-bill: the cards were admissions for the *new* play of 'Percy;' the bill, the list of the players who performed therein – amongst them, David Garrick! It was curious to see these in the hands of the author of 'Percy' after the lapse of so many years. 'It was a great temptation', she said, 'to write for such an actor; no one now can form any idea of what it was. He not only was all you could imagine, but the *reality* of whatever he undertook. Then such a face! Can you wonder at my thinking so seriously of the passing away of all these things, when I believe I am the only one living of all who are named on this paper?' She folded the play-bill and cards together as they had been, and replaced them carefully.

More than once we rose to depart. Our awe had subsided into an affectionate respect towards the fragile woman who had held fast to what she believed right – unflinchingly. We do not now adopt her opinions quite so implicitly as we did then; though we would gladly, for the sake of one so great in her day, and who must ever deserve a high place amongst the bravest and best of the women of England, do pilgrimage anew to the houses she occupied – particularly to Barley Wood, the real home of her affections.

Some time after our visit, circumstances to which it is needless to refer induced her to leave Barley Wood and to reside at Clifton. She lived for about four years at 4, Windsor Terrace, Clifton, receiving the most marked testimonies of affection and veneration from persons of all sects and classes. Her end, in the 89th year of her age, was peaceful as her life was pure; and if strangers had seen the numbers who congregated to attend her to the grave – had heard the tolling of the bells from the Bristol steeples, and observed that every shop was closed as the procession passed on its way to Wrington – if they had noted the mingling of yeomanry, clergy, and gentry, accompanied by the children of the Wrington Schools – if they could have been told that the lessons conveyed in the 'Cheap Repository' were as familiar to the people as 'Thoughts on the Manners of the Great' were to their noble fellow-mourners – they would have honoured those who so honoured the virtues of a lady of humble birth; who, by her own exertions, had realised enough to enable her during many years of her life to devote 900*l*, a-year to deeds of charity, and leave a noble property to be divided among the most useful of our Institutions.

Mrs. Hannah More died on the 7th of September, 1833; and in Wrington churchyard, within view of Barley Wood, she was buried. A flat stone, with iron railing, beneath a gnarled yew – aged, yet vigorous with branches and leaves – marks the spot which contains her honoured dust; and not hers alone, but that of her four sisters, each of whom was worthy to repose beside one of the truly excellent of the earth. [1] It is a quiet and retired spot – meet resting-place for one so good and pure; who had quitted the world long previously – except for the holy ties which linked her to it for its service. But of her, in truth, it may be aid, 'Blessed are the dead which die in the Lord; for they rest from their labours, and their works do follow them.' She has made posterity her debtor, for all time; her precepts and her examples are alike lessons that will lead to active benevolence and practical piety. The stone contains this inscription:

Beneath are Deposited the Mortal Remains of Five Sisters.
Mary More, died 18th April, 1813,
Aged 75 years.
Elizabeth More, died 14th June, 1816,
Aged 76 years.
Sarah More, died 17th May, 1817,
Aged 74 years.
Martha More, died 14th September, 1819,
Aged 69 years.
Hannah More, died 7th September, 1833,
Aged 88 years.
These all Died in Faith;
Accepted in the Beloved.
Heb. ch. xi. ver. 13.
Ephes, ch. i. ver. 6.

In these our times, unfortunately, women have in many instances been so busied about their RIGHTS, as to be forgetful of their DUTIES: as they cannot destroy, they endeavour to set aside, the laws of God and Nature; untuning the sweet and gentle voice, given for the expression of prayer, of supplication, of mercy, charity, patience, hope, and faith, in 'screaming' for more liberty: proving their unfitness, by the very temper of their demand, for an impossible equality, they lose sight of the beautiful balance which constitutes civilised society; and forget that even in savage life, it is the man who seeks the hunting ground, while the woman remains in the wigwam to nurse the infant, and prepare the food. It is solely by the softening influence of the Christian faith that women are elevated to the position they hold in Christian lands; and the only course beneficial to them is, by increasing those qualities that will enable them still more to cheer and enlighten the social system, which it is their peculiar province to guide and to adorn. A well-organised and properly harmonised woman has so much occupation in the sphere so clearly defined in the Book of Life, that she appreciates the high privileges of womanhood, in the several relations of daughter, friend, wife, and a 'joyful mother of children', too highly to exchange them for 'advantages' unseemly, out of keeping, and out of character. She values the power of forming the minds of those who are to be the great acting principle, the mental mechanists, the heroes, statesmen, rulers of our land, hereafter. Her proper sphere is so extensive, that she only fears her life may be too short, her power too limited, to fulfil its duties. What a spirit of harmony pervades her dwelling! Be her means large or small, she has still something to bestow: her humanity extends to all around her; she never keeps the sempstress waiting for her work or for her pay, and is too just to beat down the value of a necessary to obtain a luxury. A knowledge of her own defects instructs her to be merciful to those of others, and though her servants at first are not better than those of her neighbours, her patience and good management render them so at last: she has so early taught the infant at her bosom the duty of obedience, that his pliant will bends without distortion, and instead of rebellious brawls racking his father's heart, the well-trained child already imparts the consciousness of future happiness to his anxious parents: woman, in the quiet noiseless circle of her domestic and social duties, has even more to do with the future character of empires, than the mighty man, whose bolder brain and stronger muscle must fight life's battle till his life is done: for, after all, perhaps it is scarcely an exaggeration to say that

'Those who rock the cradle rule the world.'

If woman but knows herself, she can work miracles; be she high or low, rich or poor, her influence is unbounded, if it be properly exercised: it is possible to combine a perfect fulfilment of arduous, literary, or other labour, with a devout and fitting attention to the more pleasing duties of a home-cherishing life; still, those women are certainly the happiest whose occupations and pleasures are strictly of a domestic nature; but no woman pursues a safe course who calculates her happiness to consist in any but the path of duty, while she remembers that the road to *real* renown lies not through mental endowments, however brilliant, or intellectual achievements, however great. The whole career of Mrs. Hannah More is a striking example of what can be affected by *one* woman – a woman neither high-born, nor wealthy, nor beautiful, nor, in what is understood to constitute genius, as highly gifted as many others whose names are histories: her dramas have had no sustaining power to keep the stage, and her poems, as poems, are little more than amusing trifles; but her 'Cheap Repository,' her book on 'Female Education,' her 'Thoughts on the Manners of the Great', her 'Christian Morals,' her 'Spirit of Prayer,' 'Hints on the Education of a

Princess,' 'Character of St. Paul,' and her 'Practical Piety,' despite, as we have said, some occasional conventionalities, are the temples in which her memory is enshrined; and when we recall the formation of those Poor Schools, – when we remember that neither the time bestowed upon them, nor upon her literary pursuits, prevented her fulfilling her duty to the

'Great Father of all,'

in whom 'she lived, moved, and had her being,' – when we learn how faithfully her domestic duties were discharged, while she was the benefactor of the poor, and the instructor of the ignorant, – when we remember what she was to society, and recall the kind, playful, unostentatious womanliness, of her nature, we do greatly rejoice in the triumph of *usefulness*: we gaze with reverence upon the clear beacon-fire she kindled, so different from the phantom lights that dazzle and betray; and we recommend most earnestly to our countrywomen the study of such a life, and its consequences, as opposed to the malaria of those unhealthy influences which, born of a degraded woman of genius, have, of late years, crawled from France into the literature of England.

Front cover design for *Uncle Sam's Money-Box*
by Mabel Lucie Atwell (c. 1900)

VIII

A Series of Children's Books for Chambers

Grandmamma's Pockets (1849)

Anna Maria Hall had a long and successful working relationship with the firm of W. & R. Chambers, Edinburgh from 1832–1859. She worked with many different publishers during a prolific career but her output with Chambers was more prodigious than for any other publisher and showed a range of formats and subject matter over an extended period of time. The letters, ledgers and catalogues in the Chambers archive in the National Library of Scotland contribute further to our knowledge of her literary output and her financial anxieties and priorities. The ledgers prove that she was a profitable and bankable author for Chambers.

Anna Maria contributed to three distinct areas of work for Chambers: firstly her *Stories of the Irish Peasantry,* serialised in *Chambers's Edinburgh Journal* from 1839–40 – invariably top billing on the front page of the journal due to her popularity and selling power. They were published as a collection in 1840[1]; secondly the stories that were ultimately collected in the *Miniature Library of Fiction* in 1858 (serialised in *Chambers's Edinburgh Journal* between 1841–45 and originally referred to by Hall as her "Stories for English Homes" – Anna Maria was convinced that these stories were amongst her best)[2]; and thirdly, four juvenile titles included in *Chambers's Library for Young People.* The latter differs from the other two in that the children's books were illustrated and a distinctive house style was created for the series with identifiable bindings. Anna Maria contributed four stories to the series of twenty titles and they were published within a four year period from 1848–51: *Uncle Sam's Money Box* (1848), *Grandmamma's Pockets* (1849), *The Whisperer* (1850) and *The Swan's Egg* (1851).

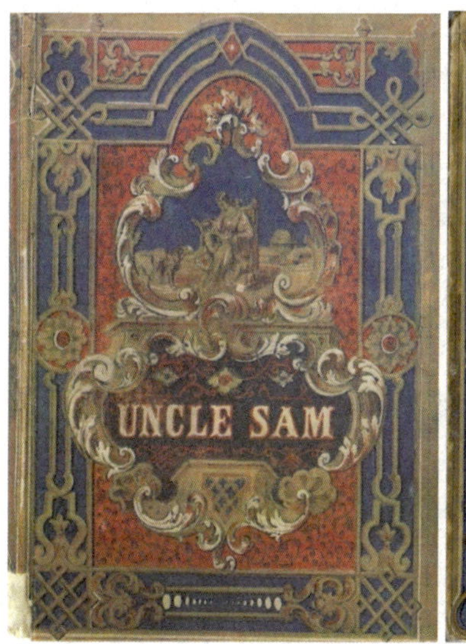

Variant front and back covers dating from 1848–1851 for *Uncle Sam's Money-Box* (1848) and *The Swan's Egg* (1851). The covers made the series instantly identifiable. In all, Chambers produced 20 titles in this series between 1848–51, the first title especially written for the series was Maria Edgeworth's *Orlandino* in1848.

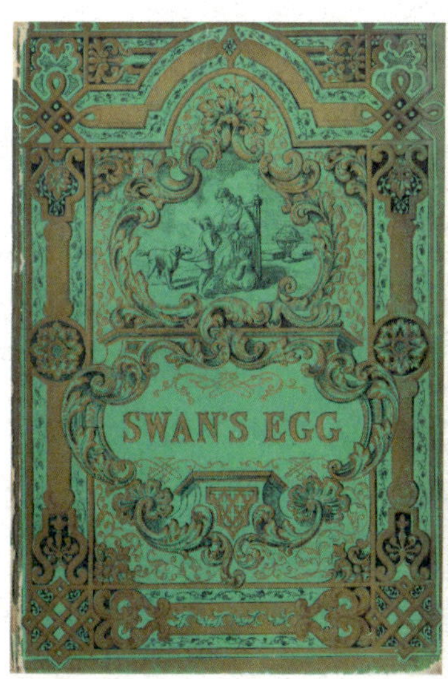

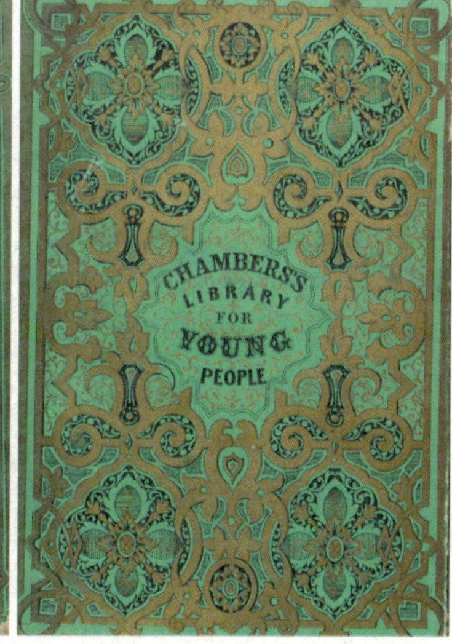

The mid-nineteenth century was a key period in the evolution of children's book covers and there was a move towards cheaper production methods with decorated paper boards and cloth bindings replacing leather. Variant covers were frequently used for the same edition of a book but it was not until the arrival of toy books in the 1860s that children's preferences were taken into account when designing book covers. Each book had a frontispiece and the artist received anything from £9 to £12 as a fee for this series. The popularity of her books was such that they were all reissued in the 1890s with new covers and many additional illustrations. The new editions were larger and were bound in coloured cloth with attractive illustrations in colour. It is noteworthy to compare the frontispieces for her titles for the earlier and later editions to gauge the publisher's preferences for visual accompaniments to her books. It is unlikely that she had much say in this process as she only travelled to Scotland on rare occasions. This contrasted with her other publications where her husband's connections as editor of *The Art-Union* were instrumental in the selection of artists chosen to illustrate her books.

The four titles by Anna Maria written for *Chambers's Library for Young People* were highly representative of her work for children. Similar themes pervade the four titles and echo many of her central concerns: changing fortunes, binary character tropes, didactic narrative devices, the role of The Big House, attitudes towards Irish characters, and resourceful women versus weak men.

The consequences of changes in family fortunes proved to be a key plot device both in *Uncle Sam's Money-Box* and *The Swan's Egg*. Both stories were set in idyllic rural environments in the Home counties of Berkshire and Surrey. Economic misfortunes brought about either by the collapse of the banks or the effects of the repeal of the Corn Laws in 1846 set the scene for dramatic change for the principal characters. Hall is concerned with the varying reactions to misfortunes. Adversity brought out the best and worst in people and the reader follows with interest "the healthful experience which a struggle gives." How the binary characters, Kate and Jane, reacted to their reduced circumstances forms the backdrop to *The Swan's Egg*. Charles Dickens' daughters read this book and he told Anna Maria that they were "devouring [it] with great delight."

Both *The Whisperer* and *Uncle Sam's Money-Box* feature a sage older male returning from travels abroad. These characters take it upon themselves to teach the young characters the importance of using their intelligence and of listening closely to their conscience. Uncle Sam was a likeable character, full of hearty good cheer, whereas Cousin Jacob in *The Whisperer* was a more intimidating tutor, too quick to humiliate the children.

Grandmamma's Pockets was the only one of the four titles to be set wholly in Ireland and there is every indication that it was autobiographical, based not only on the heroine's name ie Annie Fielder but the reappearance of many of the characters in other works. A continuous thread throughout the story was the dependence of the community on the benevolence of the inhabitants of the Big House. Annie's grandmother and mother were constantly out and about visiting schools and distributing food to the needy at Christmas and whenever necessary.

There are references to Irish characters in the other books in the series, in particular Simon, the Irish shepherd in *The Swan's Egg*. He plays a similar role to Randy the fairy man in *Midsummer Eve*, portrayed as close to nature and with an endless supply of useful tales and proverbs from Irish folklore to demonstrate important lessons to Kate and Jane. His ability to tell parables, his earthiness and affinity with nature, his inherent wisdom and unwavering loyalty are characteristics of this Irish archetype so favoured by Hall.

Strong female characters abound in Anna Maria's children's books with patriarchal figures generally in short supply. They are usually dead, ailing or away travelling. When Farmer Kemp's farm in *The Swan's Egg* failed, he was incapable of functioning. He became a confused and pathetic figure, reliant on his sister Miss Lyddy and Kate to keep him alive. Likewise when the bank collapsed in *Uncle Sam's Money-Box*, Mr Hayward took to the bed leaving his wife, elder daughter Charlotte, and son Harold to pick up the pieces. In *Grandmamma's Pockets*, the master of Dove Hall was an aloof character in the wings of the matriarchal household, dependent on his wife's good sense, "Grandpapa always seemed as if everything went ill when his wife of many years was not on the spot to be consulted." The themes in these stories therefore reflect Anna Maria's ongoing concerns with nationality, childhood and gender.

Finally, were these books successful, both for the author and for Chambers? Extensive records in the National Library of Scotland archives reveal that Anna Maria was paid well in comparison to other authors in the series.[3] Three of her four titles rank in the top five earners where she received over £50 per title. *Uncle Sam's Money-Box* fared particularly well, earning the second highest profit of £232 for Chambers, the third highest initial print run and the fifth highest total print run with 44,569 titles sold by the end of 1880. *Grandmamma's Pockets* made a healthy profit of £171 for Chambers with 37,289 copies sold.

Hall's children's books for Chambers were evidently pitched at the cheaper end of the market in comparison to a gift book production such as her fairytale, *Midsummer Eve*, published in 1848, the same year as *Uncle Sam's Money-Box*. However, it is worth noting that although her four titles for Chambers were still making profits into the new century, her expensive fairytale never recouped its costs.

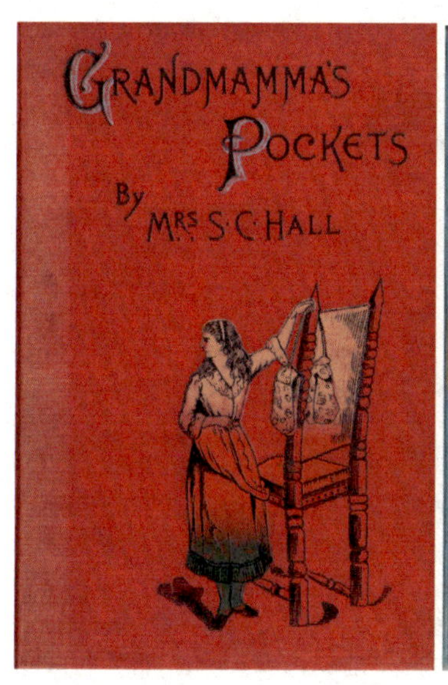

Front covers for *Grandmamma's Pockets, The Whisperer, Uncle Sam's Money-Box* and *The Swan's Egg,* dating from c. 1899–1900

Notes

1 The publisher's ledgers for 1842–45 show that it was first published on 12 June with an initial run of 6,333 copies, followed the next year by 3,164 copies with regular annual or biannual reprinting bringing it to a total of 13,956 copies printed and sold by 1850 giving a profit to Chambers of over £338. A total of 11,300 of the second edition, published initially in 1850 was printed and over the next thirty years, the ledgers show a steady 500 copies printed every two-three years to satisfy demand. Anna Maria's determination to obtain a fair return for her *Stories* is evident in frequent correspondence on the possibility of further remuneration

2 'With respect to the stories I am now writing for the Journal – I certainly do attach some importance to them – as Mr Hall thinks them the best I have ever written, and if I am to judge from the thought & feeling – I think so too.' Dep 341/313 Receipts for Literary Labour 39–40. Letter dated 26 February 1843.

3 Anna Maria's letters in the archive indicate that she had to fight her corner to gain a fair price for her work overall. In a letter dated 13 April [1841] she referred to possible payment for "The Governess" and said: 'My magazine here would give me five and twenty pounds for it. If you think this too much, do not hesitate to say so ... I do not think I should have put a price *at all* upon my productions had *you* not urged me to it.' Six weeks later in a letter dated 29 May 1841 '... my demand now is on your purse – if you will be so good as to remit me the money for these two stories this week, I shall be greatly obliged ... I want as much as I can get as I have not gone in debt but paid weekly as the work went on, the wind up however will demand a good sum.'

Further Reading

Burman, Barbara, and White, Jonathan, "Fanny's Pockets: Cotton, Consumption and Domestic Economy, 1780–1850" in Jennie Batchelor and Cora Kaplan (eds), *Women and Material Culture, 1660–1830* (Basingstoke, Palgrave, 2007).

Dickens, Charles, Letter to Mrs. Hall, 1 October 1851 in Madeline House, Graham Storey, and Kathleen Tillotson (eds), *The Letters of Charles Dickens 1850–1852*, vol. 6 (Oxford, Oxford University Press, 1988), 503–504.

Hall, S[amuel]. C[arter], Mrs, *Grandmamma's Pockets* (Edinburgh, William and Robert Chambers, [1849]).

Grandmamma's Pockets (London, W. & R. Chambers, [c. 1899]).
The Swan's Egg (Edinburgh, W. & R. Chambers, 1851).
The Swan's Egg (London, W. & R. Chambers, 1890).
Stories of the Irish Peasantry (Edinburgh, William and Robert Chambers, 1840).
Stories of the Irish Peasantry (Edinburgh, William and Robert Chambers, 1850).
Uncle Sam's Money-Box (Edinburgh, Edinburgh: W. & R. Chambers, [1848]).
Uncle Sam's Money-Box (London, W. & R. Chambers, [c. 1900]).
The Whisperer (Edinburgh, W. & R. Chambers, [1850]).
The Whisperer (London, W. & R. Chambers, [c.1890]).

W.R. Chambers Inventory Dep. 341. National Library of Scotland, Manuscript Collections Division.

Frontispiece to *The Swan's Egg*
by Swanston (1851)

Frontispiece to *Grandmamma's Pockets*
by G. Millar (1849)

Annie Fielder and Her Pets

Chapter II

'Who was Annie Fielder?' do you inquire; 'and where did she live?'

Annie Fielder was a very animated, bright-looking, light-hearted girl; and when I commence her history, she was a long way from her 'teens.' She was an only child, who never remembered to have heard her father's voice, and who loved the only parent she ever knew the more because she had so very few things to love. Her mother richly deserved this affection; living in a large, lonely house, in a lonely seaside country, she devoted herself as much to the instruction as to the amusement of her little girl, until the 'half-hour bell' called her from Annie to the drawing-room to meet her own parents, with whom they both resided. And as Annie was considered to young to sit at table, except on Sundays, she was well pleased when the old butler rang the bell which called *her* to dessert. She never loved her grandmamma and grandpapa as she did her mamma. Her grandmamma was very stately, and dignified, and particular. She had been educated abroad, and had rather a leaning towards the convent plan of education, as far as restraint went; and when Annie became a woman, she quite believed that restraint had done her a great deal of good.

The little girl's grandpapa was as particular in his way as her grandmamma was in hers; he had what would now be considered very old-fashioned ideas; he often repeated to Annie the tag of an old rhyme, which he firmly believed was the outline of a young lady's domestic duties –

Hold up your head,
Turn out your toes
Speak when you're spoken to,
Mend your clothes.

He also had lived a good deal abroad in his youth, and, to do him justice, made the most perfect bow of any gentleman in the neighbourhood. He was a high-minded, fine old man, proud and solitary, spending his whole day in the library, and seldom finding fault with Annie, except when he heard her voice in the kitchen, or saw her without a veil in the plantations. He held it to be very wrong for young ladies to go into a kitchen, and most injurious to the complexion to go out unveiled. Annie always walked along the courtyard with her veil down, and certainly desired to keep it so; for she knew it was her duty to please her grandpapa. But somehow, when she ran, it would flow back; and as Annie ran a great deal, it often streamed away like a pennon behind her. Once, when in full chase after a butterfly, she encountered her grandpapa.

'Well, Miss Annie!' he exclaimed, striking his gold-headed cane upon the gravel, 'you wear your veil at the back of your bonnet to keep the sun from your face? That is a new fashion!'

Annie had neither brother, sister, cousin, nor companions – that is to say, as she once said herself, 'human-being companions;' but a little cottage in the plantations was sacred to her favourites, and there she had a great number of birds and animals of many kinds: rabbits that would not be friends with a hare, which she considered very unsocial; and hawks that, if permitted, would destroy the blackbird, and not live on terms of intimacy with the owls. She had an otter so tame, that after a good bath in the pretty streamlet

That flowed round her cot,

he would return at her command to his kennel. She was very fond of natural history, and was permitted to indulge her taste, provided she took care of her favourites; but if her grandmamma found a bird without seed and water, she invariably released it from confinement. Independent of her regular 'pets,' Annie had a vast number of dependents. She was allowed to feed the pigeons once a day – the pigeons of the dovecot, as it was called – and it was a pretty sight to see the young girl descending the steps of the old mansion carrying the huge measure of oats and tares and beans, which the pigeons looked for regularly when the great bell had rung out for the servants' dinner at one o'clock. It was quite curious to listen to the 'whiz–z' of their wings in the air. About a minute after the bell ceased, there were always from two to three hundred–'pouters,' and 'fantails,' and 'reefers,' and 'tumblers,' and 'ruffs,' and some lovely 'snowballs,' with red eyes, that were as loving and gentle as doves. They would wheel over and over the courtyard, each circle bringing them nearer to the earth, until the space was literally alive with them. Some sage old pouters walked about with great dignity and composure; others – flirting fantails – bowed and complimented each other, and 'cooed' their admiration, spreading out their plumage in the sun, and each not so intent upon the other's beauty as to neglect the display of its own.

Then the tumblers, if their young mistress did not appear as soon as they expected, began picking up bits of gravel, as much as to say, 'Just look how hungry we are!' But the sweet patient snowballs had too much loving trust in their friend to doubt her; they of course descended with the flock, as if to show that they did not consider themselves favoured in any way; but after a minute or two they were sure to slip away from the crowd, and walk leisurely, if not gracefully, to the steps, and hop up, hop on, until they reached the square top step where Mallow, the Angora ram, and Emperor, generally called 'Emp,' the great mastiff, winked away half the day in the sunbeams. It was very droll to see the old ram butt at La Reine (that was the white hen pigeon's name) if she came too close to him, and to see her spread out her snowy wings, and give a half-fly, half-hop back, and then take her stand patiently on the scraper. If Annie tarried *very long*, La Reine and her prince-consort would stretch their necks, so as to peep inside the Hall; and after a half-coo or so of consultation, give a bold hop at once, and march into the very centre, or fly upon the top of the old organ.

At last, when Annie did really come forth, La Reine and her consort would fly boldly into the basket, begin to eat at once, and suffer Annie to carry them into the very midst of her winged favourites, who rose *en masse* as she stood on the threshold, making the air vibrate with their wings, and hardly waiting until she flung her bounty around, before they rushed to share it. It was a pretty sight: Annie loved her pigeons, and her pigeons loved her; and if any circumstance prevented her feeding them as usual, they were never satisfied with the manner in which others performed the task, but would hang about until sunset watching for her; and this made Annie very happy, for she said, 'It is such a pleasant thing to be wanted, even by a pigeon:' and Annie was right.

The poultry-yard was another source of great enjoyment to Annie Fielder: her grandmamma was very proud of her poultry. There was a turkey-house, a goose and duck house, a henhouse, and a piggery, built in a semicircle round a pond, and all kept so exquisitely clean, that they were considered quite curiosities. Two old servants, too old to work, but never so old that their services were forgotten – Molly Brown and Johnny Peter – did nothing all day long but look after the poultry, and keep their yard and houses clean.

The care-taking old gander was one of Annie's particular favourites: he was a bird of very singular character; so much attached to the steward, that during the winter, and indeed until the downy goslings were all freed from the shell, 'Gag' followed him wheresoever he went. Day and night, it was all the same to Gag – he invariably walked home with the steward, and sat patiently roosting on one leg outside the door, until he arose in the morning; when he breakfasted with his friend, and continued his attentions until the first brood of goslings were quite hatched; then he did not even acknowledge 'a divided duty,' but set himself the task of attending to the maintenance and education of the young geese, only recognising the steward, as he passed, by a gentle nibble at his heel, and a 'Ga! ga! ga!' – probably the most affectionate salutation within the compass of his language.

Old Gag was an example to all fathers of families – a discreet and painstaking gander as ever lived; and brave! So brave, that not a dog would go within ten yards of his flock; and once, between screaming and hissing, he kept a fox at bay until aid came, that preserved him and his from destruction. As soon, however, as he had seen his progeny arrive at years of discretion, when they were able to seek the stubble-field alone – and were considered 'fine green geese' – he returned to his old friend, waddling up to him 'ga-ga-ing' with all his might, and falling into his old habits of attention and affection, as if they had continued uninterrupted by the claims of wife or children. Much as Annie admired the stately peacock, who added so much to the appearance of the entrance by perching on the great pier, while his tail hung like a rainbow behind him, she often confessed to herself that the activity, industry, and domestic virtues of the smallest bantam-cock commanded more respect; for the peacock was a bad father, so cruel to his offspring, that the peahen was obliged to hide her eggs and her chicks, les he should destroy them. Despite his magnificence, he was anything but a respectable member of the feathered community, and this was not the only lesson Annie learned from her practical acquaintance with the creatures of the lower world.

Her pony, 'Blind Sorrel,' was a model of sagacity. Even if the gate of the flower-knot had been latched, he could have opened it; but all his mouthing and 'lipping' could not turn the key in the lock; and this Annie having one day neglected to do, it was left on the latch – not open, as Margate insinuated. He had generally a favourite of his own kind amongst the horses, and for this one friend he would open the gate of the clover-field, and *absolutely close it* after him, when he was munching the dewy clover. In short, he could manage to do everything except turn a key – that was beyond his art. He was so fond of milk, that the dairymaid was obliged to look after her pails, and keep the door of the dairy locked fast, for at milking time Master Pony was always on the watch – 'worse,' as she often declared, 'than any calf.' The truth was, that whenever he did wrong, he knew it; and lest he should be punished, would hide away, like a naughty dog expecting a thrashing, sometime behind the hayricks – he was only blind of one eye – sometime in a dark corner of the great coach-house; and once he was discovered, after upsetting a crock of cream, quietly standing between the half-open folds of a clothes-horse, which had been placed in the sun to air some sheets.

As to dogs, there was no end to the interest Annie took in the canine race and the amusement she derived from them: they were abundant at Dove Hall – that was the name of her grandpapa's residence. Old gray-muzzled greyhounds, the remnant of those who coursed with her grandpapa before the gout kept him an occasional prisoner; little cranky terriers, belonging more especially to the warrener; 'Emp,' the regal-looking mastiff; spaniels, from the tiny King Charles, up to the field beauties, who were starved into sporting condition from July to September; a long turnspit, so long, that (to speak figuratively) before your eyes could get sight of his head they lost sight of his tail. He had a leaden, down look, and only vouchsafed a sly glance from the drooping corner of his eye occasionally. Poor fellow! He never reconciled to his slavery, but fought hard against turning the spit, though still compelled to the duty.

Thus you may imagine that although Annie had no young companions of her own kind, she had a large circle of acquaintances; and moreover, she found them all more or less teachers. The bees in the sunshine; the birds on the bough; the mysterious swallow, with his glancing wing and his beaming eye; the careful rook; the active corncrake; the great horned owls, who had hooted at the world while the world slept on unconsciously, and insulted the queenly moon, who never winked at their reproofs; the provident ants; the faithful and sagacious dogs; the sowing and growing, budding and blossoming of every flower – were all interests and all instructions. Sometimes her mind wandered, and she would desire to see the countries her grandmamma told of. Her grandmamma had been a great traveller in her youth: had seen Madrid and the wonders of the Alhambra; visited the Holy Land, and seen St Peter's and the pope; and the old lady was very fond of talking of Windsor, and royalty, and the noble-looking princes and beautiful princesses, and the fine sights of London, the parks and theatres, and, above all, the great poets and painters she had absolutely known, and considered as friends.

And Annie had constructed, and in a degree painted, the scenery of a doll's bower, and made and dressed a number of pasteboard dolls, that danced – very much to her satisfaction – by means of a string passed through their bodies; and she often wished to be in London, to see the fine sights her grandmamma spoke of: but her mamma always endeavoured to make her understand that she ought to value the repose and opportunity, the health and calmness, the country afforded her to cultivate and concentrate her restless mind.

She told her of the thousands of town children who would rejoice to exchange – for the freedom and freshness of the green fields, and the exhilaration of the delicious breeze that came across the Atlantic, and the perpetual change that every passing cloud threw over the surface of the ocean whose waters rolled within a quarter of a mile of her home – the close-fevered heat and incessant turmoil of the crowded streets. She told her how pale and sickly the town children looked; and that though they sometimes sat up late and learned dancing – not so much to enjoy it, as to practise it before a crowd – and went sometimes to a hot theatre, and looked at the stage until their eyes ached, they had never known the delight of seeking for the early violets, or gathering ripe strawberries off a sunny bank, or listening for the blackbird's whistle, or peeping into a robin's nest, or watching the emigration of a young swarm of bees, or observing the lark climb singing into the heavens, or been tossed in the pleasure yacht upon the little waves up and down in the bright sunbeams, or watched the peasants gathering samphire, or returned home, 'wearied with pleasure.' And laden with a basketful of shells and curious pebbles, and beautiful seaweed – 'flowers of the ocean.' They could not know the happiness of visiting the cottages, and listening to the wants of the poor cottagers, with the power of relieving them. They could not experience the delight of seeing troop after troop of grateful peasants crowd to the 'harvest home,' or gather round the Maypole, or eat their Christmas feast in the great hall.

Annie knew how happy it made her to be met wherever she went with a smile and a blessing – a greeting of 'God bless you, Miss Annie. It's proud we are to see you growing so like your grandmamma.'

She liked to be told she resembled her grandmamma, who every one said had been so handsome; though she never did understand how her round rosy face, and little *retroussé* nose, and laughing eyes, could resemble the Grecian outline, so dignified and severe, of the noble old lady, whom she believed the most learned and grave person in the whole world.

Her mamma had told her that in large cities, where thousands of human beings crowd the streets, she might walk during the longest day in June and not meet one person to bid God bless her! This was a sad thought to Annie Fielder, for she was learning to be useful, and enjoyed the exchange of kind looks for kind prayers; but it very much reconciled her to a country life.

Last Paragraph of Chapter III

Annie thought her grandmamma's dress perfection; and she might well have thought so. She could not have been found guilty of bad taste: the simplest things became her, because the colours were always well chosen and arranged: and to prove that she never thought the ordinary duties of life incompatible with its refinements, I have only to mention that she always wore a very large pair of 'quilted pockets.' Let no modern lady housekeeper, who has a bag-like slip of silk inserted in the skirt of her dress – let no *demoiselle* with a three-inch pocket stitched into her pretty little apron – or a bustling country dame with a white jane pocket behind, imagine that they understand a tithe – which means the tenth part – of the utility or comprehensiveness of GRANDMAMMA'S POCKETS!

CHAPTER IV: ANNIE'S TEMPTATION

Every article grandmamma took off while undressing was carefully folded and put by – with one exception. When she unslung her pockets, as it was impossible to fold them, she reslung them with her own hands across the square, substantial back of an oak chair – a chair of dignity, which had stood with becoming gravity by her bedside for twenty years. There they hung – majestic pockets! – so broad, and deep, and long, and strong, nothing flimsy about them, quilted into a stiff border of erect vine-leaves, with a still stiffer flower-pot in the middle; then inside each of these flexible panniers were two of what grandmamma called '*leetle* pockets,' but out of each of which a pair of modern pockets might have been manufactured.

It would be impossible to tell the numerous contents of the heavily-laden right-hand pocket – such numbers of keys, with their parchment numbers; such knives, and spoons, and forks, in cases; such scissors and thimbles, not fine gold ones, set with rare stones, but solid, determined industry silver ones, with deep indentations; then such scissors, in red leathern cases; a large silver nutmeg grater, with a cunningly-devised case at one end to hold the nutmeg; a housewife, not a little tiny delicate role, with a ribbon strip of silk stitched into divisions for thread on a white ground, but a broad thread-case, with whole skeins of whity-brown and black thread, and cable-like darning cotton – the needlebook filled with needles and pins of all sizes; and such bodkins – broad and short, long and narrow! – with a line engraved upon them, inculcating some bit of actual wisdom. Inside these, as I have said, nestled two little ones, quilted to match the larger.

All her life Annie had regarded these pockets with mingled admiration and curiosity. Her grandmamma made a decided distinction between these large receptacles. The right-hand pocket might be considered an active member of society – a positive fountain pouring forth what was wanted: the left-hand pocket, on the contrary, was a reservoir wherein everything was preserved. One typified the spirit of activity, the other that of carefulness. 'I should be in a state of confusion without my two pockets,' the old lady would say. 'What I wanted to preserve, would get confused with what I wanted to use; and as I have told you, my dear *leetle* granddaughter, no matter how we *realise*; unless we *preserve*, we shall neither be useful nor rich.'

Annie always looked at these pockets with veneration; they really were venerable specimens of bygone times. Grandmamma's ordinary pockets were, as I have said, quilted so as to resemble very much what servants call a 'Marcella' quilt, all in patterns and flowers; others, of a bettermost kind, were double-stitched, and corded cotton inserted between the stitching, so as to have a very raised effect – *alto-relievo* she called them; and very pretty that was, but very hard to stitch, as Annie knew; for she had been entrusted with the task of stitching a pair of little watch-pockets to go inside a pair of unfinished large ones of this description. But grandmamma had also her state pockets: white satin, run with coloured silks to imitate natural flowers. These were put on on birth and festival days. Annie once said it was a pity, they were so handsome, that they were not seen; and upon this her grandmamma read her a very useful lecture, saying it was the fitness of things, and not the show of them, that young women ought to think of! At all times the pockets, slung across the high back of one of grandmamma's chairs, had a mysterious and imposing effect. When Annie was a very little girl, her grandmamma was ill, and at her earnest request she was permitted to sit by her bedside and watch her. The pockets seemed as they too were watching. Annie had often longed to peep into them, but was afraid. She knew their contents were numerous, and very tempting. Amongst them was a large silver bonbon box, with a puzzle top to it – and a cup and ball, which she was permitted to play with when she was very good.

Annie at last just ventured to peep into the quilted depths of the great pocket. She thought she saw the bonbon box resting quietly at the bottom – she was not old enough to know that she should avoid temptation – so she thought there could be no harm in looking again.

Grandmamma was fast asleep; and then she thought there could be no harm in stealing her hand softly into the pocket, and just touching the box with the tips of her fingers. She never had touched the box before, though she had often, very often, seen it opened. One would have thought that the box contained a magnet, so completely were the little maid's fingers drawn towards it. If she had not known she was doing wrong, she would not have peeped between the curtains, and observed grandmamma's eyelashes just resting on the pale pink of her delicate cheek; for though her cheek was thin, it was of the colour of a rose-leaf. She watched closely, her little fingers playing on and around the box all the time; and then she grew to think there could be no harm in just bringing it out to look at it close. She would not open it; she would only look at and feel it. Now, instead of a magnet drawing the little fingers to the box, you would have thought the box covered with birdlime, she held it so firmly, and grasped it so tightly. Another moment! – there hung the gaping pocket, and the box was on Annie's lap!

She thought it so handsome; and yet how the little maid's heart did flutter and beat! Again she repeated to herself she had done nothing wrong; yet still the tell-tale heart beat positively into her throat. Ah, little maids! little maids! – when fingers tremble and hearts beat, and cheeks flush, and you keep looking round and round lest any one should see you, be sure all is not right. You have done something, or are about to do something you are ashamed of, and which *if seen* you would not do. Now, when once convinced that *if seen* you would not do it, make a bold, brave resolution, and do *not* do it! Annie took another peep around the curtain at grandmamma: the old lady slept so sweetly and softly, that, anxious as she was about the box, she paused a moment to thank God for this gentle sleep, and would not have awakened her for worlds; for love and fear were mingled together in her feeling towards her grandmamma.

The box lay in her lap. 'Put it back,' suggested the RIGHT feeling to Annie.

'Why did you bring it out, if you must put it back without looking into it?' suggested the WRONG.

'There can be harm in just *looking* at the bonbons!' thought the little maid. 'They must look so pretty, white and red mingled together in that pretty box!'

She opened it – but was instantly seized with so violent a fit of sneezing, that her poor grandmamma was roused from sleep – to see that Annie had mistaken the snuff-box for the bonbon box! There she sat rubbing her eyes, into which the finer particles of the snuff had entered. Poor little maid, she sneezed, and winked, and wept altogether!

'Why did you take my snuff-box?' inquired grandmamma, looking very much astonished.

Annie was an imaginative child, and the bad spirit that is in all of us tried to turn that imagination to its own purpose, and rapidly suggested a number of excuses; but Annie was also a true child; and when she could speak, she said, 'Dear own grandmamma, I thought it was your bonbon box, and that I might just look into it.'

So the old lady placed her hand on her head, and said, 'Dear own grandchild, you have told the truth, and I forgive you for the breach of confidence. You came to watch by me, and we trusted you; but it is almost as wrong to pry with your eyes into what you know is kept secret from you, as it would be to pilfer with your fingers. If we steal a secret either with eye or ear, it is as morally dishonest as if we take things with our hands. If the eye tempts us,' continued her grandmamma, 'let us shut him up; if the ear tempts us, let us close him. If the bonbons had been there, you would have tasted them, and they would have been sweet to your tongue, but poisonous to your mind. You would have been no longer my bright-eyed honest child.

'See how you have wasted my snuff, you naughty *leetle ting*! You waste more snuff in a minute than my poor nose requires in a day. There, go along, tiny one; only first put my box in my pocket – in my *left*-hand pocket – that preserves; not my right-hand pocket – that distributes. I have a *leetle* box in my right-hand pocket, and this, my store-box, in my left. Go and send my maid. My head makes a great ache!' she added; and then Annie took her hand and kissed it, and said she was so sorry, and would never do so again. And when her grandmamma looked at her red eyes, and her little nose, scarlet as a bachelor's-button from sneezing, much as her head ached she could not help smiling. She was very glad that Annie had told the truth, and glad that she had received so practical a lesson on the evil of prying into temptation.

This was the first time that Annie Fielder had anything actually to do with grandmamma's pockets. The old lady soon got better; and when she was well, all went well in the house. Grandpapa always seemed as if everything went ill when his wife of many years was not on the spot to be consulted.

Spines of book titles by Anna Maria Fielding Hall

IX

An Irish Historical Novel

The Whiteboy: A Story of Ireland in 1822 (1845)

Any discussion of Anna Maria Hall's view on nationality must take into account the context of the political and economic union between Ireland and Britain in the nineteenth century. The issue of the Union dominated discussions of Irish nationality throughout her lifetime. Whether this shared community represented a union of all peoples of the British Isles where the cultural differences of each nation would be respected and nourished as Unionists claimed, or whether this shared community only extended to the island of Ireland was a key question.

Anna Maria's books aimed to promote a greater understanding of Ireland to English people, an awareness of its ancient past, its rich culture and its friendly people. However, the superiority of the English ways versus the Irish ways was ever-present in Hall's work and she always saw the Irish as the beneficiaries of the English, requiring help and guidance, as would an errant child. Martha Nussbaum and Caroline Levander have both explored different aspects of the dependency model of nationalism and this model is revealing when applied to Anna Maria's Irish works and her sense of a parent-child relationship between the two countries. Nussbaum and Levander argued that notions of an essential child identity codified an eighteenth-century concept which blended child development and democratic progress in nations. The child represents the possibility of autonomy yet the reality of dependency; freedom and equality on the one side yet the dangers of exploitation and subjugation as dependent beings on the other side. Anna Maria's solution demonstrated time and again in her writing was for the Irish to imitate English ways. This was problematic on many levels, not least in the firm resistance from the colonised Irish.

In the pages of *The Nation* newspaper which had an estimated readership of 250,000 in 1843, the Young Irelander Thomas Davis argued for Irish spiritual rebirth through nationhood. It was only through the establishment of the Irish nation that Irish nationality could be fully realised. Whilst liberal towards those who espoused nationalist ideas, the Halls entertained Charles Gavan Duffy at their home at Firfield, despite not sharing his ideas. Anna Maria was unwavering in her support for parliamentary Union between Britain and Ireland and consequently did not see any political conflict in her joint loyalties to Ireland and Britain. Her stories show time and again her acute awareness of the underlying political tensions: the aftermath of the 1798 rebellion in Wexford, the rapparees and the resurgents, and the escalating Whiteboy agrarian protests arising from the uneasy relationships between landlords and tenants. She frequently referred to the heroic Irish soldiers who fought in the British army against the Napoleonic forces, evidence of her acceptance of their assumed loyalty to the Crown.

Anna Maria was not blind to the political situation, the mismanagement of Ireland and religious intolerance and was fully aware of the difficulties facing the Irish peasant in the 1830s and 40s. In a tale set in Manchester entitled "The Little Fishmonger" (1841) she compared the situation endured by the lower classes.

> There is an immensity of privation endured by the lower classes. As an Irishwoman I see it less than others, because the peasantry of my own country suffer and bear so much more.

The Whiteboy was published in four parts in 1845. Anna Maria was at the peak of her powers as a writer and editor, bestselling author of many editions of her *Sketches*, successful novelist of historical novels with an English setting such as *The Buccaneer* (1832) and *The Outlaw* (1835) and enjoying the recent success of *Ireland, its Scenery, Character, etc* (1841–3). While she had returned time and time again to the question of absentee landlords and the plight of tenants in Ireland, this was her first Irish or national full-length novel on this theme. It centres on the story of a young Englishman, Edward Spencer who comes to Ireland to take over the running of his property and he is adamant that he wants to improve the lot of those living on his estate. There are many twists and turns in the tale and Edward is careful to work both with the landlords and the tenants to bring about improvements.

Another key character in *The Whiteboy* is Abel Richards the cruel middleman and Anna Maria leaves us in no doubt of her scathing regard for this character who typifies the very worst of his kind.

> In the evil days of which we write, such evil men were considered necessary to the thriftless absentee; necessary to the careless fox-hunting, claret-drinking squire, willing to pay a middleman for bearing the curses that ought to have fallen on himself.

Maureen Keane devotes a chapter to *The Whiteboy* and concludes that it is a novel where Anna Maria is 'at ease dealing with the large problems that plagued Ireland – political mismanagement, religious intolerance, legal and illegal violence and poor landlord/tenant relations'. Keane also discusses two other novelists who were preoccupied with the same themes at the same time – William Carleton with his *Valentine M'Clutchy* (1845) and two novels by Charles Lever entitled *St Patrick's Eve* and *The O'Donoghue* both published in 1845. Despite their varied backgrounds – Carleton was a peasant from Tyrone and Lever a doctor and writer of military tales – all were drawn to highlight the situation where the landlords of Ireland were consistently negligent and heartlessly oblivious to their responsibilities towards those who depended on them for their very survival.

FURTHER READING

Carleton, William, *Valentine M'Clutchy: The Irish Agent, Or The Chronicles of Castle Cumber*, (Dublin, Duffy, 1845).

Keane, Maureen, *Mrs. S.C. Hall: A Literary Biography*, Irish Literary Studies 50 (Gerrards Cross, Colin Smythe, 1997).

Levander, Caroline Field, *Cradle of Liberty* (Durham, N. C., Duke University Press, 2006).

Lever, Charles, *The O'Donoghue: A Tale of Ireland Fifty Years Ago* (Dublin, Curry, 1845).

St. Patrick's Eve (London, Chapman & Hall, 1845).

Nussbaum, Martha, "Patriotism and Cosmopolitanism," (1994) Web 6 November 2021.

Chapter VIII
The Middleman

The funerals were long talked of, and the animosities they revived still longer felt, in the immediate neighbourhood of the scene. In isolated parts of a country, impressions linger like snow on the mountain-tops – impressions that would have been obliterated by the business or pleasures of active life. Abel Richards, who acted so conspicuous a part in the transaction we have recorded, had previously been making his way in the world after the fashion of the lowest reptiles; wriggling as a worm; burrowing as a mole; wise, in his own fashion, as a serpent; poisonous as an adder – the slime of evil deeds tracking his course. As a toad broods and fattens in its rocky bed, so did this man increase and prosper – the base ideal of a class which at one time ate into the very vitals of Irish prosperity – the exacting, the selfish, the merciless – the debasing and debased – middleman.

"But how," will the English reader ask, "how was this? – how could it be?"

How it was we can hardly explain, though we have heard and seen as much of the "Middleman" as most persons; seen the character in all its various grades – from the broad, vulgar, pompous presume who dared to talk of "his family," who had his thousand acres of the absentee landlord-in-chief, to whom he was a punctual paymaster, or advancer of monies, wrung from the thews and sinews of hard-handed men, the blood and bones of a willing people – from him down to the middleman scarcely a remove in education or position from the poor vassals over whom he was a despot. It would be difficult to believe that any people but the Irish could so long have submitted to the middleman as "a system;" and alas! When they did attempt to rise against it, from its terrible and intricate ramifications, it involved them in entanglements of false-reasonings, false judgings, and crimes, which have left an awful curse upon the country.

Take Abel Richards as a specimen of the class – and, believe us, there have been many worse; a keen, cunning man – a steward's son, inheriting his father's earnings and his mother's vices – crawling about "the big house" with a bland smile, a quick car, a ready invention – a few pounds ever in his purse – to lend, when profit could be made – to buy, at every seizure for rent, either cow or pig, potato or kish, by which he could make a guinea, a shilling, or a penny – a bow and an obliging lie always at the service of his rich neighbour – a blow and a bite for his poor one. Not but that Abel shirked "the ruffian" whenever he could, especially in his latter days; for he was not given to open strife – it did not answer his purpose. He knew that land – "the bit of land" – is the peasant's existence; he has, in nine cases out of ten, no regular employment to look to; he must have "the bit of land," no matter what he promises to pay for it; he must have it, or beg and starve; if ejected, he dare not seek for ground elsewhere, for if he eject another holder, his own doom is sealed. Richards knew this – he had grown up in the knowledge, and to the calculations which such knowledge brings; at first he got twenty or thirty acres of land into his possession, which he let, re-let, divided, subdivided, until it was said he made the district " a place of poverty and potato-gardens." Then he was only an under "middleman;" – the middleman of a middleman, who perhaps (the case was by no means rare) was a middleman under yet another middleman. The wretched beings who called him "Mister Abel" (that was his *first* public step) were subject to have their pig, and their bed if they had one, "canted" by landlords – one, two, three, or more. But Abel never "got on swimmingly" until he became a convert – turned his back upon his old faith, and adopted a new, under the fostering patronage of Mrs. Spencer. This, for a time, gave him a push – a lift with the gentry. All the ill-will his avarice and cruelty had earned, it was very convenient to attribute to "his changed faith." He had been so hated previously, that we may doubt if his "turning coat" increased the ill-will; but he made people believe it did, and managed to obtain a considerable augmentation of land from an absentee landholder, who had some zeal – and much need of the money, which Mister Richards did not fail to procure.

In due course he made some speeches at meetings in Dublin, which "told" with those who have a sufficient quantity of charity to "know" that all who believe as they believe must be saved, while those who believe otherwise, will be – the contrary. While Dean Graves, and other of his acquaintances received his confessions and ejaculations, and tales of persecutions, with mistrust – in Dublin, he dined with titled ladies, learned to eat with a silver fork, obtained various presents of bitterly-worded tracts from those who had the reputation of sanctity among their own "set;" while more timid votaries bestowed on him blue and pink book-markers embroidered with words, which, strange to say, were at decided variance with their practice – thus a lady who would not suffer a "popish" domestic to enter her service, selected the motto, "Charity suffereth long and is kind;" and another, the simple word "Peace," worked in *orange* silk, as a token of her hatred of the *green*. At all the little "tea-parties" got up by this mistaken body, Abel Richards was introduced with much ceremony as, "that suffering saint from the south."

He returned to the neighbourhood of Spencer Court with added interest in the eyes of its mistress; for there are persons in the world, who, seeing others "get on," take it for granted they deserve to prosper. Abel's system, under his improved fortunes, was that of the higher grade of middleman – the agent between the necessities of one class, and the necessities and vices of another. Sometimes he let two or three acres, or even one – never of course on lease; the tenant had to build his own dwelling; this in itself stamps the place in the poor cottier's affection – he has kneaded the clay with his hands and his spade; he has raised the stones; he has cut the sods; he has carried the wattles; and if his roof be straw, he and his wife and children have borne it – perhaps as a free gift from "a strong farmer" – on their shoulders, and wrought it into a shelter beneath which he is to spend, he hopes, his life. Few think of this natural love which all men have to the work of their own hands, when they read of an ejectment, and the consequences which follow; but Abel Richards knew it, and understood it – and knew its value, when it was to be turned to account. There are some who joy to see the harrow passing over the fresh-tilled field; to whom the husbandman's whistle is sweeter than that of a wild bird; who pause in the fresh pure air to bless God that He permits them to hear the music of hopeful hearts; and to see the seed cast into the earth – a type of immortality. But Abel Richards would bit his lips with bitterness a the labourer's whistle, and inveigle the tenant who could pay and wished to pay, into his debt, that so he might have power to raise his rent or cast him forth.

An act of this kind caused the return of Mr. Spencer, who after his wife's death, had absented himself from Spencer court, making Miss Ellen's education a pretext for the change he so much needed or desired, leaving many he had protected, to the mercy of evildoers; he was, however active when roused, and this roused him for a time. A man who resided many years on the land of which Abel Richards got possession, and had hitherto paid his rent punctually, was induced by a manoeuvre of the middleman to get into arrear. Watching his opportunity, while the man was in Cork, the agent levied a distress upon his goods, and seized for the rent. His wife resisted, and was committed for assault; it is true she was liberated in a few days, but she caught the fever in gaol, and communicated it to her husband, and two out of five of their children died of the pestilence. Next "gale" day the poor man was totally unable to meet his rent.

At this time, the potatoes in the pit outside the poor man's house were distrained on, and the bailiffs were watching to seize him for the costs of a lawsuit which Richards had drawn him into in the extremity of his distress; and knowing that Mr. Spencer had influence over Richards, who still acted as his agent, he wrote to him the particulars of his case, by the hand of Lawrence Macarthy. Time, however, passed on, and no answer came; for days and nights the poor man lay out amid the rocks of Glenflesk, and the fastnesses of the higher mountains.

Abel feared Mr. Spencer's return before his victim's ruin was thoroughly accomplished, and with the sagacity of a demon he laid a trap for the man. He caused a report to be circulated through the outlawed district, where he believed he was concealed, that his wife was dead; the man rushed home, was tracked by the bailiffs to his own house, but had time to bar the door – they dared not break in! But the middleman was not to be baffled: he said to the bailiffs, "Starve them out; suffer neither bit nor sup to enter the house; he will not see his children die."

For three days they endured famine; on the first, they had a few cold potatoes; on the second, nothing; on the third, the children cried for food, and the mother looked in her husband's face. As the evening advanced, the door opened; the man, ghastly and desperate, stood armed with a pitchfork at the entrance; he said he would have food for his children, and the life of whoever touched him. The bailiffs (there were three), it might be they feared, it might be they pitied him, but they suffered him and his wife to drag some potatoes from the store. And when Abel heard it, he knew that NOW he could issue a criminal warrant against the man for stealing his own potatoes! He procured it; but its execution was prevented by Mr. Spencer's arrival. If ever Ellen Macdonnel was greeted as an angel, it was then; if ever she was cursed by a demon, it was then. It was well known that she had accelerated Mr. Spencer's return; it was believed that Lawrence Macarthy communicated with her on the subject. But the poor man was saved from ruin, while Abel blandly resigned all charge of Mr. Spencer's rents, declaring that however unworthy he believed the man to be, he was but too happy to oblige his old "patron," by proving that he bore him no ill-will for his obstinacy. But the man could not – and did not – forget his dead children!

After this occurrence it amazed many that Abel remained in the country; but, strange as it may seem, he was countenanced by some who believed the people in array against him "for his new faith;" he was still the "suffering saint of the South," "labouring in an unproductive vineyard," sowing seed on stony-ground, and "among thorns."

It may seem marvellous to those who have happily never mingled with the *ultras* of either party, much less of both parties, in Ireland, how such a man could not only live, but proceed in a course of worldly prosperity, feared by some, useful to many; useful beyond all telling to those who required the utmost penny for their land – yet despised – hated – cursed! – while thieving, thriving!

In the evil days of which we write, such evil men were considered necessary to the thriftless absentee; necessary to the careless fox-hunting, claret-drinking squire, willing to pay a middleman for bearing the curses that ought to have fallen on himself.

And so Abel Richards went on – grasping together large sums at last; yet he would still enter the widow's cabin, and if she could not pay him the interest of the two or three pounds lent to her husband before his death, he would pocket the eggs laid on the dresser for market day, or take the hanks of yarn off the peg, or the basket of chickens from the eldest girl – not as a "set off" against principal or interest – oh no! that would be mercy and justice! And Abel Richards knew neither; but as a present, a boon for his *forbearance*! And then as he mounted his horse he would fling them a tract and a "blessing." He never distrained an utterly poor man, where he could gain nothing by it. No! cases of that kind he contrived should be witnesses to his patience and charity; but like a fiend, he would watch and wait, and so despoil the tenant of every comfort – of his new hat, or his wife's shawl, or his little pig, or his hive of bees – whenever any such came: nothing was beyond or beneath, too high or too law for his grasp.

Mr. Spencer became after this, his last absence from Spencer court, his own agent and his own steward; and though he lacked perseverance and energy, he was kind and conciliating – *just*, moreover, and justice is the last thing a poor Irishman expects. Ellen, whose mind was older than her years, was his almoner, and if it had not been for the necessary, though frequently injudicious, superintendence of Mrs. Myler, would have been as happy as any ungoverned young lady could have wished to be.

The kindness of Dean Graves, and the affection of his daughters preserved Ellen from being utterly spoiled. To Mr. Spencer, Ellen Macdonnel had grown from a plaything into a companion, riding, singing, reading, and reciting with him; and to him, as was most needed, she was in every respect a fond, a most affectionate, if not altogether a very obedient child.

During the five years that Mr. Spencer survived his wife, Ellen Macdonnel's clear full brow would have been seldom overcast, but for the love she bore her brother, who was never noticed by her protector. Master Mat had become so completely crazed on the subject of concealed treasure, that he abandoned his teaching for wandering, and his pen for the pickaxe, and seldom approached the schoolhouse for weeks together; this was also a grief to her – her wise, her kind, her learned Domine! To be sure, she had free access to his small store of books, and they were, generally speaking, such as a wild, enthusiastic girl should now have made her companions. Ellen, however, must be known as she really was, a creature of warm affections; a lover of all things appertaining to her native country, which she believed had suffered beneath long ages of misrule; earnest and hopeful; determined, rash, with a temper quick enough to be called "violent" by her foes, and "very warm" by her friends. Her position was still as undefined, as undetermined as ever. Some said one thing, some another. The neighbours had long discovered, that her bright chestnut hair was the colour that Mrs. Spencer's might have been in her youth; that her eyes – deep, violet eyes – resembled those of poor Annie Cumming; that her large, full brow, was like – nobody's; but her nose and chin the "very moral" of one they did not care to name. Her figure was small, considering her years, more active than graceful; and her movements, at times, more rapid and decisive, than was in strict accordance with good breeding. But Ellen's greatest charm was the varying and eloquent expression of her mobile features; clear or shadowed, tearful or smiling, as circumstances touched her heart or excited her imagination. In her character, she was brightly and eminently truthful; not feeling her dependence, as an English girl would have done, because dependants swarmed around her, without considering it degradation, or being insulted in a poor country because of their poverty. And yet, "Nelly" was proud as a princess; at times, exalted by the highest spirits, while at others, she sank into tears, and a despondence akin to despair. Her natural habits and disposition might have been moulded into mental beauty of the rarest kind, for she was generous as upright, and brave as true; while her intense love of her country exalted her character – as patriotism, apart from all worldly and personal considerations, must ever do.

Mr. Spencer continued to live undisturbed at Spencer Court – indifferent to rumours that occasionally reached him, of evil doings among the peasantry, far off or near at hand.

Still, the Whiteboy outbreaks were becoming more frequent, and assuming more organised and determined forms. Several gentleman quitted the neighbourhood; but Mr. Spencer's want of energy and activity increasing with his prolonged existence, was his principal safeguard; he became also more kindly and good-humoured, – attributable, and perhaps justly, to Ellen's influence; and shocked some of the high-pressure people, by a declaration that he was convinced the lower class were not evil movers; that he wondered how they had borne what they had borne for so many years; that their endurance was exemplary, and that disturbance existed only amongst those who were not poverty-stricken. He muttered, also something which sounded very like "rights of the people;" and hinted his opinion, that the representative of a certain ancient family had actually committed a breach of the peace by knocking down his own coachman. These were novel doctrines in those days. He had learned, moreover, what things a landlord might do, and what things it would be much better for him to avoid. Some said his conduct proceeded from love of the people, others, that he feared for himself; and many wondered that Mr. Graves permitted his daughters to companion so much with such a girl as Ellen Macdonnel, whom nobody knew, and who was little more or less than a young rebel.

But all Mr. Spencer's plans were suddenly overturned – crushed – extinguished, by a stroke of apoplexy, which terminated fatally in a few hours. A kindly man he was, without any of the higher or holier objects of our nature, – living an aimless life; yet his funeral was "mighty grand."

His heir and nephew being abroad, did not hear of his death for a considerable time after the last "palled pageant" had faded; and did not visit Ireland, as we know, until several months after the "melancholy event."

Some said, it was a great blot on the memory of the "Master of Spencer Court," that he had forgotten to provide for a child of his adoption, who had loved, and tended, and cherished him as a parent. His wife had bequeathed her to his care, and as he never spoke of his nephew Edward Spencer, and invariably treated "dear Nelly" as a daughter, and during the last months of his life, always mentioned her as "his niece," many expected that the young, favoured, petted creature, would have been provided for; but at the last "poor Nelly" was forgotten – left upon the world without a shilling!

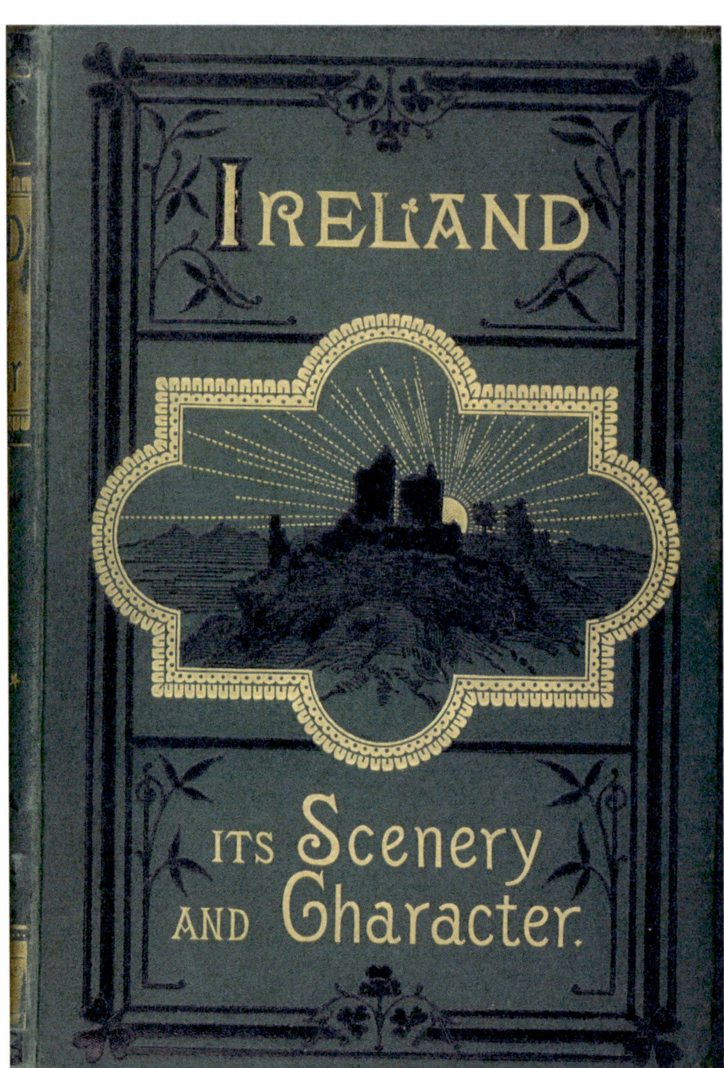
IRELAND
ITS Scenery
AND Character.

X

Travelling Around Ireland Pre-Famine

Spines of variant editions of Halls' *Ireland*, *Midsummer Eve*, also *Sketches of Irish Character* and *Pilgrimages to English Shrines* from the collection at dlr LexIcon, Dún Laoghaire

The Halls were regular visitors to their native country and, as outlined in the Introduction, they undertook at least five tours to Ireland during the period 1825–41 and again before 1865. These tours culminated in their outstanding three-volume joint publication entitled *Ireland: its Scenery, Character, &c.* published 1841–43. This work was published in many different formats in later years, some focusing on one area such as *A Week at Killarney* (1843) or the four-volume *Hand-Books for Ireland* (1853). As recently as 1984, Michael Scott's edition of the first volume reflects his preference for a more minimalist approach – removing the stories and sketches from the main text and inserting them in two appendices instead.

Travel literature was immensely popular in the early nineteenth century. Such literature proved to be a popular genre which could highlight history and social conditions, folklore and legends and indeed could provide a valuable guide for prospective tourists. Short articles were ideal for reproduction initially as essays in a series on a given topic as we have seen in Anna Maria's 'Pilgrimages to English Shrines', later compiled into volumes when the series was completed. This gave the writers and publishers a chance to test the waters, monitor sales in the periodical press and encourage audiences within their circle to subscribe to the enhanced gift book publication at the conclusion of the project. The first edition of *Ireland* was planned as twenty separate parts, each issue approximately forty-eight pages and priced at half-a-crown, the first published on 1 November 1840.[1] It was advertised in the October and November 1840 issues of *The Art-Union.*

The Halls dedicated the three volumes of *Ireland: its Scenery, Character, &c.* to Prince Albert, referring to Ireland as 'a country with which his Royal Highness is so closely, and so auspiciously, connected.' Queen Victoria and Prince Albert were avid enthusiasts of art and sought to promote living British and Irish artists with their extensive patronage. During the 1840s and 50s Prince Albert was President of the Fine Arts Commission and he was instrumental in promoting the Great Exhibition of 1851.

Diarmaid Ó Muirithe in his 1972 publication *A Seat Behind the Coachman: Travellers in Ireland 1800–1900* was effusive in his praise for *Ireland: its Scenery, Character, &c.* saying that 'it is the best account of its kind.' He praised the Halls for their deep insight and lack of religious or class prejudices compared to the 'Protestant and imperialistic prejudices' of their contemporary William Makepeace Thackeray whose *The Irish Sketch Book* was published in 1843.

The Halls readily acknowledged the work of numerous earlier scholars including the topographical writer and artist Isaac Weld, antiquarians Thomas Crofton Croker and John Windele and folklorist Thomas Keightley. At the heart of their endeavours was their oft quoted aim to encourage people to visit Ireland and to sample the unique 'character' of the Irish people. These travels around Ireland also furnished Anna Maria with ample opportunity to expand on her repertoire of stories from every county of Ireland. In Volume 1 they note:

> The Legends and Traditions of Ireland are full of interest; and its Superstitions are rich in romance. It is indeed rare to pass a single mile, without encountering an object to which some marvellous fiction is attached. Every lake, mountain, ruin of church or castle, rath and boreen has its legendary tale; the Fairies people every wild spot; the Banshee is the follower of every old family; Phookas and Cluricaunes are – if not to be seen – to be heard of, in every solitary glen. (Vol. 1 v).

Illustration and Collaboration

Most of the travel books written by the Halls were prime examples of the *livre romantique* and in addition to *Ireland: its Scenery, Character, &c.,* included *Pilgrimages to English Shrines* (1850), *The Book of the Thames* (1854), *Tenby* (1860) and *The Book of South Wales, Wye and the Coast* (1861). The Halls were avid collectors of art and they privileged contemporary British and Irish art. They were anxious to support the work of friends and colleagues and to retain art that was closely connected to their own publishing ventures.

One such artist was Belfast-born Andrew Nicholl (1804–86). Nicholl was one of the team of artists who worked closely with the Halls on *Ireland: its Scenery, Character, &c.*, contributing 114 drawings which were subsequently wood-engraved for the three-volume work. His contribution to the publication was the most extensive. As well as drawings, he evidently carried out research for the Halls, sketching the recently discovered caves at Mitchelstown, Co. Tipperary in 1834 and carrying out extensive note-taking and drawings of Glendalough on their behalf.

> Mr. Nicholl, who searched the ruins with exceeding care and perseverance, informs us that there is scarcely a stone in the vicinity that did not afford some subject for his pencil, although they were nearly all broken, and scattered without the smallest regard to their preservation (Vol. 2. pp 213–214).

In a letter dated 2 Dec. 1840, S.C. Hall showed how much he valued the work that Nicholl did for this publication in the following excerpt:

> A great many sketches of objects in Wexford county have been sent to me – but I will not use any of them until I receive yours – but I shall be glad to get them soon – Do as many as you please of this county. I have ordered parts 1 and 2 to be sent to Belfast for you; I most sincerely hope you and Mrs Nicholl are well ...[2]

Nicholl's drawings were used consistently in all three volumes. Volume 1 included his drawings of the Cork and Kerry region, Volume 2 had over fifteen drawings of the Wexford area, many of them of locations dear to Anna Maria, such as the ruins of Bannow Abbey and the castles at Johnstown and Bargy. Volume 3 included a large selection of drawings by Nicholl of scenes in Northern Ireland, his home location.

Many artists continued to work on various projects for the Halls, thereby gaining financially and enhancing their reputations through further promotion in *The Art Journal*. Another artist who provided most of the illustrations for the section on Galway, was William Evans of Eton (1798–1877).

> We are fortunate in having obtained the co-operation of so accomplished an artist; and lament that the beauty of his coloured drawings cannot be satisfactorily transferred to our pages by the aid of wood engraving. (Vol. 3. p. 456).

Evans visited Ireland in 1835 and again in 1838 and enthused about the 'primeval simplicity' of the honest peasants. 'Ireland had failed to attract the pencils of the recording brethren of the easel, and lay like a virgin soil untouched by the plough.'[3] His vignette of a young bare-footed woman in a cottage interior accompanies text that highlighted details such as the 'rude and smoke-dried chimney piece' with its plates, the saddle on a peg, a four-legged stool, the kish with its potatoes and the iron pot attached to the chimney by its crook. The Halls' descriptions and comments provide factual details on the usage of various implements and opinions about how peasants should be rewarded for the upkeep and maintenance of their cabins.

In Volume 3, the Halls urge artists to visit Ireland to experience the grandeur and sublimity and they refer to the peasant as a 'valuable accessory' to the picturesque landscape.

> Perhaps no country of the world is so rich in materials for the PAINTER; nowhere can he find more admirable subjects for his pencil, whether he studies the immense varieties of nature, or human character as infinitely varied. (Vol. 3. pp 392–393).

To emphasise the importance of this ekphrastic manner of visualising Ireland, they reproduced an extensive essay from *The Art-Union* written by F.W. Fairholt who accompanied the Halls on their tour. Fairholt reiterated the vision of the 'savage grandeur', the 'magnificent clouds ... which claim for Ireland the pre-eminence in cloud scenery' and above all the picturesque inhabitants.

> The girls in their deep red petticoats and jackets, with their healthy cheeks and richly-clustered hair ... confined beneath the ample hood or capacious mantle ... upon which a load is frequently poised, adding an 'antique grace' and dignity to figures that seem to realise Homeric times. At least, they may be said to be the 'finest peasantry in the world' for the painter; a more fortunate admixture of bright colours is seldom to be met with than they display upon themselves. A red petticoat, with a deep blue body and yellow handkerchief, aids the more sober scenery of the country not a little, and is of much value in landscapes where green and grey alternately abound. (Vol. 3. pp 393–394).

In addition to promoting Ireland in such glowingly romantic terms, the Irish peasant was objectified and seen in formal terms as a colourful accessory in his or her own landscape. The Halls created a vision of Ireland that was enticing and alluring from an artist's perspective.

As with their other publications, older wood-engravings could be used if relevant, so that not all images had to be originals. Individual publishers held onto wood-engraved vignettes, capital letter forms and tail pieces and within Anna Maria's oeuvre as a whole, this is evident. Many of the wood-engravings in *Midsummer Eve* had been used in Volume 1 of *Ireland: its Scenery, Character, &c.* which covered County Kerry and Killarney, the primary setting for her novel. One of the famous legends associated with Killarney was that of the O'Donoghue, and Thomas Crofton Croker included an account of this legend in his section on 'Thierna Na Oge' in *Fairy Legends and Traditions of the South of Ireland* (1825). O'Donoghue was a Gaelic chieftain associated with Ross Castle and there were many legends about his life and death. The image used of O'Donoghue in Crofton Croker's book was the same engraving that the Halls used when referring to the legend in *Ireland: its Scenery, Character, &c.* and *A Week at Killarney*. When Anna Maria wrote about it in *Midsummer Eve,* it was rendered by an attractive new wood engraving by John Franklin.

"The O'Donoghue"
by J. Franklin
Midsummer Eve (1848)

An advertisement to the first volume maintained that 'Their great object is to promote the welfare of Ireland – but not by a sacrifice of truth.'[4] There was a deliberate avoidance of illustrations depicting abject squalor and extremes of poverty as such images could have a lasting effect on the reader. While the authors were keen to provide facts and statistics, to recount legends and customs, it was not in their interest to portray the country in a very negative light. This would have been counter-productive to their overall aim.

The Editorial Question

Isabella Fyvie Mayo, in her account of her two friends following the death of S.C. Hall, suggested that Anna Maria ignored the dry arts of editing and proofing and that she 'owed much to the professional skill and dexterity of her husband's polishing hand.'[5] Anna Maria may have cultivated this impression in order to publicly credit his superiority as an editor and thus reinforce her own primary role as wife rather than author. Given the workload they both had, it seems unlikely that she would want or expect him to fulfil this role. Apart from the very early days when she was learning her craft, and he was a professional editor, there is little reason why she would not edit her own copy. Proof may be shown in a manuscript version of 'Waking Dreams' from the Huntington Library, California. At least 10 changes have been made to the text on one page alone, and the corrections are in her handwriting. James Newcomer, in his article on the Hall papers in Iowa, wrote of a similar experience with a manuscript copy of her sketch 'Luke O'Brian':

> On the first short page are no fewer than 20 corrections that Mrs Hall made in the original text. A glance shows that 16 pages will yield at least 320 corrections to be noted and considered. Even more interesting is the discovery that in the

printed text that I own there are, in the first 30 lines, 30 changes from the Iowa manuscript.[6]

By publicly acknowledging her debt to her husband, she boosted his self-confidence and perpetuated the idea that her success owed much to him.

Most contemporary commentators saw Anna Maria as the superior writer of the two, despite her husband's best efforts to promote himself. Even though S.C. Hall lived in Ireland until 1822 and made an invaluable contribution to the country, especially through his hard work on *Ireland: its Scenery, Character, &c.*, his wife's higher Irish profile and allegiance eclipsed his own. The consensus from commentators is that S.C. Hall contributed most of the facts and figures and antiquarian details to the three-volume work while his wife added sparkle with her tales of the peasantry, excerpts of dialogue and warmth of tone. What is undeniable is that both worked extremely hard on this project and the series of twenty-five letters from S.C. Hall to John Windele in the Royal Irish Academy demonstrate the pressure they were under to cover thirty-two counties in twenty-four parts.

Maureen Keane has drawn attention to how adventurous the Halls were, whether it was shooting through the rapids 'with frightful rapidity' at the Old Weir Bridge in Killarney, climbing the ascent to St. Kevin's Bed in Glendalough, or crawling through the caves at Mitchelstown and Newgrange.[7] She also provides detailed discussion of the reception of this ambitious work by Irish and English critics. Without doubt it was a great success with over 8,000 sales in England according to *The Nation* newspaper[8] and was reprinted and revised many times over the following decades, even translated into German in 1850. It was not unanimously celebrated in Ireland where some critics took exception to how the Irish were caricatured.

The overall plan for each monthly part-issue of *Ireland: Its Scenery, Character, &c.* was to include two steel engravings, a map of the county under discussion and approximately fifteen wood-engravings throughout the forty-eight pages of text. Initially twenty parts were envisaged but that number increased. It was a complex project and some counties were discussed in exhaustive detail whereas others were treated in a more cursory fashion. Two of the latter included Queen's County (Laois) and King's County (Offaly). Both were given a mere four pages each in Volume 2. King's County is included as a sample in the following pages and it had three wood engravings and one steel plate of Clonmacnoise. Queen's County had only one wood engraving and both counties were included on a map featuring King's County, Queen's County and Kilkenny – placed with the more extensive chapter on Kilkenny in the same volume.

By way of contrast, Wicklow is featured after King's County and it has sixty-four pages, twenty-seven wood engravings and eleven steel engravings. The short extract from the first page on Wicklow gives a flavour of the approach and passion for this county. It was not possible to give each county the same attention and Volume 1 is devoted mainly to Cork and Kerry with shorter entries on Waterford, Limerick and Carlow.

There is no doubt that *Ireland: Its Scenery, Character, &c* provides unique insights into pre-Famine Ireland, is a treasure trove of folklore and antiquarian interest and has arguably contributed to the patterns and preferences of tourists to Ireland to this day.

NOTES

1 Hazel Morris, *Hand, Head and Heart: Samuel Carter Hall and The Art Journal* (Norwich, Michael Russell, 2002), 30.

2 Martyn Anglesea, 'Andrew Nicholl and his patrons in Ireland and Ceylon,' *Studies: An Irish Quarterly Review* 71 (1982): 136–37.

3 Louisa M. Connor Bulman, 'Titian in Connemara,' *Apollo* (2004: Apr) 46. Evans exhibited 14 Irish paintings at the Old Watercolour Society, all of Counties Galway and Mayo, between 1836–37. He portrayed landscapes, streetscapes, homes, peasants and the 'unexpectedly respectable' quayside at Claddagh.
4 *The Art-Union* Nov. (1840): 172–4.
5 Mayo, 'Two Old Friends' 304.
6 Newcomer, *Books at Iowa* 43 (1985) 15 – 23.
7 Maureen Keane, *Mrs S.C. Hall – A Literary Biography* (Gerrards Cross: Colin Smythe, 1997), 117–119.
8 *The Nation*, 18 Nov. 1843, 106.

FURTHER READING

Croker, Thomas Crofton, *Fairy Legends and Traditions of the South of Ireland* (London, John Murray, 1825).

Finlay, Peter, The Irish as 'Other': Representations of Urban and Rural Poverty in early Victorian Travel Writing on Ireland, Diss. Queen's University of Belfast, 2005.

Hall, S[amuel]., C[arter]. Mrs., and S.C. Hall, *The Book of South Wales, the Wye and the Coast* (London, Virtue & Co., 1861).

A Companion to Killarney (London, Virtue, 1853).

Hand-Books for Ireland (London, Virtue, 1853).

Ireland: its Scenery, Character, &c. 3 vols (London, How and Parsons, 1841–1843).

A Week at Killarney (London, Jeremiah How, 1843).

Letters from S.C. Hall to John Windele. Windele Collection, Royal Irish Academy, Dublin.

Keane, Maureen, *Mrs. S.C. Hall: A Literary Biography*, Irish Literary Studies 50 (Gerrards Cross, Colin Smythe, 1997).

Keyes, Marian Thérèse, 'Adding Sparkle to the Dry Details: Folkloric Themes, Tales and Tangents in the Work of Anna Maria Fielding Hall' in Anne Markey and Anne O'Connor (eds), *Folklore and Modern Irish Writing* (Dublin, Irish Academic Press, 2014).

'Taken from the Life'. Mimetic Truth and Ekphrastic Eloquence in the Writings of Anna Maria Fielding Hall (1800–81), Unpublished diss., St. Patrick's College, Drumcondra, 2010.

Mayo, Isabella Fyvie, 'A Recollection of Two Old Friends: Mr. and Mrs. S.C. Hall.' *The Leisure Hour* May 1889: [303]–307.

Morris, Hazel, *Hand, Head and Heart: Samuel Carter Hall and The Art Journal* (Norwich, Michael Russell, 2002).

Ó Muirithe, Diarmaid, *A Seat Behind the Coachman: Travellers in Ireland 1800–1900* (Dublin, Gill and Macmillan, 1972).

Scott, Michael (ed.), *Hall's Ireland: Mr and Mrs Hall's Tour of 1840* (London, Sphere Books, 1984).

Thackeray, William, *The Irish Sketch Book* (London, Chapman and Hall, 1843).

"Connemara" by William Evans, engraved by Henry Vizetelly, *Ireland, its Scenery, Character, &c.* vol. 3 (1843). The page shows a particularly pleasing combination of image and text in the style of the *livre romantique*. A panorama of peasant activities depicts the picturesque and rather idealised setting of Connemara. There was a deliberate avoidance of illustrations depicting abject squalor and extremes of poverty as such images could have a lasting effect on the reader.

"The Seven Churches of Clonmacnoise" (on the Shannon)
by W.H. Bartlett, engr. R. Brandard,
frontispiece to King's County, Vol. 2
Ireland: its Scenery, Character, &c.

The King's County being, like the Queen's County, without any peculiar characteristic, may be described briefly. It received its comparatively modern appellation in compliment to Philip of Spain, the consort of Queen Mary. Its boundaries are, on the east the county of Kildare; on the north the counties of Meath and Westmeath; on the west the Shannon, which separates it from Roscommon and Galway, and part of the county of Tipperary; and on the south the Queen's County. Its population was in 1821, 138,088; and in 1831, 144,225. It comprises an area of 528,166 acres, of which 133,349 are mountain and bog – an immense proportion of which is the famous bog of Allen. Its baronies are eleven, viz: Ballyboy, Ballybrit, Ballycowen, Clonlisk, Coolestown, Eglish, Garrycastle, Geashill, Kilcoursey, Lower Philipstown, Upper Philipstown, and Warrenstown.

The King's County abounds in ruins of old castles; one of the most striking is Garry Castle, which the artist has pictured for us. It stans beside the road leading from Birr to Banagher and was the ancient forta-lice of the Mac Coghlans.[1]

We visited the King's County in one of the canal-boats which run from Dublin to Shannon Harbour; passin, for nearly the whole distance of, perhaps, eighty miles, through the bog of Allen. The boat is called a "fly-boat;" it is composed of iron, and proceeds, drawn by two or three horses, at the rate of nine English miles an hour; the country being very flat, there are comparatively few locks, fifteen miles of the journey being made without encountering one. It is, however, by no means a pleasant mode of travelling; for the boat being exceedingly narrow, the passengers are painfully 'cramped' and confined. The 'bog' commences at Robertstown, in the county of Kildare, twenty miles from Dublin, and continues, with little interruption, to Shannon Harbour.[2] In the midst of this bog are the two principal towns of the county – Philipstown the former, and Tullamore the present, capital. They are by no means remarkable either for cleanliness or picturesque character; and after visiting both, one might quote, without incurring a charge of bad taste, the old rhyme:

> 'Great bog of Allen, swallow down
> That odious heap call'd Philipstown;
> And if thy maw can swallow more,
> Prey take – and welcome – Tullamore.'

The passage through the bog of Allen, although dreary and monotonous, is by no means without interest; and as the recurrence of locks enables the passenger occasionally to walk on land, the 'voyage' will amply repay curiosity. The aspect that surrounds him on all sides is very singular; huge 'clamps,' or stacks, of turf border the canal, and here and there a cabin rears its roof a few feet above the surface, from which it can scarcely be distinguished. It is hardly possible to imagine more wretched hovels than those which the turf-cutters inhabit. The man rents usually from two to five acres; the turf he cuts with his own hands, and conveys to market as he best can. When settling, his first care is to procure shelter from the wind and rain; he selects, therefore, a dry bank a little beyond the influence of floods; here he digs a pit, for it is nothing more, places at the corners a few sticks of bog-wood, and covers the top with 'flakes' of heath, leaving a small aperture to let out the smoke. Yet the inhabitants of this miserable district, existing in this deplorable manner, are by no means unhealthy; and around their huts we saw some of the finest children we have seen in Ireland.

There can be no doubt that, in ancient times, this huge tract of country was one immense forest, although its remains are less numerous here than elsewhere, the turf being for the most part peat, with little admixture of wood – a circumstance to be accounted for by the fact that, in consequence of the difficulty of drainage, the cutters seldom work far beneath the surface. Many attempts have been made to drain portions of it, and with partial success, those which border the can having been in several places converted into good arable land. When internal peace in Ireland has been followed by prosperity, the expenditure of capital will certainly convert this immense waste, which contributes so little to the national wealth, into fertile and productive fields; the next generation may see the merry harvester taking the place of the miserable turf-cutter, and smiling and happy cottages occupying the sites of the now wretched hovels that would be contemned even by the bushmen of southern Africa.[3]

The Western parts of the King's County, where it is bordered by the mighty Shannon, are infinitely more picturesque than those we have been describing, which lie to the north and south, or rather occupy the centre of the county. On the banks of the Shannon, and also adjacent to a branch of 'the Bog,' are the interesting ruins of Clonmacnois, the school where, according to Dr. O'Conor, 'the nobility of Connaught had their children educated, and which was therefore called Cluan-mac-nois, 'the secluded recess of the sons of nobles.' It was also, in ancient times, a famous cemetery of the Irish kings; and for many centuries it has continued a favourite burial-place, the popular belief enduring to this day, that all persons interred here pass immediately from earth to heaven. The abbey is said to have been founded by St Kieran about the middle of the sixth century, and soon became 'amazingly enriched,' so that, writes Mr. Archdall, 'its landed property was so great, and the number of cells and monasteries subjected to it so numerous, that almost half of Ireland was said to be within the bounds of Clonmacnois.' The ruins retain marks of exceeding splendour. In the immediate vicinity there are two 'Round Towers.' One of the many richly carved stone crosses scattered in all directions among the ruins, we have given above; the artist also copied one of the peculiarly elegant doorways. We shall have so many opportunities of examining other relics of the magnificence of remote ages, that we must content ourselves with this meagre reference to those of Clonmacnois; taking no note of the few natural beauties of the King's County, in order that we may devote greater space to those of the County of Wicklow, to which we now direct the attention of the tourist.

NOTES

1 Of the last of the race, Mr. Brewer gives the following account, which he obtained from Colonel de Montmorency: "Thomas Coghlan, Esq. – or, in attention to local phraseology, 'the Maw' (that is, Mac), for he was not known or addressed in his own domain by any other appellation – was a remarkably handsome man; gallant, eccentric, proud, satirical, hospitable in he extreme, and of expensive habits. In disdain of modern times he adhered to the national customs of Ireland, and the modes of living practised by his ancestors. His house was ever open to strangers. His tenants held their lands at will, and paid their rents according to the ancient fashion, partly in kind, and the remainder in money. 'The Maw' levied the fines of mortmain when a vassal died. He became heir to the defunct farmer; and no law was admissible, or practised, within the precincts of Mac Coghlan's domain, but such as savoured of the Brehon code. It must be observed, however, that, most commonly, 'the Maw's' commands, enforced by the impressive application of his horsewhip, instantly decided a litigated point! From this brief outline it might be supposed that we were talking of Ireland early in the seventeenth century; but Mr. Coghlan died not longer back than about the year 1790. With him perished the rude grandeur of his long-drawn line. He died without issue, and destitute of any legitimate male representative to inherit his name, although most of his followers were of the sept of the Coghlans, none of whom, however, were strictly qualified, or were suffered by 'the Maw,' to use the Mac, or to claim any relationship with himself."

2 Excerpt from the *Dublin Penny Journal* referring to the geography of the Bog of Allen. (Not included here).

3 Note referring to the Fourth Report (printed into 1814) outlining further statistics relating to the Bog of Allen. (Not included here).

Vignette Clonmacnoise

WICKLOW

We have no design to write a guide-book; although our leading object will be to offer some observations for the guidance of those who design to visit Ireland – with especial reference to the most picturesque of its counties.[1] To picture adequately half the beauties of beautiful Wicklow would require a large and full volume. We must be content so to stimulate the appetite of the tourist, that he may long for the rich banquet which nature has abundantly provided for him. Wicklow is the garden of Ireland; its prominent feature is, indeed, sublimity – wild grandeur, healthful and refreshing; but among its high and bleak mountains there are numerous rich and fertile valleys, luxuriantly wooded, and with the noblest of magnificent rivers running through them – forming, in their course, a series of cataracts. Its natural graces are enhanced in value, because they are invariably encountered after the eye and mind have wearied from gazing upon rude and uncultivated districts, covered with peat, upon the scanty herbage of which the small sheep can scarcely find pasture. It is to this peculiar feature – its richly adorned borders, and the rugged character of its interior – that Dean Swift referred, when he likened the county to 'a frieze mantle fringed with gold-lace.' The chief attractions of Wicklow are its glens – 'splits,' as it were, in the mountains, through which the hill-torrents have burst; every one of them falling, repeatedly, from immense heights; often, for considerable space, without encountering a single break. Down the sides of each, the perpetual dripping of moisture has nourished the growth of trees and underwood. Usually, the work of nature has been improved by the skill of art, and it is impossible to imagine a scene more sublime and beautiful than one of these ravines, of which there are so many. Some of them, as the Vale of Avoca, become valleys of miles in extent;

others, as the Devil's Glen, are little more than graceful 'passages;' and in other cases, as the Scalp, the 'cuts' are barren, and covered only by the debris that have fallen from above, or been shaken from the sides – huge rocks without verdure, but of singular varieties in size and form. Every now and then, we meet with places of very gentle beauty; small rivulets that have been sent out, as young and innocent things, by the brawling and rushing river, as it forces apart all impediments that would bar its voyage to the sea – brooks that mimic their rough parents, in the rippling music they make among the comparatively tiny stones – 'brooks' such as have been pictured by the most eloquent of our living poets –

> '– whose society the poet seeks,
> Intent his wasted spirits to renew;
> And whom the curious painter doth pursue
> Through rocky passes, among flowery creeks,
> And tracks thee dancing down thy water-breaks.'

NOTE

1 And nowhere, perhaps, in the world can they be so largely repaid for so small an expenditure of time and money. A journey of twenty-four hours may place them in the centre of it – a journey by no means tedious, troublesome, or costly. A railway-carriage conveys them to Liverpool; the steamboats – the largest, safest, and best in the kingdom, which ply twice a-day – in little more than ten hours to Dublin; and Dublin is within an hour's drive of the county. The charges at all the inns in the route are so low as to astonish strangers. The inducements to a tour to Wicklow are, in fact, very strong and very numerous. If we can succeed in showing our readers how easily and pleasantly it may be made, and what a rich reward will attend those who either love to examine natural beauty, to scrutinize character, original and full of matter, or to become even partially acquainted with a country so deeply interesting, in every sense of the term, we may, to some extent, turn the current of 'travelling' from the continent to Ireland. Another recommendation, upon which we should lay some stress, is the temptation the county holds out to the angler.

ANNIE LESLIE
AND OTHER STORIES
BY
MRS S. C. HALL

Bibliography of Children's Books by Anna Maria Hall

Alice Stanley and Other Stories (London, T. Nelson, 1868).

Annie Leslie and Other Stories (London: T. Nelson, [1877]).

The Boy's Birthday Book (London: n.p., 1859).

The Cabman's Cat. Kindness to Animals' Series, No. 1 (London, S.W. Partridge, [1865]).

Chronicles of Cosy Nook: A Book for the Young (London, Marcus Ward & Co., 1875).

Chronicles of a School Room (London, Frederick Westley & A.H. Davis, 1830).

Daddy Dacre's School: A Story for the Young (London, G. Routledge & Co., 1859).

Deeds – Not Words, Fanny Murray, and Other Choice Stories (London, Milner, [c. 1900]).

Fanny's Fancies: Magnet Stories for Summer Days and Winter Nights (London, Groombridge & Sons, [1860]).

Grandmamma's Pockets. Chambers's Library for Young People (Edinburgh, William and Robert Chambers, 1849).

The Hartopp Jubilee; or, Profit from Play. A Volume for the Young (London, Darton & Clark, [1839]).

The Juvenile Budget: or, Stories for Little Readers (London, Chapman & Hall, 1837).

Little Chatterbox: a Tale (London, W.S. Orr & Co., 1844).

The Lucky Penny and Other Tales (London, George Routledge & Co., 1857).

Mamma Milly: A Story. Magnet Stories for Summer Days and Winter Nights, No. 3 (London, Groombridge & Sons, 1860).

Marian; or, a Young Maid's Fortunes (London, Henry Colburn, 1840).

The Merchant's Daughter and Other Tales (New York, C. S. Francis, 1850).

Midsummer Eve: A Fairy Tale of Love (London, Longman, Brown, Green, and Longmans, 1848).

Miniature Library of Fiction (Edinburgh, W. & R. Chambers, 1858).

Mother and Daughter, and Other Stories (London, T. Nelson & Sons, [c. 1878]).

The Mountain Daisy and Other Stories (London, T. Nelson and Sons, 1864).

Nelly Nowlan and Other Stories (London, T. Nelson and Sons, 1865).

Number One: A Tale (London: W.S. Orr & Co., 1844).

The Playfellow and Other Stories (London, T. Nelson and Sons, 1866).

Popular Tales and Sketches. Amusing Library for Young and Old (London: Lambert, 1856).

The Prince of the Fair Family: A Fairy Tale (London, Chapman & Hall, [1867]).

The Rift in the Rock: A Tale. The Rainbow Stories for Summer Days and Winter Nights, No. 2 (London, Groombridge & Sons, [1871]).

Ronald's Reason; or the Little Cripple (London, Seeley, Jackson & Halliday, [1865]).

Stories of the Governess (London, J. Nisbet, 1852).

Stories of the Irish Peasantry (Edinburgh, William and Robert Chambers, 1840).

The Swan's Egg. Chambers's Library for Young People. (Edinburgh, William and Robert Chambers, 1848).

Tales of Domestic Life (New York, C.S. Francis & Co., 1850).

There is no Hurry, and Deeds not Words: Tales, Chambers's Edinburgh Journal (Edinburgh, W. & R. Chambers, 1858).

The Two Friends: A [temperance] sketch (London, William Tweedie, 1856).

Uncle Sam's Money-Box. Chambers's Library for Young People (Edinburgh, William and Robert Chambers, 1848).

Union Jack, and Other Stories. Shilling Gift Books (London, Groombridge & Sons, 1863).

The Village Garland: Tales and Sketches (London, T. Nelson & Sons, 1863).

The Way of the World and Other Stories (London, T. Nelson & Sons, 1866).

The Whisperer, Chambers's Library for Young People (Edinburgh, William & Robert Chambers, 1848).

William and his Teacher. The Golden Casket, etc. [1861].

EDITED BY ANNA MARIA HALL

The Adventures and Experiences of Biddy Dorking: To which is added The Story of the Yellow Frog (London, Griffith and Farran, late Grant & Griffith, 1859).

Animal Sagacity (London, S.W. Partridge, [1868]).

The Drawing-Room Table-Book (London, George Virtue, [1848?])

Finden's Tableaux: A series of thirteen scenes of national character, beauty and costume (London, Charles Tilt, 1837).

The Juvenile Forget Me Not (London, N. Hailes; Fred. Westley & A.H. Davis; R. Jennings, 1829–37).

COMPILATIONS

Hall, Mrs. S.C. and Mrs. J. Foster. *Stories and Studies from the Chronicles and History of England* (London, Darton & Co., 1847).

Hall, Mrs. S.C., Wm. Howitt, Augustus Mayhew, Thomas Miller & George Augustus Sala. *The Boy's Birthday Book: A Collection of Tales, Essays & Narratives of Adventure* (London, Houlston & Wright, [1862]).

Howitt, Mary. *The Favourite Scholar, and Other Tales* (New York, James Miller, 1863), includes 'Number One' and 'Little Chatterbox' by Anna Maria Hall.

Howitt, Mary. *The Little Peacemaker and Other Stories* (London, Cassell, [c. 1890]), includes 'William and his Teacher' by Anna Maria Hall.

Hereward the Brave and other stories (London, Groombridge and Sons, [1879?]) includes 'Mamma Milly' by Anna Maria Hall.

"The Vision of the Woodcutter" by Daniel Maclise
Midsummer Eve: A Fairy Tale of Love (1848)

ANNIE LESLIE

About the Editor

Marian Thérèse Keyes has been the Senior Executive Librarian at Ireland's largest public library, dlr LexIcon since it opened in December 2014. Much of her work with her team has involved planning and programming events, festivals and exhibitions for this vibrant and exciting library and cultural centre.

Marian's first post as a librarian was at the National Art Library in the Victoria and Albert Museum in London (1991–98). It was here, when she was cataloguing the Renier Collection of Children's Books that she first came across the work of Anna Maria Fielding Hall. In 2010 she completed a PhD in Dublin City University (St. Patrick's College) on Anna Maria's illustrated publications.

Over the last 25 years, Marian has played an active role on committees including as President of the Irish Society for the Study of Children's Literature (2011–13) and Secretary of iBbY Ireland (International Board of Books for Young People). In 2021 she was presented with the CBI Award for outstanding contribution to children's books in Ireland.

Select publications by Marian Thérèse Keyes:

What's in a Name, Dun Leary, Kingstown, Dún Laoghaire, co-edited with David Gunning and Nigel Curtin (dlr County Council, 2020).

Divine Illumination, The Oratory of the Sacred Heart, Dún Laoghaire, co-edited with David Gunning and Nigel Curtin (New Island Books, 2019).

People on the Pier, co-edited with Betty Stenson (New Island Books, 2018).

Politics and Ideology in Children's Literature, co-edited with Dr Áine McGillicuddy (Four Courts Press, 2014).